Miller
shook
Lance

The people ld
a lasting ci n.
But now a horde of bloodthirsty raiders has come, and the village's guardian dragon is gone, perhaps forever.

Yala-tene's stout walls and the bravery of her people have kept the raiders at bay so far, but time is swiftly running out. They have only one last chance to survive. A handful of warriors steal away in hopes of finding the legendary Karada, the "Scarred One," who fights a never-ending war against the elves.

Up against dark magics, shifting alliances, epic battles, and a ruthless enemy from the past, civilization's last hope lies in one person—

The Sister of the Sword.

THE BARBARIANS SERIES

Children of the Plains
The Barbarians • Volume One
Paul B. Thompson & Tonya C. Cook

Brother of the Dragon
The Barbarians • Volume Two
Paul B. Thompson & Tonya C. Cook

Sister of the Sword
The Barbarians • Volume Three
Paul B. Thompson & Tonya C. Cook

THE BARBARIANS • VOLUME THREE

SISTER of the SWORD

Paul B. Thompson
and
Tonya C. Cook

SISTER OF THE SWORD

Distributed in the United States by Holtzbrinck Publishing. Distributed in Canada by Fenn Ltd.

Distributed to the hobby, toy, and comic trade in the United States and Canada by regional distributors.

Distributed worldwide by Wizards of the Coast, Inc. and regional distributors.

Made in the U.S.A.

Cover art by Corey Wolfe
Cartography by Dennis Kauth
First Printing: May 2002
Library of Congress Catalog Card Number: 2001092213

9 8 7 6 5 4 3 2 1

US ISBN: 0-7869-2789-5
UK ISBN: 0-7869-2790-9
620-88614-001-EN

U.S., CANADA,
ASIA, PACIFIC, & LATIN AMERICA
Wizards of the Coast, Inc.
P.O. Box 707
Renton, WA 98057-0707
+1-800-324-6496

EUROPEAN HEADQUARTERS
Wizards of the Coast, Belgium
P.B. 2031
2600 Berchem
Belgium
+32-70-23-32-77

Visit our web site at **www.wizards.com/books/dragonlance**

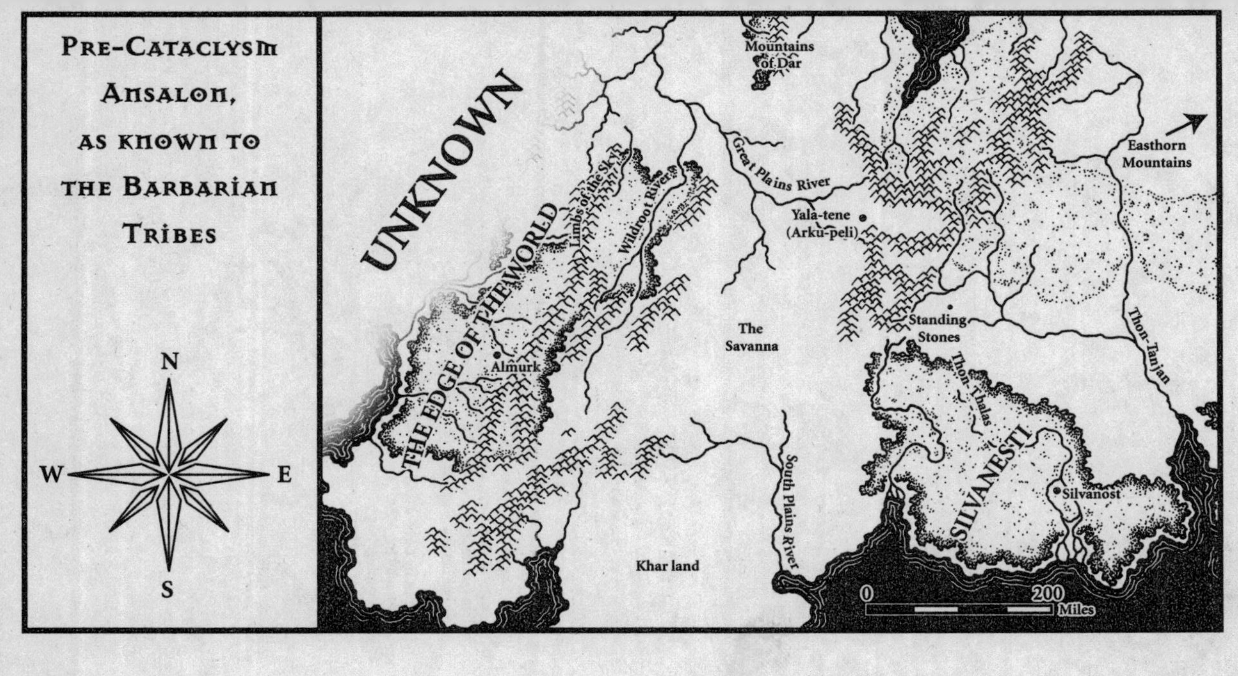

Pre-Cataclysm Ansalon, as known to the Barbarian Tribes
N
W
E
S
UNKNOWN
THE EDGE OF THE WORLD
Limbs of the Sky
Wildroot River
Almurk
Mountains of Dar
Great Plains River
Yala-tene
(Arku-peli)
The Savanna
Khar land
South Plains River
Standing Stones
Thon-Thalas
SILVANESTI
Silvanost
Thon-Tanjan
Easthorn Mountains
0
200
Miles

Chapter 1

The setting sun painted the walled town of Yala-tene in soft colors—golden yellow, warm orange, dusky red. One hue followed another until they were all swallowed by the indigo of twilight. When the day's last glow subsided, stars appeared in the darkening expanse of sky and the early summer evening took on a crisp chill.

Twenty-two pairs of eyes fixed on the scene were blind to the beauty of sky and sunset. The eyes belonged to twenty-two young men lying on their bellies on a low hill that rose from the bank of the Plains River. The sand on which they lay cooled quickly as night fell, but the youths remained completely motionless. They regarded Yala-tene intently, no hint of emotion on their faces.

They looked identical. Their hair was short and slicked down with a mixture of beeswax, nut oil, and plant dye, and their skin was stained dark green.

They were the Jade Men, raised from early childhood to worship the green dragon Sthenn and carry out his wishes without question, without fail. When their master was away, they gave obedience to Nacris, adopted mother of them all.

For three turnings of the moons, a band of seven hundred raiders, led by Nacris's son Zannian, had occupied the Valley of the Falls. They had plundered and murdered their way across the plains without opposition. Yet, in spite of Zannian's leadership, their own determination to plunder and ravage, and their terror of their mighty patron, Sthenn, they had still failed to take the village. Direct assault had not worked, and they'd been unable to terrorize the villagers into surrendering. The raiders' last resort was to choke the stubborn valley folk into submission, to cut them off from outside aid until their resolve was broken by starvation and despair.

The village, called Yala-tene ("mountain nest") by its inhabitants, was known to the Jade Men and the raiders as Arku-peli, or "place of the dragon." It had three sources of strength: the guardianship of the bronze dragon Duranix, the stone wall that encircled the town, and the leadership of the town's headman, Amero. Sthenn had lured Duranix away on an aerial chase, and no one had seen either beast since before the siege began. The wall had withstood every stratagem Zannian and Nacris devised to overcome it. That left the headman.

Amero, son of Oto, was Zannian's target. If he could be captured, the village would certainly lose heart. Zannian would achieve his lifelong dream of being chief of all the plains; Nacris would have her revenge upon Amero, brother of Karada, the woman she held responsible for crippling her and killing her first mate; and Sthenn would have destroyed the "pet" humans of his old enemy, Duranix.

That was the Jade Men's mission tonight: capture Amero.

Nacris had prepared them with a ceremony both simple and mysterious. For two days, the Jade Men had fasted. Though the rest of the raider camp still feasted on the captured bounty of Arku-peli and its lush valley, the Jade Men ate nothing and drank only water. After two days, Nacris broke their fast with a special stew filled with centipedes, cockroaches, and black crickets. Eating these night creatures, she said, would make them likewise silent, stealthy, and unseen.

At a predetermined time, the last Jade Man in line rose up on his knees. He was the leader, differentiated from the rest by a daub of yellow paint on his forehead. He pressed the thumb and forefinger of his left hand to his lips and blew. The sound he made was a high squeak, like the call of a bat on the wing. The other Jade Men stood. Each was armed with an obsidian knife, sharp as a viper's fang, and a mace whose heavy diorite head could burst a skull with a single blow.

Their leader waved them forward. In a single line, they crept over the hill toward the distant town. In the gathering darkness, against the lush grass of the valley floor, their green coloring rendered them invisible.

They passed through the remnants of previous battles—cracked spears warped from exposure, broken flint blades, the decaying carcasses of horses. The smell of death meant nothing to the Jade Men. Having grown up in the green dragon's forest lair, the rank odor of decay was part of their daily fare.

A few paces beyond the wreckage of battle the killing ground began. Where once the tent camp of wanderers who traded with Yala-tene stood, now there was a barren wasteland. The traders had pulled up stakes and fled the valley in advance of the raiders' arrival. The villagers had set fire to the grass and underbrush that remained, clearing the land to prevent sneak attacks.

The attack of the Jade Men, however, went forward. They slowed their advance to make their movements less detectable and placed their bare feet carefully, so no stray noises would give them away.

The walls bulked higher as the Jade Men drew near. They could see sentinels, long spears poised on their shoulders, walking atop the wall between trios of blazing torches. This was the baffled entrance into the town, where walls were the lowest. The normal openings through the wall had been filled with boulders and rubble. Consequently this vulnerable place was the most brightly lit and best defended.

The leader slanted off to the right, away from the light, and his troop followed. The twenty-two Jade Men headed for a spot where the wall made one of its three outward jogs. Village masons had to zigzag the wall here to find bedrock on which to anchor the structure. The notches gave natural cover to the Jade Men. Guards on other parts of the wall could not see into the corners.

A dozen paces away, the leader slowed. The high stone curtain darkened the ground here, making it hard to see ahead. In spite of their careful approach, one of their number fell into a prepared pit. The hole was filled with sharpened stakes, and the luckless Jade Man was impaled through his left thigh.

Though he made no outcry, his slide into the trap dislodged gravel and dirt. The resulting cascade seemed loud as a shout to the silent group. They froze, awaiting the blaze of torchlight, the cry of alarm, and the rain of death that would follow when the villagers spotted them.

Nothing happened. The leader crept along on his belly until he reached the pit. He made his way down into the steep-sided hole. At the bottom, his comrade lay grievously wounded, biting his own hand to keep from screaming. Feeling around in the dark, the leader discovered the sharpened stake was thrust all the way through his man's thigh.

It was a crippling injury. There was no chance he could run or climb with such a wound. Nor could he be left behind. There was too much chance he might make a noise.

Nacris had chosen purposely the Jade Men for this mission. The twenty-two green-painted fighters represented the twenty-two years since the founding of the village of Yala-tene—and the twenty-two years since Nacris's ignominious defeat at the hands of her archenemy, Karada. It was a deliberate number, imbued with secret power, yet the leader knew he must now compromise that very power. He plucked the knife from the doomed youth's waist, then reached out to rest his hand on the fellow's cheek. He felt rather than heard the wounded man sigh and give a nod of acceptance.

With one stroke, the leader cut his comrade's throat from ear to ear.

Burning with deadly resolve, the leader climbed up out of the pit. Though Nacris had ordered them to bring Amero back alive if possible, he vowed now that it would *not* happen. By the sacrifice in the pit, the fate of the village headman had been decided: a life would be exchanged for a life.

On hands and knees, the leader led the rest of the band to the base of the wall. Other pit traps dotted the ground around them. Some were hidden by branches of willow and sprinkled with dirt and ash, but no more Jade Men fell amiss. The group was soon gathered at the inside corner of the wall.

They'd practiced this maneuver many times by scaling the tall stone tower at the ruined river bridge. The two brawniest Jade Men faced each other, each butting one shoulder against the wall. Arms fully extended, they gripped each other's shoulders and settled their feet wide apart. Two of their comrades climbed atop them and repeated their stance, then two more. When the fourth pair began climbing up, the men on the bottom grunted and shifted under the weight. Two more Jade Men joined them, bracing them.

A single man worked his way to the top and leaned both hands against the inward-leaning masonry. Once in place, he was only a single man's height from the top of the wall. The twelfth youth hauled himself up, and his fingers easily reached the rim of the parapet.

The leader, still on the ground, took one last look around. All was still. Putting his slain comrade's knife in his teeth, he started up. It was not an easy ascent. The living ladder was slick with sweat and trembled under the terrible strain. He ignored everyone beneath him, concentrating on his goal, the top of the hated wall.

At last he slid onto the flat, open ledge. Off to his right three torches burned, their shafts lashed together in a tripod. He saw no sign of a watchman. Leaning over the edge, he signaled for the others to join him.

In short order, eight Jade Men lay atop the wall with him. The twelve who made up the ladder quietly unstacked themselves and huddled in the dark corner of the wall.

Nine Jade Men were now in Arku-peli. Nacris had chosen these nine (as well as the one who'd been lost to the pit trap) because they were the strongest in spirit. They would do whatever it took to fulfill her orders, down to sacrificing all their comrades.

The leader reviewed the information he'd memorized on the village layout. Tortured from villagers captured in battle, it might not be reliable, but it was all they had. Decisively, he led his men in single file along the wall away from the standing torches. At the inside of the next zigzag, they found, as they expected, a ramp leading to the ground inside.

Halfway down the ramp, they came upon an armed villager relieving himself. The sentinel never had a chance. The Jade Men rolled his corpse into the shadows at the base of the ramp and moved on.

Yala-tene was an alien world to these youths, raised in a forest and on the open plain. The streets were dark, stone-cobbled, and damp. The stone houses seemed to close in on them from all sides. An odor of burnt meat was thick as fog. Though many of Zannian's raiders ate cooked food, Nacris had raised her Jade Men to loathe such softness. They ate flesh in the way of their plainsmen ancestors: raw.

The concentration of peculiar sights and aromas was almost overwhelming, and their pace slowed as they grew confused and unsettled by the maze of streets. They collected behind their leader in the shelter of a blind alley below the town wall, unsure of their next move.

The leader's senses slowly adjusted, and he studied his surroundings with more care. The highest structures stood out against the light of the stars. One of these structures, their mother had told them, was the White Tower, where the bronze dragon was fed. The headman, it was said, lived in a dwelling four houses east and two north of the White Tower. The door of his house was marked with the sign of the turtle, painted in white.

By hand signals, the leader ordered his men to follow him. They moved down the dark street in absolute silence. Nothing disturbed their single-minded concentration, not distant voices on adjoining streets nor the barking of the villagers' tame dogs. Anything or anyone interfering with their purpose would die swiftly.

The narrow road, closed in on both sides by tall, windowless houses, ended on a much wider avenue. Lit by three large, open fires, the White Tower loomed over them. The area seemed filled with villagers, talking loudly and rattling their weapons.

The leader dropped to the ground and slowly wormed his way around the corner into the wider road. His followers waited. At times villagers walked within ten steps of him, oblivious to his prone form. Using his chin, fingers, and toes, he squirmed across the dangerous open space into the shadows on the other side. He signaled for the rest to follow, one at a time.

They proceeded without incident until the last man. A door in the house behind them opened suddenly, flooding the lane with light. A stoutish woman hefting a basket of food scraps saw the final Jade Man lying motionless in the street.

"Iby!" she called over her shoulder, shifting the basket to her hip. "Some drunkard's passed out in the street!"

A male voice inside the house answered indistinctly. Before the woman could say more, the Jade Men's leader was on her, green hand clamped over her mouth. He pushed her inside, and the rest of his band flowed in behind him.

The man called Iby rose from his hearth, a stone axe in his hand. He raised his weapon, but the Jade Men swept over him. Down he went, and the obsidian knives were put to work. Neither he nor his mate uttered another sound before they died.

Shivering with excitement, the Jade Men crowded around the dead couple's hearth, poking their meager supper with their knives. They were quickly and silently called to order by the leader. He led them out of the house by the rear door, and they moved swiftly down the black, narrow street.

The leader felt a surge of triumph when they found the house of the turtle. Not only did it have the animal totem on the door as they'd been told, but a pair of armed villagers stood guard by the door. This was certainly the headman's dwelling.

Four Jade Men worked their way around to the west side of the house. They would seize the closest guard while their leader and the other four took down the one nearest them. The signal to strike would be the leader's bat-call.

The guards, one female and one male, were not as heedless as the others they'd encountered. The woman scanned the darkness alertly.

"Something moved over there," she said.

The Jade Men froze in place.

"A dog?" the man suggested, lifting his spear.

"I don't know. It doesn't feel right."

"You're too nervous, Lyopi."

The woman's protest was interrupted by the squeaking bat-call. Before the first notes had died, several Jade

Men launched themselves at the male guard. The woman shouted a warning, and the man turned, swinging his spear. He managed an awkward parry of the trio of obsidian knives thrust at his chest, and his arcing spear-shaft connected with the head of one of his attackers.

The woman put her back to his. As the rest of the Jade Men, leader to the fore, spilled out of the shadows, she gasped, "More of them coming!"

A diorite mace hit the male guard on the knee. He gave a grunt of pain and toppled. Before he hit the ground, another club connected with his temple, knocking him unconscious. At the same time, a leaping Jade Man struck the woman in the back. The spear flew from her hand, and she went down hard, landing facedown in the lane.

Every moment counted now. There was no time to spare for killing the two unconscious guards, and the leader guided his troop swiftly through the door of the dwelling.

A fire on the hearth had burned down to embers. The interior of the single round room was dim. Nostrils flaring, the leader smelled his prey before he saw him.

The headman lay on his side, his back to the door. The commotion outside had not wakened him. Half his face was swathed in bandages—a wound earned in battle with Zannian's men.

Slaying him as he slept held no satisfaction, so the leader kicked the headman until he stirred. The fellow's single visible eye widened in shock as he rolled over and saw the apparitions surrounding him.

Before the headman could so much as raise a hand, the leader struck, dropping to his knees and using his whole body to increase the force of his blow. He drove the dagger into his victim so far the brittle stone snapped in two. The other Jade Men moved in, ringing their prey and stabbing him again and again. None would leave with an unbloodied knife.

Shouts outside ended the murdering frenzy. Time to depart. The leader gestured at the open doorway.

He was the last to leave. With a final satisfied glance at the dead man, the leader of the Jade Men went out the door. He left his broken blade lodged in his victim's ribs.

Outside, the streets were alive with villagers shouting and brandishing torches and spears. The two guards were gone, either fled or carried off.

There was no need for stealth now, so the Jade Men ran, heading for the ramp they'd used to enter Arkupeli. Near the White Tower they were confronted by a band of villagers. Stones and spears flew at them. One of the latter caught the trailing Jade Man in the back, and he went down, severely injured. He swiftly drew his knife and fell upon it rather than surrender to the outraged townsfolk.

The alleys confused the fleeing youths, fragmenting the band of eight. The leader knew the way out yet did not call to the others. Like his men, he had taken an oath to say nothing until the mission was completed. None of them violated that oath—not even those who, confused and disoriented, blundered into armed search parties and were killed.

The leader was the only survivor to reach the foot of the ramp. After racing up the ramp, he uttered his batcall from the summit of the wall. The rest of his group hastily quit the shadows to re-form their living ladder.

As he waited for them to be ready, the leader looked back over the village. Twin rivers of fire were converging on his position, two columns of torch-bearing villagers howling for vengeance. When several villagers reached the base of the ramp below him, the leader could wait no longer. He slid feet first down the sloping wall to reach his comrades.

Rough stone tore at his legs. When he hit the uppermost Jade Man, the human ladder shuddered but held.

The leader climbed quickly down his comrades' bodies. As he passed a pair, they would disconnect themselves and follow him down.

From the wall, villagers hurled stones, pots, and torches at the intruders. One pot filled with oil shattered on the wall, and a blazing stick that followed set it alight. The uppermost Jade Men were doused in flames, and the remainder of the ladder simply fell apart, burning.

"Get them! Kill them all! Let none escape!" shouted a villager. Rocks and trash were replaced by lethal spears.

Two Jade Men died in the fire. Three were swiftly impaled. Two more fell into hidden pit traps. It seemed none of them would escape. But when the leader finally threw himself to the ground, he found two of his comrades remained with him. All three lay on the lee side of the hill, panting and listening to the shouts of their furious enemy. Suddenly, one plaintive cry rose above the rest.

"They killed him! They killed the Arkuden!"

The wail was taken up by the rest of the villagers. Lying in the dirt, the searing pain of his scorched arms and back forcing tears from his eyes, the leader of the Jade Men smiled so broadly his parched lips cracked and bled.

Arkuden, meaning "dragon's son," was the villagers' name for their headman. Amero was dead.

Mother and the Master would be very pleased.

Chapter 2

Harak was a long way from home.

Not that he had a home, in the sense the people of Yala-tene did. Harak was a nomad and had always been a nomad, even before joining Zannian's army. When he thought of home—which he rarely did—he thought of the wide, grassy plains where he'd been born. He was a long way from there now.

Sitting on a cold stone slab high in the mountains of Khar land, surrounded by hostile and suspicious ogres, was not a place Harak wanted to be. He'd undertaken this insane errand at the behest of Zannian's mother, Nacris. Crazy woman, crazy mission.

Go to the mountains, she'd told him. Find the ogre tribe led by Ungrah-de. Promise them rich plunder if they will help us capture Arku-peli.

It sounded simple the way she put it, but Harak had no real idea just how dangerous his task would turn out to be. Unlike the relatively gentle mountains surrounding the Valley of the Falls, the ogre homeland was higher and colder than any place he'd ever been. By day, wind roared through the passes like a torrential river, blinding him and his horse with driven grit. The air was so frigid and dry it sucked all the warmth from his limbs and caused his exposed skin to crack like old leather. By night the wind died, but sunset brought on cold more pervasive than any he had ever felt before. Furs hardly sufficed to keep the deadly chill away.

Harak's first night in the high pass was almost his last. He was well toward freezing to death when his horse, unhappy with the raw conditions, kicked him awake. Staggering to his knees, Harak managed to get a fire going before his eyes closed forever. The horse got a double ration of hay the next morning, as well a new name: Stone Toe.

Harak's travails didn't end with the cold or the desiccating wind. He had to convince the ogres he met not to kill and rob him on sight. Some would not be persuaded, and time and again he was forced to flee. Those ogres not bent on murdering him presented another problem: how to locate Ungrah-de.

Harak quickly discovered that "Ungrah" was a common name among ogres, and "Ungrah-de" merely meant "Big Ungrah." Many of the creatures answered to that epithet. A great many.

In the end, he found the one he sought by means of a stratagem. He presented a minor chieftain with a bronze Silvanesti dagger and hinted he had a very special gift for the great chief known as Ungrah-de.

"Give gift to me," said the lesser chief, who was named Garnt. "I'll give it to Big Ungrah when next I see him."

Harak had no doubt his life would end immediately once the ogre extracted whatever goods he had. On the other hand, resisting Garnt's request was likely to be less than healthy, too.

Clapping his hands to his head, Harak howled, "Fierce One, have pity! I bear in my pack a blade cursed by the priests of the woodland elves. My master, the great chief Zannian, cannot wield this weapon himself, for the curse will strike down anyone who holds the blade, sending maggots to consume his flesh even down to the small bones! My chief seeks to rid both his people of this cursed blade and your mountains of the vile tyrant Ungrah-de. When the monster takes the weapon in his unworthy hand, the elf curse will infest him at once, and we shall be blessed by his death!"

Garnt digested this. Harak was gambling on his host hating Ungrah-de, who by reputation was the largest and fiercest ogre in the highlands.

Garnt asked to see the "cursed" Silvanesti weapon. Harak displayed a sword Nacris had sent along as part of the payment for the ogres' aid. It was a fairly unremarkable bronze weapon with a ring of smoky garnets in its pommel. Harak made a great show of handling the Silvanesti blade with scraps of leather to keep from touching the bare metal.

Garnt studied the sword for a long time. Harak could almost hear the turnings of his slow brain.

"Such a gift must be delivered right away," the ogre said at last. "One of my warriors will take you to Ungrah-de."

Harak bowed low, deliberately letting the bronze blade slip from his grasp and fall at Garnt's feet. The massive ogre shuffled backward to avoid the touch of the "cursed" weapon.

"You go now!" Garnt snapped, face paling. He sent an ogre named Ont to accompany Harak as guide and interpreter.

A day later Ont was leading Harak through a lofty crevice between two of the highest peaks in the range. The air was so thin that Stone Toe's breath came in labored, deep-chested gasps. Harak took pity on the horse and dismounted, leading him by the reins.

Even Ont found the height difficult. He rested frequently, leaning a heavy arm against the unyielding mountain and breathing hard. During one of these breaks, Harak asked why the great chief lived so high.

Ont's knowledge of the plains tongue was limited, but he explained the mighty Ungrah-de, being much bigger than his fellow ogres, could breathe effectively at high altitude. It was clear Ont considered himself a mere youth in comparison to the great chieftain.

Harak he dismissed as a "bird," the uncomplimentary epithet ogres used to describe any small and insignificant creature.

Harak assumed the ogre was exaggerating. Ont was two full spans taller than Harak's own considerable height and much more heavily muscled than any human. However, when they reached Ungrah-de's camp, situated on a plateau below the highest peak in the entire range, he realized his guide was only relating the truth. Ungrah-de proved to a towering creature, and the males of his tribe all topped Ont by at least a handspan.

With Ont interpreting, Harak greeted the celebrated Ungrah-de and offered him the gifts Nacris had sent. In addition to the Silvanesti sword, there were various other pretty items stolen by the raiders on their sweep across the plains.

Painted pots and leather goods did not interest the ogre chief. Ungrah-de kicked through the pile of gifts at his feet until he came upon a rare item—a bronze scale. Cunning Nacris had included it intentionally. It was the same scale Duranix had sent to Zannian as a warning to turn back from Yala-tene.

Ungrah-de picked up the scale in one hand, sniffed it, and said a single word to Ont.

The smaller ogre, translating, turned to Harak and asked, "Dragon?"

"Yes," Harak said, "a scale from a bronze dragon." Kneeling before this gargantuan ogre, he felt exactly as Ont had characterized him, like a bird, a sparrow in a ring of vultures.

Ungrah asked a question, and Ont relayed. "You take from dragon?"

A little embellishment never hurt a story. "No. My chief, the mighty Zannian, struck this off the dragon Duranix."

"Where is dragon now?" the chief asked, through Ont.

Harak looked up at the hulking ogre. "Flown away, to the setting sun. The powerful Zannian chased him away."

Ont translated this. Ungrah responded with a sharp-sounding query.

"He says, if your chief so strong, why need Ungrah-de?"

"Tell the dread chief my people are worn down from long days of fighting. The villagers have chosen to hide behind walls of stone and refuse to come out and fight, face to face, like men—ah, like ogres."

Ont conveyed this reply. More of Ungrah-de's warriors gathered around them. The chief thrust his jutting jaw forward, clacking his lower tusks against his upper fangs. He asked what was in the alliance for him.

"Plunder," Harak said loudly, spreading his hands wide. "All the horses and oxen you can carry off. Cloth, furs, and anything else in the village."

"Humans?" Ungrah asked slyly.

Though it made his stomach churn, Harak nodded. "Yes. As many as you can take."

When Ont translated this, the ogres began talking all at once, bellowing, pointing, and gnashing their prominent teeth. Harak tried to interrupt but it was like whistling against thunder. Ungrah-de noticed the human trying to speak and roared for quiet.

Ogres are taciturn and slow to speak, but once they get going, they're equally hard to silence. When his bellow failed, Ungrah snatched a club from his belt and laid about with this huge persuader, knocking some of his warriors out cold. Others retreated out of reach, nursing bloody noses or spitting out cracked teeth.

Ungrah shoved the end of the club in Harak's face and roared a question. Ont, after shouldering his way out of the mob, translated.

"He says what else do you have for him?" Ont added in a low voice, "Give cursed blade now. I pick you up and run when Ungrah die!"

Harak nodded, feigning agreement, but he also noticed Ungrah watching them both warily. The chieftain, he was certain, had understood Ont's words.

Harak opened his fur coat and drew out the wrapped bundle. As he pulled the leather away from the sword, ogres around him grunted. Lacking metal themselves, they greatly prized the few pieces they acquired by raiding or trading.

Obvious appreciation showed in Ungrah-de's dark eyes, and one taloned paw moved as if to touch the blade. He hesitated.

"It's all right. Ont thinks it's cursed." Harak pulled away the rest of the wrapping and held the sword in his naked hands. "But it's not."

Ont's shaggy brows arched upward, and his wide mouth fell open in surprise. In the next instant, Ungrah took hold of the long sword (in his huge hands it resembled a dagger) and ran the keen point through Ont's throat. Dark blood welled out of the wound. His knees folded and, gurgling, he toppled. Ungrah withdrew the blade smoothly. The treacherous ogre writhed on the icy turf until a pair of Ungrah's troop finished him with their clubs.

Harak was still staring at the dying Ont when he felt the warm, sticky tip of the elven sword pressed against his jawbone. Without moving his head, he shifted his eyes to the wielder.

"Great, dread chief," Harak said carefully, "surely you won't kill me after I have gifted you with such a blade?"

"Why shouldn't I?" Ungrah said, and Harak quickly realized his command of the plains language was far better than Ont's had been. "Was this not a plot by little Garnt to murder me?"

"Yes and no, great chief. My story was true. I am here to persuade you to return with me to the Valley of the Falls to fight alongside my chief, Zannian."

The sword moved forward a hair, breaking Harak's skin. "What was this foolishness about the Silvanesti blade?"

Despite the debilitating cold, sweat formed on Harak's brow and slowly trickled down behind his ear to sting the tiny cut the ogre had given him. With the blade still pricking his jaw, he explained how he had duped Ont's chief into helping him find Ungrah-de.

"It's good you slew Ont," Harak finished. "If he had gone back and told Garnt you were not struck down by the curse, there might have been war between your bands."

Ungrah took the sword away from Harak's face. "As I am a wolf, they are rabbits," he scoffed. "Garnt's tribe is no threat. Someday I will eat them."

Harak wondered queasily if that was a boast, or merely the simple truth.

The chieftain bellowed commands, and the ogres erupted into action. Harak thought they were breaking camp, preparing to march to Zannian's aid, and he grew puzzled when they began piling up a great heap of broken tree trunks and dry brush in the center of the camp.

"Great chief, what's happening?" he asked.

"We go to your fight, but first we punish ourselves."

Harak's questions were lost in a forest of giant, fur-clad bodies, dashing about the high, arid plateau in busy preparation. Though brutally strong, for their size the ogres were surprisingly agile and plainly inured to their harsh environs. He counted close to a hundred, of both sexes. They would be a powerful reinforcement for Zannian. Too powerful, perhaps. He wondered what would happen if the ogres decided to turn on their human allies.

Embers were brought from the recesses of the ogres' cave to the enormous pile of wood and brush in the center of the camp. Driven by the incessant daytime wind, the woodpile rapidly caught fire. Harak wondered if the creatures planned to immolate members of their own band.

Pairs of female ogres appeared, carrying ox hides tied to poles. The skins had been sewn back together in the shape of their former owners, and they sloshed significantly.

Harak's brown eyes widened. The ogres used whole ox hides as wineskins!

Wine proved to be too grand a description of the beverage that soon poured forth. The dark, brown brew smelled something like old ox hide and something like sour grain. They didn't use drinking vessels but crowded around the skins, which were each held by a pair of females. The drinkers received a spray of brown brew in their gaping mouths. Harak learned an ogre's prowess for drink was judged as much by the amount he could swallow in a single gulp as by how well he stood up to the wildly intoxicating effects.

A muscular hand thumped his back. Regaining his balance, he turned to find Ungrah-de glaring down at him.

"Man will have *tsoong,*" he rumbled, gesturing at the wineskins.

It was obviously a test, not of manners but of strength. Offering his most charming smile, Harak doffed his fur cap and said, "After you, great chief."

Ungrah snorted; vapor streamed from his flat, leathery nostrils in the frigid air. He preceded Harak to one of the waiting ox hides, swatting warriors aside like so many pinecones.

The ogre females held the skin as high as they could to reach the chief's gaping mouth. At a wave of his meaty hand, they pressed the sides of the hide together, directing a stream of *tsoong* into Ungrah's mouth. The chieftain's cheeks and throat ballooned as a river of brew flowed and flowed into his mouth. Harak's own mouth hung open in shock. He was so amazed that he forgot to be disgusted.

The females drained half the hide into their chief, stopping only because they needed to adjust their grip in order to dispense more. Ungrah stepped back and wiped his tusks with the back of one hand. His warriors roared his name.

Whirling, the ogre chief took Harak roughly by the front of his fur cape. His pupils had shrunk to the size of jet beads.

"You next," he said. His breath was indescribably foul.

Harak swallowed hard. "Thank you," he said. He winked at the burly *tsoong* carriers, saying, "Ladies, be kind to a stranger and a human. Don't drown me!"

Ungrah repeated his remarks in his own tongue, and the females giggled, a sound only somewhat lower than an ox's grunting.

Harak offered a prayer to his ancestors, though he thought it highly unlikely any of that wayward crew could help him now. Opening his mouth, he shut his eyes and waited. A stream of brew hit him. The force of it drove him back a step. Gulping rapidly, he managed to keep up with the flow. Then it doubled.

Tsoong washed over his face and down his chin. He tried tilting his head back, but that just allowed the liquid to run up his nose. Choking, he swallowed what he could, then finally turned aside, face purpling.

The flavor was . . . well, awful didn't even begin to describe it. Intensely bitter, *tsoong* had an aftertaste so sweet it made his jaw lock tight. And the smell! He was sure they must ferment it in the ox hides to get such a strong smell of putrid meat.

His stomach roiled. *Tsoong* threatened to climb back up his throat, but he held it down with a trick he'd learned in Zannian's band—he rolled his tongue backward, blocking his throat. The intoxicating effects of the brew hit him and lightened his head. A fiery aura enveloped him, the first warmth he'd felt since coming to the high mountains. His nausea faded.

A powerful hand spun him around. The camp whirled about his head. The blurry visage of Ungrah-de swam before Harak's eyes.

"You did not lose the *tsoong!*" the chieftain exclaimed with dawning respect. All around them grown ogre warriors were on their knees, retching. "You are a warrior indeed, little bird! Have you ogre blood in you?"

Shame on my ancestors if that's true, Harak thought groggily, but was sober enough not to say it out loud.

"A spicy . . . drink, great chief, but I've had stronger," Harak said. Anything stronger would have loosened his teeth.

Ungrah picked him up by the back of his cloak and shook him playfully. "I like you, man. What are you called again?"

"Harak, Nebu's son."

"The night is long and cold, Harak Nebu's Son! You will tell me of your battles, of the enemies you have slain! Come, let us punish ourselves again, to make our spirits angry and our future battles sweet!"

It was a long night. Harak was obliged to drink more of the foul brew but was able to fool the drunken ogres into thinking he was keeping up with their excesses. Ungrah passed out near midnight, the last of the ogres to succumb. Hoarfrost was forming on the snoring ogres, so Harak crawled close to the dying bonfire before blessedly losing consciousness. When morning came at last, he well understood why they called their revels "punishment." The aftereffects of *tsoong* proved to be even worse than the ordeal of swallowing it in the first place.

* * * * *

Beramun lay on her belly in the high grass. All around her, scouts from Karada's band of nomads were likewise hidden. It was early afternoon and hot. No shade softened the glare of the sun on the open savanna. Sweat pooled in the small of her back, but she ignored it, as she ignored the fly buzzing around her face and the maddening itch on her ankle.

The rest of the band was half a league back, hidden in a dry wash. Since leaving their camp on the eastern plain, Karada's people had covered better than fifteen leagues a day—an amazing distance considering a third of them were not horsed.

Continuing that pace would have brought them to Yala-tene in six and a half days, but just after dawn Karada halted everyone. Her scouts had come galloping back reporting fresh signs of strangers on horseback ahead.

"Could be Zannian's men," Beramun said, her heart racing.

Beside her, Karada was reflective. "Or Silvanesti. Were the tracks shod?" Elves put copper shoes on their horses' hoofs. Humans rode unshod animals.

The scouts reported the horses were unshod, and Karada ordered the band to take cover in the dusty ravine. She placed her old comrade Pakito in charge of defending the children, old folks, and baggage, then picked two dozen riders to follow her forward to investigate the strangers. Beramun was included in the scouting party since she knew Zannian's men on sight.

Before they rode away, a girl of eighteen summers dashed out from the line of baggage-bearing travois. Long auburn braid bouncing on her back, she ran to Karada and clutched the nomad chieftain's leg.

"Take me!" the girl demanded. "I'm too old to remain with the children!"

Karada shook her leg, breaking the girl's hold. "Get back, Mara," she said sternly. "You're not a warrior."

"Neither is she!" The girl pointed to Beramun.

"She's a hunter, and she knows the enemy. Go back to Pakito." When Mara showed no sign of moving, Karada pushed her away with her foot. "Do as I say! Go!"

The column of riders trotted away. Beramun looked back. Mara glared at her, tears staining her face, then whirled and walked back to the waiting band.

Beramun wanted to feel sorry for the girl. Her life, like Beramun's, had been difficult. Captured and enslaved by Silvanesti, Mara had been freed by Karada. Beramun had suffered likewise at the hands of Zannian's raiders. They had killed her family and forced her to labor in their camp, but she had escaped and made her way to Yala-tene. Though she could sympathize with what Mara had suffered, Beramun found it impossible to like her. The girl's jealousy was all too plain.

Half a league west, they found the trail of the unshod horses. Karada examined the signs. Whoever they were, they rode in a double line, keeping precise intervals between each horse. Beramun felt the raiders were too wild to keep such order and wondered who this could be.

Karada, cinching her sword belt tightly around her waist, ordered Beramun and ten scouts to dismount and search westward on foot for fresh signs. She and the remaining mounted scouts strung their bows and followed at a distance.

Time passed. The sun climbed to its zenith then began its journey down to the west. Beramun walked slowly, constantly scanning the horizon for movement. Her thoughts wandered back to Yala-tene.

How many days had it been since she'd left—twelve, fourteen? Did the walls still stand? Did Karada's kindly brother Amero still lead the village? Or had he and the rest already fallen to the raiders, never knowing she had reached her goal?

Unconscious of the gesture, Beramun rested her hand against a spot high on her chest. Beneath her fingers was the green mark placed there by Sthenn—a smooth, iridescent triangle, a bit larger than a human thumbprint. The mark had nearly been her undoing when she first arrived in Yala-tene. She had no memory of receiving it, but Duranix said it stamped her as Sthenn's property and had urged her immediate death. Amero had defended her against his powerful friend. Had her long absence changed Amero's mind? Perhaps the people of Yala-tene now believed her to be doing the evil dragon's work.

Beramun kept the mark hidden from Karada and her people. She couldn't bear the thought that the same hatred and loathing she'd seen in the bronze dragon's eyes might bloom in Karada's clear hazel gaze.

The nomad on her immediate right, a dark-skinned fellow named Bahco, suddenly dropped to one knee. All along the line the scouts followed suit. With the pronounced heat-shimmer in the air, Beramun and the others would be invisible behind tall grass so long as they remained still.

She glanced at Bahco. His ebony skin was sweat-sheened, like her own. By following the line of his gaze, she saw dark figures moving against the bright horizon. The objects grew larger as she watched. They were closing. She and the other scouts dropped to their stomachs. Bahco crawled back to warn Karada.

Raising her head slightly, Beramun could make out six figures on horseback and, between them, four people walking on foot. Each pair of walkers had a long pole on their shoulders. A butchered animal carcass swayed from each pole.

Beramun sighed and relaxed a little. They were probably not Zannian's men. Such a hunting party would likely not be scouting for a force of raiders.

They were approaching from the northwest, heading southeast, which would bring them obliquely across Beramun's hiding place from right to left. As they drew nearer, sunlight flashed off the metal they wore, and Beramun fretted anew. Hunters avoided wearing metal, as the glare and clatter of it scared away game. Who were these people?

Someone came sliding through grass behind her. A dry, callused hand touched her forearm. She turned and saw the nomad chieftain crouched behind her.

Karada held a finger to her lips. Her bow was in her other hand. Beramun looked a question at her, but Karada's face was like a mask of seasoned wood. The marks on her face and neck, which had given her the name "Scarred One," stood out whitely against her tan.

Faintly, the strangers' voices could be heard. One of them laughed. The odor of freshly killed game was strong now. Beramun didn't dare lift her head higher for a better view. Instead, she slowly parted the grass stems in front of her, trying to peer through the summer growth.

Her caution was for naught. Karada suddenly rose to her knees and in one swift motion, nocked an arrow and loosed it. Beramun heard the flint-tipped shaft strike flesh; the sound was unmistakable.

Shouts erupted, and the riders urged their horses to a gallop even as Beramun wondered why Karada had given them away by attacking. All around her, the nomads rose from hiding places and picked off the mounted strangers. It was over in a few heartbeats, all six riders slain.

"Stand up, Beramun, and see who we've found."

The nomad chieftain bent over the one she'd shot, turning his lifeless face to the sun and pulling off his helmet. A shock of pale hair was revealed—and sharply pointed ears.

"Elves," Beramun breathed. "How did you know, Karada?"

The four bearers on foot had thrown down the deer carcasses they carried and stood in a huddle. They were elves too, dark-haired and more sunburned than their mounted comrades. When they heard the name of their captor, they fell to their knees in the trampled grass.

"Spare us, terrible Karada!" one cried. "We are not soldiers. We bear no arms!"

"You're elves," she replied coldly. "Why should I spare any of you?"

"We're poor folk from the south woods," said another, "hired to work for the great lord. Spare our lives, great chieftain! We will leave your land and never return!"

"What lord?" Karada asked. "Who leads you?"

"Lord Balif."

Bahco, leaning on his bow, was startled. "Out here? Why would the commander of Silvanos's host stray so far from home?"

"A hunting expedition, sir. Lord Balif delights in the hunt."

"Don't I know it." Karada prodded the nearest elf with her bow. "How many soldiers are with him?"

He shook his head, exchanging a frightened look with the others. "I don't know the number, lady."

"More than what you see here?"

He looked around at the watching nomads, then said, "Yes. Twice this many, could be."

Karada's eyes shone. "So Balif goes hunting with fewer than a hundred retainers?" She punched a fist in the air. "I'll have him! I'll hang his head from my tent post!"

"But what about Amero and Yala-tene?" Beramun cried.

"What about them?" Karada said coolly.

Beramun was stunned by her indifference. "We have to help them. Now!"

Karada tossed her bow to Bahco and folded her tanned arms. "Amero can hold out a half day longer. I've waited too many years to get Balif at sword point!"

Beramun tried to argue, but the rising color in the nomad chief's face told her it was useless. Love for her brother had given way to a dream of vengeance, a dream Karada would not deny herself.

From the bearers, they learned Balif's camp was two leagues southeast. Karada sent riders to tell Pakito to bring the rest of the band forward. Her plan was to wait for nightfall, then surround the elves' camp and take them while they slept. Beramun's worry that it might be a trap was dismissed outright, reasoning the Silvanesti had no way of knowing the nomads had come so far west.

"As far as they know," Karada said, smiling a bit, "we're still in the foothills of Strar, where you found us. Everyone has been chased out of this region, right down to Miteera and his centaurs." Her smile widened into a fierce grin. "Balif thinks he's safe!"

The nomads rounded up the slain Silvanesti's horses and prepared to join up with Pakito. Beramun was relieved when Karada ordered the captives bound rather than killed, and the woodland elves were led away by rawhide halters looped around their necks.

"I ought to burn them, as their masters tried to burn us on Mount Ibal," Karada muttered. Her hazel eyes narrowed. "But I won't. I've learned many things from the Silvanesti, but they are not my teachers in war."

Beramun was relieved, then startled as Karada's demeanor lightened abruptly. "I'll have him at last! Balif will fall to me!" the nomad chief exclaimed. "It's you, Beramun. You're my good luck. Your coming has been a portent."

Beramun shook her head sadly. "I did not come, I was sent."

Unmoved, Karada turned her attention to the elves' game. "Someone pick up that meat! Balif's hunters went to the trouble to kill those deer. The least we can do is eat them!"

* * * * *

They found Balif's camp just where the bearers said they would, by a small tributary of the Thon-Tanjan. A palisade of sharpened stakes surrounded the tents, and a few mounted warriors stood guard, but the eighty-odd elves in camp were sleeping as Karada closed in around them.

Beramun had never seen bows used at night before. The effect was terrifying. With no more sound than the snap of the bowstring, lethal arrows came flying out of the darkness. Highlighted by the campfires behind them, the mounted guards had no chance. They quickly went down, and Karada sent ten nomads forward to break a hole in the hedge of stakes. Only a small gap in the palisade was opened before the nomads were seen. The rattle of bronze gongs roused the Silvanesti from their slumber.

"Form on me!" Karada called, placing herself at the head of a close column of riders.

"Do we give quarter?" asked Pakito, a giant on a mammoth horse.

The chief's wheat-colored horse reared as her hands tightened on the reins. "Spare all who lay down their arms!" Karada shouted. "Now, at them!"

Three abreast, the mounted nomads charged through the gap made in the line of stakes. At first there was little resistance. Hastily donning what armor was at hand, the Silvanesti hung back around a central cluster of tents. Several javelins flew at the nomads, emptying a few saddles, but Karada was too canny to ride straight into the center of an aroused enemy camp. She sent half her warriors off to the left, circling just inside the palisade, while she led the rest to the right. A second wave of nomads, headed by Pakito, brought in torches and set fire to the outer ring of tents.

Fire blazed up, revealing the confusing scene. Beramun, armed with an unfamiliar sword, tried to keep pace with Karada. She did not strike a single blow, for the elves had done her no harm, but Silvanesti on foot around her did not realize this. A half-clad elf threw a spear at her. It seemed to leave his hand slowly, then gain frightening speed as it plunged at her face. She brought up her sword to deflect it, but a heedless, howling nomad rode in front of her and took the Silvanesti javelin in the ribs.

Shaking off her battle lethargy, Beramun rode through a gap in the churning crowd toward Karada. The Silvanesti adopted an interesting way of fighting their mounted foes. Instead of trying to make a line, they grouped into small knots of four to six warriors each, presenting a circle of sharp points all around them. They might have held off Karada's band with this tactic but for the nomads' bows. Whenever a knot of Silvanesti proved too tough to break, bows were called for and the defending elves picked off.

Between the two biggest campfires, a large contingent of elves had collected, led by a tall, fair-haired Silvanesti clad in a white shift stained with blood. Shouting in unison, the elves charged their mounted enemies and drove them back.

Karada shouldered through the melee. "Balif! It's Karada! Yield or perish!" she cried.

The fighting continued, however, so the nomad chief called on the archers beside her, ordering them to spare the tall elf leader.

A quick thrum of arrows cut down several Silvanesti standing beside Balif. When he saw his companions felled, the pale-haired elf snapped an order. Within moments, the remaining Silvanesti grounded their arms. A few on the far side of the camp did not hear the command or would not obey it. They fought on until they were overcome, and more died.

By midnight, the fighting was over. Half the elves and a score of Karada's warriors had been slain. The surviving elves were plainly shocked by the swift battle, and they sat disconsolately on the ground, lords and commoners alike.

Balif, slightly wounded, surrendered his sword to Pakito, who presented the elf lord to Karada.

Looking down on Balif from horseback, she relished the ironic change of fortune that had brought him into her hands.

"So, your life is mine now," she said. "What do you say to that?"

Balif mopped sweat and blood from his high forehead. "I say I am wiser than even I knew," he answered in a subdued voice.

She frowned, plainly at a loss. "What do you mean?"

"Years ago I spared you after the battle of the riverbend. Had I killed you, the leader of your band of nomads now might have no reason to spare my life."

Some of the nomads laughed at this surprising reasoning, but Beramun was still puzzled. "If you'd killed Karada back then, this whole battle might not have happened," she pointed out.

The elf lord turned to her, and she was struck by the strangeness of his eyes. They were like a cloudless sky or watered rock crystal. . . .

"Do I know you?" Balif said, pale brows rising. Even in defeat his manner was winning. She gave her name. "Well, Beramun, consider this: felling a single tree does not bring down an entire forest."

The nomads laughed again, but Beramun was as mixed-up as ever, both by his subtle words and by his demeanor.

"You still talk too much," Karada said harshly. "Stand where you are and keep silent!"

The captured elves were bound hand and foot and their camp thoroughly looted. Stores of fine bronze weapons, helmets, and breastplates were distributed to nomads who had distinguished themselves in the fight. Karada offered a long, yellow dagger to Beramun, but the girl declined.

"I'd rather learn the bow," she said.

"Then you shall." Karada tossed the dagger to Mara. "Put that in my baggage." Mara slipped into the crowd, the bronze dagger clutched in her fist.

When Balif was separated from the rest and led away, it became obvious not all the nomads were in favor of sparing him. A man named Kepra, whose face bore the old marks of severe burns, argued forcefully for the elf's death.

"Have you forgotten this?" he hissed, gesturing at his own face. "My mate and children burned to death at Mount Ibal in the fire *his* soldiers started!"

"Those Silvanesti were commanded by Tamanithas, not Balif," Pakito said.

The elf general Tamanithas had long pursued Karada with fanatical fury. His soldiers had set fire to the dry grass on the slopes of Mount Ibal, killing over half her band eight years ago. Tamanithas did not long enjoy his victory. He perished in personal combat with Karada, two years to the day after the fiery destruction he'd inflicted.

"Balif is no better!" Kepra insisted, his voice rising. "Cut off his head, I say! You've spoken of doing just that many times!"

During the debate, Balif had sat quietly at the center of the emotional nomads. He now asked if he could speak, and Karada gave him leave.

"In the plan of life it matters little whether you kill me or not. The Throne of the Stars will continue, and Speaker Silvanos will find a new servant to carry out his will."

The humans around him muttered and swore.

"That said, I must admit I do not want to die."

His declaration was followed by loud suggestions the elf lord be mutilated or blinded. Beramun noticed that for all his seeming calm, Balif's pallid face grew even whiter as he listened.

Karada let her people rant a while, then said, "A hunter does not injure an animal on purpose. She kills it or lets it go. There is no third way."

"I could be ransomed," Balif said. The word meant nothing to the nomads, so he explained. "Send word to Silvanost of my capture, and demand payment in exchange for my freedom. I'm certain the Speaker will barter for me, if the price is not too high."

Nomads greeted the notion with enthusiasm. Once more there was much noisy wrangling, this time over what to ask for. It wasn't lost on Balif that Kepra and a good number of other nomads remained silent, staring at him with unconcealed hatred.

Karada called again for silence. "As I am chief of this band, so your life belongs to me," she said to the elf lord. "Eight years ago I was in your place, and you spared my life—"

"No!" many nomads shouted, interrupting her. "Kill him!"

"Ransom! Ransom!" chanted others.

The tumult died down, and Karada's gaze bored into Balif's. "You won't know the day you're meant to die. That will be my choosing. Until then, we shall see if your great lord Silvanos values you as much as you say he does."

Balif nodded solemnly.

"Take any four of the well-born captives," Karada told Pakito. "Give them clothes to cover their backsides, a skin of water each, and a strip of jerky. Tell them to return to Silvanost with this message: Lord Balif will live only if I receive five hundred bronze swords, five hundred fleet horses—mares and stallions in equal number—and five hundred pounds of purest bronze."

Gasps arose at the huge price named. None of them had ever seen so much metal, and the band had never had five hundred horses at one time before.

"Will they be able to pay it?" asked Bahco, awed.

"They will pay or receive Balif's head in a pot of salt," said Karada flatly. Her bloodthirsty remarks did not seem to worry Balif as much as the silent anger of Kepra and those who sided with him. In fact, the elf lord smiled at Karada. She turned brusquely away.

"It'll take time to gather such wealth," Pakito said. "We're riding west. How will we ever get the ransom, if the great elf chief agrees?"

Karada pondered for a moment. Her eye fell on Kepra, scarred inside and out by fire.

"We will give them one year's time," she said. "Let the Silvanesti meet us then on the south slope of Mount Ibal. There the ransom will be given over . . . if Balif still lives."

The last four words were added in a mutter, but the elf lord agreed with surprisingly little rancor. Four noble elves were cut loose to deliver the message. At first they were reluctant to present such shameful words to the Speaker of the Stars, but Balif convinced them. They were given their meager supplies and sent off. The hoofbeats of their mounts faded quickly into the night.

The nomads dispersed to make preparations for night camp. Soon Karada and Beramun were alone with the captive elf lord.

Balif sat down on the ground. "Congratulations, Karada," he said.

"For what?"

"You are treating with the mightiest ruler in the world," he said, almost bemused. He looked past the nomad chieftain standing over him, focusing his gaze on the starry sky. "By doing so, you and your people cease to be a band of scavengers and vagabonds. Now you are a nation, like mine."

"Like yours?" she said, spitting the words. "Spirits preserve us from such a fate."

Chapter 3

At first, the flashes in the clouds below puzzled him. They couldn't be lightning. When a bronze dragon was aloft, any lightning in the air would naturally collect around him, not far beneath in some broken clouds. If not lightning, then the flicker of fire in the air had to be something else, something unnatural. This possibility filled his tired limbs with new energy.

Duranix had been airborne eleven straight days, keeping on the trail of his mortal foe, Sthenn. More than a thousand leagues had passed beneath his hurtling shadow: ocean, islands, continents, and more ocean. His days had been a grim routine of flying, eating on the wing, and straining his senses for clues.

Some five or six days into the chase, Sthenn had switched to a spear-straight course due west, no longer dodging and doubling back to confuse his younger adversary. Just as Duranix was adjusting to his foe's headlong flight, the aged serpent tricked him again. Losing the trail completely, Duranix wove north and south for several days, seeking remnants of the green dragon's passage.

There were a few signs—a small blasted area in a dense forest, the half-eaten carcass of a whale floating in the ocean, an errant smell of decay on the high winds—yet never an actual sighting.

Sthenn's new elusiveness was disturbing. Until now the green dragon had been careful *not* to lose Duranix. By keeping him on the chase, by leading him farther and farther from the Valley of the Falls, Sthenn was clearing the way for Zannian to destroy Yala-tene.

Duranix accepted those risks—the possibility of his own death and that of Amero—in order to sink his claws and teeth into his ancient enemy.

Now, thousands of leagues from Amero, Duranix sensed Sthenn's purpose had changed. Perhaps the ancient creature was growing tired. Maybe he thought enough time had elapsed for his human minions to ravage Duranix's territory. Whatever the reason, the green dragon was no longer leading Duranix astray, offering tantalizing glimpses of himself and leaving obvious markers to his passage. He seemed genuinely to be trying to evade his pursuer.

Scarlet and yellow flashes rippled through the lower clouds again. A distant boom arrived a little later. Duranix knew the air was too dry and cold to birth a thunderstorm. Perhaps he'd found Sthenn at last.

Shortening the spread of his wings, he dropped swiftly through the clouds. White lines of surf were visible to the north, evidence of a beach. Sunlight slanted through the tattered clouds, illuminating the tossing waves. The sea was shallow here, shallow and green as emerald.

Duranix emerged from the lowest level of clouds and found himself buffeted by searing flashes and loud claps of thunder. Heat flashed over his metallic hide.

Slitting his eyes to shield them, he saw the sea below was thick with boats, like the canoes made by humans but larger and more elaborate. Some were very long, with many slender oars protruding from the sides. They resembled giant centipedes. Other craft, shorter and blockier, pushed through the frothing waves propelled by a paddle wheel on each side. The centipede ships were roofed in timber and painted with stripes of red and black. The paddle-wheelers were sheathed in bronze plates. Duranix couldn't see what sort of creatures were operating the craft, but they were fighting each other, centipedes versus paddlers.

The strange thunder and lightning came again, and he immediately saw the source of the fury: machines, mounted on platforms atop the paddle vessels, were hurling pots of fire at their foes. When a pot hit a black-and-red centipede boat, it burst apart with a loud report and the craft, burning, sank.

There was no sign of Sthenn here, so Duranix pointed his nose west again. His wings had not flapped three times before the ocean exploded behind him. He thought it was more of the sea battle until he heard a reptilian shriek of fury. Craning his long neck around, he spotted Sthenn protruding from the waves. Water streamed from his neck and tree-trunk sized nostrils.

Got you! Duranix exulted. The craven Sthenn had tried to hide by lying submerged in the shallow, green waters, but had misjudged Duranix's position and emerged too soon. Now he was caught!

Duranix came diving back, chin barbels whipping in the wind. He thrust out his foreclaws and let his mouth gape wide. Too often on the chase Sthenn had managed to dodge Duranix's energy bolts. He'd always been airborne, able to maneuver. Now he was chest-deep in wind-tossed waves, standing on the sea bottom. Duranix let fly.

The sizzling blue bolt caught the green dragon squarely in his ancient, withered throat. He erupted in a howl of pain. Heat from the blast caused the water around Sthenn to steam. Slowly, like a great tree falling, he toppled backward into the waves.

Duranix flashed over the spot so low his wingtips flicked saltwater onto his back. He sped past a line of black-and-red boats, which back-oared frantically to avoid him. The paddle-wheelers hoisted pennants and closed in to finish their opponents off.

Duranix turned and strove hard to gain height. Strange, there was no sign of Sthenn. He couldn't possibly have succumbed to a single strike . . . but then, the green dragon had been traveling hard, and he was not as young or strong as Duranix.

The sea battle continued to rage beneath him, but Duranix ignored it. He had no time for anything but the destruction of his enemy.

The water was a perfect cover for the green dragon. Cursing his inadequate vision, Duranix tried to probe the surging depths with his other senses, but the scene was too confused.

Just as Duranix banked left, Sthenn reared up in the midst of the paddle craft. The green dragon had a deep wound in his chest that bled black ichor into the sea. Bilious jets of toxic fumes billowed from his mouth. The poison couldn't kill Duranix, but it did mix with the clouds to form a murky vapor. What effect it had on the creatures in the boats Duranix didn't know.

Sthenn reached down with both foreclaws, grasped the nearest boat, a flag-decked paddle-wheeler, and hoisted it into the air. The paddles on each side of the tubby hull continued to turn, water sluicing from them. Wheezing with pain, Sthenn hurled the vessel at Duranix.

The bronze flapped vigorously for altitude. The boat tumbled end over end as it came. Duranix dodged, and the craft plummeted back to the sea. When it landed a huge spout of green water was thrown up, and the battered boat rapidly sank.

A curious thing happened next. The boats ceased battling each other and attacked the dragons! Not just the paddle-wheelers but the centipede vessels as well—scores of craft turned their attention to the giant beasts in their midst. The centipede boats were equipped with sharp metallic prows, which they tried to ram into Sthenn. He swatted the craft aside while spewing poisonous breath over them.

The paddle-wheelers tossed firepots at Duranix. He twisted and turned, keeping his vulnerable wings away from the exploding pots. He had no quarrel with these unknown beings, but they were hampering his more important contest. Without the strength to loose another bolt of lightning, he directed his repelling force against the firepots arcing toward him. The pots rebounded, falling among the very ships that had launched them. Two of the craft were shattered by the ensuing blasts, rolling over and plunging beneath the waves. The remaining paddlers scuttled away.

By this time Sthenn had waded free of the sea battle. Striding laboriously on his hind legs, the green dragon rose higher and higher out of the water.

"Sthenn!" Duranix bellowed. "Stay and fight!"

The old beast continued his plodding progress toward land, still more than a league away. "Not today, little friend," he wheezed. "Not . . . today!"

Duranix tore after his fleeing foe. So intent was he on the chase that he didn't notice a second fleet of paddle craft just below his right wing. At a range of a hundred paces, eight vessels flung their firepots. On converging courses, the pots collided directly beneath the bronze dragon.

The shock of the blast flipped him upside down. Sulfurous fumes filled his chest. He plunged to the water and struck hard, headfirst.

The impact stunned him. He was conscious for a few moments, feeling something encircle his neck, sensed he was moving through the water, being towed. Then he blacked out.

Time passed. The sun climbed higher, its heat thinning the early morning clouds. Blue reclaimed the wide sky. Sea birds, leery at first of the enormous creature beached on their turf, slowly came out of hiding and began to wheel and dive for food again.

Duranix awoke slowly, slitting his eyes against the blinding brightness of sky. He lay on his back in the surf, wings extended but buried in wet sand. His tail drifted side to side with the motion of the tide. Cold seawater gurgled in his ears.

He raised his head, and the web of fiber lines wound around his neck snapped and fell away. Having stunned him, the paddle crafts had wrapped him in a stout net, towed him ashore, and hastened away. Why they didn't try to harm him further he couldn't guess.

The ocean was dotted with wreckage—broken timbers, oars, the shattered remains of boats. Underneath the pervasive smell of sulfur and niter was the tang of burned flesh. Whether his, Sthenn's, or that of the warring creatures on the boats, he couldn't tell.

Rolling onto all fours, Duranix shook off the netting and damp sand. A look up and down the beach showed him Sthenn was gone, so he set about putting himself to rights so he could resume the chase.

Each wing had to be preened of sand. If the sand was allowed to work its way under his scales, it would cause painful sores. The preening was a cautious operation, requiring concentration. His claws and horns were hard and sharp, and his wing membranes were delicate.

When he was finished, Duranix spread his wings a bit to dry them. He strode up the shoreline to the highest dune. From this vantage, he saw a green line of trees inland. More importantly, he saw Sthenn's narrow, three-toed claw prints. The old dragon had come ashore here, and his prints led directly toward the distant forest. He must have been hurt if he wasn't flying—or could this be another of his endless tricks to put Duranix off guard?

It scarcely mattered. Duranix had no choice but to follow his tormentor's mincing tracks. The trees were still a long way off when he found the ancient stone marker.

It stood in the midst of the dunes, a sandstone column carved flat on four sides. It was old and weathered, and its base was askew, causing the tall column to lean. Strange figures were carved in deep relief on all four faces.

Duranix started to walk around the column but paused. The carvings caught his attention.

The reliefs showed a crowd of two-legged beings (vaguely like humans or elves) swarming ant-like up the side of a mountain. They toppled large round objects—boulders perhaps—off a cliff while others of their kind fought a pair of large, four-legged creatures with long, serpentine necks.

Duranix stared hard at the worn images. Were those wings folded on the creatures' backs? Was he looking at some kind of memorial to a battle fought against dragons?

The shrieks of gulls spiraling overhead broke his contemplation. With Sthenn still roaming free, this was no time to puzzle over artifacts. The green dragon's trail led without deviation to the forest; he must be seeking the kind of cover he knew best.

Duranix flexed his wings experimentally. They were dry and free of sand. He leaped into the air.

From this height, he could see the woods were wide and dense, separating the beach from a series of cliffs beyond. The escarpment was composed of a light blue stone, making it hard to distinguish from the hazy sky.

When he reached the trees, Duranix spread his powerful senses wide in search of Sthenn. Immediately, he picked up the scent of a dragon—but, surprisingly, it wasn't Sthenn.

The old wyrm exuded a putrescence Duranix knew as well as he knew the smell of Amero (poor soft-skinned humans could never get truly clean). This new scent was certainly draconic, but metallic and clean. There was something else, a difference he couldn't quite fathom. The closer he came to the escarpment, the more pronounced the distracting scent became.

Extending his rear claws, Duranix landed on a ledge of blue stone. It was a pretty species of slate, only slightly darker than a summer sky. He put his back to the plateau and studied the forest below. He had an excellent view of the land, and in that position he remained, unmoving as the stones around him, while the sun passed its zenith and began its descent.

Many animals and birds passed beneath his gaze, but not Sthenn. Puzzling. The green dragon's presence should have disturbed the local animals greatly, yet he saw little sign of it. Predatory birds circled in the warm air. Tree-climbing rodents cavorted among the leafy branches. Clouds of insects swarmed over the narrow stream flowing through the heart of the woods. The largest beast Duranix saw was a kind of long-legged pig, with a ruff of stiff, white fur around its neck and a pair of vicious-looking tusks. About half the size of a wild ox, the ruffed pigs left the shade of the trees in twos and threes to dip their long snouts in the stream. If Sthenn was around, he was being extremely discreet. The pigs looked completely untroubled.

They also looked quite tasty. Duranix's stomach rumbled. His last meal had been a school of leaping sailfish two days ago, and he found his attention fixed by the prowling pigs.

Then came that feeling again, the sensation another dragon was near. A broad shadow flashed overhead. Acting purely on instinct, he sprang straight up at the shadow. He had only a glimpse of bright scales and slender wings before he slammed into the belly of another dragon.

The stranger bleated in surprise. Duranix knew immediately it was not Sthenn. He tried to disentangle himself but was firmly held by the other. Together they dropped from the sky and crashed into the forest. The spicy, resinous smell of fractured cedar filled the air.

Powerful clawed feet kicked at Duranix's chest. Nothing like the vicious attacks he'd weathered from Sthenn, they still hurt. Tired, frustrated, and ravenously hungry, Duranix lost his temper. He seized the other dragon's hind legs, reared, and flung him into the trees.

There was a glint of bright metal. The dragon hit the cedars and flattened them. Rolling over several times, the stranger came quickly to his feet.

Duranix blinked, his eyelids clicking down and up several times. The stranger was not a he but a she—a bronze dragon, smaller than himself.

She shook off the effects of the crash and faced him, back arched like an enormous wildcat, horns, spines, and barbels rigid with fright and fury. Extending her neck, she opened her jaws and hissed.

He was surprised, having expected her to loose a bolt of lightning. Assuming a passive stance, he relaxed his coiled muscles. "Greetings." he said. "Who are you? What's your name?"

"Greetings!" She growled angrily, deep in her throat. She was half Duranix's weight and two-thirds his length. Thin, too, but well muscled. Her scales were bright and well buffed.

When he failed to get any further response, Duranix asked, slowly and deliberately, "What is your name?"

The female bronze finally lowered her back and raised her head. "Blusidar. Blusidar is my name."

"I'm sorry I attacked you, Blusidar. I mistook you for an enemy. There is a green dragon in your territory, a creature of great evil. I've pursued him around the world to this spot. When you flew past me, I thought you were him."

She stepped over broken tree stumps, carefully keeping her distance from the imposing stranger. "I see no dragon but you, and I did not see you till you struck."

She was young, Duranix realized. Very young. Still, she was the first bronze dragon he'd encountered since the death of his mother and clutchmates many centuries ago. In his travels around familiar lands, he'd met other dragons: the loquacious brass Gilar, who dwelt in the far eastern desert, and the copper twins Suphenthrex and Salamantix, who lived on twin mountains northeast of the Valley of the Falls. Other dragons he had known had dwelt on the borders of the great savanna, but one by one, they'd been killed or driven off by Sthcnn.

"This green dragon—his name is Sthenn—is here somewhere close by, hiding," Duranix told Blusidar. "I wounded him in the sea and I tracked him ashore. You're not safe with him here."

She pondered that for a moment, then asked, "What? I am safe with you?"

"Certainly!" he said indignantly. She flinched when his voice rose. Schooling himself to calm, Duranix added, "What land is this? Who dwells here besides you?"

"This land is the land. I know no other," Blusidar said. "Came you through the *Zenzi?*" At his obvious lack of understanding, she explained, "Zenzi—walk on two legs, like birds, but have no feathers. So big." She held her claw off the ground at about the same height as a human child.

"These Zenzi, do they use large boats to cross the sea?" he asked, and she nodded. "Then I saw them, fighting others or among themselves. Who are they?"

Haltingly, pushing the limits of her vocabulary, Blusidar told him about the Zenzi and this, her homeland.

It was an island, quite large, with a ring of blue stone mountains in the center. She was the only dragon on the island, though once there had been others. The Zenzi had confined the dragons to the island long, long ago.

"How is that possible?" Duranix demanded. "Creatures no bigger than humans imposing their will on dragons? I don't believe it!"

"Not big dragons like me, you." She cupped her foreclaws around an imaginary sphere. *"Vree-al."*

Duranix was startled. The sound Blusidar made was the one clutching females used to comfort their unhatched offspring.

She continued, relating an amazing tale that explained the weathered column he'd seen on the beach. Ages ago, the Zenzi had dumped fertile dragon eggs on this remote island. After hatching, the dragons grew up in isolation and ignorance, having no idea of the wider world beyond the shores of their island. Over time, a few had taken a chance and flown away, certain there must be more to their world than this island. None had ever returned, and the rest had lived and died here. Blusidar was the last.

"You go," she said, finishing her story. "This place is mine. You go back where you came."

She seemed unmoved by the fact that Duranix's very existence confirmed a wider world beyond her tiny island.

"I shall leave," Duranix said, "but not until I find Sthenn. If I leave him here, he'll kill you."

Blusidar backed away, keeping her dagger-shaped pupils fixed on Duranix. "Then go soon. Too many dragons are trouble. Find your Green and go!"

She slipped between the closely growing trees and disappeared. Duranix advanced a few steps. Pigeons rose in a cloud from the trees, marking the fleeing bronze's path.

Something hard jabbed his foreclaw. Duranix lifted his leg and saw a bright bronze scale embedded in the trunk of a shattered cedar. He worked it loose with his talons. One of Blusidar's. Unlike his own scales, which were large, curved, and shaped like an acorn in silhouette, Blusidar's were flatter and almost circular. The edges were smooth, another sign she was less than a century old. From the scale wafted the clean, bright smell he'd sensed while flying over the island.

The image of Blusidar staring fearfully up at him, knowing he was larger and stronger, yet facing him with foolish bravery, caused Duranix to close a powerful claw around the scale.

Here was one dragon Sthenn would not harm, he vowed. He would not allow it.

Chapter 4

Dawn arrived in awesome silence. A light morning mist filled the low places below the walls of Yala-tene and hung over the clear waters of the Lake of the Falls. Despite the early hour, the parapets were lined with people—somber, gray-faced, as stony as the wall on which they stood.

On the valley floor, lines of horsemen were deployed in a great arc around the besieged town, from the rocky flats below the waterfall to the now empty ox pens on the north end of Yala-tene. In places the line was only a single rider deep, but they were there, armed and ready.

A small party of raiders rode out from their camp by the river, making straight for the western entrance to the town. In their wake came a dozen raiders on foot, four of them bearing a litter on their shoulders. Showing off their best horsemanship, the approaching raiders wheeled about just out of throwing range. The morning sun flashed off their purloined weapons and armor.

Four raiders put ram's horns to their lips and blew a flat, wavering note that carried from one end of the valley to the other. A single man on a pale gray horse rode forth a few steps from the group, then stopped. Like most of the raiders, he was masked—his was an elaborate creation fashioned from the skull of some horned beast and adorned with leather flaps and paint. He removed his skull-mask, revealing a surprisingly youthful face and light brown hair.

"People of Arku-peli!" he called. "I am Zannian, chief of this band! Do you hear me?" A shower of stones spattered the ground a pace in front of his horse.

His lips thinned in a grim smile. "I see you do. I have words for your headman! Bring him out, so I may speak with him!"

The crowd atop the wall stirred, and two people shouldered to the front. One was an elderly man with thinning gray hair and a long nose. The other was a woman half his age with chestnut hair drawn back in a thick braid. She leaned on a spear.

"Say what you need to say to me!" the woman called.

"Begone, woman! I will speak only to your Arkuden!"

"Begone yourself then, butcher. The Arkuden is too busy to waste words on you!"

Puffing under their load, the litter bearers arrived alongside Zannian. Seated in the contraption of hide and poles was a woman of forty summers, though she looked much older. Her fair hair was liberally streaked with gray, a shade reflected in her dark, flinty gaze, and her face was deeply lined. Once a warrior herself, she traveled now by litter because her right leg ended at the knee, the limb lost years before to a shattering injury.

"Go back, mother," Zannian said to her under his breath. "You're not needed here."

"I want to see their faces," Nacris replied. "I want to be here when they admit Amero is dead!"

"Bring out the Arkuden!" Zannian shouted once more. "Bring him out, if any of you want to survive this fight!"

The woman and the elderly man conferred, then the old man called down in a quavering voice, "The Arkuden has been wounded. He can't yet stand on his injured leg. Speak to us, raider. We will carry your words to him."

Nacris pushed herself up on her hands, screaming, "Show us his corpse, you liars! We know he's dead! I want to see the work done by my Jade Men!"

Furious, Zannian leaned down and shoved the crippled woman back into her seat.

"Meddling old vulture! Shut your mouth!" To the men holding up her conveyance he barked, "Take Nacris back to camp!"

"No! I deserve to see his blood! Stop, men! I killed him, Zan! You couldn't do it, but I could! Stop right now! Take me back—"

Wary as they were of the formidable Nacris, the litter bearers were more afraid of their leader. They continued down the hill with the woman ranting at them all the way.

"Listen to me, foolish people!" Zannian declared loudly. "This is your last chance! By Moonmeet, we'll have the means to overcome your wall! When that happens, no one in Arku-peli will be spared! Do you hear? You'll all die! Tell that to your *wounded* Arkuden—you have until the morning of Moonmeet to yield. After that, no mercy!"

In answer to his ultimatum, many villagers on the wall turned their backs and lifted their kilts in contempt.

Zannian laughed despite himself and donned his skull-mask again. He rode back to his waiting captains. The eldest of them, Hoten son of Nito, greeted him.

"Any sign of the Arkuden?" the elder man asked.

"No. Mother's assassins may well have succeeded."

Another raider said, "She promised they would submit if their Arkuden died."

"My mother says many things. You'd be wiser to listen to me, not her."

The raider chief and his captains rode back to their band. Hoten pulled the skullcap of bear and panther teeth from his head and rubbed a hand over his sweaty pate.

"I don't like it, Zan," he said. "What if the mud-toes don't give up in time? Will you really set a pack of ogres on them?"

"Assuming that rogue Harak returns with any, yes." Zannian glared at Hoten's shocked expression. "Did you think I wouldn't?"

"But ogres, Zan! How can we ally ourselves with such monsters?"

Zannian's laugh was as sharp as a bronze sword. "Are they any worse than a green dragon?"

He kicked his horse's flanks and cantered away. Raiders eager for his favor followed him, leaving Hoten behind. The camp by the river soon rang with Nacris's shrill denunciations, punctuated by her son's deeper-voiced replies.

* * * * *

By the time the first mountain peaks appeared on the western horizon, Beramun was beside herself with worry. So many days had passed since she'd left the Valley of the Falls—days without word of Zannian's raiders or the fate of Yala-tene. She chafed at the deliberate pace Karada set for her band. When she complained at their slowness, Karada told her the horsed contingent couldn't leave behind the unmounted members. If the band became strung out, both the head and tail of the line would be vulnerable to raider or Silvanesti attack.

Beramun saw the wisdom of this, yet understanding did nothing to ease her anxiety. Her riding skills had improved on the long march, and she was able to concentrate less on maintaining her seat and more on the distant ghostly peaks ahead. Her anxious eyes remained fixed forward, watching the mountains grow slowly more distinct in the hot, hazy air.

To distract herself from the slow pace and her own dark worries, Beramun left Karada's side and circled back through the dusty column. Eventually, she passed the ranks of the elf prisoners, marching in the center of the nomads' column under the command of their own officers.

The elves had proved surprisingly docile. Aside from plenty of sullen faces in their ranks, they kept pace and caused no trouble. One or two glared at Beramun as she rode by, but she ignored them.

Balif had been given over to the custody of Pakito. The elf lord was mounted on a good horse, the better to keep pace with Pakito's large steed. Balif's hands were bound in front of him so he could hold his reins, and a stout rawhide thong was slung under his horse's belly, hobbling the elf's ankles. The horse he rode had been trained by Samtu, Pakito's mate. It responded to whistled commands like a dog. If Balif tried to gallop away, Samtu's shrill whistle would bring the animal trotting obediently back.

"It would be simpler if you'd give your oath not to escape," Pakito said.

"All captives have the duty to escape," replied Balif. "Karada would agree with me."

A grunt. "Try it then. Karada would slit your throat."

Balif smiled thinly. He knew the big man spoke the truth.

Beramun rode up to them, falling in beside the elf lord's mount. Though she said nothing, her curiosity was so obvious Balif addressed her.

"Are you Karada's daughter?" he asked. The nomads had taken his helmet and suede hat, so his fair face was rapidly turning red-brown under the broiling sun.

Beramun shook her head. "No. I come from a different place, a different clan."

"Yet, she favors you like a daughter. Don't you think so?" This last was addressed to Pakito.

"This one interests her," the giant agreed. "And Karada does not give her attention lightly."

Balif looked back at Beramun, his pale eyes frankly assessing her. "Why, I wonder? What does she see in you?"

"All that black hair and those big dark eyes—she is pretty," Pakito said thoughtfully, and Beramun's blush was more fiery than the elf's sunburn.

"For a human, I suppose so. I'll concede it as a matter of taste."

"Don't talk about me as if I were a prized mare!" Beramun snapped. "I came from Yala-tene with a message from Karada's brother, Amero. His town is besieged by vicious raiders. I was one of several scouts sent to find Karada and fetch her back to Yala-tene."

"Yes? Why doesn't the dragon of the mountain help his friend the Arkuden?"

Beramun explained Duranix's absence, then said, "Elf, you seem more talker than fighter. How did you and Karada become such dire enemies?"

"In my country, one may be a poet, a dancer, or a painter, as well as a warrior. Thinking and fighting are not like fire and water, mixing to the destruction of both. As commander of the host of the Speaker of the Stars, I am obliged to carry out his will and make war on his enemies. Karada understands this. We've fought many times. Once I won and spared her life. I thought showing leniency to their chief would dispirit the nomads, but . . ." He shrugged and shot a sidelong glance at Pakito, who was listening carefully. "Many times I regretted not killing Karada. The Speaker's soldiers have hunted her for twenty seasons. In that time, many brave warriors have perished."

"On both sides," put in Pakito.

"How do you know Karada won't kill you, if the ransom isn't paid?" Beramun asked.

Balif leaned toward her. His sky-blue eyes bored into her dark ones. In a voice deep and vibrant, he said, "You won't let her kill me, will you?"

Startled, Beramun pulled back on her reins, halting her horse. The moving column flowed around her. Balif's light chuckle, joined by Pakito's booming laugh, came clearly back to her. Wrenching her mount's head around, she rode back toward the rear of the band, her crimson face hidden in the swirling clouds of dust.

When Beramun finally returned to the head of the column, she found Karada surrounded by scouts. Trotting in the flattened grass behind the nomad chieftain's horse was the girl Mara, her face and auburn hair yellow with dust.

"Have a good talk with Balif?" asked Karada as Beramun arrived. Beramun's surprise was evident, and Karada added, "I know everything that happens in this band. A horse doesn't stumble or a child cough that I don't hear about it eventually."

"I've never met an elf before," Beramun said defensively. "I wanted to see what they're like."

"Stay away from Balif. He's too wise for you, too cunning. Listen to him long enough and you'll end up wanting to free him."

"I would never do that!"

"Yes, you would," Mara put in airily. "The Good People can change a mind or turn a heart around as easily as the wind finds a new course."

Beramun had no chance to dispute this, as Mara added quickly, "Please, Karada, may I have a horse?"

"None to spare," was the terse reply.

Mara, panting between the mounted nomads, looked so downcast Beramun felt sorry for her.

"Climb on," she said, extending a hand. "We can ride double."

Mara looked from Beramun's outstretched hand to Karada's stern face and back again. Without another word, she turned and merged back into the dusty stream of horses and dragging travois.

* * * * *

The dry wind switched directions, becoming damp and heavy as it blew down from the north. By late afternoon, the hazy white clouds had clotted into piles of mighty thunderheads, filling the northern sky. The nomads plodded on for a while, but night and the threat of rain finally convinced Karada to halt her people. While the first campfires were being laid, the clouds broke open and dumped a torrent of water, dousing all hope of warmth. Cold jerky and journey bread were everyone's fare that night.

A few tents were dragged out and unfolded before Karada rode by and ordered they not be put up. The band would move out at first light, and she wanted no time wasted pitching and striking tents. Many grumbled at having to spend the night in the rain, but every nomad in the band knew their leader would be out in the weather herself, just as wet and miserable as the rest of them.

Beramun had lost sight of the chief when the rain closed in, so she wandered the camp, looking for some spot to spend the night. The elf prisoners had a novel method for beating the weather. Their cloaks were made with several small metal hooks and rings along their edges and could be joined together into a large, lightweight fly. As the rain poured down, the elves sat on the ground in a tight circle, facing outward, shielded from the worst of the downpour by their ingenious cloak-tent.

After a long search, Beramun spotted Karada's wheat-colored horse tied to a picket line. Below the animal's nose was a dark hump in the grass. Someone was squatting there, wrapped in a large ox hide. Beramun hurried over. She lifted one edge of the hide and shoved her head under.

"Room for another?" she asked, then saw it was not Karada under the hide, but Mara.

The girl said nothing but moved slightly to one side, giving tacit assent. Warily, Beramun crawled in.

It was dark as Sthenn's heart under the hide, but with their knees drawn up to their chins, the two girls were able to stay dry. The air was heavy with cold rain and Mara's palpable jealousy.

The silence stretched between them until Beramun asked, "Where's Karada?"

"With that elf. She's spent every night with him since he was caught." Beramun gave a low exclamation of surprise, and Mara added, "Not alone. Pakito's with them."

"Oh." Beramun dismissed the alarming fantasies she'd conjured up. "Is she afraid he'll escape?"

She felt the other girl shrug. "Pakito says they argue about everything, from the best way to raise horses to who's the best leader. This goes on until one tires and goes to sleep. Karada's won every night. That elf sleeps first."

Rain trickled down Beramun's collar. She pushed away from the edge of the hide until her feet bumped Mara's.

"Is it a game?"

"Karada doesn't play games," Mara said, her tone a mixture of pride in her leader and animosity for her own treatment. "It's a fight. Karada is pitting her spirit against that elf's."

In a comradely way, Beramun replied, "She's in no danger, I'm certain."

The sharp chime of metal sliding against metal, the sound of a dagger being drawn, froze the words in her throat. She tensed as a cold, bronze point touched her ankle.

"No one will harm Karada!" Mara announced. "Not while I live!"

Beramun was silent, unmoving and barely breathing. Her lack of response had the desired effect: the weapon was returned to its sheath.

"I think I'll get some rest," Beramun said mildly and curled up on the damp ground. A spot between her shoulder blades tingled at being exposed to one so troubled who carried a dagger, but Beramun felt she had Mara figured out. The girl worshiped whoever ruled her—first Tiphan, leader of the destroyed Sensarku, then her Silvanesti masters while she was a slave, and now Karada. Those her ruler favored, Mara would not harm, but woe to anyone Karada hated!

As she drifted off to sleep at last, Beramun reflected on Balif's predicament. Being in the hands of his long-time enemy didn't seem to worry him, and he didn't appear to chafe at waiting as long as a year to see if his lord Silvanos would pay his ransom. Yet if he knew the danger he faced from this single, strange girl, things might be different. "That elf," as Mara called him, might know true fear.

* * * * *

The rain pounded the walls of Yala-tene. It ran in streams down alleys, washing away the dust of many dry days. In the lane before the House of the Turtle, it also washed away a great deal of blood.

Within, Lyopi sat quietly by the fire, her tears spent. Her thick chestnut hair, freed from its usual neat braid, fell past her waist.

"Pitiless children," she said.

"What?"

Two men knelt on the other side of the hearth, the flames between them. One was Tepa the beekeeper, oldest of the remaining village elders. With him was Hekani, a young man lately thrust into the position of leading the defense of Yala-tene. Not quite twenty, Hekani wore his brown hair in a long horsetail, in the fashion of the men who still wandered the savanna. Until the raiders invaded the valley, he'd never spent a night in Yala-tene. He was a wanderer who had dwelt in the tent camp outside the walls. Like the rest of the camp's inhabitants, he traded, bartered, and hired out his labor for two days or ten. When the wanderers in the tent camp pulled up stakes and departed under threat of Zannian's arrival, Hekani was the only one who'd remained. His common sense and loyalty had won the trust of the Arkuden and, even more difficult, of the Arkuden's woman, Lyopi.

"What did you say?" Hekani asked again.

"The ones Zannian sent after Amero—they were barely more than children. How do you make children into such pitiless killers?"

"I hope never to know," Tepa murmured. He rested his forehead in the palm of one hand and sighed deeply. His own son, Udi, had been one of those sent out with Beramun several weeks ago to find the Arkuden's sister. The raiders had caught Udi, and his dying body had been displayed on stakes before the walls of Yala-tene. As yet there was no word of Beramun.

As the old man dozed, Hekani slipped around the hearth to be closer to Lyopi. He was very tall, all knees and elbows. Fate had shown him to be a formidable fighter. He'd slain two of the invading Jade Men by himself.

"What shall we do?" he asked, voice low out of deference for the sleeping man. "Our food won't last twenty days. There's been no sign of the last scout the Arkuden sent out. Unless the dragon returns to save us, I doubt we can hold out much longer."

Lyopi nodded her agreement and prodded the dying fire. The fact that Beramun's body hadn't been exhibited by the raiders had given Lyopi hope the girl had made it through. But perhaps the girl wanderer had taken to her heels, leaving the certain death of Yala-tene behind.

The flickering flame went out, leaving only a shoal of glowing coals. "There are," Lyopi said slowly, as though choosing her words with care, "tunnels in the mountain."

"The storage tunnels? What of them? They're all dead ends."

"Two are; *one* isn't. Amero found a fissure in the rock while hunting for copper ore. He had some men widen the cleft. It runs all the way to the cliff top overlooking the village. Amero had both ends concealed with slabs of rock."

Hekani was stunned. "Why haven't you spoken of this earlier? We can escape!"

Lyopi shook her head and said, "The passage is too narrow to allow more than one small person through at a time. It would take days for the population of Yala-tene to get out—those who would fit—and the tunnel could collapse at any time. Escape was never the plan. It was too risky even to consider, but now . . ." She lifted hollow eyes to his. "The children. We might get some of the children out. They could escape over several nights, scatter in the mountains. It will be dangerous, but at least something of Yala-tene might survive."

Hekani rocked back on his hands. "I say, fight it out! You saw them out there yesterday—there aren't so many left! We can beat them!"

"Moonmeet is in two days. They claim they'll have a way to tear down our wall."

"They're bluffing! They can't overcome our wall. All they can do is threaten and scare us."

"I am scared," Lyopi said softly. "How many do we have left who can fight?"

Hekani thought a moment, then answered, "Able-bodied men and women—one hundred and sixteen. Old folks and children who can help—one hundred forty and nine. Hurt or sick ones who can't fight at all—two hundred and eighty-eight."

"And how many have died?"

He turned away from her intense gaze. "I don't know. I've only been war chief since the night of the Jade Men."

Lyopi rose suddenly. She draped a horsehair blanket around the sleeping Tepa. Hekani took his leave, throwing on his cloak and retrieving his spear.

"Be strong, Lyopi." he said proudly. "We're not lost yet!"

He strode away in the rain. Once he was gone, Lyopi discovered a well of tears she had not yet exhausted. She leaned her head against the door and wept. The sound of her crying was lost in the rush of rain down the dark, empty street.

Chapter 5

"This had better not be a jest."

Zannian sat on his horse, flanked by Hoten and four other captains of his band. To his right, Nacris reclined in her chair, hands folded together and pressed against her lips. The morning sun was behind the group, filling the mountain pass with long shadows and tinting the peaks crimson.

A scout had returned earlier that morning with an odd report: In the lower end of the pass leading out of the Valley of the Falls, he'd encountered a lone rider. The rider identified himself as Harak, son of Nebu, but would not approach. When the scout tried to approach him, the supposed Harak had told him to come no closer but to bring Zannian and Nacris at once.

Irritated by the lofty command, the scout started to argue, but movement on the slope behind Harak caught his eye. Something stirred, sending a shower of pebbles down the mountainside. The scout's horse pranced amidst the cascade of stones.

Harak cast a glance at the slopes behind him and snapped, "I've been on a mission for our chief! Go now and do what I tell you! Bring Zan and Nacris here!"

The scout went.

He found Zannian in a black mood. Five raiders had deserted the night before, while patrolling the passes east of Yala-tene. In the past three days, more than twenty men had abandoned the siege.

The scout's report caused the raider chief's hazel eyes to narrow suspiciously. "Are you sure it was Harak? What's he playing at? Why didn't he just ride in?"

Though Zannian had accepted the necessity of Nacris's plan to send for the ogres, most of the band knew nothing about it.

Nacris gave her son a significant look and, glancing at the men in earshot, said, "Harak doesn't know what's happened since he's been gone. He's a cautious, clever fellow, that one."

"Yes," Zannian muttered, "too clever."

Without explanation, he rounded up two dozen raiders and led them to the western pass. Most he left at the mouth of the ravine, as only he, Nacris, Hoten, and a handful of favored captains continued deeper into the pass.

Hoten hadn't been nearby when the scout made his report, but the elder raider was observant. When they had left the other warriors behind, he said quietly, "Harak's back, isn't he?"

"Seems to be," Zannian replied.

"Do the men know what's coming?"

A sharp look. "What difference does that make?"

Hoten reined to a stop. "It makes all the difference, Zan! We're the Raiders of Almurk. We follow the Master and do his will, but we are still men!"

Zannian swung his horse to one side, his hand resting on the hilt of his sword. "Are you questioning my command?" he asked calmly.

Hoten stared at his leader, jaw flexing as he ground his teeth.

Four other captains, following behind, caught up to them and stopped, uncertain what was happening. When Nacris arrived in the next moment, she sized up the situation immediately.

"You two going to fight?" she asked.

"And if we did?" Hoten asked his mate through clenched teeth. "Who would you favor?"

"You're both too important to this band to waste your lives fighting each other. Open your eyes! Can't you see victory before us? It's just down this pass, a league or so away. Do you really want to kill each other now, when the spoils of success are nearly in your hands?"

Zannian relaxed as she spoke. "You're my mother's mate, Hoten. Killing you wouldn't be respectful." Tapping his heels to his gray stallion's flanks, the chief moved on.

Hoten glared from Zannian to Nacris and back for the space of a few heartbeats. Then he too started his horse moving again. When he caught up to his chief, he said in a low voice, "This is wrong, Zan, and we'll all suffer for it."

Zannian's reply was loud and confident. "As the Master says, the only wrong in this world is failure. I won't fail."

They arrived at the spot the scout had indicated, but there was no sign of Harak. They waited. The morning sun pushed higher and higher, warming the shadeless canyon. To shift Zannian's mind from his growing impatience, Nacris spun out old stories about her youth, her days with Karada, and her first mate, Sessan. The air grew hotter, and biting flies beset both horses and men.

"This had better not be a jest," Zannian repeated

"Zan! Look!"

Far down the trail, shimmering in the heat-soaked air, a rider came. His pace was slow, and the steady clop of his horse's hooves echoed off the high stone walls around them. Hoten wanted to ride out to meet him, but Zannian refused to let him go. He'd come this far at someone else's beck and call. Now that someone would come to him.

The wavering image slowly resolved into a lanky, tanned rider with long, dark brown hair, riding a dappled brown horse. At Zannian's command, the raiders fanned out in a semicircle. Nacris, unafraid, ordered her bearers to carry her out in front of the mounted men.

Her vision was still acute. "Harak!" she called.

The young raider urged his mount to a canter and loped in, nodding to his comrades. He stopped when his horse was head to head with Zannian's.

"Greetings, chief," he exclaimed, "and to your wise and ferocious mother."

"Where are they?" Nacris asked eagerly, eyes alight. "Are they with you?"

Mischief danced in Harak's deep brown eyes, but a look at the sweaty, impatient faces around him caused him to quell his normal impulse to be flippant. He twisted sideways on his horse, one arm sweeping out to gesture behind and above. He gave a loud, guttural call.

In unison, the raiders' heads lifted. One man let out a hoarse yell.

"Ogres!"

Stepping out of cover, hulking figures ranged on both sides of the pass. The raiders were surrounded. Hoten, the captains, and the litter bearers were obviously alarmed. Swords and spears came up. Only Zannian, Nacris, and Harak remained calm.

"Be careful," Harak said quickly, as several of the raiders brandished their weapons. "Ungrah-de is wary of humans. He says you can't trust creatures with such small teeth."

"Which one is he?" Zannian asked.

A sly look crossed Harak's features. "Leadership among the ogres is determined by size—a most sensible practice." He was himself a span taller than Zannian. "Ungrah-de is the biggest ogre here."

Zannian picked him out immediately and raised his hands in the plainsman's traditional greeting. "Great Chief! I greet you with open hands!"

Ungrah folded his tree-trunk sized arms. "Huh," he called down. "You're very small—smaller even than little Harak. How can you be chief?"

"I am chief by my wits, by my skill with arms, and by the will of my Master, Sthenn Deathbringer of Almurk."

"Talking of old Sthenn, is he here?" asked Harak.

"Do not speak his name so lightly!" Zannian barked.

"He hasn't returned yet," Nacris told Harak. "We don't know where he is."

Ungrah clattered down the slope, followed by his towering warriors. Reaching the bottom, he strode toward the anxious raiders. The top of his head was even with Zannian's, though the raider chief was on horseback.

"It's well," said the ogre. "Dragons are not fit company for warriors. They plot and plan and talk too much. I don't fight beside dragons, only against them."

The horses rolled their eyes and shied away from the ogres as they congregated around their leader. Ungrah-de noticed Nacris in her litter.

"Cripple," he said bluntly. "Better to die than live less than whole. If I was crippled like that, I'd crawl off a cliff." He translated this for his followers. They grunted in approval, sounding like a chorus of enormous boars.

Harak noted Nacris's anger at the ogre's high-handed words. "Ungrah-de, it was her idea to enlist your aid," he said.

The raiders exchanged surprised looks at this bit of information. The ogre chief grunted deeply and shouldered a huge axe. Its head was an enormous chunk of grayish agate veined with lapis.

"Lead us to the place of stones," Ungrah-de commanded, "to Arku-peli."

He started down the canyon, his troop at his back. Zannian yelled, "Wait! We must bargain first, so you know what's expected of you."

Ungrah paused. "He made promises," he said, and lifted a gnarled, hairy finger to Harak. "I agreed. The bargain is made. We will kill the enemies you failed to conquer."

He and his monstrous warriors resumed walking.

Zannian turned, swift as a striking snake, and whipped out his sword. The point came to rest on Harak's chest. "What did you promise them?" he growled.

Wincing, Harak tried to push the blade away, but Zannian dug in the tip. "Your mother said I should promise them anything for their help!"

"You will not sell my victory to those monsters!" Zannian snapped at Nacris.

"Then win it yourself!" she replied hotly. "Get on your horse and use that bronze blade on your enemies and not your followers!"

She spat a command to her bearers. They hoisted her onto their shoulders and started after the ogres. Harak carefully leaned away from the sword at his breast. Zannian, his eyes on his mother, allowed the blade to drop.

"By my blood, I will take the mud-toes' village myself!" Zannian vowed. Silence answered his rousing declaration. He looked to his men. They were staring at him with expressions that mixed shock and horror.

"Ogres, Zan?" murmured one, his voice hoarse. "Are we to fight with ogres now?"

Another spoke up. "The spirits of my ancestors will rise in outrage if I fight alongside their murderers!"

"We dishonor ourselves, siding with those monsters!" Hoten said firmly.

Without warning, Zannian struck. The flat of his sword connected with Hoten's head. The elder raider toppled sideways off his horse, stunned. One captain brought his sword up and thrust it at Zannian. The young chief swung his own weapon; at the end of its arc, the captain's severed hand fell to the ground, still grasping his sword. The man gave a harsh cry of pain. He fell from his horse.

Zannian whipped his bloodied sword around and snarled, "Any one else dare draw on me?"

The other raiders pulled back out of reach. Only Harak held his ground.

Zannian turned on the smirking young wanderer. "I should slay you as a lesson to the rest!"

Harak lost his affected good nature for once. "Slay me? You should thank me! It wasn't easy finding Ungrah-de or convincing him to help!" Zannian continued to regard him with hatred, and he added, "You know, if I were you, Zan, I'd hurry after those ogres. If the band doesn't know they're coming, they might attack Ungrah when he reaches the river. That would be bad in many ways."

The truth of those words turned Zannian's fury into action. "After them!" he ordered. Sullenly, his captains galloped after the marching ogres.

"I'd better go, too," Harak said mildly. "Ungrah likes me, you see. I can keep things calm between you and the ogres."

Zannian sheathed his sword with a clang. "Don't cross me, Harak, or you'll not live to see the end of this siege."

"It's a very bad habit, Zan, threatening your friends."

"You're not my friend!"

Harak looked down at the dying raider and the unconscious Hoten sprawled on the ground. "Thank my ancestors for that," he said, and rode away.

* * * * *

Karada was riding across the high plain with her entire band at her back when the lead riders flushed six men on horseback.

The strangers tried to flee, but Karada's superior horses overhauled them. Karada herself joined the brief melee, trading spear thrusts and sword cuts with a wildly painted rider. None of the strangers tried to surrender. All fought to the death.

Karada had the six dead men laid out for Beramun to see. The girl needed only a glance to recognize them.

"Zannian's men! The men who killed my family painted their faces just the same!"

Karada shaded her eyes. "We're still two days from the Valley of the Falls. Why would Zannian waste men scouting so far east? Is he expecting us?"

"All the messengers from Yala-tene were taken but me," Beramun said thoughtfully. "Zannian could have learned of our mission from those he captured."

Karada changed the marching order of her band. Those not fighting—children, elders, the captured Silvanesti—were sent to the rear. Instead of a long, slender column of riders, Karada's warriors spread themselves out in a wide line, two ranks deep. This would allow them to sweep the savanna as they rode and shield their families, too. Karada kept Beramun by her side, since the girl could help guide them through the mountains. It had been many years since the nomads had traveled so far west.

She divided her fighting force into three parts. Pakito was summoned, and he arrived with Balif still in tow. Karada gave the giant charge of the right wing. Bahco was to have command of the left, and she herself would lead the center. Pakito left Balif with Karada and took his place on the north end of the nomads' line.

The elf general looked trailworn, his long hair windblown and his fine clothes unkempt. Unlike some of the well-born elves, Balif never complained about his comfort or treatment. He seemed to regard his captivity as an interesting outing, like a prolonged hunting trip.

He looked down at the six dead raiders. "We had word of men like these in the west. Their deeds drove many humans into land claimed by the Speaker of the Stars."

Karada spared him but a scornful glance. The nomads took up their new formation and surged forward. The wide line scared up all sorts of animals and game. Rabbits, wild pigs, deer, and every bird known on the plains took flight before Karada's band. Edible game was taken down with arrows and the meat passed back to those on foot. Beramun expressed concern that their bold approach would warn Zannian they were coming.

"Maybe if they know we're coming, they'll get on their nags and clear out," Karada said.

She had a stem of sweet grass in her teeth and a woven grass hat on her head to keep the sun off her face. Beramun marveled at her calm demeanor. She looked like a middle-aged hunter's mate, foraging for roots. Of course, when she lifted her head, the light shone on the web of scars at her throat and in her hard hazel eyes, and she was again Karada, famed nomad chieftain.

"Do you have a plan of action?" Balif asked. Karada wouldn't answer him, so he went on, "You're a fine natural tactician, but you're fighting an unknown enemy. They may outnumber you. They may have traps set for you. Stealth and surprise will greatly aid your cause."

"This is not your fight." Karada spat out the grass stem. "Once I beat this Zannian and get your ransom, I'll have blades, mounts, and warriors enough to wrest the south plain from your leader, and all the elves in Silvanesti will not be enough to dislodge me!"

Balif pursed his lips and said nothing more.

The terrain began to break apart and rise. Rocky hills pushed through the green grass, and stands of trees appeared, pine and cedar mostly, with a few wild apple trees mixed in. Bahco and the left wing of the band, a hundred sixty-three strong, were lost from sight as they bore south around an intervening hill. Pakito's wing, a hundred forty-four riders, forded a wide stream and disappeared into a grove of trees. Karada allowed a short rest for her part of the band. Horses were watered in the stream and noisily munched windfall apples.

Karada dipped her hand in the creek and brought the clear water to her lips. She swallowed, made a face, and said, "I forgot how stony the water is here."

Beramun looked north and south, past the idle nomads. "I remember this stream," she said quietly. "I crossed it lower down, the day the raiders caught Udi."

Because Balif couldn't dismount without help (his legs were still hobbled under the belly of his horse), Beramun filled a hollow gourd and took it over to him.

"Thank you, girl." He drank deeply, then suddenly dropped the gourd. Beramun caught it before it hit the ground.

"Careful!" she chided. "Break the gourd and you'll have to lap your water like the horses."

"Will you ask Karada to come here, right away?" Balif's polite words sounded more like a command than a request, but his tone was urgent and his face wore an odd expression.

"Don't run or shout," he added calmly. "Go to her slowly and return the same way. Do it *now,* Beramun."

She put aside her surprise and did as he asked. Karada was enjoying the feel of the cool creek water on her feet, and it was hard to pull her away. Beramun persisted. When they returned to Balif, the nomad chieftain was still barefoot, her doeskin leggings draped over one shoulder.

"What do you want, elf?" she said, annoyed.

"You're being watched from that stand of pines over there. At least two men, maybe more."

Karada did not so much as glance in the direction he indicated. Her hard grip on Beramun's arm kept the younger woman from turning.

"Raiders?" Karada asked.

Balif grimaced. "What am I, a dragon? I can't see that far. Find out yourself."

The word spread softly through the band. Slowly, casually, groups of three and four slipped into the pine copse. They circled wide, seeking hidden horses or spies on foot. They found nothing. When they reappeared empty-handed, Karada took the matter into her own hands. She nocked an arrow and loosed it at the tree Balif said housed the spy.

The missile had its intended effect. With a shriek, a figure tumbled from the pine. Karada ran to the spot. By the time she arrived, two more figures had appeared, weeping.

Beramun joined her. "Children!" she exclaimed.

They were two young boys and a girl. The older boy had been in the tree, and Karada's arrow had scared him so badly he'd lost his hold. The younger pair tried to comfort him, but they were so frightened they could do little more than cling to each other and cry.

"Be still!" Karada snapped. The weeping trio flinched and tried to obey.

Beramun knelt beside them, patting heads and cheeks. She recognized the beadwork on their dusty kilts. "You're from Yala-tene, aren't you?" she said.

"Yes," the smaller boy quavered.

"How did you get here?" demanded Karada. "How did you avoid the raiders?"

"Please, Karada," Beramun said. "Be patient. They're young and scared." The nomad chieftain grunted and walked away to retrieve her arrow.

The children followed her movements with wide eyes. Beramun spoke kindly to them, shifting their attention back to herself.

Little by little, she drew from the children the story of how they had come to be here. They'd been sent by the elders of Yala-tene, they said, "through a crack in the mountain." The elders had sent other children like themselves through this narrow tunnel and told them all to run away and hide from anyone on horseback.

When Karada rejoined them, Beramun related what

the children had said, then asked them, "How long ago did you leave?"

"A night, a day, a night, and today," said the smaller boy.

"Things must be bad for them to send children out alone," Karada remarked.

The little ones began sobbing again. "Monsters have come!" wailed the girl. "The painted men have monsters to help them! They'll pull down the big wall!"

"Monsters? You mean the green dragon?"

"No. The monsters have legs and arms like us, but they're big and ugly, with teeth sticking out their mouths, and long, floppy ears—"

Karada inhaled sharply. "Ogres?"

Beramun jumped to her feet. "The Arkuden needs us. We must go to him right away!"

"Lady." The little girl was tugging at Beramun's kilt. "Lady, there is no Arkuden any more."

The child's declaration was like a spear through Beramun's heart, and she froze.

Karada's sunbrowned face turned paler than Beramun had ever seen it. The chieftain grasped the poor child by her shoulders and shook her hard.

"What do you mean? Where is the Arkuden?" she cried. The child could only sob.

A blow on her leg broke through Karada's shock. The smaller boy had struck her with his walking stick. She set the girl down.

"What happened?" she asked, striving to keep her voice calm. "What happened to the Arkuden."

"They killed him," said the boy, pulling the girl away from her. "The green-skinned men killed the Arkuden!"

Chapter 6

Blusidar's island was no mere rock in the midst of the ocean. From high above, Duranix could just barely see it in its impressive entirety. Both shape and terrain were surprisingly regular. Though the coast had been etched by centuries of tides and tempests, the island was a nearly perfect circle. The outer edge was bordered by a wide band of sand dunes. A ring of steep mountains sat in the center, and a heavy belt of forest filled the area in between.

The odd regularity was a puzzle to be pondered at a later time. For now, Duranix remained convinced Sthenn was hiding somewhere in the forest. Days had passed without any sign of the green dragon. He must have been badly injured by Duranix's lightning strike to remain hidden so long. Though a satisfying theory, it was also troubling. Wounded, Sthenn might be more desperate, more dangerous than ever.

Duranix floated on high, riding the steady winds available over the island. The sky was bright and cloud-free. Though he could see the natural life of the island with his usual clarity, he detected no visible trace of Sthenn. His deeper senses did not lie, however. His old enemy was near.

He descended to the mountain where he'd first encountered Blusidar. He hoped to see her again and scrutinized crags and crevices as he swooped in. She was nowhere around. Disappointed, Duranix alighted atop a forked pinnacle, balancing on the narrow peak with his tail spread out behind him.

Stop being a fool, he chided himself. Why waste time looking for the female? She was backward, awkward, and blind to the danger Sthenn represented. It was dangerous to divide his attention between the two. Better to concentrate on his green nemesis and leave Blusidar to fend for herself.

Cast-off scales glittered on the slope below his perch, and he realized Blusidar must have used the notch in the peak for preening. The thought birthed an irresistible itch between his shoulders. His wings, numbed from his long vigil over the island, were regaining feeling, and it felt as though a hundred brazen-toothed vermin were gnawing at him. Leaning to one side, he lowered his shoulder and scraped his back against the sky-blue stone.

Instead of a dull, stony scratching sound, the air was filled with a sonorous droning, like the organized noises the humans in Yala-tene called "music." Duranix stopped scratching and the sound ceased. Experimentally, he rubbed his shoulder again on the rocky crag. The noise resumed. The spire of heavily crystallized stone vibrated in sympathy when scraped, creating an impressive sound.

He tried striking the spire with his horned head and tapping it with a talon. Each method drew a different note from the rock.

Movement in the air interrupted the performance. Extending his wings, Duranix prepared to pounce or fly.

Blusidar flashed past him, close enough that he felt the wind from her wings. He called to her.

"Why are you still here?" she said, passing close behind him. She was a swift flier, he had to admit. Young dragons often could outfly their elders. Mature dragons were stronger but also much heavier.

"I'll stay until I find Sthenn," he replied. "I have pledged to put an end to him, whatever else happens."

Blusidar extended her rear claws and landed on a lower prominence. "Make not the sound," she said, shifting from one clawed foot to the other with evident agitation.

He looked from her to the pinnacle. "Rubbing the stone? Why not?"

"It is for *ji-ri-ni,* not for play!"

In the ancient dragon tongue, *ji-ri* meant "hatchlings." The syllable *ni* indicated "to make." So *ji-ri-ni* meant "making hatchlings."

Taken aback, Duranix tilted his huge, horned head to one side, regarding the spire. Apparently the dragons confined to this island in the past had used the sonorous stone as part of some sort of mating ritual.

"Forgive me," said Duranix, embarrassed. "I don't know your customs here."

"Dragons of your land, they do not do this?"

"I have never seen it."

His own mother had mated just once and subsequently laid three eggs. Duranix's father was an ancient bronze known as Venerable Ro. (It had once been customary for each new generation of dragons to gain a syllable in their names—Duranix and Blusidar, having three, were of the same generation. Sthenn and the Venerable Ro were of the eldest generation.)

Blusidar settled down, flaring her nostrils. "You will not go until the green is found? Then follow, and be quiet."

She leaned sideways and fell silently from her ledge. Spreading her wings, she glided over the jagged lower slopes and soared up a hundred paces. Hovering in an updraft, she waited for Duranix to join her.

Feeling more than a little old and clumsy in her wake, he opened his heavier wings and pushed off his perch. Stones loosed by his talons clattered down the mountain. Blusidar gave him a disdainful glance and flew on.

She traveled some way, paralleling the cliffs. He flew slightly above and behind her. The woods below presented an unbroken canopy of intertwining branches, alive with thousands of birds.

When at last a break appeared in the tree cover, Duranix saw a shallow river meandering through the forest. Blusidar dropped her tail and landed on a stout fallen tree. He settled on the sandbar beside the tree. His claws promptly sank into the damp, loose sand.

He didn't have to be told why they'd come here. The stink of Sthenn was strong in the air. Across the river lay the remains of a herd of wild pigs, recently slaughtered. Blood from their mangled carcasses mingled with the flowing water.

Duranix waded into the river, holding his wings up out of the mud. He counted six dead pigs and signs of at least that many more devoured by Sthenn. A great heap of brush and logs was scattered in all directions behind the herd. The blood was still fresh; the kill wasn't very old.

He hadn't flown away, or Duranix would have seen him. He must have crawled away. In the river—yes! The flowing water would conceal his trail, and the open air above the stream would help disperse his fetid odor.

Duranix pondered which way Sthenn might have gone, until the sound of sloshing broke his concentration. Blusidar waded to the pig carcasses. She hoisted one of the more intact ones by its hind leg and skinned back her lips to take a bite.

Like lightning, Duranix swatted the dead pig from her claws before she could sink her fangs into its flesh. She snarled at him, dropping on all fours and shrinking back to present a smaller target.

He snapped, "Calm yourself! You don't want to eat that. Sthenn doesn't leave gifts behind. What he couldn't finish, he tainted." Duranix picked up the carcass and sniffed. "Yes, poisoned with one of his vile secretions. Eat this animal, and you'll wish you could die!"

Blusidar uncoiled herself and sniffed the dead pig cautiously. She blinked rapidly, eyelids clashing like swords. "This smell . . . is poison?"

"The worst sort. It would rot you from the inside out, and nothing on this island could save you."

Duranix piled up all the carcasses and incinerated them with a lightning bolt. Blusidar watched closely.

"How do you do that?" she remarked. "I cannot make fire."

"It's not born into us. You must find the fire in the clouds, breathe it in, and keep it here." Duranix tapped a single talon against his chest. "I could teach you."

She hesitated then replied, "I need it not. Find the green one and go."

Blusidar launched herself into the air and vanished beyond the treetops. Duranix found himself staring after her. His experience with females was nonexistent.

Silver-sided fish flashed between his motionless legs, and he looked down. Sunlight glinted on their iridescent scales. Along with the speeding trout came swirls of gray mud. Something was churning the river upstream.

Duranix did not return to the air. Too long he'd delayed doing the obvious thing: combing the forest for Sthenn at ground level.

Sleeking his wings back tight, he bounded up the shallow river, raising enormous splashes with every leap. The streambed wandered this way and that, descending from the high ground at the center of the island to the low-lying shore. He slammed around the bends, scraping against trees and skittering over boulders buried in the river. The water grew thicker with mud the farther he went. Something big was floundering upstream, and he was certain he knew what.

Duranix rounded a tight bend and crashed into a heavy tree trunk lying across thc river. It yielded, sliding off the bank into the water. The tree had fallen very recently. Wood in the break was still white, and the tree's leaves were still green.

A loud splashing sounded nearby, followed by roars of reptilian anger. Duranix stepped over the big tree and assumed a more stealthy pace as he made for the sounds of conflict.

He'd come to the foot of the ring of mountains. Here, the river was born, cascading down a series of short steps made of fractured slabs of blue stone.

When he reached the edge of the forest, Duranix beheld a shocking sight: Sthenn and Blusidar violently entwined in the lower falls. The green dragon's elongated claws gripped the female's neck just behind her head. Her wings were splayed out, pummeled by the waterfall. She kicked at Sthenn's belly with her hind feet, but the old monster had her pinned against the rock table, the greater length of his back and tail wrapped around her like a rope snare.

Sthenn's head snapped around. He opened his mouth and hissed, drawing the warning out into a dry, withered laugh.

"Little Duranix!" he wheezed. "Good of you to join us!"

"Hang on to him, Blusidar," Duranix called. "Don't let him go!"

"You know each other, do you? How interesting." The joints in his long foreclaws worked. Scales squealed on scales, and Sthenn's claws sank into Blusidar's throat. Her tongue fell out between her parted lips.

"Stand where you are, dear friend, or I'll tear her head right off!"

Duranix strove to conceal his concern, knowing Sthenn would only use it against him. "She's just a child, no more than a nymph with wings."

"Hehhh, hehhh." Again, the dry-as-dust laughter. "Is that supposed to dissuade me? You forget, my darling enemy, I killed your clutchmates, and they were mewling newts."

Duranix advanced two steps. Sthenn twisted away from him, trying to keep his distance and not lose his grip on Blusidar. It wasn't a simple task. She was still resisting and hampered Sthenn's mobility.

"Stay back!" Sthenn cried shrilly. "Stay back! I'll kill her!"

Duranix sat back on his haunches and prepared himself to leap. "I can't stop you. But know this: I can reach you in a single jump. You'll die far more slowly than she, old wyrm."

"You frighten me," Sthenn sneered.

"I notice you're not using your teeth. Why not? Surely an elder like you could bite through a young dragon's throat far faster than you can strangle her. Ah, I remember. Back on the plain, when we grappled, you didn't use your teeth then either." Duranix's eyes narrowed. "You're so old, you're more than half dead. Everything about you is decayed. Those yellow fangs of yours are as brittle as icicles, aren't they, Sthenn? That's why you don't use them. They'd shatter on hard bronze scales."

Sthenn heaved himself and his captive a step farther away, gurgling hatred deep in his throat.

"Shall I bite through this fine young throat to prove you wrong?" he wheezed. He opened his narrow jaws and rested his long, eroding teeth on Blusidar's neck.

"Go ahead, if you can. Blusidar, if you can hear me, keep fighting! You're a tenth his age. He's vicious and cruel, but he's too feeble to hold you down forever."

Her tail thrashed once from side to side. Sthenn shifted one of his back feet to restrain it, wavering a bit as he sought his balance again.

"Are you afraid yet, Sthenn?"

Blusidar twisted violently against the grip of her larger foe. Duranix tensed himself to strike, but Blusidar and Sthenn were too much in motion for him to aim his attack precisely. They rolled under the steplike waterfall and out again. Blusidar's tail, freed from Sthenn's grip, lashed out, whipping across his side and back. The spiked center ridge caught him in the face, and black blood flowed.

Furious, the green dragon let go Blusidar's neck with one claw and raked his thick talons across her eyes.

Her high-pitched trill of pain was Duranix's cue. He sprang, aiming his whole body at Sthenn's head. When he landed, the stone ledge beneath them shattered, dumping all three of them into the deep pool at the base of the falls.

For a while all was swirling water, rushing bubbles, and reptilian limbs striking and clutching. When Duranix emerged at last from the tangle, Sthenn was scrambling ashore, wings outstretched. The raw wound on his chest was bleeding again, and the lacerations on his face and back oozed steadily. His decrepit lungs gasped for air as his sides heaved in and out. He looked back at Duranix.

"Come for me, old friend, and the female will bleed to death!" he panted.

It seemed too true. Blusidar lay motionless on a broken slab. Blood stained her bright scales and hid her face completely. Duranix couldn't tell if her throat had been slashed, but dark blood was rapidly covering the stone on which she lay.

Sthenn labored into the air. He did not circle but simply called, "I've won, little friend! You've been gone too long from your pet humans. Return home and see my victory!" Then he flew away, his course erratic, his belly skimming the treetops.

Duranix went to Blusidar. Her right eye was badly cut, and there was a deep wound from her right earhole to the bottom of her left jawbone. Blood pulsed slowly from this terrible gash.

He rinsed her face and neck gently with cool water. Through these ablutions, Blusidar never moved. She barely seemed to breathe.

There was nothing Duranix could do for her eye, but the throat wound had to be closed, or she would surely die. Arching his neck and inhaling deeply, he called on the lightning deep within. It would require extraordinary precision to seal the gaping wound without incinerating Blusidar or burning off his own foreclaw.

Duranix gazed skyward for a moment, feeling a fearsome calm settle over him. He lowered his head and breathed blue-white fire on the dying dragon's wound.

* * * * *

Deer were plentiful on the island, and it didn't take long for Duranix to catch four. He carried them back to the headwaters of the river and seared a brace for his dinner. The other two he left raw. Having little experience of fire, Blusidar would be accustomed to eating her meat uncooked.

She had not stirred from where he'd laid her after closing her wound. Day passed into night and then into day again, and still she did not move. After catching the deer, Duranix never left her side. He coiled himself on a rock ledge, watching over her and listening to the wild things in the woods.

At twilight two days after the battle with Sthenn, Blusidar twitched. The tremors became aimless movements of her limbs. When her head moved side to side, Duranix's own head lifted.

Her eye opened, and she rolled onto her side. After a pause, she crawled to the water's edge and dipped her parched, swollen tongue in the stream.

"How do you feel?"

She spasmed hard with fear at the sound of his voice. "Why are you still here?" she said, her voice a hollow whisper.

"I waited to see you through."

"The green . . . is dead?"

"No, but he's gone."

"Then why stay? I thought you want to kill him."

"There's time. He'll be returning to our homeland to see his humans triumph over mine. He's old and injured. I can catch him."

Blusidar examined her reflection in the water. "My eye," she whispered, claw waving helplessly before the ruined socket. "I cannot see with it."

"Sthenn put it out. I can't heal it, but in time a new one will grow in its place." He had to reassure her of this several times before she turned her attention from her damaged face to her empty belly.

"You spoke true," she said as she devoured the raw venison. "The green wanted to kill me. Why are such creatures living?"

"Sthenn defies explanation. In some hearts, evil arrives at birth. He's as craven as he is wicked, and I thought if you fought him he'd flee, but I made a mistake. He felt trapped, and even a trapped rat will bite."

She said nothing more but curled up at his feet and fell into a profound slumber. Duranix stood over her for two more days, bringing fresh game from the forest. When Blusidar awakened again, he told her he was leaving.

She considered this in silence, eating part of a deer and then moving to the stream. Once she'd drunk her fill, she said, "The green is far away. Why not stay?"

Duranix was amazed by this reversal. "I must make sure Sthenn doesn't hurt anyone ever again," he told her quietly. "I have to finish him."

Blusidar rose her feet. She was steadier now, and her injuries had acquired a healing crust.

She flexed her wings several times and tilted her head, fixing him with her good eye. "When the green is dead, come back. Live here."

The same thought had entered his mind as he watched her lie motionless by the pool, teetering between life and death, but he had dismissed the idea as absurd. She wouldn't be much of a companion—too wild and ignorant.

And there was Amero. How could he explain to her of his friendship with a mere human—creatures Blusidar had never seen—a friendship more important to him right now than mating or offspring? It was irrational to care more for a soft-skinned, inquisitive, two-legged pet than the furtherance of his blood. Yet, he had to admit, he did.

"My life is in the Valley of the Falls," Duranix said. "I must protect my domain from Sthenn and his like for the rest of my life." He regarded her closely. "You could come with me."

"I cannot fly far," she replied. Duranix realized it was true. Blusidar had neither the size, strength, nor stamina to fly all the way back to the Valley of the Falls. After another century's maturity perhaps, but not now.

A shadow fell over the ring of mountains. Clouds, larger than the island itself and pushed by the sea wind, blotted out the setting sun.

The clouds gave Duranix an idea. He opened his wings. "Come aloft, and I will show you something wondrous."

She was weak but able. When they reached a certain height, Duranix turned his face into the wind. The powerful current of air filled his wings, and he shot up into the clouds. Blusidar followed warily. She seldom flew so high and did not enter clouds if she could help it. Some deep, unexpressed fear made her dread the billowing white walls.

Duranix lowered one wing and banked tightly, then flapped steadily to increase his speed. Blusidar came alongside him, wingtip to wingtip. Before long sparks of blue fire began to play over Duranix's wings. Blusidar shied away, flitting off into the mist. Duranix followed, lightning crackling as he flew.

He mischievously maneuvered on her blind side. The sky was exceptionally charged, and a corona of incandescent blue formed around his bronze body. When their wings brushed, the lightning passed from Duranix to Blusidar with a loud *crack!* Thunder rolled. She promptly folded her wings and dived.

Duranix dropped after her. She was spiraling slowly, wings limp. Chagrined, he realized the bolt had knocked her senseless.

He dropped beneath her and spread his wings to their fullest extent. She landed heavily on his broad back, and his muscles coiled with the strain. He held them both aloft until she recovered.

"Bad trick!" she snarled immediately. Rolling off him, she flapped hard to support herself.

"Try again," he urged. "If you can take the fire in, it will be yours!"

Blusidar followed at a reluctant distance as he climbed again into the cloud. Lightning was already snapping from sky to sea. Two bolts hit Duranix in quick succession. The power surged through him, and he made a loop in midair out of sheer delight.

Blusidar appeared close by, gliding on his left wing. She too was limned in blue radiance, and sparks formed on the tips of her horns, claws, and wings, flashing off into the storm-laden atmosphere.

Unconsciously, they matched rhythms, wings rising and falling in perfect unison. Lightning leaped from one dragon to the other and back again. Duranix roared his full-throated cry, and to his surprise, Blusidar answered. Her voice was high and shrill with youth, but he was glad to hear it. She had found fire at last.

Catching her attention, he opened his mouth and loosed a bolt at the sea. She tried to do the same, but no lightning emerged. He showed her how to arch her neck, inhale, and let the lightning form deep in her throat.

On her third try, a spear of white, forked fire burst from Blusidar's mouth. Ecstatic despite her exhaustion and wounds, she rolled and banked and looped all over the sky. Her maneuvers left Duranix speechless. She truly was a peerless flier.

The sundered cloud surrendered its rain. Pelted by the downpour, both dragons slowly lost their surcharge of fire. Duranix circled the center of the island, taking his bearings from early stars glimpsed through the upper clouds. Finding west at last, he hovered in place a moment, bowing his long neck. Blusidar circled him.

Saying farewell is a human custom that dragons do not share. Duranix merely changed the angle of his wings and flew on. Blusidar dropped away. The last he saw of her were the tips of her slender wings as she vanished in the clouds below.

Chapter 7

After so many days of sullen siege, the day of Moonmeet arrived with flourish and fanfare: blaring horns, shouts, and pounding hooves. Zannian formed his men into three large units separated by wide lanes. For some time after dawn, slaves ran back and forth in these lanes, carrying hanks of vine rope and tree trunks trimmed of branches. To the defenders of Yala-tene, it looked ominous.

The villagers spoke in low voices, speculating on what the raiders would do next. Only one woman was silent. Lyopi was hard-faced and pale in the morning light. She had not slept at night since the Jade Men entered Yala-tene. Catnaps in daylight were all the rest she could manage.

Young Hekani, now leading the defenders, said to those around him, "Looks like they mean to try to scale the walls again."

"Stupid!" declared Montu the cooper. "It didn't work before!"

"Maybe they have some new plan," Hekani said. Lyopi remained silent, flexing her sore, callused hands around the shaft of her spear.

A boy came running up the ramp from the street below. He whispered into Hekani's ear, and Hekani nodded to Lyopi. She shouldered her spear, took up her shield, and followed the child down to the village.

The raiders' noisy preparations came to an end at last. A hush fell over the valley. From the wall, the villagers could easily see Zannian front and center in the middle block of horsemen. He raised his long spear high in one hand for all his band to see. Dust rose behind him, and the open lanes between the squares of mounted raiders began to fill with men running toward Yala-tene.

Villagers shifted their weapons to throw. Hekani reminded them not to cast too early, to wait until the targets were close enough to hit.

Behind the first wave of raiders on foot came a slower-moving mob of ragged prisoners. Each bore a fascine, a large bundle of brush and twigs, on his or her back. Driving these fascine bearers were several raiders on foot. Whipcracks could be heard.

The villagers held off throwing their weapons at the fascine bearers, realizing that some of their own captured neighbors were likely among the pitiful prisoners.

The running raiders drew closer, as did the stumbling crowd of captives. Hekani was grim as he said, "Make ready!"

Lyopi ran up the ramp, resuming her place on the wall as the raiders reached the line of ditches and pits dug by the villagers. Not many fell in, but the ditches were only meant to slow an attack, not stop it. While the obstacles hampered the attackers, the defenders pelted the raiders with stones and javelins—simple wooden stakes with sharpened tips, rather than the hard-to-replace flintheads. Raiders fell, skulls cracked by heavy stones or stabbed by javelins.

For a moment the attack hovered at the line of pits, then the captives arrived with their fascines, and the charge flowed on. As they neared the foot of the wall, the bombardment intensified. This was the moment the raiders' previous attacks had always broken. Unable to climb the wall or batter it down, they would endure torment from above only for as long they could, before fleeing.

They did not flee this time. Goaded by whips and clubs, slaves hurled bundle after bundle of brushwood into the corners on each side of the west baffle. The villagers responded with a furious barrage, trying to avoid hitting the slaves with their missiles but forced to fight anyone they could reach.

Lyopi took aim at a wildly painted raider who was prodding forward a gray-haired woman, stooped by the weight of a large fascine. The old woman heaved off her burden, and it rolled down the slope, coming to rest against the foot of the wall. Lyopi was about to knock the raider behind her down with a well-placed javelin when the old woman lifted her eyes skyward.

"Jenla!" Tepa yelled, gripping Lyopi's arm and halting her cast. "It's Jenla! She's alive!"

Sister of his deceased mate, Jenla was the beekeeper's best and oldest friend. She'd been lost in one of the early battles outside the wall, and everyone in Yala-tene assumed she'd been killed.

Heedless of the spears flung by the raiders, Tepa ran to the edge of the parapet, calling for Jenla. Lyopi yelled at him to get back just as a stone-tipped missile hit the edge of the wall at his feet and shattered. Tepa reeled back, face bleeding from cuts caused by flying shards of flint.

Lyopi caught him by the shoulders and hauled him back. "Jenla's down there! We must save her!" he moaned, pulling at her hands.

"There's nothing we can do!" she snapped.

The attack seemed to be getting nowhere. Bundles of brush filled the corners of the baffle, but the pile never mounted very high. The fascines tended to roll down rather than build up to any height. Even so, the raiders continued to drive their reluctant prisoners forward to dump their loads. The ground around the western baffle was thick with bundles of dry brush and senseless or dead attackers.

Their loads delivered, the slaves ran away, still hounded by their pitiless taskmasters. Jenla was carried along by a gang of fleeing prisoners, but those on the wall could see the tan square of her face turn back to them as she was borne away. Tepa remained huddled on the ground, weeping, until Hekani stood over him with a spear.

"Tepa, get up and take this," Hekani said. "Jenla's best hope lies in our victory, and we need you for that." Tepa stared up at the young man for a moment then stood, wiping the tears from his stubbled cheeks. He took the offered spear and gripped it tightly.

"This isn't much of an attack," Hekani said as the raiders retreated. "I guess Zannian was just talking big again."

"They're not done," Lyopi told him. She shaded her eyes with one hand and surveyed the enemy horde. "Something else is stirring."

A line of horsemen approached at a slow trot, dragging travois. Pairs of captives, empty-handed now, ran along behind them. The travois were laden with what looked like large wicker baskets plastered over with river mud.

The defenders were so puzzled that they allowed the horsemen to approach unchallenged. Seeing their slack-jawed confusion, Hekani exploded into profanity.

"What are you staring at? Let them have it! Fight! Fight!"

Pain and death rained down on the raiders. Their response was to ride faster. Bouncing wildly on the travois, a few of the baskets lost their lids. Smoke rose up from the open baskets, plumes of gray playing out behind the galloping riders.

Lyopi lowered the javelin she'd raised to throw. The meaning of the smoke struck her, and she screamed, "Fire! Everyone get back from the wall! Away from the baffle, now!"

The raiders galloped to the piles of fascines and stopped. Orders were shouted, and the prisoners grabbed the trailing ends of the travois and dumped their contents on the brush heaps. Hot coals scattered everywhere. Streamers of smoke rose, followed by the first flickers of flame.

Hekani shouted for water, and children waiting in the street below hurried to comply. Before any of them could return, the dry fascines began blazing. Two bonfires, one on each side of the baffle, drove the defenders off the parapet.

As they retreated along the wall to escape the flames, Hekani said, "This is new, but I don't see the point. They can't burn down stone walls!"

"Zannian's driven us away from the entrance, hasn't he?" Lyopi barked angrily. "They must mean to isolate it for further attack."

The travois-dragging raiders rode away. From their positions by the river, the assembled raiders cheered the success of their new tactic. The cheering quickly faded when a new sound filled the battlefield—the deep, rhythmic pounding of many large drums.

* * * * *

Ungrah-de rested his giant axe on one shoulder. "Let the storm drums sing," he rumbled.

Nacris, seated in her litter next to her towering ally, couldn't stop an involuntary flinch as ten ogres behind them began to pound on hide-covered drums. The deafening sound was loud enough to be heard all over the Valley of the Falls. It rattled Nacris's teeth.

The ogre chieftain nodded and added, "The power of the drums will fill the humans' hearts with fear."

Nacris did not remind him that his allies were human as well. It seemed impolite and not a little dangerous. Ungrah-de was dressed for battle in lapis-studded leather, the skulls of his victims hanging from his chest by thongs. More than a few of these trophies were human.

Since arriving in the Valley of the Falls, he and his ogres had killed sixteen of Zannian's men in brawls—all of them provoked by foolish humans. Ungrah made no secret of his scorn for his frail, treacherous allies, and his barbed comments and contemptuous manner had goaded the hotheads into making stupid challenges. The worst incident had occurred on the ogres' second night in camp. Two of Ungrah's warriors asked for provender, and lazy raiders told them to find it themselves. The ogres took them at their word, went to the prisoners' pen, and dragged out two young men. When the raiders realized what was going on, they stopped the ogres from slaughtering the humans. Words ensued, then a sharp fracas that cost the lives of eight of Zannian's men. Half the raider band would have deserted then and there, but Nacris cajoled and threatened them into staying. Her performance that night had not been lost on Ungrah-de.

Now, looking down at her, he said, "You are the only one here I worry about."

"Really?" she replied, flattered.

"These others"—he waved a dismissive hand at the raider host—"are wolves, eager to swarm over the weak or the few. Not you. You care nothing about danger. Your heart is dark. You would do anything to get what you want."

"You're right, great chief. I shrink from nothing."

Surrounded by the punishing sound of ogre war drums, Nacris could hardly contain her excitement. Emboldened by his backward praise, she asked Ungrah if one of his ogres would carry her into battle on his back. The chief responded to this notion with a withering glare.

"Females and cripples don't belong in battle. A warrior of mine would stamp the life out of you before carrying you."

As Ungrah did not offer idle warnings, she let the matter drop.

Gradually another more threatening sound joined the drums: The ogres were banging their axe heads against the bosses of their shields. The ominous *clank* was deliberately off the beat of the drums: *boom, BOOM, clank; boom, BOOM, clank.* From a monstrous heartbeat the noise now sounded like the advance of massive metallic creature—a dragon, perhaps.

Nacris shifted in her seat. Sweat broke out on her face. She could not miss the final destruction of Yala-tene! She had to be there for the kill. Her Jade Men would carry her litter anywhere she ordered, but, jealous of their success in slaying the Arkuden, Zannian had left them out of the attack. They languished in the river camp, guarding the raiders' slaves.

Ungrah watched impassively as flames licked up the steep walls of Yala-tene. When he judged the flames were at their height, he raised his shield and joined in the cacophony. His thunderously deep voice broke through the uproar as he commanded his warriors in their ancient tongue. The drumming ogres finished with a flourish and joined their comrades.

"Now we go," he said to Nacris.

Striding through the dust and smoke drifting back from Yala-tene, the ogres appeared even bigger than they were. Even Zannian's hardened fighters edged their horses back, leaving a wide path for their savage allies.

Unable to bear being left behind, Nacris struggled to her feet and braced herself on her crude crutch. She would see the final fight, she vowed, even if she had to crawl all the way to the battlefield.

She hobbled after the ogres.

* * * * *

Crouching behind the parapets upwind of the burning brush, Lyopi and forty-odd villagers could hear a distant, regular booming. It didn't get louder or closer, and after a while they dismissed it as another of Zannian's ruses.

Smoke from the fires obscured much of the open ground between the village and the river. This made Hekani more uncomfortable than the fire itself. He sent runners down to the street to circle behind the baffle and warn the defenders on the other side to be wary of any raiders who might emerge from the smoky cover.

"What's happening, Lyopi?"

Those behind the parapets looked up to see a small knot of elders coming up the ramp from the street below. Montu was there, along with Adjat the potter and the mason Shenk. With them was another person in a hooded cloak.

"You shouldn't be here," Lyopi told them. "It's too dangerous."

Adjat spoke again. "We heard drums. We came to see what's going on."

Hekani said, "I think they mean to storm the ba—"

"Hai! Hai! Look!" Cries echoed along the parapet. Hekani, Lyopi, and the rest strained to see what the shouting was about.

Advancing through the smoke were many large figures, far taller than any human. At first, Hekani thought they were masked raiders on horseback, but when they cleared the smoke he saw they were walking on their own two legs. His mouth fell open in shock, and he turned wide eyes on Lyopi. Her face was pale as snow. The elders crowded around trying to see.

"What is it?" asked the cloaked man. "What do you see?"

"Ogres," Lyopi gasped, her voice barely above a whisper. "He's brought ogres to the valley."

Ten of the jut-jawed monsters were in view, and more were emerging from the smoke. They arrayed themselves in an irregular line behind the tallest of their kind—evidently the leader. Catcalls and insults usually hurled at the raiders were absent, as those defending their homes simply stared in horrified disbelief.

"Twenty-four, twenty-five," Hekani counted.

"We're dead!" Adjat proclaimed. "We're done for!"

"Shut up!" Lyopi snapped. "We did not bow down to them when they had a dragon fighting on their side. Why would we give up now?"

The villagers held a hasty council on the ramp. Every able-bodied person—young, old, male, and female—gathered in the street behind the closed western baffle. A barricade of timbers and scrounged stones would be thrown up inside the wall, closing both blocked entrances. If the ogres managed to gain the low wall atop the baffle, they would face a fresh barrier beyond.

The largest and strongest men in Yala-tene were rounded up and armed with the heaviest weapons available: stone hammers, axes, and stout, wooden clubs. The last pots of burltop oil in the village were assembled in the street north of the baffle, and Hekani called for fishermen's nets. Puzzled but obedient, gangs of boys dragged the nets out of storage and passed them to the defenders on the walls.

The word from the lookouts was that there were thirty ogres.

"Only thirty?" Lyopi tried to make a joke.

From a hundred paces away, the ogres raised their weapons high and shouted, *"Ungrah-de! Ungrah-de!"*

They broke into a run, heading straight between the blazing piles of brush. A thick hail of stones and javelins fell on them, but they shrugged off the barrage and kept coming. Nearer the wall, heavier stones stunned a few ogres, but the rest came on like an avalanche.

"Get ready!" Hekani called down to the street behind the wall. The barricade was still taking shape.

"We're not done yet!" Montu shouted. "You must hold them!"

* * * * *

Ungrah-de, as befitted a chief, reached the baffle first. He sprang up and used his axe to hook the top of the wall. Gripping the axe handle in both hands, he walked up the sloping stone barrier. A small boulder hit him at the base of the neck. His left hand lost its grip, but he hung on with the right. His followers leaped up beside him, one throwing a beefy arm around his chief's waist. Thus supported, Ungrah took hold of his axe again and levered himself onto the baffle wall.

For a moment the villagers' barrage dwindled as they beheld the terrible spectacle of armed ogres standing on their wall. Ungrah-de brandished his huge axe and urged his warriors onward. He jumped down from the baffle wall onto the heap of boulders Duranix had piled up to block the entrance. Skidding in the loose rubble, Ungrah clambered across the gap to the undefended stretch of wall bordered by fire. More ogres followed him. The fifth one to gain the top of the baffle arrived in time to receive the brunt of a renewed bombardment. Larger and larger missiles struck him. With a grunt, the ogre toppled backward, knocking down several of his comrades.

Whatever glee the villagers might have felt with this small victory was lost when Ungrah marshaled his four warriors and charged through the flames. By chance he chose to go to his left, away from Hekani, Lyopi, and the village elders.

With two sweeps of his broad stone axe, Ungrah cleaved aside the villagers in his path. Smelling victory, he bellowed for his warriors to follow.

The villagers gave ground, retreating along the wall until they came to the ramp leading down into the town.

There they stood, shoulder to shoulder, many openly trembling as the ogres advanced. They were joined by townsfolk carrying bundles of fishing net and pots of oil, hurrying up the ramp.

Ungrah waited for more ogres to join him. When his strength reached ten, he charged. The ogres came bellowing at the terrified villagers.

Up went the fishing net, held aloft on long poles. Ungrah had never seen a net before, but it didn't look like any sort of barrier that could resist the stroke of his mighty axe.

They were almost in chopping range when the net fell forward, covering them. The ogres thrashed and hacked at the heavy cordage. While they were engaged, villagers upended two tall jugs of nut oil.

Ungrah slipped in the oil, and fell heavily on his back. A stone-headed spear buried itself in his right calf. He roared with anger and plucked the puny weapon out.

All around, his fighters were struggling with the fishing net and treacherous oil. The thick liquid lapped over the edges of the wall and ran down, leaving dark stains. Out on the plain, Zannian had advanced his horsemen to within a hundred paces of the wall. He watched the ogres' charge, the ensuing melee, and the oil seeping over the stones.

"The walls are running with blood!" he declared. "What monsters those ogres are! They're wallowing in the mud-toes' blood!"

Then the liquid reached the burning fascines. Blue flames raced up the wall.

A few of the ogres had almost freed themselves from the net when it suddenly caught fire. Ungrah saw the danger and, ignoring heat and pain, chopped his way out. He stood erect, bathed in fire, and saw the humans dumping a fresh amphora of oil on the parapet.

"Back!" Ungrah roared at his troops in the ogre tongue. "Go back!" So saying, he leaped feet first to the ground. It was a long drop even for him; he hit hard, rolled, and took a few seconds to shake off an impact that would've killed a human. A torrent of rubbish fell on him—rocks, wood, mud bricks, and, most insulting of all, offal and dung.

Outraged, mighty Ungrah heaved himself to his feet and struck Yala-tene's wall with his axe. A stone shard six hands long flew out, leaving a deep crevice in the block. It was a fell blow, and it also cracked the head of his axe.

Screaming from their burns, more ogres jumped off the wall, hair singed, skin blistered, and leather armor smoldering. The rest of the ogre force, still embroiled at the baffle, saw their leader's jump from the wall and abandoned the fight.

* * * * *

Nacris had crossed the battlefield alone, leaning on her crutch. She saw the repulse of the ogres and felt curiously elated at their overthrow. Served them right for leaving her behind, she thought.

A horse cantered up behind her. She heard someone dismount, but before she could turn around, strong arms encircled her.

"Why are you out here?" Hoten asked. Her mate for less than a season, Hoten had grown more and more protective of Nacris as the siege dragged on, even as she felt less and less need of him.

"This is my fight. I had to see it! Why doesn't Zan attack? Ungrah-de can't carry the day alone!"

"The ogre chief insisted we stand back and witness the prowess of his warriors. Zan agreed, and now they've learned a lesson. The villagers are not fools, nor are they weaklings. But the battle isn't done. While the ogres drew the enemy's eyes to the west, Zan has sent half the band to storm the north entrance."

She took his arm in a painful grip and her flint-colored eyes narrowed. "This is my battle, too, Hoten," she hissed. "I won't remain in camp like some doddering ancient."

"I know, I know. Come with me. We'll fight together."

He lifted her to his horse's back and mounted behind her. He laced a broad leather strap around both their waists, tying them together.

For the first time in many, many days, she smiled at him. "Don't untie me until I'm dead," she said, taking the reins.

Hoten closed his hands over hers. "Not even then," he vowed.

Chapter 8

No one could remember ever seeing Karada so shaken.

The news brought by the village children changed everything. Karada called in Bahco and Pakito, gathering the whole of her band in a hollow beneath three stony hills. She related what the children had told her, that ogres had joined the fight against Yala-tene and, even worse, that the Arkuden had been slain.

"The raiders," she went on, tendons standing out in her throat, "have a small of band of young, handpicked warriors who wear green face paint. They're called Jade Men. They entered the village by night and murdered my brother. He was wounded in the leg in an earlier fight and was lying helpless on his bedroll." Her hazel eyes, normally sharp and clear as melting snow, were rimmed red and filmed with unaccustomed tears.

"They slew him where he lay, stabbed him with obsidian knives . . ." She could not finish.

After a long and pain-filled silence, Pakito stood. "He was a good man, Karada. We grieve with you."

She shook her head. "Save your grief." She raised her dusty, tear-streaked face skyward. "Turn it into rage to expend on the treacherous ones who killed my brother and seek to destroy all he worked for."

"Aye, Karada." Hundreds of solemn voices repeated Pakito's affirmation.

She glanced at Beramun, sitting on the ground between Mara and Balif, and saw the girl's lovely face was pale and strained from mourning. She turned back to the sea of faces watching her.

"If any of these green-painted killers fall into our

hands, I want them slain at once. Do you hear? Take no Jade Men prisoners." There were nods and shouts of agreement. Karada went on, "With ogres in the field, I'm going to change our order of battle. Those not fit for fighting will stay behind. You'll not enter the Valley of the Falls until the battle is over."

There was grumbling among the elder nomads at being left behind, but they understood the wisdom of her plan. If they remained out of reach, they could not be caught and held hostage against Karada. Only one voice rose in protest.

"What are we supposed to do here?" Mara demanded. "Where will we go?"

Karada swept an arm out to encompass the terrain. "Build a hidden camp on the summit of one of these steep hills. Stay there until I return."

Mara said no more, but her expression was mutinous.

Balif rose. "May I speak, Karada?" he asked.

"No. Yes. Be brief."

The elf lord folded his arms across his lean chest. "Despite the valor and skill of your warriors, Karada, the odds are lengthening against you. According to Beramun"—he bowed to her—"the raiders already outnumber you. Add to that an unknown number of ogres, and you're facing a far more potent enemy than you reckoned on."

"It doesn't matter," Karada said. "My honor and my duty to my brother demand that I go." Standing on the stump of a storm-toppled tree, her bronze helmet glinting in the late day sun, her braid of sun-streaked brown hair falling across her shoulder, she looked like the spirit of war made flesh.

"Will you lead your loyal band to such an uncertain fate?"

"Fate is never certain, as your presence here proves."

There was chuckling in the crowd, and Balif smiled

thinly. "Which brings me to my point: I would like to offer my arm to you, Karada, for the duration of this campaign."

General astonishment reigned. Beramun reacted first. She clutched Balif's arm and declared, "Well said! Well done!"

"Quiet!" Karada barked. She crossed the open ground to the elf lord. Beramun quickly withdrew, yielding to the formidable nomad woman.

Nose to nose and eye to eye with Balif, Karada said fiercely, "This is some trick. Do you think I'll give you back your swords and horses so you can attack us from behind?"

"That's unworthy of you," he said calmly. "Don't be stupid."

Karada's hand went to the hilt of her sword. There were gasps from those gathered around; they were sure the insolent Silvanesti was about to die.

"I have not tried to escape," Balif said. His calm in the face of Karada's ire amazed Beramun. "I chose to stay with my soldiers and share their fate, whether ransomed or not. What I now propose is that I fight alongside you against these painted raiders and their ogre allies—I and as many of my soldiers as will join me."

"Ha!" Karada walked away a few steps, whirled, and presented the tip of her sword to Balif's face. "I see your plan! No. You and your elves will remain behind with the children and elders!"

He shrugged. "As you wish, Karada, but consider: My soldiers are trained warriors. You've never defeated Silvanesti troops in open battle—not once in twenty years. Can you afford to ignore so ready a weapon placed at your disposal?"

"Why would you want to help us?" asked Pakito suspiciously.

Balif lifted his head, speaking to everyone in earshot.

"We've fought each other a long time," he said. "We know each other, know our motives and goals. Though we've sometimes dueled without quarter, I believe there is an understanding between us—even respect."

Karada said nothing. Balif forged ahead.

"The raiders represent a grave threat, different from you nomads. For humans to serve the whims of a green dragon is very troubling and would distress the Speaker of the Stars. Add to that their new alliance with ogres, and I see a common cause for us: to defeat these savages and keep them as far from the borders of Silvanesti as possible."

Pakito's expression showed he found the elf's explanation sensible.

It made sense to Beramun, too. "Shouldn't we stand together on this?" she said quietly to Karada.

The nomads muttered among themselves, some agreeing with Beramun and others hotly ridiculing even a temporary alliance with the Silvanesti.

"Karada, maybe we could—"

"Not a word!" she snapped at Pakito. Lowering her blade, she gazed steadily at the fair-haired elf. "Even if I trusted you, can I trust your lieutenants? Surely they can't all be as honorable as you."

"My officers are no less loyal than yours. They will follow me to death or to victory."

"Will you obey my commands, even if you don't agree with them?"

"Certainly." She looked surprised, and he added, "You took me by force of arms and spared my life on condition of ransom. I am honor-bound to obey."

Her sword declined farther, until the point was hovering just above the ground. "I won't put you on horses," she warned him. "You'll march and fight on foot."

He nodded his acceptance.

Karada slipped her sword back into its leather scabbard. When the hilt slid home, Beramun leaped to her feet and cheered. A surprising number of nomads did likewise.

Puzzled by the acclaim, Karada said, "All of you, listen. This is a temporary alliance! When the fighting ends, the elves must give up their weapons again."

Balif's pale brows rose. "One way or another, we'll be disarmed. Either we triumph and our arms belong to you, or we perish and our bones belong to the crows."

The rest of the band saluted his brave good humor, but Karada did not smile.

Alone in the excited crowd, the girl Mara sat quietly, looking first at her chief, then at the cool and confident Balif. Her face contorted briefly, but whether from fear or hatred or something else only Mara could say.

* * * * *

While her people prepared themselves for the hard ride ahead, Karada rode off into the hills alone. In a lonely ravine, she dismounted, tying her horse to a scrub elm. She'd taken only twenty steps up the gully before, clasping both hands around her stomach, she doubled over in agony.

Amero is dead.

She'd lost siblings before. One sister had died before learning to walk, and marauding yevi had killed her baby brother Menni. Yet the news—*Amero is dead*—burned through her body like a blazing brand.

Putting her back to a tree, she fought for breath. Though she hadn't seen her brother in a dozen years, it had always been enough to trust he was alive and well in Yala-tene, protected by his steadfast people, the bronze dragon, and a stout stone wall. Now that he was gone, it felt as if something inside her had been torn out.

She knew the depth of her feeling was unnatural. Long ago, a jealous member of her band named Pa'alu had used spirit power on her, trying to compel her love. The talisman miscarried, and instead of undying passion for Pa'alu, she was stricken with an unsisterly love for her own brother. Ever since, she'd grappled with the insidious influence. The struggle had nearly driven her insane, but from deep within she found the strength to live with the impossible compulsion. Live with it. Not conquer it.

Karada slid down the tree trunk, rough bark snagging her buckskins. She would never love again. She knew this in her heart. The abnormal flame she'd carried concealed for Amero had consumed her. It could never be kindled for anyone else. Lifting her eyes to the empty sky, she grieved, weeping for Amero and for herself.

The tears went on for a long time, too long. She found she couldn't stop them, couldn't command the gulping sobs that wracked her. At last, disgusted by her weakness, she drew the bronze dagger from her belt. Baring her left arm, she pressed the keen-edged blade against the tan skin between her wrist and elbow. Blood stained the golden blade as she drew it across her arm. The wound hurt, but not enough, so she made a second cut above the first. And then a third.

* * * * *

With a few exceptions, the Silvanesti supported their lord's offer to fight Zannian. The common soldiers volunteered to the last elf. After all, it was better than being left behind, sitting in the dirt and wondering when one of these angry, unpredictable nomads would take it into his head to slay them. However, all six of Balif's noble officers declined to fight. They objected to taking orders from Karada—a human, a woman, and an enemy. Balif listened to their arguments then dismissed them to idle captivity.

"Guard them well," he told Pakito. "They're honorable elves, but once I'm gone, they may not feel inclined to sit by and await ransom. I wouldn't want their lives wasted."

Leadership of the nomads remaining behind was given to Karada's old friend, Targun. Though the oldest man in the band, his once-black hair nearly all gray now, Targun was one of the chieftain's most trusted lieutenants. Only Pakito and his mate, Samtu, had been with Karada longer. Old Targun had his charges organized in no time.

Children were told to use pine boughs to sweep away their tracks as they departed, hiding their whereabouts even from their own people. If the battle went badly, none of Karada's warriors could be forced to tell where their loved ones were hiding.

Warriors watched in silence as their families disappeared into the hills. Many wondered where Karada was. No one had seen her since the elf lord proposed his startling alliance. The nomads knew better than to look for their leader. She often went off on her own, and there was no questioning her when she did.

Beramun found herself standing next to Samtu, as the woman waved farewell to her children. Bearing five children in twelve years had left Samtu's short frame rather stout, and her dark hair bore strands of gray, but she still rode at Pakito's side and fought like a nomad half her age. Now, though, the warrior woman's face reflected her sadness at seeing her children depart.

The obvious pity on Beramun's face seemed to embarrass Samtu, and she busied herself with freshening the spirit marks on her face. Beramun asked about the significance of the marks and, obviously grateful for the distraction, Samtu explained. The nomads wore the painted streaks as a sign of unity. The marks were meant to resemble the scars Karada had received in her fight with the yevi so many years before. It was that first fight that had made their leader strong.

Beramun didn't understand why Karada painted the marks on herself, since she had the real scars after all.

Samtu, shrugging, repeating what Karada had told her people: "Some scars can't be seen unless you draw them on your skin."

As the last of the family members disappeared around a low hill, Bahco discovered Mara crouching among the tethered horses. He told her to go with Targun, to run and catch up, but she refused, digging in her heels and fighting him as he tried to pull her out of hiding.

Karada reappeared on the other side of the camp, her left forearm tightly wrapped with a fresh strip of doeskin. The altercation between Bahco and Mara drew her, and she arrived in time to see the girl bite Bahco's hand. Furious, the warrior pushed the combative girl to the ground and planted a foot on her back to hold her there.

When Karada gestured at him to let the girl up, Mara scrambled to her on hands and knees and clung to her chief's leg.

"I serve you, Karada," she pleaded. "Let me go with you!"

"Stand up, Mara," Karada said severely. "You're not a dog."

The girl stood. Her doeskin shift was dirty and her curly hair matted. Impatiently, Karada combed through the rusty brown tangles with her fingers.

"Such a strange girl," she said. "What do you think you can do with us? We don't have a travois for you to ride, and you'll never keep up with us on foot."

"Let me ride with you!"

An impatient shake of her head, then Karada said, "I could burden Balif with you. He'll be walking with his elves—"

"No!" Mara shrieked, jerking away from Karada's hands. "I won't go with them! I hate them! Let me ride with you!"

Beramun came forward, leading her own horse. She took in the situation immediately.

"Mara can ride with me," Beramun said. "My horse is big enough to carry us both."

"She'll only get in the way," Bahco said, glaring and rubbing the hand Mara had bitten.

Green eyes narrowed at the dark-skinned man, Mara shoved her hands into slits cut in her shift, reaching for something inside. Nomad women often carried seeds and roots they gleaned in a pouch inside their shift, but Beramun doubted the girl was going to offer Bahco food.

Grabbing her elbow, Beramun pulled her away, saying, "Come. Ride with me or go with Targun. That's your choice." She got on her horse and put out a hand to Mara.

Mara looked away from Karada's unhelpful expression to the outstretched hand. Finally, with Beramun's assistance, she mounted awkwardly. The two girls rode away.

Karada sighed, rubbing her red-rimmed eyes. "That girl's touched, Bahco. Don't be so rough on her."

"She loves you like a jealous mate, Karada," he said, shaking his head. "Watch out for her. Some day she'll do something rash."

* * * * *

Night fell in the valley, but the battle continued. Ungrah-de reformed his ogres and, fighting like lions, they stormed the west baffle again, this time holding it against all the villagers' counterattacks. The defenders were fewer in number now because Zannian had drawn some away with his attack on the northern entrance.

From atop the wall, the ogres could see across Yala-tene to where the raiders battled the villagers, highlighted by flaming fascines. Ungrah could not get any farther because a barrier of logs and stone slabs had been thrown up behind the baffle. Three times the ogres had rushed the barrier, trying to break it down with axe blows or their massive bare hands, and three times they were repelled by large, bronze-tipped spears hurled down at them. The villagers attached lines to the butts of these oversized weapons, to recover them after they were cast. The ogres' leather armor could not turn aside the sharp spearheads, hastily formed from Duranix's cast-off scales.

After these three failures, Ungrah ordered his warriors to tear down the baffle wall and dislodge the boulders heaped inside it. This they did far into the night, sending huge sections of carefully placed masonry crashing to the ground.

On the north side of Yala-tene, the situation was just as dire. While the villagers' attention was focused on the ogres, Zannian personally led an assault on the north baffle, isolating the entrance with bonfires and sending his men up the wall on ladders fashioned from trees taken from the village's spirit-enhanced orchard.

Once, when Yala-tene's newly planted orchard was threatened by ice and cold, the proud leader of the Servants of the Dragon, Tiphan, Konza's son, had used the power of ancient spirit stones to save them. The orchard not only grew at an unnatural rate thereafter, but twigs cut from its branches put down roots and became full-grown trees within days. His success with the orchard had fueled Tiphan's arrogance, impelling him to take the entire company of Sensarku out to face Zannian's men before they reached the Valley of the Falls. The Sensarku had been destroyed, down to the last acolyte.

Now, Zannian's raiders cut down dozens of the spirit-enhanced apple trees, hewed their branches off short to serve as footholds, and carried them to the northern baffle. Thrust in the dirt by the wall, the amputated trees took root and began to grow again. After a day, it was impossible for villagers to topple them from the wall. The raiders cut their way to the top and kept their toehold on the wall despite fierce counterattacks by the villagers.

"One more day should do it," Zannian said, slumping under the overhang of the town wall. From there, he and his men were shielded from most of the bombardment. "One more day, and Arku-peli will fall."

The sweaty, soot-streaked warrior beside him opened his eyes. "One more day like today and there may not be enough left of the band to capture anything," he said.

Zannian, his face and arms covered with cuts, bruises, and blood (not his own), peered at the gloomy raider's dirty face and recognized him. "Harak? Of all people to share a respite with!"

Harak ran a scrap of leather down the length of his bronze sword, wiping the blood away. Both edges were deeply nicked, and the tip had acquired a distinct bend. "I've been fighting at your side since sunset, Zan. Saved your life at least three times."

"Liar." Zannian found it unbearable that Harak might be telling the truth. He was good with a horse and deadly with a blade but so smug and sneaky Zannian could not help but distrust him.

A thrown mud brick, heated in a fire, hit the parapet above them and shattered, raining hot fragments over both men. Yelping, they brushed off the burning shards. Two other raiders sitting beside them didn't move. Harak leaned over and patted their faces. They toppled sideways, falling facedown in the dirt.

"Dead, both of them," he reported.

"Who are they?"

Harak squinted through the smoke and darkness. "That's Othas. I knew him. He was a good horse-healer." He leaned across dead Othas to inspect the other man. "Don't know this one."

Somewhere in the darkness, a death scream rent the air. It wasn't possible to tell if it was friend or foe. Unperturbed, Harak took a grass-wrapped gourd flask from his belt and pulled the stopper with his teeth. The spicy smell of cider reached Zannian.

"Give me some of that."

Harak passed the gourd. His chief upended the flask, gulping rapidly. "Ahh!" he gasped, handing it back to Harak. "That's wretched cider!"

"Tastes like spring water to me." He sipped it lightly. "You should try the ogres' brew, *tsoong.* Whew! Strip the skin from your throat, it will. It's so bad they call getting drunk 'punishment.' "

"Maybe I'll try it someday," Zannian retorted. "If you can drink it, I can. Speaking of ogres, I'll be glad to see the back of Ungrah-de. Bloody beast! You know he vows he will claim his choice of villagers after the battle? Not to ravage or enslave, but to eat! Filthy monster!"

"The Master's been known to dine on our delicate kind."

Zannian snatched the gourd from Harak. "The Master is not bound by human customs. He is above them all."

Harak took the gourd back and drank. "Tell me. Do you miss Sthenn? Not his power or the terror he brings, I mean. Do you miss his guidance, his company?"

"No."

The single word, firmly declared, surprised Harak. He said so.

"You know nothing about being chief," Zannian replied. "I owe my place to the Master, but I have been more of a chief to my men since he left than I ever was in Almurk."

A loud sound of pottery smashing made both men flinch. Zannian reclaimed the gourd of cider.

Harak said thoughtfully, "At the horse pen, I talked to villagers we've captured. They said the Arkuden and the bronze dragon were linked in spirit—one could call the other, even from many leagues' distance. Do you believe that?"

The raider chief hawked and spat. "I know I never knew the Master's mind, spoken or unspoken. I only did his bidding."

Harak leaned his head against the warm stone wall. "I wish he were here to do our fighting for us."

Zannian drained the last drops from the flask and tossed the empty vessel into Harak's lap. "Fool. You have no sense of glory."

Seated beside two corpses, surrounded by screams, darkness, and destruction, Harak had to admit his chief was right.

Chapter 9

~

The time before dawn is so quiet, plainsmen say, because that's when the spirits of their ancestors are about, observing the world and the descendants they've left behind. Humans and animals alike are quieted by their gaze, and when the disk of the sun first breaks the horizon, the spirits vanish like dew on the grass—until the next night and the next dawn.

Lyopi dozed, standing up. She and the elders of Yala-tene had taken refuge on the sloping ramp below the town wall, a few score paces from the north baffle, now in Zannian's hands. Hekani and his beleaguered comrades were still holding off Ungrah-de at the west entrance.

She scrubbed her face with her hands and gazed across her threatened town. Early rays of sunlight slanted in over the wall, highlighting the drifting smoke hanging over most of Yala-tene. The streets were deserted, and Lyopi wondered how many people still lived within the wall of Yala-tene. Everyone not fighting had been told to stay inside. Many of the children had already been sent through the narrow tunnel in the eastern cliffs. The anguish of the parents, consigning their young to an uncertain fate, had been terrible to see.

All along the ramp, the defenders stirred. Everyone was armed now, even the elders and the wounded. Lyopi squatted and prodded the cloaked figure lying curled at her feet.

"Wake up," she said quietly. Beneath the brown homespun, the sleeper jerked awake, then groaned. "Come on," she said, dragging the cloak aside. "It's light already. The raiders will be coming soon."

Amero lifted his head and squinted against the early morning light. He stretched and flexed until the blood began to flow again in his tired limbs, then got stiffly to his feet. He smiled at Lyopi, but the smile changed to a wince as he put weight on his right leg. The thigh wound he'd received in battle still ached.

"Any word? Any movement?" he said, peeking over the top of the ramp. Six steps away, a hasty barricade of stones and wood blocked the parapet. On the other side was ten paces of open wall, littered with the casualties of the night's battle. Bracketed by twin columns of smoke was the north baffle, firmly under Zannian's control. The tops of his tree-ladders could be seen sticking up above the baffle wall. In the midst of death, the trees were already leafing out in tender green.

"No movement so far. They had a hard night, too," Lyopi said with a snort. "Shall we let them sleep?"

"I wish we had the people to charge down there and wake them properly," Amero said bitterly. His beard was no longer neatly trimmed, but long and uneven. Dark circles ringed his hazel eyes, and like the rest of the survivors in Yala-tene, he'd lost so much weight that his clothes hung loosely on his frame.

He looked out over the north end of the valley. All there was to be seen were raiders' horses and tents clustered around the captured baffle. No Nianki. No Duranix. How he longed to see either of them riding or flying over the intervening mountains, ready to strike the enemy and scatter them to the winds!

Montu and Tepa arrived on their hands and knees, anxious not to expose themselves to the raiders' deadly throwing sticks.

"What's the enemy doing?" whispered the cooper huskily.

"Snoring," said Lyopi in a normal tone.

"Shouldn't we be getting more of our people out of the

village?" Tepa asked. "While things are quiet, I mean?"

"Most of the young children are out," Amero said. "The older ones want to stay and fight."

"You must order them to go, Arkuden!"

"How can I? We need every pair of hands we can get."

"They'll be slaughtered."

"We survived the ogre attack, didn't we? And everything Zannian has thrown at us?"

"But can we continue to hold out?" Tepa wondered aloud.

"Yes, we can," Amero said, helping the exhausted old man stand erect. "Go wake the others, and see if there's any water to be had. Don't give up, my friend. Our enemies are strong, but they're not without weakness. We thought Jenla was dead, and she still lives. They thought they could murder me, but I survived."

"Unar didn't."

Amero sighed. Unar, Lyopi's brother and one of Amero's foundry workmen, had died in his place, slain by the Jade Men who'd mistaken him for the Arkuden.

Since the night of the Jade Men's attack, however, Amero had kept out of sight. If the raiders thought him dead, they wouldn't make other attempts to kill him. Moreover, Zannian and Nacris no doubt believed the people of Yala-tene would crumble without their headman. Their continued stout resistance must have taken some toll on the raiders' fighting spirit.

"*Many* good people have died, Tepa," Lyopi said quietly, her grief for her lost brother evident. "But the only way to save the rest is by saving Yala-tene. Do you want to surrender?"

Tepa shook his head dumbly. Leaning on Montu, he turned to go and rouse the others.

At that moment, a brace of throwing spears banged into the barricade, and hoarse shouts rang out.

"Hurry," Amero urged the men, hefting his spear.

Raiders on the baffle pelted the barricade with missiles for a short time, shouting dire threats. With quiet determination, thirty villagers filed in behind the barrier, spears ready. From the edge of the wall, Amero could see scores of raiders milling about beneath the baffle, waiting for their chance to climb the trees and join the attack.

"I'd give all the bronze in Yala-tene for just six jars of oil!" Amero cursed softly. He knew there was none to be had. Hekani had the town's remaining few jars on his side to use against the ogres.

Spearpoints thickened below the parapet as the raiders mustered. Amero had his people leave small holes in the barrier, just large enough to run a spear through. Another thirty villagers crouched on the ramp, ready to reinforce the line if the raiders pressed too hard.

A raider's face, chillingly painted to resemble a grinning skull, popped up above the parapet. He raised his spear and shouted, "Go!"

Leather-clad men with similarly garish visages poured over the wall and ran helter-skelter at the makeshift barrier. Villagers lobbed stones and lumps of broken pottery at them, felling a few. The rest came on, howling for blood. The lead raiders threw themselves on the barricade, bracing their arms against it so their comrades could climb their backs.

"Now!" Amero yelled. Villagers shoved javelins through the prepared chinks in the wall, spearing the human ladders where they stood. When they collapsed, the raiders on their shoulders fell too, some tumbling right off the wall. Furious, those remaining pounded on the barricade with fists and spearshafts, making the hastily erected structure shake ominously.

Amero stuck his foot in a likely niche and climbed the barrier. Keeping his head below the top, he held on with one hand and reached over with his spear, jabbing at heads and shoulders. He wounded several raiders, and the attack fell apart. Still screaming threats and obscenities, the raiders retreated to the baffle.

They attacked twice more before midday. On the third attempt, the villagers came under fire from spear-throwers on the ground. Raiders thrust the butt ends of their spears into the holes in the barricade and tried to lever it apart. Timbers and stones fell on both sides, and the struggle degenerated into a contest of grunting, straining muscles and unyielding stubbornness.

Zannian, masked and helmeted, appeared on the wall behind his men. He recalled his troops to him, and the raiders withdrew, panting in the heat of the day.

Amero thought the raider chief might want to parley, but this hope died almost instantly. At Zannian's nod, two raiders raised ram's horns to their lips and blew a loud, bleating signal. The plain below filled with horsemen.

The villagers' hearts fell. They were barely a hundred strong, and Zannian had just called in twice that number of reinforcements. Up and down the lines, spears were lowered, shoulders drooped, and heads bowed.

Amero knew what he had to do. He'd been saving a last trick, a final stratagem, for their most desperate hour. This was it. He climbed the barricade again. This time he kept going until he reached the top, and he stood upright. Dropping the hood from his head for the first time since his reputed assassination, Amero stood in clear view of the enemy.

"Zannian!" he cried. "Zannian, here! I am here. Come and get me if you can. It's Amero, Arkuden of Yala-tene!"

The horn blasts died away. The raiders stared up at the shouting man. More than one took a step back in surprise, as if facing an apparition.

Zannian slowly removed his mask. "So. Mother's little pets failed after all?" His youthful face, scratched and streaked with soot, split into a grin. "Good! A man like you should not die in bed, stabbed by green-faced children. Your blood belongs on my sword!"

His words brought a frown to Amero's face, but the Arkuden forged on. "Will you parley?" he called.

"This is our parley. Speak your piece! It's the last chance you'll have!"

Amero glanced at his gray-faced, exhausted followers. Taking a deep breath, he said, "Let's speak of surrender."

The raiders broke into ragged cheers. Zannian tossed his skull-mask to one of his men and strode forth until he was only few paces from the barricade.

With a sweeping gesture to silence his men, he said, "Throw down your weapons, people of Arku-peli!"

"I want guarantees first," Amero told him, over renewed raider cheers. "You must protect my people from the ogres."

"I guarantee nothing. Ungrah-de expects certain rewards in exchange for his help. I can't go back on my agreement with him."

Amero's disgust was evident. "How can you treat with ogres? You know what they are, what they'll do!"

Zannian drew his bronze elven sword, holding it up to let the bright sunshine flash off the naked blade. "A warrior uses whatever weapon he can to win. The ogres are just weapons."

"You can't believe that! What's to stop them from returning to their country and bringing back more of their kind? Will you be strong enough afterward to resist an attack by a horde of ogres? You must know the ancient tales—how their kind enslaved all of humanity, and scores of our people died seeking freedom. It's said they *devour* their enemies!"

His words struck home, at least among Zannian's men. None of them had been happy to find ogres in their midst, allies or not. Amero's words reinforced their fears.

They could be heard muttering among themselves. Their leader glared at them.

"No more talk!" Zannian shouted. "And no guarantees. Surrender or die!"

"That's no choice," Amero replied. "To surrender *is* to die."

"Very well." Zannian walked confidently back to his waiting warriors. He donned his skull-mask again and, whipping a hand over his head, signaled the attack to resume.

There followed an eternal interval of bloody struggle, a seemingly endless clash over possession of the last barricade. Dismounted raiders climbed the apple trees to bolster Zannian's assault while those on horseback peppered the villagers with thrown spears. The defenders dwindled. Soon Amero and Lyopi had only a handful of wounded comrades around them.

More horns blared out in the valley. Amero felt his heart shrivel with despair. Were even more raiders coming to trample them into the dust? Where did Zannian get his endless supply of men?

Packed shoulder to shoulder, the raiders pushed and heaved harder at the barricade. Afraid of being trapped when everything fell, Lyopi grabbed Amero by the collar and dragged him to the ramp. Grunting in unison, the raiders as one slammed against the tottering barrier.

The horns sounded again, closer. Lyopi pushed sweat-drenched hair from her face and peered out over the wall. Columns of horsemen filled the eastern valley. She felt numb as she watched them charging down from Cedarsplit Gap. Numb and hopeless. It was all over now.

What was this? She blinked suddenly, not crediting the evidence of her eyes.

Were the horsemen fighting each other?

She shook the dazed Arkuden. "Look, Amero!" she cried. "Look!"

He forced himself to follow her pointing hand. A mass of riders, most on tall, light-colored horses, were pouring into the valley. The mid-afternoon sun showed their faces were clean of paint, and many wore bright bronze on their heads. With sword and spear and ringing cries they attacked the mounted raiders already pressed against the walls of Yala-tene. To his confusion and shock, Amero saw many of Zannian's men fall from their horses as though clubbed, yet no enemy was close enough to strike them. What spirit power was at work here?

Then the barricade came down with a crash, and Amero, Lyopi, and the surviving villagers were forced to concentrate on the battle closer to home. They braced themselves for a final onslaught.

It never came. A few intrepid raiders leaped over the ruined barrier, now a heap of rubble, but the majority hung back, shouting and pointing at the battle raging beneath them. One by one they abandoned the wall, streaming across the baffle to the tree-ladders. Amero saw Zannian himself urging his men *away* from Yala-tene and back to their tethered horses.

"By all our ancestors," Lyopi said, sinking to her knees, tears glistening in her hollow, dark eyes. "We are saved!"

"But who can it be?" murmured a battered man behind her.

"Spirits, elves . . . I cannot tell, and I do not care," she said weakly, then slumped to the parapet, unconscious.

Though equally exhausted, his wounded leg throbbing with every beat of his heart, Amero flung his arms wide and shouted, "No, not spirits! Not elves! Nomads! They're nomads! Nianki's band has come at last!"

* * * * *

From the moment he'd risen, Hoten knew the day was an ill-omened one. Raider dead, slain in the previous day's battle, lay in heaps outside the camp. Though it was a grim sight, he'd seen much death since joining Zannian's band. It was the eerie silence hanging over everything that had halted him in his tracks. Crows and vultures should have been circling, but the sky above was as empty of scavengers as it was of clouds. It was as though nature itself was rejecting the dead, and this troubled Hoten deeply. Such a thing had never happened. Never, until the ogres came.

After washing himself in the river, Hoten had awakened his mate and found her different this morning. Nacris came to life unusually animated. She told him of a wager the men had going, on whether it would be Zan or the ogres who entered Arku-peli first. Though betting favored Ungrah-de, Nacris wagered on her son.

"Losing faith in your allies?" Hoten asked, helping her rise and placing the crutch in her hand.

"Gaining faith in myself," she replied. "I will lead my Jade Men to Arku-peli today. With them as his spearhead, Zan will prevail."

"But Zannian commanded the Jade Men to remain in camp."

"A stupid order. I shall lead them to victory!"

All the remaining raiders were summoned to Zannian a short time later. Hoten lingered at the rear of the formation, watching Nacris in her litter and the Jade Men surrounding her. Though Zannian offered him command of this attack, Hoten let the fiery young captains lead the morning's assault. Shouting war cries, they galloped off to the north baffle to help storm the fading village defenses.

Still Hoten hung back. Nacris did not follow the horsemen when they turned toward the town. She led her twenty-two surviving Jade Men into the center of the valley and halted, facing the rising sun.

Hoten cantered to her. "What are you doing?" he called. "The battle is there. Why have you stopped out here?"

Nacris's lean, lined face was alight with rapturous excitement. Her normally cold, flinty eyes glowed with a strange happiness. She looked years younger. It was astonishing how the emotion transformed her, yet the sight only added to Hoten's feeling of nameless worry.

"She's coming," his mate said. "She's coming, and I'll be here to greet her."

"Who's coming? Nacris, what are you talking about?"

She looked up at him with shining eyes. "Karada."

"Karada's dead and gone, like her brother," he said with a disgusted snort. Then, in spite of himself, he asked, "What makes you think she's coming?"

"I feel it. Here." The crippled old woman pressed a fist to her heart. "All night I dreamed I could hear the hoof-beats of Karada's band, riding and riding. When I awoke I could still hear them. I know it is true, Hoten. The Great Spirits have granted me this boon. This is the day I will see Karada again, and one of us is fated to perish!"

He couldn't tell if she was mad or inspired. In either case, Hoten felt he was losing the woman he loved. He palmed the sweat from his blistered brow and made one last attempt to reach her.

"If what you say is true, then you shouldn't be standing out here, alone. Karada always led a band of superb warriors. If she comes, you and the Jade Men will be trampled into the dirt."

Nacris drew a light javelin from a socket in the frame of her litter. She laid the weapon across her lap. In the same strange, lilting voice, she replied, "We will fight and we will win. The spirits are with me. Haven't you understood this? Everything that has happened in my life has been done so to bring me here! You don't believe me?

Broken, lame, I was found by you and spared. The Master enlisted me in his cause, not knowing he was really serving mine! Zannian raised a mighty band to fulfill his ambition, but it was mine he was achieving!

"The bronze dragon abandoned his people, why? Because I willed it! The Dragon's Son was slain—by *my* Jade Men! Even Ungrah-de has subordinated himself to my design. All that remains is to destroy Karada herself, and my revenge will be complete! I cannot possibly fail now."

Hoten stared at her. He had lived too long to believe in anything so childish as heartbreak, but at that moment he knew, win or lose, Nacris was lost to him forever. The knowledge left him feeling empty.

He dismounted and came to her side. Her glittering eyes were fixed on the eastern horizon. Bending down, he kissed her gently on the forehead. She paid him no heed whatsoever.

Back astride his horse, Hoten turned toward Arkupeli, already ringing with the sounds of combat. "Farewell, Nacris. Hoten, son of Nito, salutes you."

She did not look up as he rode away.

Chapter 10

By the time the nomads entered Cedarsplit Gap, day was well advanced. Though tired from their all-night ride, not one wanted to stop. Before sunrise they had flushed a party of raiders camped on a ridge overlooking the pass. From them, they'd learned the ogres and raiders were close to capturing the town. Karada united the different segments of her band and set off immediately for the Valley of the Falls.

The Silvanesti, on foot, had fallen behind during the night but caught up at the ridge. Ironically, it was the elves who had the stiffest fight in the mountains.

As Karada had ordered, Balif led his soldiers to the cliff top and immediately ran into a force of five-score raiders. Outnumbered three to one, Balif attacked. The raiders had detected Karada's large, mounted band moving through the pass and closed ranks in expectation of an assault on horseback. They did not expect thirty metal-armed Silvanesti on foot.

Balif spread his elves out in skirmishing order, taking a small pinnacle above the plateau first. From there, the Silvanesti hurled bronze-tipped javelins down on the tightly packed raiders.

Outflanked, half the raiders bolted there and then. The rest charged the elves with their long stabbing spears leveled. Balif drew his soldiers back on the crag where the raiders' horses couldn't reach them. The undisciplined raiders broke into small groups and attacked at will, which allowed Balif to pick them off, equally at will. By midday, the elf lord was master of the plateau.

Sending a messenger on a dead raider's horse, Balif informed Karada he held the cliff tops. To his surprise, the messenger returned with Karada herself and an entourage of twenty nomads.

She looked over the field of Balif's small victory. The elf lord, long hair tied back with a leather strap in nomad fashion, was sweating in the heat but as composed as ever.

"Well done," she said. "How do they fight?"

"They're fell foes. With better leadership, they'd have driven us off the mountain."

They went to the edge of the high precipice and looked down on Yala-tene. Smoke drifted over the beleaguered town, and a mass of horsemen was milling about below the wall on the north end of the village. Whatever pangs of memory and loss Karada felt looking at her brother's home she quickly suppressed.

"Pakito!"

"Aye!" The giant appeared at his chief's side.

"Take two out of three in the band and hit those yevi-spawn! Go now!"

"Aye, Karada!" Pakito kissed Samtu and started shouting orders. His booming voice carried across the open plateau, putting the heat of battle into everyone's veins.

"Bahco! Wait here with the third that Pakito doesn't take," Karada ordered. The young nomad grimaced with disappointment but did as she said.

Beramun slipped in beside Karada. "Can you see the ogres? How many do you think there are?"

Karada shaded her eyes with her hands. Her vision was proverbially keen, but even she couldn't distinguish ogres from men at this distance, and she said so.

Hawk eyes still fastened on the scene below, she suddenly exclaimed, "By my ancestors! On the valley floor, there—folk on foot. Do you see?" Beramun and Balif agreed they did. "Do they look *green* to you?"

Balif frowned. "They do."

"The Jade Men!" Beramun breathed.

The grim calm of the nomad chieftain gave way to the fury of Amero's sister. "Bahco!" Karada said, voice cracking with rage. "Take the rest of the band down there and get them!"

"Yes, chief. Do you want prisoners?"

"I want corpses! Those are the snakes who killed my brother! Not one of them is to live, Bahco! Kill them all!"

The dark warrior nodded gravely and departed.

Beramun stared after him, her hand resting on the mark on her chest. Strangely, when she'd escaped Yalatene to search for Karada, the green brand had saved her life. The Jade Men had captured her but, seeing their master's sign, had let her go, thinking she was one of them. Their calm assurance had frightened her, but she'd proven she was not Sthenn's tool, hadn't she? She was returning with Karada and her nomad warriors.

"I must get to the village as soon as possible," Beramun said. "May I go with Bahco?"

Karada glanced at Beramun and at Mara, standing behind her and quietly observing everything. "All right," the chieftain said. "Leave Mara here, and mind what Bahco tells you. He leads in my place."

Soon only Karada, Mara, Balif, and his elves remained on the cliff. Anyone else might have felt vulnerable being surrounded by armed former enemies, but not Karada. She knew Balif well enough by now to know he would not try any treacherous coup.

They remained overlooking the scene until Pakito's column hit the raiders from behind. Zannian's men were crowded in close to the wall, awaiting their chance to come to grips with the weakening villagers, and they never knew what hit them. Pakito, disdaining the use of bows, closed with spear and sword.

"That's it!" Karada cried, racing along the edge of the cliff, following the fight. One wrong step, and she would have plunged hundreds of paces down the mountain. She was oblivious to the danger. "Drive in! Keep them against the wall, Pakito. No room to maneuver! Give them no room!"

Turning suddenly, Karada sprang onto her horse. "Why am I here? To battle!"

Mara said, "Take me with you!"

Karada gave the girl her hand. "Hold on!" she said as Mara scrambled aboard. "If you fall off on the way down, I'm not stopping to pick you up!"

Mara wrapped both arms around Karada's narrow waist. The nomad chief waved to Balif, who mustered his elves and started them jogging into Cedarsplit Gap. At a bone-jarring gallop, Karada passed the Silvanesti and hurtled down the slope, drawn by the intoxicating tumult of battle.

* * * * *

The Jade Men formed a circle around Nacris, each facing outward. The youth who'd led the killers after Amero said, "Mother, we await your will."

"Good boys. Be patient. She will come."

The din of battle waxed and waned behind them as Zannian tried to bludgeon his way into Yala-tene. More distant was the noise of Ungrah and his ogres resuming their attack, having now demolished the west baffle and part of the outer wall. The sound of ogre war drums could be heard again throughout the Valley of the Falls.

It was high summer, and the Jade Men suffered in the heat, though they wore nothing but green kilts and leggings. They made no complaints and kept formation as the hot sun beat down on them. The ground around them became stained with their dripping sweat.

A strong breeze blew down Cedarsplit Gap, driving eddies of dust before it. The Jade Men on the east side of the circle sniffed the air and immediately stiffened with alarm. They looked to Nacris, reclining in the litter, the javelin still on her lap.

"Mother—"

"Yes, my child. I know. Horses are coming. Are you ready?"

They were.

"Present your arms."

Each Jade Man knelt on one knee, butting the end of his long spear against his foot. Their circle was now a fence of keen points.

Tiny mounted figures appeared on the cliffs overlooking the valley. Their horses were taller than the ponies the raiders rode, and most were light-colored—tan, gray, white. They stood out boldly against the darker stone of the cliffs.

A heavy cloud of dust rose from the pass, soaring as high as the cliffs around it. The drone of massed hoofbeats gradually overcame the tumult of the battle for Yala-tene, and the first riders emerged from Cedarsplit Gap. Obviously scouts, they took in the scene and reentered the pass. Moments later, a column of riders six abreast burst into view. They thundered down the trail, making for the rear of Zannian's band and veering away from the Jade Men's position. Nacris said nothing. The Jade Men held their places.

The moving column of nomads passed within a hundred paces of the Jade Men. The riders saw the strange, green-painted youths on open ground but held their course to hit the engaged raiders hard. A gigantic melee developed, with hundreds of horses churning up the dry earth, filling the air with dust.

A second band of nomads descended the pass in a more leisurely fashion. They halted briefly, then came toward Nacris at a steady walk.

"Steady, children," she said. "Remember your Master! He will hear of how well you fight today!"

The nomads spread out, plainly seeking to encircle their unmoving enemy. Nacris admired their tall mounts, their buff deerskins, and tanned, healthy faces. She'd been one of them once and remembered how it felt to have sound limbs, a good horse, and the endless plain as your domain.

At a distance of forty paces, the nomads halted. They put aside their spears and swords and took strange devices in their hands—slender staves of wood, their two ends joined by a taut length of cord.

Nacris furrowed her brow. What was this?

Each rider fitted a little spear to the cord. That was enough to warn Nacris these were weapons of some sort. She cried, "Jade Men! At them!"

With a concerted shout the green-skinned youths threw themselves forward. The nomads waited, implacable, drawing back the cords on their odd weapons, stretching the staves into deep arcs. When released, the little spears were thrown with incredible force. The air was filled with the thrum of tight strings and the hiss of flying feathered-tufted missiles.

It should have been over in a few heartbeats—two hundred nomads loosing arrows at less than twenty-five targets. Yet, the fight did not go that way. Slender green bodies twisted and spun, dodging the first volley of arrows sent at them. Screaming in high-pitched, boyish voices, the Jade Men came on. Unnerved, the nomads hesitated before loosing a second hail of arrows.

This time many of the arrows found their marks. Jade Men toppled, chests sprouting with slender wooden shafts. Those not hit dropped to the ground and scrambled forward on all fours, each with a spear clenched in his teeth. Horses reared as the weird youths scampered under them. Some nomads were thrown down and slain by the waiting Jade Men. Others dropped their bows in favor of spears and swords to better combat their strange enemies.

From her litter, Nacris watched and laughed. With a hundred Jade Men, she could have wiped out the nomads before her. With a thousand, she could have ruled the plains. How well they moved and fought! Those mortally stricken lay in the trampled weeds, she noted with a pang, like exotic flowers cut down by a scythe.

The surviving Jade Men swarmed over the confused riders, dragging them off their horses, stabbing, choking, even biting them into submission. A hollow space opened in the midst of the nomad formation as Karada's warriors drew back from the bizarre green killers. When the dust cleared, the bows went to work again, this time with carefully aimed arrows. Jade Man after Jade Man was hit.

A loud murmur arose from the nomads. Even bristling with arrows, some of the green-skinned youths struggled to rise and carry on the fight. Nacris strained neck and arms trying to lift herself to see what was happening. As the breeze swept the dust aside, she saw a dark-skinned man with a bronze sword in his hand. On foot, he went among the wounded Jade Men, dispatching them with well-placed thrusts.

By the time Nacris hauled herself up to stand with her crutch, it was all over. Tears coursed down her weathered face, though she did not make a sound. Her ploy of waiting in the open had drawn Karada, just as she hoped. Her Jade Men had died well. She was so very proud of her children.

The dark swordsman remounted and rode through the nomad line. Leaning hard on her crutch, Nacris pulled her gaze from the sprawled forms of her young Jade Men and presented the point of her spear to the enemy.

Among the lead riders Nacris noticed a strikingly pretty girl with long black hair and jet eyes to match. Nacris knew that girl. Her name was . . .

"Beramun," the girl supplied, seeing the crippled woman struggling to remember.

"You came back. Zannian will be pleased."

"I don't think so. I've brought friends, many friends." To the dark man at her side, Beramun added, "Watch her, Bahco. She's a snake!"

Nacris smiled through her tears. "And Karada? Where is she?"

Beramun turned and pointed to the cliff. "There. She sent us to fetch you."

Nacris drew back her arm and flung the javelin. Unsteady on one leg, her cast was awkward, and the weapon flew low. It landed in the dirt in front of Bahco's horse.

"Take her," he said. Four nomads seized Nacris but found her unresisting. In fact, she broke into wild laughter.

"My design is almost complete!" she chortled. "Obey my will! Take me to Karada!"

* * * * *

Zannian couldn't believe it. Victory had been his—the Arkuden himself was talking surrender—and now everything was falling apart! What capricious spirits were at work here? How could his glorious destiny have splintered so thoroughly, like a stick of rotten wood?

He abandoned the north baffle, for which so many had died, and got on his horse. The bulk of his once-numerous band was hotly engaged, and every man, every weapon, counted. He rallied his demoralized men and they pushed their new enemies back a bit, gaining room to breathe. The newcomers were not too numerous. Zannian guessed they totaled perhaps four hundred, similar to his on-hand strength, but they were powerfully armed, rode bigger animals, and both horses and riders were fresher than his own troops.

Slowly his men retreated westward, forced away from

the village. During the running fight, Zannian rode through the site of another skirmish. The bodies on the ground were green-skinned.

Jade Men. This was his mother's work. Only she or the Master could have commanded the Jade Men into battle, and Sthenn was certainly nowhere about. Zannian had no chance to look for Nacris's body among the others before the swirling fight carried him and his men away from where the Jade Men perished.

He spotted Hoten in the fray, trading blows with a sturdy foe on a tall horse. The old raider was having the worst of it, so Zannian charged through the press and speared the nomad on his blind side. Hoten saluted wearily. Zannian started to ask about Nacris, but new enemies appeared, and he and Hoten were driven apart.

A new column of nomads appeared on the raiders' left. Though smaller than the first group, they still numbered nearly two hundred robust warriors. Outnumbered and outridden, the raiders began to lose heart. Some threw down their weapons and whipped their exhausted mounts westward to the empty camp by the river. Zannian boiled with fury. The cowards would not dare quit the battle if Sthenn were present!

As one trio of deserters cantered away, watching anxiously over their shoulders for pursuit by nomads or Zannian's loyalists, they failed to see a line of ogres stalking toward them. The biggest ogre raised his chipped stone axe and knocked the lead rider off his horse, cleaving him from shoulder to waist with one blow. The other horses reared, throwing off their startled riders. Two ogres picked up a deserter by his ankles. The terrified raider screamed as he was flung back into the churning battle. He vanished into the mass of fighting humans and stamping horses. The last deserter saw none of this. He ran like a rabbit. Sneering, the ogres let him go.

Ungrah-de hailed Zannian, saying, "We heard the fight

coming our way and came to join you." His brawny arms were stained to the elbows with his enemies' blood. "Your men are running away."

"Kill as many as you like, great chief!" Zan snarled. "It will encourage the rest to fight!"

Nearby, the nomads broke through the raiders. Upon seeing the ogres the nomads wavered, but they were many and the ogres few, so they resumed their charge. Ungrah's warriors did not look as though they could withstand a mounted attack, but they turned the nomads' spears with their stone-faced bucklers and chopped them down with broad sweeps of their axes. Zannian reorganized his remaining men behind the firm line established by Ungrah-de. The nomads made a few forays against the formidable monsters, but these were bloodily repulsed.

Horns blared, and the nomads drew back several score paces, forming into two blocks. Zannian saw the larger block, on his right, was commanded by a huge man riding an equally tall horse. The nomads on the left seemed to be led by a muscular young man with richly brown skin and short, black, tightly curled hair. There was no sign of a female chief, the Karada of legend.

There was much posturing and spear shaking, but as horses and riders calmed, the two bands drew farther apart. The sun was not long from setting, and the nomads had the blazing light in their eyes. Across from them, many raiders were reeling on their animals, nearly overcome by exhaustion.

Into the open ground between the two forces rode five nomads on four horses. The giant and the dark man were two of them. The third was a slender woman with long black hair. In the midst of the ruin of his dreams of conquest, Zannian felt a surge of fire in his veins when he recognized Beramun.

His elation was tempered by the sight of the fourth horse. It carried two women: one, a red-haired girl Beramun's age,

Zan dismissed immediately; the other, older and browned by years of sun, merited a longer inspection. The older woman wore a fine bronze helmet of elven make. Her jaw and throat were streaked with livid, white scars.

Beside him, Hoten drew in a breath sharply. "Karada!"

"Are you certain?" Zannian demanded.

"In my youth I rode with her band," was the awed reply. "That's her."

Zannian gave a low growl of annoyance. "First the Arkuden and now Karada. Too many dead people are still alive."

He and Hoten rode out together with Ungrah-de striding along between their horses. They came within six steps of the nomads and stopped.

No one spoke. The only sound was the ogre's loud breathing and the sound of horses' tails switching away flies.

Hoten broke the impasse. "Greetings, Karada," he said, hailing his former chieftain.

She squinted against the flare of the setting sun. "I know your face. You're . . . Hoten, son of Nito. You were in my band, many years ago."

He nodded, thinking it strange that her recognition should please him so.

"Now you ride with these savages?" Pakito growled at him. "Yevi-spawn!"

So much for old memories.

Zannian said, "Speak, Karada. Why have you come here?"

"To save my brother and his people. I may be too late for one but not the other."

Zannian did not enlighten her that Amero lived. "You don't belong here. Go back to the east. Battle the Silvanesti, and leave this land to us."

"You are the invaders!" Beramun spoke up. "Murderers and looters! Go back to the stinking forest you call home and tell your dragon master you have failed!"

The raider chief turned his horse's head toward her. "I saved you from the Master more than once, girl. Have you no gratitude?"

"Speak to *me,* raider," Karada said severely. "I give you this leave: be gone from the Valley of the Falls by sunrise tomorrow, or your corpse will rot where it falls."

"This one is a warrior," Ungrah said suddenly. His dark eyes had not left Karada's face since she'd first spoken.

Hearing the imposing creature speak their language startled the nomads. Ungrah went on. "Even in the high mountains we have heard of the Scarred One. I see now the tales are true."

"This is not your fight, ogre," she replied. "Withdraw, and none shall hinder you."

"My fight is any I choose. Killing the wall-people was just work, but now I think this fight will be good. I will wear your skull with pride, Karada." He rattled the trophies hanging from his armored chest.

In answer, she drew her long bronze sword. Zannian and Hoten tensed, ready to fight. Ungrah stood his ground, feet planted firmly, both massive hands resting on the head of his axe, unmoving as a mountain.

"To the death then, is it?" said Karada, looking from the ogre to the raider chief.

"It is," Zannian said.

Ungrah and the raiders turned to go. They'd taken several steps before she spoke again.

"I have Nacris."

The simple words halted them. Hoten tried to see his mate's fate in Karada's expression, but the nomad chief's face was like the eastern cliffs—hard and unyielding.

"Does my mother live?"

Something flickered across Karada's face. "Mother?"

"Does she live?" Zannian snapped.

"For now. If I return her to you, will you leave the valley?"

"No." Hoten's protest was overridden as Zannian said,"We did not come all this way to fall short now! Karada is my mother's blood foe. Nacris would rather die at her hands than be spared by her!"

The raider chief kicked his mount into motion, leading his sullen men back to camp.

Before he turned to follow them, Ungrah-de said, "When the sun is next overhead, we will meet here and test our strengths, arm to arm. Until then, savor your blood, Karada. Tomorrow it will stain the soil at my feet."

Though the other nomads, even giant Pakito, were visibly affected by the threat, Karada turned her back on Ungrah and rode back to her band.

* * * * *

High atop the walls of Yala-tene, Amero and his companions watched the nomads and raiders parley, unable even to discern who the participants were. Yet, Amero was almost certain that one of the nomads was his sister. She was on a wheat-colored horse, and something about the way she sat the animal struck a chord in his mind.

When the two groups rode away from each other, he was filled with joy. Surely the raiders were defeated! What else could they do but abandon the siege and leave the valley?

Amero saw the nomads return to the north baffle and set up camp beneath the walls. A body of men marching in close order down Cedarsplit Gap joined the nomads. It wasn't until they were much nearer that it became apparent the warriors on foot were elves.

"What does this mean?" asked Hekani, who'd come over from the west baffle once the ogres had retreated. "Silvanesti fighting alongside nomads? Such things don't happen!"

"What about men allied with a green dragon and with ogres?" replied Lyopi tartly.

"I don't know what's possible, and I don't care! It is a great day!" Amero declared. Worn down to raw courage and sheer nerve, the other villagers could only agree.

Amero hurried to the north baffle, eager to see his sister after so long a time. Beramun would be there, too—brave girl! He longed to see her again and do honor to her courage. Alone of the scouts he'd sent to find Nianki, she had survived and brought the nomads back to save them.

By the time he arrived at the entrance, nomads had already swarmed onto the baffle and were making their way into the village. The people of Yala-tene lined the walls to cheer them. Gratitude poured out of every hoarse throat.

Beyond the wrecked barricade, Amero stopped. He could see them coming. His throat tightened, and his hands trembled. Beramun's raven hair was painted dark crimson by the setting sun. In front of her, a tawny woman of forty summers clambered over the boulders and rubble. It was Nianki indeed, and how strong she looked!

Where the obstructions ended and the wall began, Karada and her party halted. She looked up and saw the assembled villagers waiting for them. Standing on the wall directly above her was a bearded man in tattered clothes. He was hollow-eyed, battered, and cut about the hands and face. A handsome woman with a thick chestnut braid of hair stood at his side, gripping a much-used spear.

Karada felt her heart beat hard, the pulse pounding in her ears. The setting sun was behind the people on the wall, leaving their faces in shadow. Yet she knew the bearded man. Though her voice, when at last she could speak, sounded questioning and strained, she knew him.

"Amero?"

"Nianki!" the man called joyously, spreading his arms wide.

No one else in all the world called her by her birth name. It was Amero. He was alive.

She didn't remember climbing the last bit. Next thing she knew she was on the wall, arms around the apparition of her brother. He was solid and real, no spirit, and when he drew back from her, she saw the old gleam of wit in his hazel eyes.

"I can hardly believe it! You saved us!" He was grinning so wide his face seemed ready to split.

"You called me," she said quietly, moved. "I came."

Chapter 11

Vast was the relief felt in Yala-tene that night. The desperate, hungry villagers poured from their homes, embracing any nomad who would stand still for it. Though not plentifully supplied themselves, the nomads shared what provender they had with Amero's people. It was not a celebration—everyone was too tired for that—but the feeling of doom over the valley had eased.

Beramun was enthusiastically greeted by all. Even Lyopi, not overly fond of the nomad girl, honored her courage and perseverance. When Beramun told them Karada's band had met the three children from Yala-tene and that the children were safely hidden with the noncombatants outside the Valley of the Falls, the villagers gained hope that the rest of their young might have made it as well.

Amero, Lyopi, and the village elders left the safety of the wall for the first time in many days and went to Karada's camp. There they met Bahco and renewed their acquaintance with Pakito and Samtu, both of whom Amero had known from his sister's last visit to Yalatene a dozen years before. The villagers were presented to Balif, who greeted the Arkuden and his people with great courtesy.

Unlike his hard-riding captors, Balif had taken the time to wash after the day's fighting. Dressed in a skyblue robe and girded by a cloth-of-gold belt, he looked every bit the elf lord.

"How is it you're here fighting alongside my sister?" Amero asked.

"It's the fault of the moon," was Balif's reply.

Conversation around the great campfire died. "Moon?" asked Lyopi.

"Just so. I was on a hunting expedition north of the Thon-Tanjan during the dark of the white moon, and the catch was meager. My hunt master recommended we return to Silvanost and try our luck later, but I knew the moon would return soon and the hunting would improve. I insisted upon staying on the plain a few days longer." He squared his angular shoulders and tried not to look irritated. "Two nights later we were taken unawares by Karada's band."

"You might as well blame Beramun as the moon," Karada said, sipping cider. "It was she who brought us west."

Sitting in the circle behind Karada, Beramun blushed as all eyes turned to her.

Balif explained that the ogre threat had persuaded him to offer his sword to Karada's cause.

Amero gripped his sister's hand and smiled. "I always believed you were alive," he said. "I knew you would come."

"Yes, he only feared you'd arrive after the village was razed," Lyopi said dryly.

Amero protested amid general laughter. While he was distracted, Karada freed her hand from his and moved away, ostensibly to refill her cup.

Talk continued, with confessions of faith balanced against admissions of doubt. The conversation remained light until Pakito said, "Tomorrow, will the raiders really stand and fight?"

The camp grew quiet. Burning wood hissed and popped in the fire.

"They will, and so will the ogres," Karada said.

"How many ogres are there?" asked Bahco.

"You saw them all today," Hekani said. "About two dozen are still breathing. There were thirty, once." Hekani smiled grimly. "We took care of a few already."

"Beating them will take new tactics," mused Karada. "Maybe new weapons . . ."

"Filthy monsters," Samtu muttered. More loudly, she said, "These raiders are outnumbered. If they were wise, they'd ride out tonight and leave the ogres to fend for themselves!"

"You can't count out the raiders," said Beramun. "Zannian has spent his entire life preparing to conquer the plains. It's all his mother and the green dragon have trained him for. He won't give up that dream. As long as Zannian lives, there will be no peace on the western plain." Since she knew the raiders better than anyone, her words carried weight.

In the silence that followed her harsh pronouncement, Amero yawned widely. Apologizing, he said, "I think it's time for rest now. I know we villagers will sleep easier tonight." Lyopi was already asleep, her head resting on his shoulder. He shook her gently awake.

Lyopi and the elders went ahead while Amero remained to thank their saviors again. He clasped Balif's hard, slender hand. The elf's face reminded him of painted pottery—attractive, yet cool and stiff. Amero could not fathom what lay beneath.

When he stood before Pakito, the genial giant disdained the hand he offered and instead grabbed the Arkuden by both shoulders and gave him a hearty shake. Once Amero regained his balance, Samtu kissed his bearded cheek, then departed with her towering mate.

Amero found himself facing Beramun. In the firelight, the black-haired girl was as achingly beautiful as ever—more so, he decided. Life with Karada seemed to agree with her. When she first stumbled into the Valley of the Falls, she'd looked gaunt and hunted. Now she had fleshed out and acquired the tan worn by all Karada's nomads.

"How can I thank you?" he said, not daring to touch her. "You saved everything."

"You've thanked everyone enough," she joked. "And I was but one of many. The spirits were with me, and I lived to find Karada."

"Tomorrow should see the end of it."

She didn't look convinced, but she nodded, smiled briefly, and left.

Last to receive his good-night was his sister. She stood a few steps away, looking awkward, almost shy. Amero knew of the curse she lived with, but he could not treat her like a stranger. He held out his arms. She didn't move, so he stepped forward and embraced her.

Her heart hammered against her ribs. He could feel it, so he drew back. "I'm sorry," he said for her ears alone. "I don't mean to distress you."

She only shook her head, so he added, "I'll see you in the morning."

Amero tried to leave, but he found he couldn't. Karada was gripping the front of his shirt in her clenched fists. She looked at her hands in surprise, as though they belonged to someone else, and released him.

"Watch yourself tomorrow," Amero said, then his gaze slid past her. "It's no victory if I lose you."

The campfire was at his back, and its light reflected off a pale face in the shadows behind his sister. Karada had told him how she'd released Mara from Silvanesti bondage. He'd greeted the girl with relief, surprised and pleased to know she hadn't died as the villagers had thought—on an ill-fated journey to find spirit stones out on the plains. Mara hadn't returned his good feelings but had regarded him with an odd wariness.

Now the fire's dying flames illuminated anger in her green eyes.

Karada noticed his frown and glanced over her shoulder to see what caused it. She spoke sharply to the hovering girl. Silently, Mara stole away.

"What was that about?" he asked.

"It's nothing. A girl's misplaced affection."

Amero left his sister and caught up with his people outside the nomad camp. The elders chatted idly, still excited by their sudden deliverance.

"The only thing missing," Amero said, "is Duranix."

He looked up at the night sky, brightly washed with light by the conjunction of the red and white moons. "I hope he finds what he's seeking," he added.

"I hope he kills that green dragon!" Lyopi said.

Amero smiled. "That's what I meant."

"I'm not being amusing. If Duranix fails, our battle here means nothing. The green dragon will return and destroy us."

Amero's step faltered. What Lyopi said was unbearably true. All their suffering and striving would be for nought if Duranix lost to Sthenn.

They ascended the timber ramp lowered from the wall and reentered the village. Amero bade the elders a good night. He did not accompany Lyopi to her house but walked the streets of Yala-tene for some time, trying to escape the remorseless bonds of her words.

* * * * *

Karada's head ached from too much heat, noise, and raw cider. She should sleep, but an important task remained undone.

Alone in her dark tent, she removed her heavy riding clothes, sword, and leggings. She washed her hands and face quickly, then donned a clean buckskin shirt and wraparound kilt. Tying the sash in place, she thrust a flint knife behind the knot. When she stepped out again, she found Mara waiting for her.

"Why aren't you asleep?" she snapped. "If you're restless, clean my gear for tomorrow!"

"Yes, Karada."

Walking away, Karada made a silent resolution to do something about the girl. Mara's excessive devotion had once been amusing. Lately it had become annoying.

Years ago, Karada had found an orphan child wandering the plain and had raised her like a daughter. That orphan was Samtu. Their relationship had been stormy, as Samtu was as strong-willed and fiercely independent as Karada herself. Mara's slavish worship was another thing entirely.

Thoughts of Mara vanished when she reached her destination. Two nomads guarded the small tent, leaning on their spears. Spotting their chief, they straightened up and hailed her.

"All quiet?" she asked.

"Not a sound's come out of there," said the female guard.

"All right. Go elsewhere for a while."

The guards departed, and she lifted the flap and stepped inside.

"I knew you'd come," Nacris said. "What took you so long?"

"I had more important things to do." Karada let the flap fall. There were cutouts in the fabric around the top. The white light of Soli, combined with Lutar's red glow, gave the tent's interior a pinkish cast. Karada stood over her crippled captive.

"You must think I'm very dangerous," said Nacris, lifting the heavy bronze chain coiled around her waist. The other end was attached to a stout wooden stake a pace long, driven into the ground by Pakito. Gesturing at her crippled leg, she added, "You know I can't run away."

Karada nudged the chain with her foot. "I learned from the Silvanesti troublesome things are less troubling when you chain them up."

She sat down cross-legged in front of Nacris, just out of arm's reach. She and her old foe were of an age, but Nacris's hard life had taken its toll. Nacris looked years older than her former chief.

Bluntly, Karada spoke her thoughts. "You look like a day-old corpse. What curse has afflicted you?"

"A curse with your name."

"You made your own misery, woman. Don't blame it on me."

Instead of biting back, Nacris smiled. She extended her good leg and stretched luxuriously.

"I've learned much in the years since your friend Duranix saw fit to maim me for life. That was the start of my journey to wisdom. It's taken a long time and much bloodshed, but I've nearly reached my goal."

"What goal?"

"Your humiliation and death." When her words brought no response from her hated enemy, Nacris added, "And a painful death for all you love, starting with Amero."

Karada lashed out, taking Nacris by the throat and forcing her down on her back. With her free hand she brought the flint knife to her enemy's throat.

"I *am* your death!" Karada snarled. "Why do you think I let you live this long? My warriors could have slain you with your green-skinned killers, but I reserved that deed to myself!"

"Then do it!" Nacris hissed. She continued grinning widely, eyes bulging from their sockets.

Karada let the flint blade bite a little. Nacris felt the sting and started to laugh. Furious, flinging the knife aside, Karada tightened her grip on the woman's throat.

Nacris's laughter choked off as the pressure increased. She gasped, "If I die . . . you'll never . . . find . . . your brother!"

"Fool! Amero lives in spite of your plots!"

"Your *other* brother!" Nacris gurgled.

The world went black before Nacris's eyes, and a

terrible roaring, as loud as any dragon's cry, filled her ears. She felt herself falling down a deep pit like the one Sthenn inhabited in his forest lair.

Then the air lightened, and she could see again and breathe. The face of her hated enemy was still above her. Nacris drew in a long, deep breath. Her throat felt as raw as an open wound.

"Speak, hag," Karada said. "Explain your words, and I'll grant you the mercy of a swift death."

After another ragged inhale, Nacris rasped, "Like your dragon's mercy—flinging me into the lake and breaking my leg in three places."

She said nothing more, merely struggled back upright and sat glaring at Karada.

The nomad chieftain stood and regarded her without pity. "Why say these things if you don't care whether I understand you?" she said and turned to go.

"You did have another brother, didn't you?" Nacris finally murmured.

"What of it? He died long ago, killed by the same yevi pack that slew my father and mother."

"Did he?" Eyes of bloodshot gray locked with hazel. "Did you see his body? No? You believed Amero dead for many years, too, didn't you?"

Karada gave a disgusted snort. "Your lies know no limits, viper! I came here to offer you an honorable death, but I see you're not worthy of it. I think I'll have Pakito toss you in the lake again. If we tie a stone around your neck, maybe this time you'll stay down."

Nacris grinned. "You cannot kill me, Karada. Not while I know something you must find out!"

She continued to shout as Karada lifted the flap and went out. The guards were just returning, and Nacris's obscene threats against their chief were so awful the two warriors blanched.

"No one else is to see her," Karada told them. *"No one."*

The shouted imprecations grew even louder. "I'll send wine. Drink it yourselves or give it to her, whichever leads to peace sooner."

* * * * *

After eating with the villagers, Beramun wandered away. Pleased as she was they'd reached Yala-tene in time, knowing the bloodshed was going to continue tomorrow oppressed her deeply.

Her mission was over, her duty to Amero fulfilled. Zannian's plans were undone. She once vowed to see him die as payment for the deaths of her family, but her lust for blood had dimmed. Neither a resident of Yala-tene nor a member of Karada's band, Beramun wanted most to be back on the open plain and far away from the Valley of the Falls.

So what was keeping her here? The wide world was waiting. Why not go now?

She'd wandered aimlessly away from the great central campfire, passing through ring after ring of nomad tents. By the time she looked up from her musings, she was on open ground east of camp. Cedarsplit Gap was clearly in view under the combined light of Moonmeet. The way was not clear, however.

In front of her was a ring of stakes and vines, like a temporary ox pen. Huddled figures filled the ring, most lying on the ground under scraps of hide. Nomads on horseback rode slowly around the ring.

She accosted one rider. "What is this?" she asked.

"Raiders we caught today," said the nomad. "We spared them when they threw down their arms."

The surrendered men, no more than forty in all, looked utterly beaten. Stripped of face paint, weapons, and horses, they had ceased to be fearsome raiders.

Beramun slowly circled the pen, studying the men she'd

feared for so long. She wondered if the ones who'd killed her family were present. She tried to see their nightmarish faces in the tired, pathetic prisoners before her.

Most of the captured men were sleeping, curled up in tight groups for warmth. A few, sick or wounded, whimpered and coughed. Near the fence, one man sat alone. He'd removed his torn leggings and was patiently trying to mend them by the light of the two moons.

Seeing her, he called out a greeting. She moved quickly to get past him. He stood and started paralleling her on the inside of the fence, but she kept her eyes straight ahead and walked faster.

"You look like you're escaping from someone," he called. "With a face as beautiful as yours, it must be a lover."

"Mind your own troubles!" she snapped, halting.

He was tall and well made, with hair almost as long as her own, though somewhat lighter in color and tied back with a scrap of leather. His feet and ankles were badly scraped. No wonder his leggings were in tatters, she thought.

"You look kind, fair one," he said. "I need to mend my leggings. Have you a bone needle to lend a wanderer like yourself?"

She snorted. "You should have stayed a wanderer, *raider.*" Beramun resumed walking, though she couldn't remember where she'd been going.

"My name is Harak, fair one! I come from Khar land, in the south."

She stopped, turned around, and came back. Without explanation, she unwound her own leggings. Harak watched silently, and when she handed them to him, he smiled and thanked her.

Just then a guard rode up. "What are you doing?" he asked Beramun.

"This man needs leggings," she said. "I lent him mine."

"He's a raider!"

"Not by choice!" Harak declared. He placed a hand over his heart. "Taken by Zannian, I had to join them or become a slave. I couldn't bear being held captive, so I rode for Zannian as a scout. Is that so terrible?"

"Pay him no mind," said the guard. "He's been talking like that since we caught him. Anyone who speaks so well must be a liar."

"I think you're right," she said dryly, and started to walk on.

"Where are you going?" asked the guard. "The mountains are not safe yet, what with ogres in the valley."

Beramun looked back at the moonlit camp and the walled town beyond it. "I was just out walking. I'm going back to camp."

The guard nodded and rode away. Harak pressed against the vine fence and said, "What's your name, lovely one? You know mine now. You saved my feet and I'd like to thank you."

She cast a glance over her shoulder. "Beramun."

* * * * *

When she was gone, Harak sat down and wound the buckskin strips around his legs. So that's Beramun, he thought. Zan wasn't a total fool. If he had to be obsessed with a female, at least he'd found a pretty one—beautiful in fact. Fortunately for Harak, she also had a good heart. The leggings were a little short, but they would do.

Harak stretched out on the ground and tucked his hands behind his head. Clouds were creeping in from the east, blotting out the stars and softening the glory of the two blazing moons. Thoughts of the lovely nomad girl gave way to more practical concerns.

Clouds like those meant rain was coming. Harak sighed. He hated being out in the rain. Maybe he could talk his way into a tent tomorrow or one of those piles of stone the villagers lived in. He'd like to see the inside of one of those.

* * * * *

Hoten studied the encroaching clouds. "Storm coming," he said.

He and the surviving captains sat around a crackling fire, passing a skin of pulpy wine back and forth. There was little talk, and no boastful war songs were sung.

They'd left Almurk with a thousand fighting men and over four hundred slaves. The Master, their own green dragon, had flown overhead, terrifying everyone in their path. No one could stand against them—single families and entire bands alike fled or succumbed. The raiders had taken weapons, oxen, goats, and anything else they had wanted. Everything had been fine until they'd entered this accursed valley.

Sthenn had abandoned them. The mud-toes of Arkupeli were beaten in the field, but they refused to submit like normal folk and hid inside their stone pile. What sort of fight was this, Hoten grumbled silently, with women, children, and old people throwing rocks down on your head? Real men, real warriors, got on horseback and did battle face to face.

Only three hundred raiders were left. The rest were dead or had deserted. True, Ungrah-de and his ogres were still there. Six of the brutes had perished in the fighting, leaving twenty-four ready for the final battle. The raiders could hear the ogres in their own camp on the stony hill, pounding their drums and grunting like the beasts they were. Though astonishing fighters, twenty-four ogres weren't any guarantee against hundreds of hard-riding nomads—and Karada.

Hoten shook his head. Karada herself stood against them! Many of the raider captains around the fire would have preferred to ride with her than with Zannian, even before fortune had brought them to this sorry state.

He drank and remembered his own days in Karada's band. He'd been at the battle of the Thon-Tanjan, when Silvanesti cavalry stole victory from Karada's hands. He'd ridden away with the rebel leaders Sessan, Hatu, and Nacris, all of them thinking Karada would perish fighting hordes of armored elves. Sessan had died in single combat with Karada, and Hatu had vanished one day, just after they left Arku-peli; his blood-spattered mount returned riderless a day later.

Karada survived, of course. She always survived. Many plainsmen believed she was a spirit and couldn't be killed. Mutterings to that effect could be heard this very night in the raiders' camp.

Nacris was gone now too, probably dead. Hoten did not grieve for his mate. She was so consumed with hatred that death would be the only rest she could know. Tomorrow he would join her. Their spirits would dwell together forever on the endless, high plain of the sky.

Zannian walked into the circle of firelight. He glittered from head to toe in bronze armor and bright body paint. The sullen raiders, eyes downcast, turned toward him, like flowers to the sun.

"Well, here's a proper funeral," he said. "Who's dead?"

"We are," groaned one raider.

Zannian drew a long sword from his scabbard. The scrape of metal made the assembled warriors flinch. A few edged away.

"Then leave!" Zan shouted. "Pick up your packs, mount your horses, and be gone! I would not die in the company of such weaklings and cowards!" He smacked the blade against the elven breastplate he wore. "You heard me! Leave! If I have to fight tomorrow with only Ungrah-de at my side, I shall!"

"We're not cowards, Zan," said a weary captain. "Six

hundred nomads *and* the villagers! The odds are too great against us."

"And when were they not? When we began our ride, the whole world was against us! How has anything changed?"

"But Karada—"

He laughed. "Are you scared of a scarred old woman? I'm not! She bleeds and dies like anyone. Ungrah has sworn to take her head home to his mountain lair. Anyone here want to wager against the ogre chief?"

No one spoke. Zannian laughed again.

"What did you think your lives would be like?" he went on, walking round the fire. When he found a raider nodding with drink or sleep, he kicked the man awake. "Did you think you would grow old riding the plains, fighting and taking the land's bounty in your hands? Idiots! Any of us, any day, could stop a lucky spear thrust. So what if we die tomorrow? What does it matter, so long as you've lived as a true warrior?"

The chief dragged a burning limb out of the fire and held it up. "Better to see death coming than let it sneak up on you," he declared.

Their leader's words began to sink in. The raiders lost their slouch and regained some of their confidence.

Hoten asked quietly, "Have you any regrets about the way things have gone, Zan?"

Zannian's wild grin fled. He tossed the flaming brand back on the fire. "Only one—the black-haired girl. I would've liked to have had her, at least a while." He shrugged broadly, then said, with another grin, "Will you let the ogres outshine us? Listen to them rant and roar! Can't the Raiders of Almurk do better than that?"

Two of the captains stood, a little unsteady from minor wounds and raw brew. Arms linked around each other's shoulders, they began to sing. Their voices were ragged as they wove their way through "The Endless

Plain," but Zannian circled around the fire and joined them. One by one, raiders still sober enough stood and joined in. In the rest of the camp, sleeping men awoke to the sound and crawled out of their bedrolls to lend their voices. Soon all the remaining raiders were bellowing out the old song—all but one.

Hoten had no voice left. He stared into the fire and nourished his nerve with dreams of his own death. It could not come too soon.

* * * * *

From the walls of Yala-tene, restless Amero heard loud singing rising from the raiders' camp. It drowned out the inhuman rumble of the ogres and echoed weirdly off the cliffs behind the village.

Alone on a hillock outside her camp, Karada heard it too. She'd gone out alone to prepare herself for battle. Stripped to the skin, she washed in cold spring water. While her hair was still damp, she applied spirit marks to her face, stomach, thighs, and feet. Without realizing it, she hummed along with the song the raiders were singing. The strangeness of it struck her as she finished applying the last of the marks to her feet. "The Endless Plain" was a song her mother, Kinar, used to sing to her children to cheer them on their wanderings. Strange she should hear it now, after so long.

Her damp skin dimpled with gooseflesh. Donning her buckskins, Karada sat down to await the rising sun.

Chapter 12

Beramun woke slowly. The small tent, normally stifling in the summer, was pleasantly cool. She turned her head and saw the top flap waving in a stiff breeze. Clouds were rushing past in the patch of sky she could see.

She got up, disentangling herself from Mara. The girl had crept in silently late last night, lain down beside Beramun, and gone to sleep. She remained huddled against Beramun's back all night and did not wake even when Beramun pushed her aside.

Her left shoulder twinged when she stood, and Beramun drew in breath sharply at the sudden discomfort. She must have strained her muscles during the hard ride here, or perhaps she'd slept awkwardly on her arm. She'd hardly been able to move at all, so close to her had Mara slept. With a glare at Mara, Beramun worked her arm in slow circles and walked outside.

The whole camp was stirring. Dawn was breaking, and the nomads were on their feet, grooming horses and gathering their weapons.

As she looked around for Karada, Beramun noticed the nomads weren't preparing their bows and arrows as they usually did. A chilly, damp gust of wind swirled past her, and she realized why. A storm was coming. Rain made bowstaves soft, strings stretch, and warped arrows, rendering the weapons useless. Karada's band would have to fight the old way, with spear and sword.

A stronger gust of wind rattled tents and snuffed cooking fires. The peaks south of the waterfall were partially obscured by low, white clouds. In their wake came heavier plumes of gray, gravid with rain. The cold wind made Beramun's aching shoulder throb. She made a disgusted face. The old folks always complained of pains when the weather changed.

North of the nomads' camp, the Silvanesti had finished their preparations for battle. Armed and ready, they stood in a neat line behind their lord. The elves had made a banner from a scrap of white doeskin. Tacked to the skin was the starburst crest from Balif's helmet. Though fighting under Karada's command, they would go into battle under the standard of their sovereign, Silvanos, Speaker of the Stars.

Beramun saw the elves arrayed and was struck by their calm manner. Behind her the nomads fairly boiled with activity, and she was sure the raider camp was in a similar state. These elves were curious folk.

Pakito's voice sounded, booming orders. Where the amiable giant was, Karada was sure to be near, so Beramun headed in that direction.

Amero arrived with a small group of villagers to fight beside his sister. Though he looked bone-weary, he walked confidently at the head of his little troop. With him were Lyopi, Hekani, and forty-eight villagers still willing and able to lend their lives to the final battle. They were raggedly dressed and armed with a motley collection of weapons, but one glance at their determined faces told the nomads the villagers were not to be discounted.

Amero led them to the high ground west of Karada's camp, a stony knoll formed by years of rain washing gravel down the valley. Once the villagers were in place, the Silvanesti marched out, taking up a position on the north side of the same hill. The two groups looked at each other across open ground, awkward and curious at the same time. Still, it was comforting to have the ordered ranks of Silvanesti standing with and not against them.

"I will speak to Balif," Amero said. "Stay here, Hekani, and keep watch for the raiders."

He started toward the Silvanesti position, feet crunching in the loose gravel. He heard someone behind him. It was Lyopi. She'd already told him in a tone that brooked no discussion that she would not leave his side this day.

He smiled and took her hand. "Let us greet the elf lord."

The lightness of Balif's arms and armor surprised the Arkuden. He'd assumed a noble Silvanesti would fight encased in costly bronze, but all Balif wore was a modest breastplate, helmet, sword, and shield. After greeting him, Amero commented on the elf lord's light armor.

Balif explained mildly that he'd been on a hunting expedition and hadn't come prepared for war. He looked past Amero to Lyopi.

"The females of your settlement fight, too? Are most human females warlike?"

"No more nor less than men," Lyopi replied sharply. "Courage is not determined by sex."

He bowed his head. "As one who has fought and pursued Karada for twenty years, I know the truth of that."

The first roll of thunder broke over the valley. It was far away and only barely made itself heard over the intervening mountains, but it was an unsettling portent of things to come.

Balif eyed the darkening sky with a frown as he drew on a pair of leather gauntlets. "I dislike fighting in the rain," he said. "My lord Silvanos used to bring priests with him when he traveled to insure fine weather by their art. I wouldn't mind having one or two with us now."

"Like Vedvedsica?" said Amero.

Recognition flickered across Balif's face. "You know him, do you?"

"Only by his deeds. My sister met him once."

"A talented fellow, but unreliable. He no longer serves my house."

"What became of him?" Lyopi asked.

Balif feigned indifference, but strong emotions plainly lurked behind this façade. "He overreached himself and so was dismissed."

In view of his past services, Vedvedsica's life had been spared, but he had been banished from Silvanos's realm. Where he lived now, Balif knew not.

Shading his pale eyes, the elf lord changed the subject. "This open ground will suit Karada and the raiders. Not good for us on foot, though. We won't have much shelter from attacking horsemen."

The rumble of massed hoofbeats announced the approach of Karada's band. The nomads emerged from camp in a column divided in three forces, each roughly two hundred strong.

Karada rode to the crest of the knoll where her brother, Lyopi, and Balif stood. When she stopped, the horsemen behind her halted. The middle section swung right and filled in the gap between Karada and the Silvanesti. The third rode out to their left, aligning itself beside the villagers. Bahco and two lieutenants rode out from the left wing to join Karada, as did Pakito and two riders from the right. Everyone dismounted, and greetings were exchanged.

"Bad weather for battle," Balif remarked dryly.

"Bad for the enemy as well," Karada replied, looking toward Zannian's camp.

They all turned to follow her gaze. The pulsing wind scoured away the usual spires of smoke from campfires, leaving the western half of the valley looking barren. Sunlight, visible only intermittently through the thick clouds, flashed over the panoramic view. By the river, the raiders' camp appeared deserted.

"Have they fled?" Bahco wondered.

Amero did not think so. "Their campfires burned until dawn. I could see them from the wall."

"They're there," said Karada. "If I judge this Zannian right, he won't run away. The ogres will be here, too. Of that I'm sure."

She went to the forward edge of the knoll and looked over the ground between there and the low hills shielding the river. Except for a few odd boulders buried in the soil, and a tree or two, the land was level and without cover.

"Amero, your people and the elves will go there," she said, pointing to the west baffle of Yala-tene. "Hold the ground between the village and the lake."

"Just hold?" asked Balif.

"Yes. Between my band and the raiders, there will be nearly a thousand riders in the valley. Your fighters on foot number less than a hundred. You could get trampled by either side."

"Good point," Balif said, just as Lyopi muttered indignantly, "No one's going to trample us!"

The elf lord added, "What if the ogres array against us? What then?"

"They won't," Karada said. "Chief Ungrah wants my head. He'll come after me."

"We'll hold our place unless chance beckons us to go elsewhere," said Balif.

"Don't get adventurous on me, elf! The last thing I need in the midst of a melee is to have to break off and ride to your rescue!"

"I hardly expect you to rescue—" Balif began, but Amero signed for him not to argue, and Balif understood. It was her brother, fighting with the elves, whom Karada would feel compelled to rescue.

"Now," Karada said, "I expect Zannian and his ogre friends to come for me as hard and fast as they can. I'll make myself plain and invite them. In fact, I'll give way to them, draw them in. Once they're fully engaged, I want the wings to close in on their sides and rear.

No one is to escape." To illustrate her meaning, she drew a simple plan in the dirt. Pakito and Bahco avowed their understanding.

More thunder rolled across the valley, chased by heavy gusts of wind. Whitecaps danced on the Lake of the Falls. Balif returned to his soldiers and marched them where Karada had decreed.

"Good luck," Amero said, clapping his sister firmly on the shoulder. A smile teased the corners of her mouth, then she gruffly sent her brother on his way.

With the villagers in the lead, Balif and Amero's groups descended the knoll and passed under the walls of Yala-tene. The plain was littered with the burned and broken remains of previous attacks—weapons, travois, dead horses. Fallen raiders were always cleared from the field by night, so no human corpses haunted their march. At one point Amero happened to look up and see the village wall, lined with his people. Some waved, but all were silent.

The west baffle was little more than a mound of rubble. Ogres had torn it apart, using slabs of rock and loose stones to make a crude ramp leading up to the main wall. Hekani pointed out the soot marks on the wall where he'd used fire to repel Ungrah-de. They also saw the bodies of four ogres, killed earlier, which still lay in the shadow of the town wall.

Amero arranged his people in a double line from the ruined baffle out toward the lake. Balif deployed his trained soldiers in a single, widely spaced line. The elves knelt on one knee, spears out. Balif stood behind them with the elf entrusted to carry the standard.

They waited.

Karada's force spread out across the top of the knoll, and she took her place at the center of the front line. Horses pranced and pawed, sensing the nervous excitement of their riders. Overhead, the unsettled air added its own fuel to the tension. Birds roosting on the cliffs abandoned their nests in the swirling wind. Flocks of sweeps and starlings filled the sky, their dark bodies swooping and circling several times before being carried off on the wind.

It seemed a bad omen to Beramun, and she said as much to Karada.

"We make our own fates," the nomad chief said. "No one else."

"Do the Great Spirits mean nothing to you?"

"I have no time for them now." Her gruff voice took on a more caring tone. "Be careful, girl."

Beramun vowed she would. Her shoulder still twinged, but at least the pain was in her left shoulder and not her right, where she wielded her spear.

As part of Karada's plan, a line of riders filed out on each side of her position, making it appear from a distance as though the whole nomad band was on the hill. On the reverse slope, Bahco and Pakito kept the bulk of their warriors secreted out of sight.

With the thick clouds churning it was hard to read the time of day, but it wasn't long after Karada had deployed her various troops that the first stirrings on the riverbank could be seen. A deep drum sounded a steady, repeated note. Wind stole the sound and played it falsely off the rocky crags lining the valley. The drumming seemed to come from the east, then the south. Scouts sent in those directions reported no enemy in sight.

By the lake, Amero and his people tried to see what was happening. Even the disciplined elves were curious, a few daring Balif's displeasure by breaking formation and standing erect and straining to see. A single word from him recalled them to their places.

From the village wall, people began shouting and waving. They had a longer view than anyone on the ground and could see what was coming.

The drumbeat grew louder. Something was moving on the riverbank. Swinging into view above the sandy hills came a great ogre, half again as tall as any man, festooned from head to waist in leather armor studded with chunks of stone the size of a human man's fist. Skulls of past victims dangled from his chest, and a giant single-bladed axe rested on his shoulder.

"Ungrah-de," said Amero under his breath. Merely speaking the name made him sweat. All of the villagers fighting with him closed in until their shoulders nearly touched. They'd fought the ogres for days from the wall, but it was quite another thing to face such monsters toe to toe on open ground.

More fanged faces appeared, striding along behind their leader. To warn Karada, villagers on the wall chanted, "Ogres! Ogres!"

They came forth in a broad spearhead formation, with Ungrah-de at the front. They crossed the old road from Yala-tene to the river, making straight for the open ground north of the village. When the trailing ogres on the right end of the line spotted Balif and Amero by the lake, they ignored them and kept going.

"Karada was right," Lyopi said. "The ogres are going after her."

All twenty-four ogres were in sight when the first raiders appeared. A tight square of riders, no more than fifty men in all, climbed the riverbank and rode forward slowly, filling the space behind the ogre spearhead.

"Is that all of them?" Hekani wondered.

"Maybe the rest ran away?" Lyopi offered.

Signals from the lakeshore caught Amero's eye. Balif's standard bearer was waving the white doeskin banner back and forth. Amero hurried down the hill to see what had alarmed the elves.

It was a column of raiders, several hundred strong, following the shoreline, coming right at Balif's position. Amero hailed the Silvanesti.

"Zannian isn't doing what Karada wants," Balif said dryly.

"We can't hold off so many! Should we retreat into Yala-tene?"

Balif examined the land, the sky, and the slow-moving column of raiders. "Not yet," he said. "I don't think they realize we're waiting here. Send some of your people up the ramp. Let them be noisy, make sure they're seen. I'll hide my soldiers in the hollow behind the ramp. Join me there, and we'll see if they pass us by."

"We can attack them from behind if they ride past!"

"Exactly."

Amero sent a dozen villagers scrambling up the broken-down baffle, yelling and clattering their weapons. The rest of his people and the Silvanesti quietly slipped out of sight behind the mound of rubble. They waited there anxiously until it became clear the raiders were turning east well short of the village.

"Good," said Balif. "Zannian will think your people were foragers or scouts. I wonder what Karada will do when she sees the raiders are not following her plan."

Amero sat down on the heap of stones and watched the end of the raider column disappear north of the village.

"She'll do what she does best," he said. "Fight."

* * * * *

Daylight saw the raider band diminished further, despite Ungrah's threats and Zannian's exhortations. When they mustered around their captains, only two hundred forty-four men were present. Hoten reported the rest had deserted, including all the men without horses.

Zannian was livid. "Wretched cowards! After the battle

I'll hang every one of them from the walls of Arku-peli!"

Hoten clenched his heavy jaw. "There's more, Zan. The slaves have escaped, too. All that's left are those we captured in this valley. I don't know why they stayed."

"They think they'll be free soon," Zannian muttered. "Summon Ungrah-de."

The ogre chief was fully decked out for battle, which on this special day included drenching himself with a foul-smelling oil the ogres called *kunj.* The acrid oil was supposed to weaken the enemy with its terrible odor while strengthening the ogre who wore it. Fighting the famous Karada demanded all the warrior rituals the ogres possessed.

Upwind from Ungrah, Hoten still had to hold his nose. Grim-faced, Zannian ignored the stench.

"I have a task for you," he said.

"You do not give a great chief tasks," Ungrah replied.

"Call it a favor then—a favor I'm doing for you."

The ogre's yellowed eyes narrowed. "What favor?"

"There are a score or so captives in our camp. Win or lose, they're yours. Our other slaves ran off in the night, but those from Arku-peli stayed behind, thinking they'll be free soon. I want them to know staying behind was a mistake."

Ungrah looked over Zannian's head at the depleted ranks of the raiders. "Many humans ran during the night. Why did you not?"

"Because I am Zannian!" He shook with fury. "Because I will conquer or die!"

Ungrah nodded his heavy head. "You have the proper spirit. Like Harak-ta." *Ta* was an ogre epithet meaning "small." He added, "Where is that one, since I speak his name?"

"Dead," Hoten said. "Taken when the nomads first struck us."

Zannian snorted. "Deserted, more like. Smooth-talking snake."

Hoten asked the ogre chief his plan for the coming battle.

"I will kill as many of the enemy as possible, starting with Karada. That is my plan," Ungrah said, then left to organize his warriors.

"Let the monsters do as they will," Zannian said, seating the skull-mask on his head. "As for us, Hoten, I want you to take fifty men and follow Ungrah-de. If he breaks through, ride hard and exploit any openings you find. The rest of the band will follow me. I'll show Karada how the Raiders of Almurk fight!"

With this ringing pronouncement, Zannian swung onto his gray horse. Hoten's hand on his animal's reins caused him to look down. The old man looked as though he wanted to say something but didn't. Finally he bowed stiffly to his chief and watched as Zannian cantered away to the head of the column.

Not long after, under writhing clouds and punctuated by the sound of ogre drums, the raiders rode to their final battle. Hoten led just forty-five men. He sent the other five—all older men he knew well and trusted—on a special task of his own creation. If they succeeded, he would face his death with a calmer spirit.

* * * * *

The drumming ceased.

Ungrah-de stood at the head of his warriors, wind rattling the bones decorating his chest. His patchy gray hair, coarse and long, streamed out behind his massive head like a personal standard. He raised his terrible stone axe—still chipped from the blow he'd given the walls of Yala-tene—and bellowed. Like an answer from on high, a bolt of lightning flashed overhead, and the ogre's cry merged into a ferocious clap of thunder.

The rearmost ogres began running. When they drew abreast of their comrades, these also started moving, and so on, until the line of running creatures reached Ungrah himself. The ogre chief, axe held high, hurled himself forward. Twenty-four ogres came storming up the knoll at Karada's waiting line of horsemen.

Behind the nomad leader, Beramun swallowed hard. "Karada?" she said unsteadily.

"Wait."

A white shaft of lightning struck the mountains north of the valley. The ground beneath their horses shook, and fat drops of chilly rain hit Beramun. The sky was full of black, billowing clouds.

Karada held her sword up. Every eye was on her.

"Now," she said quietly.

The horsemen stirred into motion. They didn't pitch headlong down the hill but moved at a steady trot. Inexperienced in mass maneuvers, Beramun found herself dropping back through the ranks as more skillful riders pushed by. She tried to keep Karada in sight, but it was difficult.

She heard no command, but at the same moment all the horses broke into a canter. The ranks were close-packed, and she had no room to lower the long spear she carried against her shoulder.

Rain thickened, pelting the soil and purging the air of dust. Lightning flashed again, and Beramun saw with terrifying clarity the heads of the ogres looming above the mounted nomads.

The canter became a full gallop. The ogres were less than forty paces away, running hard toward the hurtling mass of riders. It seemed impossible they could stand against the nomads, powerful as they were.

Rain fell in a torrent, and Beramun was blinded when it struck her eyes. She heard loud grunts and groans, and the screams of horses. Flinging water from her eyes, she saw the front rank of riders slam into the ogres. Succeeding waves of nomads piled up against those halted ahead of them. She hauled back on her reins, trying to turn her mount, but it was too late. Her horse collided with the animal ahead of her. The shock of impact almost unseated her.

Karada rode straight at the biggest, ugliest ogre on the field, assuming he was their leader. He in turn ran right at her, confirming her belief. Coming closer, she recognized Ungrah-de from their brief encounter the day before. He held his huge axe in a two-handed grip over his left shoulder. She shifted her horse a little to the right. As they came together, the terrible stone blade crashed against her shield. It was an oblique blow, and though her arm stung from its force, the weapon slid harmlessly down her shield.

The muscular monster recovered his swing and drew back in time to parry her sword cut with the stout handle of his axe. She cut again, aiming for his fingers. Her bronze blade bit deeply into the thong-wrapped handle held by Ungrah. He threw the axe over in a wide arc, forcing Karada's hand to follow or lose her sword. The upper edge of the axe sliced into her horse's neck. The wheat-colored stallion reared, lashing out with its front hooves. One dealt Ungrah a fierce blow to the forehead. The ogre stumbled back, recovered, and laid about on either side with his axe, hacking empty air.

A nomad on Karada's right pushed in and tried to spear Ungrah. The ogre chief snatched the head of the spear in his bare hands and snapped the shaft. An ogre beside him thrust with the spiked tip of his axe handle and caught the nomad in the ribs. The nomad dropped his spear and reeled away, clutching his bleeding side. With another sweep the ogre lopped the man's head off. His triumph was short-lived. A brace of spears hit

Ungrah's comrade, one finding the gap between his tunic and his breechcloth. Dark blood fountained. The second spear buried itself in the fleshy junction of his neck and shoulder.

Ungrah turned to the wounded ogre and plucked both spears out. The bleeding ogre staggered backward and sat down. He was immediately trampled by five eager nomads, who used the weight of their horses to hold him down while they speared him to death.

All along the line the struggle continued, drenched with rain and blood. Grips grew slick. Horses slipped. Ogres fumbled. Though the fighting pressure was not too great, Karada stuck to her strategy and slowly withdrew up the hill. Ungrah followed, still trying to connect his jagged axe with the nomad woman's neck. She eluded his blows and teased him on.

Hoten's small force of veterans was on the scene at last. The ogres, fighting as individuals, were engulfed by the nomad horde. Zannian had ordered Hoten to exploit any gaps the ogres made, but he couldn't even see all of Ungrah's warriors, much less any gaps.

The raiders with Hoten shifted restlessly in the pouring rain, watching the bloody fracas occurring just in front of them.

"Are we going to fight or sit and soak up rain?" one asked Hoten.

Hoten looked up and down the enemy line. Attacking now would be futile, like flinging grapes against a stone. He wrapped the reins around his hands. He thought of Nacris and of the dreams he had, which she would never share.

"At them, men!"

They galloped up the hill, shouting the way they had in the good old days out on the plains. Hoten aimed himself at the only landmark he could see: the back of Ungrah-de's head.

The center of the nomads' line fell back. Karada let them come, luring ogres and raiders over the crest of the knoll. The press was so great that she lost contact with Ungrah. Off to her right another ogre had cut a clean circle around himself, slaying any nomad who came within reach of his axe. She crouched low over her horse's neck and rode at him. He heard the fast rattle of hooves and whirled in time to receive Karada's sword in his eye. Transfixed, he nonetheless seized her sword arm in both his broad hands and tore her from her horse. She hit the muddy ground the same time as the dead ogre.

The legs of horses and ogres churned around her. She leaped up, planted a foot on the dead ogre's chest, and recovered her sword. Her favorite horse had disappeared. Buffeted on all sides, she found herself propelled through the crowd until her back bumped into something large and solid.

Karada looked up into the face of Ungrah-de.

He was bleeding from sword and spear cuts on his face and shoulders. Seeing Karada, he bared the yellow tusks in his protruding lower jaw. Up went the chipped axe. Her blade could not deflect such a massive weapon. With no other choice, she whirled away from the downward swipe, spinning on one heel like a dancer. Completing the circle, she brought her blade down on his axe arm, only to watch the bronze blade skid off the polished chunks of lapis attached to the ogre's sleeve.

Ungrah backhanded his axe, narrowly missing Karada's chin. She ducked, rolled, and came up standing. She felt something snag her back and jumped aside. The ogre's axe head came away with a triangle of buckskin on its tip.

The fight had shifted so that Karada had to run uphill to battle Ungrah-de. Behind him, raiders with painted faces traded cuts and thrusts with her warriors. She saw friends and foes fall, horses floundering in the mud or lying still in death.

A nomad with room to maneuver bolted in front of his chief and shoved a stone-tipped spear into Ungrah's chest. The flint head shattered on the ogre's breastplate. With a roar, Ungrah impaled the brave fellow on his axe tip, hoisting him off his horse and into the air. Lightning played on his face as Ungrah lifted the slain foe over his head. He roared back at the following thunder and hurled the nomad's body into the battling swarm.

The nomad's sacrifice was not without benefit, however. Karada sprang onto the dead man's sorrel mare and shouted for Pakito and Bahco. Her warriors took up the cry, transmitting it through the din of battle and thunderstorm. Word reached both men, and they spurred their forces to action.

Hoten's small band had disintegrated within moments of colliding with the nomads. He found himself alone, dueling with capable foes on all sides. A spear butt struck him in the mouth. He spat blood and teeth and fought on. A bronze sword chopped the head off his flint spear, leaving him with only a knife. Hoten put the stone blade in his teeth and jumped from his horse onto the back of a nearby nomad. One stroke of the knife, and the woman's horse was his.

He had no idea where he was or where his men were. He had no idea where he was going. Rain came in waves, drenching him to the skin and making his oxhide garments stiff. He drove his horse through the crowd, and many nomads let him pass, thinking from his mount he was one of them. Emerging at the base of the stony knoll, Hoten spied a large body of enemy horsemen sweeping around, closing in behind his little band and the ogres. They were solidly trapped.

Despairing, he briefly considered falling on his own knife, but thought better of it. Why throw his wretched life away when he could still sell it dearly?

He yanked a lost spear out of the mud and rode hard to the head of the nomad column. Leading them was a giant warrior, Hoten's old comrade Pakito. When he drew near enough, he shouted to the big man. Pakito turned his horse and received a spear jab in the face.

Pakito was quick as well as big, however, and the tip only tore a gash through his left earlobe. Hc countered with a stone-headed mace, caught Hoten's spear, and sent it spinning away.

"Yield!" Pakito said.

Hoten spat. He held out his too-short knife. "Do your worst!"

Gripping the club in both hands, Pakito easily parried Hoten's slashes. Then came the opening he needed. He let go with his right hand of his two-handed grip and punched Hoten hard in the ribs. Then Pakito slammed the flat stone head of his mace into the raider's chin. Hoten's vision exploded in a haze of red. He fell from his horse.

Pakito had no time to make sure of the death of his former comrade. The chaos was shifting again. After losing several warriors to overwhelming numbers, the ogres belatedly had closed together and formed a tight ring, back to back. From there, the seventeen survivors were fighting off every attempt by the nomads to ride them down. Hoten's men were not so lucky. Isolated and outnumbered, they succumbed like their leader until none were left standing.

Karada caught sight of Pakito and worked her way to him. They clasped arms.

"No raiders remain!" Pakito cried. "We've won!"

"Not yet! The ogres!"

"If only we had our bows!"

Karada lifted her eyes to the sky. The storm showed no signs of abating. Indeed, the clouds fast approaching from the south were even lower and blacker than the ones currently dumping heavy rain over the entire valley.

At this point, a nomad named Patan, who rode in Bahco's band, galloped to Karada.

"What news?" she demanded.

"Bad! The raiders hit us before we reached the top of the knoll," said Patan, breathing hard. "Bahco is down, maybe dead! Kepra now commands, and he sent me with word!"

"Pakito, ride to Kepra's relief!" Karada said quickly. "You'll have to swing 'round and take the raiders in the back."

"How many are there?" Pakito shouted above the din.

"Two hundred, seems like," said Patan.

While Pakito's band worked free of the ogres and made its way south to help their embattled comrades, Karada urged her mount back into the melee. She found Beramun, on foot, handing spears to nomads in front of her to throw at the ogres. The girl's face was covered with blood.

"You're hurt!" Karada yelled.

"It's not my blood." Beramun handed two recovered spears to the nomad ahead of her. These were passed forward until they reached the fierce struggle surrounding Ungrah.

"Give me those," said Karada when the girl was handed two more spears. Beramun did so.

Karada dismounted and tied a rag around her forehead, under the visor of her dented elven helmet. Hefting the spears to her shoulders, she started toward the ogres.

"Wait! Your horse!" Beramun cried, catching the reins of the sorrel mare.

"No room." Karada cracked a smile and disappeared, shouldering her way through the crowd.

Panic shot through Beramun. Lifting her face skyward, the rain mingling with her tears, she froze in fresh surprise. Something huge and dark wrestled with the heavy clouds. Thick, serpentine coils appeared and disappeared in the lowering storm. As she looked on, spellbound, the pain in her shoulder flared to life, lancing her sharply.

Jolted from her daze by the sensation, Beramun put a hand under her buckskin shirt, expecting to find blood or broken skin. Instead her skin was smooth and cold to the touch. She knew then what it was: the green mark. It had never given her any twinge before, but now . . .

Her gaze lifted skyward once more. Though she'd seen the strange aerial vision for only a moment, she knew now what it was. Despair welled up in her heart like a great dark wave.

Sthenn had returned.

Chapter 13

The raiders streamed by, a wall of men and horses. Amero and his small band waited to see if any turned back to deal with them, but none did. If Zannian saw them, he discounted any threat from a handful of villagers on foot.

Balif and the elves came out from behind the ramp. The villagers who'd run up the ramp hastened down again, and the mixed band of elves and humans slogged after the raiders. It was hard going. The rainfall was heavy, and the terrain itself obstructed progress. Beneath the walls the ground was broken by ditches and pits intended to hamper raider attacks. The pits now brimmed with muddy water, and ditches had collapsed in the downpour. All semblance of order was lost as the humans and elves were forced to pick their way through the morass.

By the time they got to higher ground, Zannian's men had reached the stony knoll and attacked. The momentum of the column punched through the thin line of riders screening the hill and carried down the other side into Bahco's waiting force. The raiders drove deep into the waiting nomads, their long spears giving them an advantage over the nomads' shorter weapons.

The fighters on foot ran up the gentle slope to the top of the knoll. A fantastic sight greeted them: Spread out across the valley northward was a sprawling battle, with waves of nomad riders charging a ring of stoutly fighting ogres. Scarcely more than a dozen ogres were holding off two-thirds of Karada's band, some four hundred seasoned fighters. Behind Ungrah-de, a small band of raiders was thoroughly torn to pieces, their riderless horses galloping from the scene.

Amero waited until his people and the elves were together atop the knoll. "Let's attack!" the Arkuden shouted to Balif over the rain.

"Not wise," the elf lord countered. "We may slay a few, but when they realize how few we are, we'll be swallowed up like those raiders behind Ungrah-de!"

Lyopi shouldered by the elf to stand beside Amero. "You need not come!" she said to Balif.

The villagers ran down the back slope, aiming at the end of the raiders' column. Balif watched them slip and skid on the wet gravel. His soldiers bunched around, waiting for the word to follow.

Ten steps from the raiders, Amero raised his spear and let out a yell. The little band of villagers echoed his cry, then fell upon the enemy. The nearest raiders were speared in the back before they could face about. Behind them, the rest of Zannian's men had time to turn and meet the new threat. Amero's people quickly found themselves in desperate straits, dueling with a ruthless mounted foe that was better armed. Surrounded, the villagers coalesced into a circle.

When Balif saw the raiders encircle Amero, he finally gave the order to advance. Twenty paces from the enemy, the elves paused and lobbed their metal-tipped javelins. These emptied many horses. Then the Silvanesti resumed their advance.

To the raiders, it seemed as if waves of enemies were materializing out of the rain, and their exact numbers were impossible to judge. They had developed a grudging respect for the tenacious fighting abilities of the people of Arku-peli, so some of the raiders tried to pull away, seeking room to maneuver. However, they were hemmed in by all the disparate forces.

Zannian trotted in front of his men. "What's this?" he demanded. "Why are you bunching together like a herd of frightened elk?" His horse reared, as the villagers advanced. Hoarsely he yelled, "Mud-toes? You gave way to mud-toes? At them, you gutless dogs! Trample them into the mud they live in!"

Driven by his exhortations, several dozen raiders charged toward the two leaders, Amero and Balif. The elves locked their shields together and crouched low, spears bristling in front of them. Seeing the hedge of bronze points, the raiders angled toward the less-threatening villagers.

Lightning flashed overhead. Amero knelt, presenting his spear to the enemy. Lyopi and Hekani followed suit, as did the rest of the villagers, making a formidable thorny square.

Amero swiped a hand across his face, slinging rain-water from his eyes. The raiders' horses seemed to slow as he watched, each hoof rising and falling in strangely languid fashion. Small sounds rang loudly in Amero's ears, while great noises faded. The sound of the storm diminished, and he heard every breath Lyopi took. Hekani, nearby, muttered, "I think I like fighting from the wall better."

Lightning crackled across the sky again. The charging raiders were closer now, looming hugely in the down-pour. This is it, Amero thought. Here is where I die.

After all this time? You'd better wait just a bit longer!

The voice filling his head was unmistakable, but for a few heartbeats, Amero did not believe it. It was a dream, the waking dream of a doomed man. It couldn't be Duranix!

The raiders' were closing in. The voice spoke again.

I'm a little busy at the moment, but I'm not far away. Try to stay alive, will you?

Amero jumped to his feet and shouted. "Duranix!"

A spear plunged toward his chest. Feeling as though he was swimming in honey, Amero brought his own weapon over to deflect the thrust. Wood met wood for an instant, then Amero's feet suddenly slipped out from under him. He fell flat on his back in the mud.

Surprised by his victim's tumble, the raider failed to adjust and blundered past, narrowly missing tripping over Amero. Hekani brought his spear around in a wild, wide swing, striking the raider across the shoulders. Down he went. Then many other riders crashed into the villagers' square. One by one the villagers went down, knocked off their feet by colliding horses.

Amero regained breath enough to roll over, and he found Lyopi beside him. She'd knocked him down to save him from being impaled. Bruised and caked with mud, he nonetheless grinned at her.

"What's so funny?" she demanded, dodging the hooves of a runaway horse.

"Duranix! Duranix is coming! He spoke to me!"

Word spread among the villagers. Some had been lost in the first rush, but the rest joined together again, buoyed by the news their Great Protector was near. Still trapped in a ring of determined raiders, Amero's people fought furiously, fending off solo forays and small group attacks. A few paces away, the Silvanesti repulsed two heavy attacks with no loss, causing the raiders to turn away from them. Free to move, Balif formed his men and marched to Amero's relief.

Once the Silvanesti joined with them, Amero climbed onto a nearby boulder and gazed skyward. The clouds over Yala-tene were a mix of black and gray, swirled together by winds. With increasing frequency, bolts of lightning lanced from cloud to cloud to mountaintop. Amero took this as a sign the bronze dragon was indeed near, drawing lightning to him out of the clouds.

Duranix! he shouted with his mind. *I'd almost given up hope you'd ever return!*

Don't celebrate just yet, the dragon's mental voice replied. *Sthenn is here, too.*

To illustrate the point, a serpentine tail, covered in dark green scales, whipped through the clouds, followed by a flurry of leathery wings. Thunder boomed and rolled, and the green dragon writhed amidst the boiling clouds. Rain flew in Amero's face, and when he could see again, Sthenn was no longer visible above. His heart hammered at the sight of the green dragon. Were Lyopi's fears coming true? Had Sthenn come to steal victory from them at the last moment?

On the ground, the outcome was still in doubt. Zannian organized another attack. The spear throwers tried to shake the elves' line, but the deluge of rain felled the missiles short of their targets. Regardless, Zannian drove home his charge. This time there was no swerving or stopping short. Horses and men piled on the flimsy line of spears, trapping humans and elves under them.

Amero saw Balif lose his spear, draw his sword, and trade cuts with the raider chief. His rapid thrusts forced Zannian back. The raider chief's horse became entangled with another, already flailing in the mud, and the horse toppled, throwing Zannian to the ground.

Amero jumped off the boulder and ran to where Zannian had fallen. Balif beat him there. With a single backhand slash the elf tore the sword from Zannian's grasp. It spun away into the melee. Before the raider chief could stand, he found the tip of the elf lord's blade pressed hard against his neck.

"Cease, or forfeit your life!" Balif declared.

Zannian, face twisted in fury, grabbed the blade with his bare hand. Balif snatched his sword back, cutting the raider's hand to the bone, then raised the keen blade high—

"No! Don't!" Amero cried, waving his hands. "The green dragon is here! We need Zannian alive!"

He didn't know if Balif heard him or not, but the elf lord brought his sword down in a fast diagonal slash.

Zannian's hands flew to his face, and he stumbled back, blood pouring between his fingers. Balif advanced.

Amero leaped over fallen friends and foes shouting, "Stop! Balif, don't!" He collided with the elf, knocking him away from the man writhing in the mud.

"Let me finish him!" Balif demanded, eyes wide with battle rage.

Amero held him fast and explained Zannian could be valuable barter if Sthenn gained the upper hand.

Balif lowered his sword. The fire left his eyes, as he gazed impassively down at the beaten man.

Amero knelt in the mud and wrestled with Zannian. It didn't take him long to determine that the raider chief had lost one eye, possibly both, to the elf's savage slash.

Their leader down, nearby raiders wheeled their mounts and rode away. In less time than it takes to tell, the battle at the south end of the knoll ended. Nomads chased the escaping raiders a short way, only to be called back by Karada's lieutenant, Bahco. The young warrior, unhorsed early in the fight, had spent much of the battle dodging raider spears. Once the enemy was defeated, he had found a horse and taken control of his band again. Bahco decided he wouldn't risk losing more men and women by trying to hunt cowardly raiders in the pouring rain.

As it was, few raiders escaped. Those who high-tailed it over the knoll ran right into a fresh contingent of nomads under the redoubtable Pakito. The giant had led his third of Karada's band all the way across the valley, arriving in time to cut off the remnants of Zannian's raiders.

Pakito and Bahco hailed each other as they rode up to greet Balif.

"Well, elf lord, you look like you've had a hard day!" Pakito said heartily.

Unamused, Balif replied, "Harder for those who died."

Bahco, a sling around his neck to support his sprained right arm, asked, "What of the Arkuden? Does he live?"

Balif pointed to the two men at his feet. One was an unconscious Zannian. The other was Amero. The Arkuden was squatting in the mud, catching rain in his cupped hands and using it to wash the raider's lacerated face.

* * * * *

In nine successive attacks, Karada had been unable to break the ring of ogres. She led each foray herself and tried all the maneuvers she knew to shatter the monsters' resistance. They rode straight in, circled left and right, threw spears and axes, yet nothing made any lasting impression. Ogres went down, and some undoubtedly perished, but Ungrah-de remained, as durable as stone. He bled from a hundred wounds, and still he fought on. Taking an axe from one of his fallen warriors, he wielded a weapon in each hand, shredding any nomad foolhardy enough to come within reach of those two terrible stone blades.

Pakito had ridden off with the right wing of the band, leaving his chief to battle the ogres. It hadn't seemed like such a challenge at first; after all, she'd slain an ogre with her sword earlier. Surely two hundred nomads could wipe out a dozen or so of the creatures.

The storm hadn't helped. Horses lost their footing as they churned around the monsters' ring, pounding the loose gravel into the mud. Standing in place, Ungrah's warriors did not face that problem. Still, as midday came and went, the ogres wearied and stood with shoulders hunched, hairy hands braced on their thighs during the short intervals between waves of nomad attacks. Karada thought a few more attacks would leave them too exhausted to continue.

She forgot about Pakito and Bahco, forgot Zannian and his raiders, and even let the ever-present shadow of Amero slip into the background of her thoughts. The world shrank to this muddy hill. Her only task was the destruction of Ungrah-de.

Into the haze of rain, mud, and war rode Beramun, shouting, "The dragon, Karada! I saw it! He's here!"

Karada glanced skyward. "Duranix?"

"No, the green dragon—Sthenn!"

One hand shot out like a striking viper, snagging the front of Beramun's shirt. Karada dragged the girl close and hissed, "Are you sure?"

Beramun nodded, wet, tangled hair molded to her skull. "I saw him, in the clouds! He is there!" She didn't take time to mention the jade-colored mark on her chest and how it seemed to be sensing Sthenn's presence.

Karada scanned the roiling, cloudy sky and saw nothing, yet she knew Beramun was no excitable child, like Mara. If she said she saw a dragon, it must be there.

"We must finish this quickly, before the dragon can intervene! Find Amero if you can, and tell him what you saw!"

She released Beramun and shouted to her warriors, "Once more! Form up, once more! This time we'll take them!" Her voice was raw from yelling. "Give me two groups! We'll hit from two sides at once!"

Stunned by her deep-rooted fear of Sthenn, Beramun sat frozen on her mount, the nomads' horses jostling her to and fro. Her dark eyes were huge as she stared at the nomad chieftain.

"Beramun!" Karada said sharply, and the girl jumped. "Find Amero! Do you hear? Find Amero!"

The girl nodded once and set off at a gallop.

For a moment, Karada stared after her. The dark-haired girl was one she was pleased to call friend. Strong, loyal, and free-minded, Beramun was gifted with beauty even the nomad chief could envy. Karada had never thought much about her own looks, though she'd known some beautiful men. Pa'alu, the author of her curse, had been handsome, in a lean and wolfish way. The rebel Sessan, with his blond hair and easy laugh, was pretty, even if he had loved the wretch Nacris. Scarred and hard of mien, Karada knew she was not beautiful, nor was that something she worried about. Yet Beramun made her wonder what it would be like to be beautiful.

As Beramun disappeared into the pouring rain, Karada recalled herself to the battle at hand. Her borrowed mount danced as she flung orders left and right.

* * * * *

Find Amero.

Karada's command echoed in Beramun's mind. Desperately afraid that Sthenn would swoop down on her at any moment, she held on to that simple command as a drowning man clings to a floating log. Unconsciously, she kept looking up, but there was no sign of the dragon.

It was no mystery to her why Sthenn might be overhead and yet not intervene to save his followers. The cruel, perverse dragon was probably enjoying the horrific battle. Every stroke of sword or axe weakened the nomads. Sthenn was probably reveling in the pain and death.

As the ceiling of clouds parted briefly she spied something large moving against the wind. Claws, scales, and wings . . . breath caught in her throat when she realized their color wasn't green.

Bronze! Duranix was aloft, battling his ancient nemesis! Now she had good news for Amero!

* * * * *

At that moment, Karada was hurtling across the valley toward Ungrah-de. She led her half of the warriors north, while the other half rode wide to the south. Their movements were plain to the ogres, who rose from their crouching rest and prepared to face the circling onslaught. Holding her nicked and bent elven blade out straight in front of her face, Karada stared down its length at the ogre chief's broad chest. Most of his trophy skulls had been knocked off, and his leather and stone armor was slashed and peeling. Karada aimed the point of her sword at the base of Ungrah's thick neck. She imagined four spans of bronze penetrating his spotty, grayish hide, piercing veins and muscles as it went. Leaning forward, she thumped her heels against the sorrel mare's flanks, kicking the gasping beast for more speed. Though she didn't know it, she was screaming. Everyone in the fight forever after would remark on how she screamed on and on, uninterrupted.

Ungrah waited for her, arms crossed, an axe lying on each shoulder. When she drew near, he raised both weapons, holding the smaller one forward to ward off her sword while keeping his own massive weapon back to chop her down.

Her sword never found Ungrah's throat, and his axes never touched Karada's flesh. For when the two were almost in reach of each other, a column of fire struck the ground between them. Witnesses on the village wall described the bolt as white as mountain ice and broader than an ox. It forked in all directions, but the center branch touched the ground between the hard-riding nomad woman and the mighty ogre chief.

The world exploded around them. Stones and mud flew, and the sound of the thunder deafened everyone.

Falling free from the clouds came two enormous dragons, one green, one bronze, so closely entwined they might have been one creature had not their hides been of such radically different hues. They plunged to earth, twisting and turning in deadly embrace, and crashed down on the exact same spot where the lightning bolt had struck a few heartbeats earlier.

Nomads and ogres scattered. Just before impact, the green dragon freed his head from the tangle and shrieked in skull-splitting agony. Then they hit.

Yala-tene shivered to its foundations. Inside the wall, weakly built houses collapsed. Boulders caromed down the cliffs, and avalanches rumbled through the mountains ringing the valley. A torrent of blackened mud was flung high in the air, and when it came down, it drenched everything, even the captured raiders in their pen beyond the nomad camp.

All fighting stopped—all fighting between two-legged antagonists, that is. Rearing up out of the crater created by their crash, Duranix bared his gleaming fangs and roared. The sound echoed through the valley. Sthenn's long tail was wrapped around the bronze dragon's throat, squeezing tightly. Duranix sank his foreclaws into the green dragon's tail, cracking his corroded scales and rending the ancient flesh beneath. Sthenn flailed in pain, and his tail whipped free. Clawing at the torn-up soil, Sthenn came slithering out of the crater on his belly.

The green dragon was grievously hurt. One wing was clearly broken, bent backward at a sickening angle. Livid burns earned from Duranix's lightning breath dotted his back and flanks, and fearsome wounds leaking dark blood ran along his brisket, belly, and tail.

Duranix did not emerge from the hole undamaged. One of his eyes was battered shut, and his face was terribly disfigured. Two talons on his right foreclaw had been torn off in the struggle, and some of his wounds were already festering from Sthenn's fetid, pestilent claws.

Sthenn wriggled free and crawled rapidly away from

his tormentor, eastward toward the nomads' camp. But Duranix was far from finished with him.

The bronze dragon used his longer rear legs to catch the fleeing Sthenn in a single bound and seize him by his right hind leg and tail. Enormous muscles straining, Duranix hauled the loathsome beast back.

During the dragons' battle, the constant sheets of rain gradually slackened and finally quit. A circle of blue sky had formed over the warring dragons. Sunlight slanted in, striking Duranix's bronze hide, making it glint like gold.

"Zannian! Nacrisss!" Sthenn hissed as he was dragged backward. "Help your master, now!"

"No one can help you!" Duranix bellowed. "This is the end, old wyrm!"

When he released Sthenn's tail to grab his other hind leg, the green dragon rolled quickly, snatching his leg from Duranix's grasp. He lashed out, biting Duranix's throat. He was powerful, but old, and his decayed fangs broke on Duranix's heavy scales. Next thing he knew, Duranix was on top of him, huge incisors sunk into Sthenn's long neck. The green dragon thrashed wildly in pain and panic. He managed to get one foot against the bronze dragon's belly, and with all the strength left in his febrile limbs, he thrust Duranix off.

Duranix flew backward several hundred paces, stopping only when he crashed into the wall around Yalatene. The heavy masonry sagged, then collapsed along the bronze dragon's entire length. Terrified villagers fled to the far side of the village.

Sthenn could not fly. Though only one wing was broken, the skin of the other was shredded. Quaking, he crawled slowly away to the west. He kept looking back over his tattered left wing, and when Duranix rose from the rubble of the broken wall, Sthenn fell on his belly.

"Enough!" he quavered. "Let me be, you stupid hatchling!"

Duranix shook off his hard landing, spread his wings, and made a gliding leap. He alighted in front of Sthenn. The green didn't try to attack but coiled himself in the mud in a tight ball.

"If you kill me, Duranix, what reason will you have to live?"

Standing upright, the bronze dragon planted his right hind foot on the groveling Sthenn's head.

"I'll find a reason," he said coldly.

All through his massive body, the bronze dragon's muscles knotted. His clawed foot gripped the green dragon's narrow skull, each bronze talon embedding itself. Sthenn let out a shrill scream. His tail whipped from side to side, striking blows against Duranix's back that would have crippled a lesser creature. Duranix stiffened and tightened his grip. He leaned to one side, putting all his great weight onto his foe. Brittle bones as old as the towering mountains began to crack. The grind of splintered bone could be heard throughout the valley.

"This is for my mother," Duranix snarled, bearing down even harder. "For my clutchmates . . . for Blusidar . . . for all the innocent creatures you've tormented and murdered over the centuries.

"And this is for me!"

The great talons closed remorselessly. Filthy ichor gushed around them. The loudest crack of all reverberated off the cliffs, and Sthenn's tail ceased thrashing.

Duranix slowly opened his claw and backed away a short distance. He came to rest on all fours. His wings were folded tightly against his back. He stayed that way, not moving, not blinking. He might have been cast in cold bronze for all the outward signs of life he displayed.

The last clouds flew away on the south wind, and the

late afternoon sun filled the valley with bright warmth.

From different parts of the valley, small parties of people converged on the crouching dragon. Beramun and Karada arrived together, riding double. From the village came Amero, Lyopi, and the surviving elders of Yala-tene. On Amero's heels came Balif, alone. From the raiders' riverbank camp streamed prisoners, freed by the five men Hoten had sent away from the battle. At their head was Jenla, the old gardener. When she and Tepa caught sight of each other, they rushed forward, weeping, to engulf each other in a fierce embrace.

Karada and Beramun met Amero and his people well before they reached Duranix. The nomad chief dismounted and dropped to the ground. Without a word, she approached her weary brother and threw her arms around his neck.

Amero pulled back. To his surprise, he saw his sister's cheeks were streaked with tears.

"It's all right," he said. "We're alive. Don't cry."

"I'm not crying," she retorted. "It's the rain."

Balif appeared beside Beramun.

"Greetings! You're well, I see," he said in his usual courtly manner.

"I feel like I've died many times today," she replied.

He looked past her to the sibling chiefs. "An amazing day!" said the elf. "I've seen dragons before, but never two at the same time, much less joined in mortal combat! I thought Karada was dead when the dragons fell out of the sky. From where I stood, it looked as though they landed directly on her."

"They did," Beramun said, smiling wryly. "Don't you know Karada can't be killed?"

The four of them rejoined the elders and freed captives. Jenla was regaling her friends with tales of her captivity. After greeting Jenla, Amero moved on, anxious to see Duranix. Karada followed him, but when Beramun tried to go too, she sternly ordered her back. Lyopi remained behind as well.

Brother and sister closed on the motionless dragon.

An awful stench, like a corpse too long unburied, filled the air around the green dragon. Thick, black ichor dripped from Sthenn's wounds, staining the ground. Amero wondered if anything would ever grow in soil polluted by the green dragon's blood.

He gave the carcass wide berth, coming up on Duranix's right rear flank. Karada, less intimidated, strolled within arm's reach of Sthenn.

"Duranix," Amero said quietly. "Can you hear me?"

"Of course I can." Though he spoke, Duranix remained motionless, his uninjured right eye fixed on his ancient enemy.

"What are you doing? Are you hurt?"

"I'm keeping a vigil."

At that moment Sthenn shuddered and expelled stinking yellow bile from his nostrils. Amero recoiled, prepared to flee, and Karada stepped quickly away.

"It's still alive!" she declared.

"Ssstill," Sthenn hissed.

"Why don't you finish him off?" Karada asked sharply.

Duranix said, "He doesn't deserve it. Centuries before you were born, he sat on top of my mother's body and enjoyed her death. How many days did it take, Sthenn?"

Breath rattled through the dying beast's rotten lungs.

"Ten? Eleven? How long was it before she finally died?" To the humans he said, "I'll stay here until he's dead."

There was no reasoning with him, and Amero was too spent to try. Brother and sister turned to go. Before they did, Sthenn roused himself to speak.

"I have a gift for you," he wheezed. He was so feeble the simple sentence took him a while to voice, but Amero stood by, waiting for him to finish.

"Don't listen to him," Duranix said. "He lies."

"He's right," agreed Karada. "Leave him, Amero."

Amero could not leave. There was a tingling pressure inside his head, like a headache yet unborn. He realized it was Sthenn, trying to touch his mind the way Duranix did.

"Say what you want to say," Amero told him. Though disgusted, Karada remained with her brother.

"My yevi hunted you," Sthenn said. "D'ranix saved you. Girl saved herself. I saved the other."

"What 'other?' " Amero whispered.

"Boy. Smallest one."

Karada clamped her hand on Amero's arm. She pulled him strongly. "Come away!" she said with unusual anxiety. "Don't listen to that monster. You heard Duranix—it lies!"

Sthenn's voice rasped on, feeble, weak, yet unstoppable. "I spared him. Never seen a human close up. I kept him. My pet."

Amero resisted his sister's urging. "Go on," he said to Sthenn.

"Raised him . . . gave him a mother." Wet, rattling sounds emanated from deep within the green dragon's chest. Sthenn, dying by moments, was laughing. "Loving mother Nacris."

Furious, Amero shouted, "What do you mean? What happened to Menni?"

"It's Zannian. Zannian is our brother," Karada said, and nodded when Amero's face reflected his disbelief. "It's true. Nacris hinted as much, but I didn't believe her. I have her prisoner, back in camp."

Sthenn's leathery eyelids fluttered. "Black-hearted woman. Never thought she'd outlive me."

"She won't by much," Karada vowed.

Amero yanked the sword from his scabbard. It was

ruined as a weapon—deeply notched, cracked through to the fuller—but he ran forward and stabbed it deep into Sthenn's neck.

"Why!?" Amero stormed. "Why do that to Menni, and why tell us about it now?"

Sthenn laughed until more feculent fluids rose in his throat and choked him. Amero drew back, afraid to let the poisonous slime touch him.

"To see the look on your face," Sthenn said when he could speak again. "To smell your heated blood go cold. To . . . to bring you pain on the day of your triumph—"

The ravaged head lolled to one side.

"What about Beramun?" Amero said quickly. "Release whatever hold you have on her!"

Sthenn could not or would not say more. His left eye, half-shut, took on a dull and lifeless stare.

Karada took hold of Amero's arm, and he let her lead him away. As they passed Duranix, Amero said, "I'll come back in the morning. Shall I bring food?"

"Don't bother. I'll find you when this is done."

Brother and sister walked away. Karada pondered Amero's last words to Sthenn, wondering what hold the green dragon had on Beramun and what hold Beramun had on her brother. The two reached their waiting friends before she could ask him anything, and she remained silent.

Amero led them all back to Yala-tene. On the way they were joined by Karada's comrades, Pakito, Samtu, and Bahco. Beneath the crumbling north baffle, Amero halted next to the unconscious young man lying on the ground, his head swathed in bandages. His fearsome skull-mask and weapons stripped away, Zannian now looked no different than scores of others in the valley, wounded or dying.

Should the blame be put on Zannian or on Nacris? Amero wondered. Or was Sthenn the instigator of all this misery?

The Arkuden shook his head, banishing those thoughts for now. To those around him, he said, "This is Zannian. He is my brother, mine and my sister Nianki's."

Chapter 14

The days that followed were hard. Peace was restored, but it was a peace of exhaustion and pain. Much of the valley was wrecked or ruined, and many people were dead or severely injured.

Duranix stayed in the west end of the valley, keeping his somber vigil. Though he'd told Amero not to bother, the headman of Yala-tene sent several oxen to his great friend, who had to be famished after his long journey.

The raider band was utterly destroyed. When Zannian was finally taken, most of his remaining men rode out of the valley, trying to put as much distance as possible between themselves and the vengeance they imagined awaited them now that the bronze dragon was back. A few others lingered in the mountains, curious to see how matters were resolved. Karada sent patrols to flush them out of the passes. Once they had been dealt with, all that remained were the raiders who had surrendered and those, like Zannian, who were sorely hurt.

Amero adamantly refused his sister's suggestion that all captured raiders be put to death. He was heartily sick of bloodshed and wanted no more of it in the Valley of the Falls. Instead, he put the healthiest of the former raiders to work repairing the damage they'd done. Able-bodied men were set filling in the pits and ditches, rebuilding houses in the village, and restoring the despoiled orchards.

On a bright, sultry afternoon, four days after the dragons returned and ended the battle, a crew of ex-raiders filling the huge crater where the dragons had fallen found the answer to a great puzzle.

Word of their strange find spread quickly, and Amero, Karada, Balif, and Beramun hurried to the yawning pit. Karada was once more astride her favorite wheat-colored horse.

The pit was more than thirty paces wide and at least eight deep. A gang of ex-raiders, stripped to the waist in the heat, were standing around the crater rim, gazing down in the hole. Beramun recognized one tall fellow with dark brown hair who leaned on his shovel at the edge of the pit. It was Harak, to whom she had given her leggings.

Near the bottom of the pit a gray, oblong object lay embedded in the black mud. It looked like a block of limestone, but Harak, who'd made the discovery, said the so-called stone was in fact the top of Ungrah-de's head. The combined weight of two dragons had driven him into the ground like a tent peg. Six other ogres had been found crushed in the pit, but their chief wasn't discovered until the level of rainwater filling the hole had lowered.

Though the rest were content to take Harak's word that this was in fact Ungrah-de, Karada wanted proof. She unbuckled her sword and handed it to Balif.

"Is this a formal surrender?" asked the elf.

Amero chuckled, but his sister did not. She descended into the pit. Her feet sank into the soft sides of the crater, and by the time she reached the bottom, she was muddy to her knees. Unperturbed, Karada bent down and probed the mud around Ungrah's head.

She found the proof she sought in the form of a great stone axe. It was buried alongside the ogre, and it took her some time to work it free. Wiping away the thick mud that coated it, the head was revealed to be a massive chunk of grayish agate shot through with veins of lapis lazuli.

"It's Ungrah's all right." Karada grunted, holding up the weighty weapon. "Send some men down to dig him out."

"Why bother?" Harak asked, shrugging. "Why not just fill in the hole?"

Karada glared at the raider. "He was a mighty warrior. He deserves a warrior's pyre."

Harak's wasn't the only skeptical expression. Amero seemed about to comment, but the sight of his sister's tired, drawn face halted him.

She climbed out, dragging the axe with her. When no one moved to carry out her wishes, she glowered at the idle prisoners.

"Well, dig him out!" she barked. Jerking her head at Harak and another fellow, she added, "You two—go! Bring his body out."

With an impertinent shrug, Harak picked up his shovel and started down after the other fellow.

Karada sighed deeply, and Amero said, "You're worn out. Why don't you go to the lake and wash up?"

She nodded wordlessly. She asked Beramun to take her sword to her tent and to have someone carry the heavy, dirty axe there as well. Then, mounting her horse, she left.

Despite Karada's instructions to get help, Beramun decided to carry Ungrah's axe back herself. She had dragged it only a few paces, however, before Amero picked up the blade end, knees buckling from the weight, and helped her carry it.

Balif stayed at the crater to examine the dead ogres. He'd never encountered the creatures before, and he was eager to study their weapons and physique.

Amero and Beramun walked parallel, carrying Ungrah's massive weapon between them. Normally hip-deep in grass and flowers by this time of year, the valley floor had been trampled flat by masses of horses and men. The customary smell of growing things was over-powered by the sweet-sour aroma of decay and death. Ahead, hundreds of round tents covered the center of the valley, sides tied up to admit cooling air. Though the nomads' camp had been flattened by Sthenn during his battle with Duranix, the hide tents were easy to repair and re-pitch.

"I can't believe it's over," Beramun said, sweat dripping from her brow. Though shared, their burden was considerable. "How long has it been?"

"From the day you arrived in the valley to today," Amero replied, "four turnings of the white moon—one hundred twelve days." Shaking his head, he added, "Such a waste! Think of all the lives cut short! All the crops not planted, animals not tended, lost days of work in the foundry—and for what?"

"So we could live free," she said, a little surprised. "Wasn't that why you were fighting?"

"Sometimes I forget. By the end, we were fighting just to stay alive."

When they reached the outer tents in the nomad camp, their strange cargo attracted a limping, bandaged crowd. Injured nomads had remained in camp while others went to search for their children and old folks, hiding out in the eastern foothills. Others had been sent by Karada to scour the highlands south and east for the children of Yala-tene who had been sent out through the secret tunnel when it looked like the village would fall to Zannian.

Beramun and Amero located Karada's tent. They edged through the entry flaps and hauled the monstrous weapon into the dark enclosure.

After they deposited the axe by the wall near the entrance, Beramun went into the shadowed depths of the tent to find water so they could wash up. Not only was Ungrah's weapon muddy from being buried, it was smeared with gore from the furious battle.

Amero waited by the entrance. It appeared the large tent served as a storehouse as well as his sister's dwelling. He couldn't see very far inside, and he didn't want to stumble around the dark interior, tripping over casks, sacks, and fragile amphorae.

Ghost-like, Beramun appeared before him. She held an obviously weighty leather bucket in front of her.

"Hold out your hands."

He did so, and she doused them. When his hands were clean, they switched places so she could wash her own.

While she scrubbed and sluiced away the mud, Amero spoke, his voice low and serious. "Beramun, I want to tell you something." She looked up quickly, eyes wide and worried. He shook his head, adding, "It's not what you think. A lot's happened since you left Yala-tene. I've learned many things since then. Important things. I learned . . . I belong with Lyopi."

Beramun's smile was like the sun flashing through dark clouds. Her hand gripped his. "That's good," she said gently. "I'm glad you found out. I knew it all along."

When they were back outside, Amero asked, "Will you stay with us in the valley or join Karada's band? I know she'll take you in if you ask."

"I can't stay here," she said. "I'm a wanderer. Other places call to me. I could never be happy seeing the same land, the same faces, for the rest of my life."

Amero recalled how he'd once bemoaned that very fact of his own life in Yala-tene. Having nearly lost it all had made him realize just how precious those same faces and this place were to him.

"As for joining Karada . . ." Beramun said, her voice trailing off.

Amero saw her hand had come up to touch a spot high on her chest. "Beramun," he said, gently pulling her hand away, "you saved us all by finding my sister. Whatever Duranix may think, you're no tool of Sthenn."

He took his leave of her. The walk back to Yala-tene was pleasant, despite the heat. Though his heart had gone in a different direction for good, Amero was filled with admiration for Beramun. He was sure of one thing: whoever her future mate might be, he would be a very lucky man.

* * * * *

From the shore of the lake, Karada could see sunlight gleaming off the bronze head and arching back of Duranix, a league away. He was still keeping his death watch over the green dragon. She approved of what he was doing and understood it well. When she entered the valley, she had ordered the extermination of the Jade Men, thinking they had murdered her brother. It was the duty of blood kin to avenge wrongs against family, no matter how long it took. It was a law of nature, as irreversible as night being dark and day being bright.

Wading out to her knees in the cold water, she stripped off her muddy outer clothes and rinsed them in the lake. She filled her cupped hands and dashed clear water on her face. The lake hadn't lost its hard, mineral tang. Licking droplets from her lips, she remembered the first time she'd tasted it, all those years ago.

Thoughts of the past reminded her of Nacris. The madwoman was still chained, and by Karada's order no one had told her what had happened. Karada was still trying to figure out what to do with Zannian, and his fate was linked to that of his demented "mother."

"What about me?"

Karada looked up from her reflection in the shallow water. Balif stood on the pebbled shore, a pace or two away.

"What about you, elf?"

He sat, stretching his legs in front of him. "Do you still mean to ransom me to my sovereign?"

"Certainly. Why wouldn't I?"

"Well, we did fight for your cause," he said, leaning back on his hands.

"You asked to fight."

"So I did. I was thinking I might have earned my freedom in the bargain."

Karada rose and wrung out her sodden buckskins. She sloshed ashore and sat down on the rocky beach to let the hot sun warm her. It felt good on her face.

"You're right," she said at last.

Balif seemed genuinely surprised. "I am?"

"Yes. You can leave the Valley of the Falls when I do. I'll escort your people to the Thon-Tanjan, to make sure you leave the plains. Just don't come back to my land ever again."

She closed her eyes and turned her face to the sun again. Tiny waves, stirred by a soft western breeze, lapped the black and tan stones of the shore.

Balif watched the rippling water. He had captured Karada once and freed her. He'd done it to demonstrate his superiority over his human antagonist, to show her elves understood mercy. Karada had been furious the day he set her free. She had thought Balif was mocking her. In fact, he had been discounting her. Bereft of her followers, he'd thought she would be finished.

How far he had come from the cool halls and gleaming crystal spires of Silvanost. No pampered child of capital and court, he'd been born under the trees, within sight of the Thon-Thalas. He'd been part of a band of hunters called the Oak Tree Alliance for his first hundred years. By the time of the Sinthal-Elish—the great council at which Silvanos Goldeneye was chosen to rule the elven nation—he was leader of the Oak Tree elves. Balif's followers wanted the throne for Balif, and they had the power to make it happen. He wondered what these barbarians—these *people*—would think if they knew he might have been Speaker of the Stars.

In those days he had two thousand forest elves at his back, and the chief of a powerful society of priests, the Brown Hoods, came to him, saying he would also back

Balif as Speaker. That was a fateful meeting. The Brown Hood's chief was Vedvedsica.

It wasn't lack of support that kept Balif from accepting the crown. He knew, deep within, he was not hard or ruthless enough to rule others. Lead them, yes, if they lodged their confidence in him. But rule? No.

To confirm his belief, he asked Vedvedsica to send his spirit to a future time. He wanted to see what would become of the nation if he agreed to be Speaker. For seven days Balif sat in the depths of a cave, breathing the fumes of smoldering herbs. The Brown Hoods used their power to send his spirit out of his body. He was shown what the future would be if he ruled and what would come to pass if Silvanos wore the crown. When the vision ended, he remained in the cave a full day, trying to come to grips with what he'd seen. The choice was plain, of course; reconciling himself to his own future, though, had been difficult. At the Sinthal-Elish, Balif threw his support to Silvanos. He never told anyone, not even Vedvedsica, what he'd seen in the shadows of things to come.

Karada's sunbath had turned into a nap. She snored loudly beside him.

Savage, he thought not unkindly. Of all the people in the world, Karada would probably understand his decision. She knew what it was like to lead and to live with a curse. One day his destiny would overtake him and transform him into . . . something else.

Balif shook himself slightly, pulling his mind back to the present. "Wake up," he said, nudging the nomad chief. "You'll blister, lying in the sun like that."

Karada draped an arm across her closed eyes. "Why does an enemy care whether I burn?"

"We are not ordinary foes, you and I. I'm not certain what we are. . . ."

Not wanting this line of conversation to continue, Karada rolled suddenly to her feet.

"I don't have time to waste idling here," she said, snagging her horse's dangling reins. "Don't you have tasks that need doing?"

"I do," said Balif, squinting into the afternoon sun. "I am curious about one thing: What's to become of Zannian?"

"He'll be dealt with. He at least is still a true enemy."

* * * * *

Late that night, unable to sleep, Amero wandered out of Yala-tene. He went up the shoreline toward the falls, pausing to inspect the ruins of his foundry. So many days he'd labored here, seeking the secret of bronze. They had been good days, and he wondered if he would ever know their like again.

As he kicked around the broken and blackened stones, the rhythmic thump of wings sounded overhead. He turned toward the noise and saw the dark shape of Duranix alight on the shore. The dragon bent his long neck to the water and drank deeply. Amero ran down the hill, calling to him.

"Duranix! Old friend, how are you?"

The dragon raised his head, and Amero skidded to a stop. One draconian eye regarded him solemnly; the other had been battered shut in his battle with Sthenn.

Taking stock of Duranix's various wounds, Amero asked quietly, "Will you be all right?"

"Right enough." Duranix turned away and began walking toward the cliff behind the falls which contained his cave home. Amero trotted after him.

"Is Sthenn dead?"

"He is."

"You should be happy, then—or at least relieved."

Duranix stopped suddenly and swung around, facing the far smaller human trailing him. "Happy?" he rumbled. "He cheated me again! Four and a half days! He lived only four and a half days. My mother was three times as long dying!"

"Does it matter now? Sthenn can do no more harm. You've avenged your family and saved us all."

The dragon considered him silently for a moment, then said, "And now I'm going to my cave. I will sleep a while, and heal, and when I waken, I have a decision to make."

Amero's brow knotted. "What decision?"

"I don't know whether I shall stay here any longer."

If Duranix had used his fear-inducing breath on Amero, he couldn't have shocked him more. Choking, Amero asked his mighty friend what he meant.

"I've flown around the world," Duranix said, lifting his horned head to the stars. "I've seen places and things no creature of this land, dragon or human, has ever seen before. Chasing Sthenn, I could not stop to study these distant countries. Now that he's dead and the danger to Yala-tene defeated, I no longer feel at home in the Valley of the Falls."

Duranix switched his steadfast gaze from the sky to the stone-walled village behind him. "My home is polluted," he said flatly. "One human was stimulating. A nest of five hundred humans was barely tolerable, but this—hundreds of humans, horses, elves, *ogres* . . ." He flexed his battered claws. "I shall rest, then decide."

Amero watched helplessly as Duranix spread his wings and flew to the mouth of his cave. The words, the arguments that came so easily to him a hundred different times a day, refused to form in his throat or his mind. How could Yala-tene continue without Duranix? How could he?

In a spray of phosphorescent foam, the bronze dragon pierced the rumbling waterfall and vanished into his lair.

Chapter 15

When next the gang of former raiders went out to the crater made by the falling dragons, they found it gone—which is to say, completely filled in. In fact, it was mounded with earth to the height of a horse's back. The ex-raiders leaned on their shovels and pondered this while their nomad guards muttered among themselves about spirit power.

Karada was sent for and arrived a short time later with Pakito, Samtu, and Bahco.

"You've been busy," Pakito remarked to the prisoners. "Did you work all night?"

"Don't be daft," said his mate. "Two hundred men working all night couldn't pile up this much dirt. What does it mean, Karada?"

Their chief rode slowly around the new mound, looking for clues to its formation. Her comrades and the defeated raiders trailed behind her. The ground around the pile was well tracked with the raiders' footprints and the marks of the nomads' horses but no other prints.

Two-thirds of the way around the mound, she stopped. "Do you smell that?" she asked.

Fetid but faint came the smell of decay from the heap of dirt.

"I know that stink."

The speaker was the same tall, impertinent raider from yesterday. Harak, was it? He was leaning on his shovel behind the mounted nomads. When Karada turned to him, he gave her an impudent grin.

"What is it then?" she snapped.

"The green dragon's den in Almurk smelled like this."

Karada told Bahco and Pakito to ride to the west end of the valley to see whether Duranix and the green dragon were still there. The two men galloped off.

"Why bother?" Harak said. "Sthenn's in that hole, moldering away."

"Shut up, raider."

They waited in silence until Pakito and Bahco returned. Both dragons were gone, Pakito reported. Duranix must have buried Sthenn's body in the pit.

Since the prisoners' task had been done for them, Karada ordered their shovels be exchanged for axes. They would cut wood—a great deal of wood—to construct a funeral pyre. Not only for villager dead, she intended it for Ungrah-de as well. She ordered it built here, next to Sthenn's burial mound, and square, ten paces to a side.

"It will take many days to cut that much wood," Pakito noted.

Karada reined her fractious mount about and said, "You have two days. Corpses can't lie around forever; we'll have disease."

She rode off, leaving the giant in charge of the prisoners. Sullenly, the captive raiders marched back to camp to get stone axes. On the way, two of Zannian's former lieutenants sidled up to Harak.

"Listen," one hissed. "To cut that much wood, they'll have to take us into the mountains."

"Hmm," Harak responded, keeping his eyes straight ahead.

"We can escape!"

The raider on Harak's right, a runty bully named Muwa, said, "A lot of our men have already gone away! Why should we stay here and work like slaves? Let's go!"

Harak glanced back over his shoulder at Samtu, riding nearby. "You won't get half a league," he murmured, lips barely moving. "These people know the mountains, we don't. They'll be on your backs like hungry yevi."

"So we'll kill them and take their horses! Are you afraid, Harak? What would Zan say?"

"Zannian's in Karada's hands. He put us here, so I don't much care what he has to say about anything." Harak spat on the trampled grass. "I don't intend to live out my life as a slave, but I do plan to live longer than tomorrow."

Scowling, the two raiders moved away. Harak saw them whispering to the other men, pouring their bitter poison into more eager ears. Fools, he thought. They still don't know who they're dealing with! Karada's people could hunt them down and kill them without breaking a sweat.

Nevertheless, he said nothing to the nomads about his fellow prisoners' plots. He lived by a simple code: Eat when you can, sleep when you need, and let those with power do as they will. When they clashed and fell, it was Harak who would survive, Harak who would thrive.

He was so lost in thought he didn't hear the command to halt. He continued on, not noticing the quick clatter of hooves behind him. Someone dealt him a stunning whack across the shoulders, and he pitched face-down on the ground.

"Stop that!"

"The fool didn't do as he was told—"

"That's no reason to strike him! Will you be like the raiders and abuse your captives?"

Struggling to regain his wind, Harak rolled over. A slender, strong arm braced him as he tried to sit up. Towering over him was the dark-skinned nomad with one arm in a sling: Bahco. He held his spear reversed, and it was obvious he'd hit Harak with the shaft. More intriguing was who had helped him. It was the beautiful black-haired girl, Beramun.

"Are you all right?" she asked.

"Aye, soon as my vision straightens," he mumbled. In

fact he could see just fine and had to force himself not to stare at her.

She helped him get to his feet, then rounded on Bahco. "I'll speak to Karada about this!" she said. "It's one thing to fight warrior to warrior, but you can't beat your captives just because they're slow or disobedient!"

"Don't be a fool, girl," replied Bahco sharply. "Any one of these men would cut your throat if they thought they'd get away with it."

"That was Sthenn's teaching. We must show them a better way," she insisted.

Bahco shook his head at her foolishness and resumed herding the ex-raiders to their pen.

Beramun stood staring after Bahco, a frown on her face, until Harak spoke.

"Sitting high on a horse starts you thinking those on foot are just another kind of ox, to be goaded and beaten," he said.

She turned her thoughtful gaze on him, but he pretended not to notice. Taking a step forward, he feigned pain, and Beramun rushed to his side to bolster him. She fit neatly under his arm. Harak settled his weight against her, and she easily bore up under the burden.

A fine girl and well made, he thought. Strong, too—in more ways than one.

"Is that better?" she said.

"Better." Her eyes were like beads of jet, swept by long, soft lashes as black as her hair.

He must have looked too long or too hard, for Beramun grew nervous and slipped out of his grasp.

"You!" Pakito's powerful voice carried all the way from the prisoners' pen. "Tall one with the fast mouth! If you're through pawing the girl, get over here!"

Beramun blushed and hurried away. Harak smiled slightly and started toward the towering nomad. He affected a stoop, exaggerating the effect of Bahco's blow.

Risk death in some foolish escape attempt? Harak would have none of it. Things in the Valley of the Falls were much too interesting to leave, and they promised to get more interesting in the future.

* * * * *

Karada had to hunt a bit to find Amero. He wasn't with the villagers reconstructing demolished houses, nor was he across the lake with those trying to save the gardens and orchard. To her surprise, she found him in the ruined foundry between Yala-tene and the waterfall, and he wasn't alone. Riding up the rocky slope, she heard voices ringing loudly off the cliff walls behind the broken building. Thinking there was trouble, she drew her sword and kicked her horse into a trot.

". . . can't possibly make that much heat!" Amero declared.

"With bellows you can," said an unknown, Silvanesti-inflected voice.

"But how can the melting point of bronze be higher than the melting point of tin and copper? Shouldn't it be somewhere in between?"

Balif interrupted the discussion by raising a hand and calling, "Greetings, Karada."

Sitting on her stalwart horse, sword bared, she looked every bit the nomad hero. When she realized Amero and the five elves clustered around him were arguing about metal-making, she felt a little foolish. She started to sheathe her blade.

"No, wait," said Amero. "Your sword—may we see it?"

Face hard as granite with embarrassment, she dismounted and handed her brother the weapon. It was a spare, taken from Balif's tent when he was captured—which she wore while the sword she'd used in the great battle with Ungrah-de was repaired.

"This is elven bronze," Amero said, holding up the sword.

"A fine example," Balif agreed.

His ironic tone was lost on Amero, who was frowning at the weapon. "How do you manage to make your blades so long? I know about wax and sand molds, but I've never been able to cast copper blades more than two spans long."

"Copper *is* difficult," said a mature elf with hair so darkly gray it was almost blue. "In molten form it tends to form bubbles, and it doesn't like to flow into sharp corners—"

"What is all this?" demanded Karada.

"Meet Farolenu, a master bronzesmith of Silvanost," Amero said enthusiastically. "I happened to mention my metal-making woes to Lord Balif, and he said he had an experienced smith in his company. We've been talking bronze all morning."

"How exciting." She took the sword back and slid it slowly into its sheath. "Why is a master bronzesmith carrying a spear as a common soldier?" she asked Balif.

"All my soldiers have other skills," he said. "House Protector, our caste of warriors, is not large enough to provide all the fighters the Speaker requires. When needed, warriors of the house raise retinues from the Speaker's other subjects. Males of fighting age serve under those captains to whose house they owe allegiance. Master Farolenu belongs to the Smithing Guild of House Metalline. They lend service to House Protector. On this hunting expedition, he repaired weapons and metal tools."

"Two years after you're dead, words will still be spilling out of your mouth," Karada commented, bored by the complexities of Silvanesti society.

Amero returned to the subject at hand. "So bronze flows better into molds than copper?" he said.

Before the elven bronzesmith could reply, Karada interrupted. "Arkuden, I have something to ask you. Come away, will you?"

Curious, Amero followed her on foot down the slope. Halfway to the lake, Karada stopped.

"Sthenn is dead," she said.

"I know. Duranix told me last night."

"Did he tell you what he did with the carcass?"

Amero shook his head, so Karada told him about the newly formed mound where the crater had been, then asked, "Do you think the body will taint the valley's water supply?"

He scratched his bearded chin, and she noticed for the first time there were gray hairs scattered among the brown ones.

"There's a ledge of solid stone under that spot," he said. "It should be safe for Sthenn to remain there. Anything else? No? Then I'll get back to Master Farolenu—" A sudden thought struck him. "Nianki," he said, using her old name, which no one else dared do. "You never told me. When the dragons fell, how did you escape being crushed like Ungrah-de?"

His hardened sister looked uncharacteristically amused. "It was the craziest thing," she said, grinning. "I knew nothing, saw nothing, but Ungrah before me. A bolt of lightning struck the ground between us, and I turned away to shield my eyes. Next thing I knew, a wave of mud picked me up and carried me away. I fetched up in the top of a pine tree a quarter-league from where I'd been."

Amero blinked in surprise, then began to laugh. Thanks to the all-day rain, his sister had been splashed to safety. The ogre chief, a few steps closer to the center of impact, had been killed outright.

She laughed. "Don't spread the story, Amero. It was just stupid luck."

Since she was still seated on her horse while he was on foot, he clapped a hand to her leg as he said, "What you call luck, I call the favor of our ancestral spirits! But let the tale-tellers in your band invent some romance or other. It won't be as wonderful as the truth, though." Still chuckling, he added, "Dine with Lyopi and me tonight, Nianki?"

She nodded, and Amero started up the hill to the ruined foundry. "Come at sunset!" he urged. "We'll have venison!"

He ran back to his conversation about metal. Karada noted with fondness the smudge of soot on the seat of his trews. His woman, Lyopi, would give him what for if he got soot on her fur rugs.

His woman.

Her light mood evaporated like dew on a summer morning. Amero had a right to companionship, but the phrase had a bitter taste. Karada had heard of his infatuation with Beramun, but that was no great concern to her, since the girl obviously didn't return his affection. Lyopi was quite a different fox in the den.

Lyopi had fought bravely at Amero's side. Half mother, half mate, she'd defended him with her life. Her love for Amero was something Karada understood. She had loved him too for a long, long time. Could she ever escape her curse? Short of death, she couldn't imagine how.

* * * * *

Lyopi was a fine cook. They ate well on venison and spoke of trivial things—cooking, hunting, which region of the plains had the most flavorful game. Each of them chose a different point on the horizon—Amero the north, Lyopi the south, Karada the east—and defended it to the amusement of all.

Lyopi stirred the embers on the hearth and set a clay kettle on the resulting fire to heat water for mulled wine. Talk veered from game to the weapons used to hunt it.

"These bows are very interesting," Amero said. "You say the seafarers showed you how to make them?"

"Yes. Bahco's people. We traded flint and furs with them for the knowledge. Our bows have made the elves' lives a lot harder."

Warming to her subject, she picked up a stick and drew lines in the cool ashes at the edge of the hearth. "At Thorny Creek some years ago, Balif's host pushed us back across the stream, thinking to drive us into a trap made by the soldiers of Tamanithas, coming up at our backs. We shot down so many elves at the creek ford we could have ridden from one bank to the other across the bodies and never gotten our horses' hooves wet—"

Mention of bloodshed took the good humor out of Amero and Lyopi. Sensing their disapproval, Karada cut short her war story and brushed away the map in the ashes.

"I talk too much," she apologized.

"Never mind," Lyopi said. "We've seen too much battle of late. What else did you learn from the seafarers?"

Karada leaned back against the warm hearthstones. "They make this thing Bahco calls 'cloth.' They wear it and use it to make the sails of their ships. Bahco says it's not hide or wool, that it's made from shredded leaves."

Lyopi lifted the steaming kettle from the coals and set a tall beaker of red wine into the hot water. "Like thatch?" she said. "Sounds scratchy."

"It's not," Karada assured her. "I've handled it. It's softer than doeskin and more flexible."

Lyopi was openly doubtful. Amero smoothed over the potential argument by raising an important, if painful subject.

"What's to be done with Nacris and Zannian?" he asked.

"I'll deal with Nacris before I leave this valley," Karada said firmly. "How is my business."

"And Zannian?"

"Brother or not, I know him no more than I know that insolent Harak. Zannian has done great harm to the people of Yala-tene and elsewhere."

"But he's your family," Lyopi protested. "How can you think of killing him?"

"What do you propose?" said Karada. "Shall we let him go if he promises to be a good boy?"

"He's blind! What harm can he do?"

"Nacris is crippled, and look what evil she wrought. I know you both are sick of blood, but it's weak and foolish to let Zannian or Nacris live. The woman's mad. She'd do anything to harm me or Amero. Zannian was raised to think of her as his mother, so he believes as she does. He called that green monster 'master' and did its bidding! How many people have died for his ambition? Any man who does things like that is not my brother!"

Karada folded her arms and looked away into the dark periphery of the house. Amero gazed at the fire. Lyopi looked from one to the other, then turned her attention to the warmed wine. She filled three cups and handed them out.

Amero sipped, feeling the gentle heat pervade his limbs. The aching wound in his leg felt better.

"Nacris is lost," he said after a long silence. "Like a mad dog, it would be a merciful thing for her to die. Since Nianki took her, she's Nianki's to deal with."

Lyopi nodded her agreement. Karada said nothing.

"Zannian's different," Amero went on. "I don't believe he's completely lost to madness and evil, like Nacris. He's young, and he is our brother. I believe we can turn him back from the path Sthenn and Nacris put him on."

Karada drained her cup dry. "You give speeches like an elf. Speak plainly."

"Let Zannian remain in Yala-tene. He may be blind forever. Perhaps I can find Menni somewhere, deep inside him."

Karada put her cup down. The clay clinked loudly on the stone hearth.

"The man who obeyed a green dragon, murdered his own kind, and made an alliance with ogres deserves death," she said. The flat certainty of her words brought a worried frown to Lyopi's face. Karada, however, had decided to argue no further, for she added, "But if you wish it, brother, I won't challenge you. I'll take Nacris, and you can keep Zannian."

The strange bargain was made. Amero felt lightened by the decision. Watching him smile and take mulled wine from Lyopi, Karada felt cold. He thought the danger was past, but as long as Nacris drew breath, Karada sensed the hag's venom was still working.

Chapter 16

The hills west of the valley echoed with the thud of axes on wood. Forty-one captive raiders had been brought to the wooded slopes to harvest trees for the great funeral pyre. The captives were accompanied by five villagers, led by Hekani, who showed the prisoners how to roll logs into the river and haul them upstream by means of long straps.

Guarding the captives were a dozen nomads, commanded by Bahco. He'd formed a harsh attitude toward the ex-raiders and kept them hard at their task all through the morning.

Just after midday, the puffs of breeze from the west ceased. It grew glaringly hot, even though the sun was blunted by a whitish haze spreading from horizon to horizon. Work slowed as captives and captors alike wilted in the heat.

Hekani returned from the pass with the men who'd taken in the last load of logs. He mopped his brow and studied the sullen, lifeless sky.

"Something's going to happen," he said to Bahco, shaking his head. "The air is heavy, but it doesn't feel like rain."

From their vantage point, they could see the beginning of the open plain. It was high summer, and the savanna was hip-deep in grass, a great, rippling sea of green. Even the lightest zephyr would start the grass nodding, but at this moment, not a stem was bent.

The raiders sensed the strangeness, too. Harak and five others had been lopping branches off felled trees with blunt stone axes. They halted and stood staring at the sky and hills.

"This isn't good," said one raider. "It's like the Master was here again.

"Don't be stupid, Muwa," Harak replied. "Sthenn's dead and buried. There's no need to dig him up to explain the weather."

"Then tell us your explanation, wise one!" taunted Muwa.

"I saw this kind of sky before—nine years ago, up north. An Ember Wind is coming."

The captive raiders exchanged looks of disbelief. "That's only a fable!" Muwa declared.

"I'm telling you, I went through it once when I was a boy. The wind blew for six days, and ten people in my clan died. It blows hot and dry and brings pestilence sometimes, and other times, madness." Harak smiled. "Which would you boys prefer?"

"I prefer a change of scenery!" exclaimed Muwa. "We won't wait for dark. Who's with me?"

A pair of nomads rode up. "Why have you stopped working?" one demanded.

"They're afraid of the Ember Wind," said Harak. He wove his fingers together and cracked all his knuckles with a single flex.

"Get back to work!"

Muwa held up his axe threateningly. "I'm a free plainsman, you can't force me to work like a slave!"

"Seems I heard those same words from Zannian's slaves," said Harak dryly.

"Shut your mouth!" Muwa bellowed and charged at him, swinging the axe. The nearest nomad tried to interpose his horse between the men, but before he could do so, two raiders jumped from the log at him. In moments, the second rider found himself beset by angry raiders. They grabbed his ankles and dragged him to the ground.

Harak dodged Muwa's clumsy attack. The axe hit the elm's trunk and stuck there. Bracing his hands behind himself on the felled tree, the lanky raider kicked out, his feet finding the center of Muwa's chest. The man went flying, and Harak tossed the axe away.

The rebellion spread quickly. All over the hillside, ex-raiders attacked their guards. Isolated and outnumbered, the nomads were overthrown and subdued. Shouting wildly, raiders claimed the nomads' horses. They galloped away, often two men on one animal, ignoring the pleas of their comrades on foot.

The last pair of nomads still mounted turned tail and rode back up the pass. Raiders jeered and threw stones after them.

Harak put two fingers in his teeth and whistled loudly. The raiders' chatter died.

"They're going to fetch Karada," Harak announced. "Are you going to wait here for her or make good your escape? Don't think about it too long, friends."

Back on his feet, Muwa said, "Let's go, men! Scatter!" Harak did not move. He kept his place astride the elm tree trunk.

"Harak! Aren't you coming?" asked a raider breathlessly.

"No," he replied.

Nearby, a nomad groaned and pushed himself up on his hands. It was Bahco, who'd been knocked senseless and his horse taken.

"That one's still breathing," Muwa said. "Somebody finish him off!"

Two men moved to carry out Muwa's suggestion. Harak rolled off the log to intercept them. The nearest raider was unarmed, and Harak easily threw him to the ground. The other man had a lopping axe, which he swung clumsily. Harak spun away, grabbing the axe handle behind its heavy stone head. He thrust out a foot and tripped his opponent. The raider fell and rolled over in time to see the blunt axe head coming straight down at his face. He screamed and clenched his eyes shut.

The killing blow never landed. When next he opened his eyes, he saw Harak standing over him, grinning. The axe head was embedded in the ground, just brushing his left ear.

"The others left you," Harak told him. "Better run if you want to catch them!"

Harak laughed as the raider scrambled to his feet and ran.

The leading edge of the wind reached the woodcutting camp. It was hot, from out of the north, and dry as a lizard's dream. Harak's prediction was coming true, and his good humor vanished.

Nomads and villagers, recovered from their beatings, were rising to their feet. Everyone clustered around Bahco, sheltering in the lee of an oak.

"Where are Tanik and Harto?" Bahco asked.

"Two of your men rode off," Harak said, raising his voice above the wind. "I guess they went for help."

Angry the raiders had escaped, some of the nomads began to shove Harak and upbraid him.

"Leave him," Bahco said sharply. "This man saved me and maybe all the rest of you." He told them how Harak had fought off the men coming to kill him, then frightened the rest away by reminding them Karada would be coming to avenge their rebellion.

"Why'd you stay behind?" Hekani asked.

"I've seen what Karada does to her enemies. I'd rather be her prisoner."

Hekani laughed, but the nomads openly sneered. They had more respect for the escaped raiders, who had fought for their freedom, than for this slippery character.

The hot wind coursed steadily, not gusting like a normal breeze. Sheltered only slightly from the desiccating air, the men grew parched. Though Harak warned them not to venture forth, one by one they slipped down the hill to the river to drink their fill. Fighting back through the Ember Wind, they returned drier than if they'd stayed put.

Soil once rain-soaked now dried to powder and rose into the air as dust. Coughing, the men huddled together behind the tree, flying grit stinging their exposed flesh.

After an interminable time, a column of riders came thundering out of the pass. At their head was Karada, face wrapped in doeskin against the vicious wind. Bahco went to greet her. He explained what had happened, and how Harak had fought to save their lives, yet called himself a coward to explain why he didn't flee with his raider comrades.

Karada's eyes narrowed. "Watch him closely. I don't trust clever men."

The horseless nomads and villagers doubled up with Karada's riders. She gave the order to return to their camp. The horsemen faced about and started back up the pass. Soon, only she and Harak, still on foot, remained. She looked down at him from her tall horse.

"Why didn't you escape?"

"It's not my time yet to go," he said. "Aren't you going to bring them back? They're flouting your authority."

"You mistake me for Zannian. I don't command, I lead. My band follows me out of loyalty, not fear." She shrugged, adding, "And if they live through the Ember Wind, perhaps they deserve to be free."

"You know the Ember Wind?"

"There isn't much on the plains I don't know."

She extended her hand. Harak took hold, and she hauled him up behind her.

"You're strong," he remarked, settling in close.

"Don't forget it," she said.

He didn't. All the way back to the valley, Harak kept his hands carefully at his sides.

* * * * *

The Ember Wind could not sweep directly through he Valley of the Falls, as the valley ran east-west hrough the higher range of mountains, but it closed in bove the valley, creating a strange and strained atmoshere. The air inside the valley grew still and unnatually humid. Overhead, clouds tore by at a reckless rate, lowing yellow by day and deep orange at sunrise and unset. The sky appeared to be on fire, which is why the ame Ember Wind had arisen.

Much wood had been gathered for the funeral pyre, hough not enough for the grand mountain of flame Carada had envisaged. Logs and brush were laid in ourses around the mound where Sthenn lay buried. The lead slain in battle were brought out by the remaining aptive raiders. Wrapped in hides or shrouds of birch ark, the bodies were put on each course of kindling. No listinction was made between raider, nomad, or villager. Some of the Yala-tene elders objected to this, but Karada ilenced them, saying, "Anyone who died fighting is a varrior. Causes mean nothing to corpses—they're all in he land of the dead now."

Two days after the Ember Wind's arrival, the pyre vas nearly complete and a method to ignite it needed to e found. There wasn't any oil left in Yala-tene to soak he timbers, and the freshly cut wood wouldn't be easy o light, especially in the unnaturally humid air. While he preparations continued, the elders sought out Amero. They found him on the village wall with Lyopi, Balif, and everal elves. Lyopi suggested Duranix, and Amero agreed o ask the dragon.

The Arkuden walked to the top of the ramp leading lown into the village. Lyopi, the elders, and the elves tayed back, watching him. Amero folded his arms and losed his eyes.

Duranix. Duranix, can you hear me? He repeated hi call three times before the dragon answered.

I can always hear you, was the testy reply.

We need your help. We need to burn the bodies of thos who died in the battle, only we don't have the means to mak so great a fire. Would you help?

I will if you'll stop pestering me.

Amero backed up a step, taken aback by the dragon' harsh tone. He thought, *It will mean a lot to everyone. W must do this, or face plague and wandering spirits.*

Very well.

"He's coming," Amero said quietly.

A long interval passed, so long that Amero felt hi face redden.

Finally the thundering falls burst apart as the power ful bronze body punched through to open air. Durani spread his great wings. The elders let out a concerte gasp. Though they had known Duranix a long time, he' not been seen much recently. Duranix had grown enor mously during his time away as a result of being infuse with wild spirit power by Tiphan, the ill-fated leader o the Sensarku. The bronze dragon had been poisoned b Sthenn, his limbs rotting away, when the misguide young villager released the power he barely understoo to heal Duranix. Heal him it did—and accelerated hi growth by almost a hundred years.

The villagers were filled with awe, but the Silvanest were no less impressed, though they tried harder t conceal their amazement. Duranix flew toward them swelling rapidly in size. Repair work in the streets o Yala-tene came to a halt as the shadow of the drago fell across the town. Nomads and ex-raiders placin the last bodies on the timber terraces of the funera pyre paused and looked up when the great beast hov into view. As the dragon drew closer, they could se that the injuries he'd sustained in his battle wit

Sthenn were healing well, and his left eye was no longer swollen shut.

The remaining raiders were stricken with fear. Some of them fell to the ground, terrified Duranix might be as capricious and vindictive as their former master. They had often seen their master in his hideous disguise as Greengall or in his natural, decrepit form. But no face the ancient green dragon ever presented could match the power and majesty of Duranix in his prime.

Duranix paid no heed to any of them. He landed on the pile of masonry rubble left by his collision with the town wall. The funeral pyre was complete, and Duranix ordered everyone back.

He opened his wings and vaulted into the air. It was late afternoon, and the weird orange sky glow reflected red and gold from his bronze hide as he climbed almost vertically. Golden fire trailed from the tips of his wings and his horned head, making a shimmering path many paces long in his wake. People below exclaimed in wonder, and even the elves could not hide their astonishment.

"Is he always so flamboyant?" asked Balif, coming up to Amero's side.

"No," Amero said, gawking along with everyone else. "He usually draws lightning from the clouds. I don't know where this new yellow flame comes from."

The dragon reached the underbelly of the scurrying clouds and hovered. Silent orange fire rippled up and down his wings, flying off the tips in streams of bright fiery balls. Abruptly Duranix tipped to one side and plunged down, his jaw dropped open, and golden fire burst forth.

The mound trembled, then erupted into flame. Duranix held his mouth agape for some time, playing a stream of fire to and fro across the heap of logs and kindling. When he finally snapped his jaws shut, the pyre was blazing from end to end.

No one cheered, wept, or made any sound at all. A thousand pairs of eyes—villager, nomad, raider, and elf—stared at the mountain of fire billowing up from the flat valley floor. Even after Duranix landed on the west side of the pyre, brilliant orange lightning continued to flicker down from the Ember Wind clouds, striking the funeral pyre time and again.

Against the low roar of the flames, a lone voice could be heard singing.

Come walk with me, lonely one
In summer sun or winter rain,
From mountains high to rivers low,
Across the open, endless plain.

Amero strode to the edge of the parapet and tried to spot who was singing the tune his mother had used to soothe him to sleep as a child. Ringed around the pyre were hundreds of people, mostly from Karada's band. He hurried down the ramp. Lyopi called after him, "Where are you going?"

He clambered down the broken wall, slipping and teetering over slabs of shattered stone. The voice was still singing, but the words were indistinct this close to the crackling, popping bonfire. Amero pushed among the nomads. He spotted Karada some distance away, seated on her tall, wheat-colored horse. They exchanged a look, then his sister quickly glanced away.

More voices joined in the song. All were former raiders. Hearing the slow, soothing melody issuing from the throats of the hardened men moved him deeply, and he wondered how they could know his mother's song.

Amero broke through a line of nomads still gazing at the fire and reached Karada. On the ground at her horse's feet was Zannian, his head still swathed in bandages

His was the clear, strong voice leading the singing of "The Endless Plain."

A sharp pang touched Amero's heart. He knelt beside Zannian. His nearness caused the sightless man to flinch and stop. The song went on among his former followers.

"Who is it?" said Zannian hoarsely.

"Amero."

"Ah, with Karada, then we are all together." Using her horse's leg as a guide, Zannian got to his feet. "Strange custom you have, burning the dead."

"Necessity taught it to us. Graves are hard to dig in the mountains, and when there are so many to bury, fire is an honorable solution."

"What do nomads do with their dead?" Zannian asked, raising his voice and face to Karada.

"Bury them," she said tersely. "The plains are wide, and all can sleep within."

Amero looked from her to their newly found brother. "We must talk. The three of us."

Karada was silent for a long moment, then said, "Let us go to my tent." She guided her horse away, back to camp. Amero took his brother's arm and followed.

Though it seemed every person in the valley was at the pyre, at least one was not. When Karada entered her tent, she found Mara waiting by the campfire.

"I am making food, Karada," the girl said.

A silent nod. "Go now. I want to be alone."

Mara slunk out. She'd just entered the shadows when she saw the Arkuden arrive. He was leading an injured man in raider's clothes. They went into Karada's tent without calling for permission.

Mara had never trusted the Arkuden. Since the age of eight, when her family had given her over to the Sensarku, she had been steeped in the philosophy of Tiphan, "Tosen," First Servant, of the Sensarku. The Arkuden always opposed the Tosen's plans to improve Yala-tene and bring glory to the dragon and the Servers of the Dragon. The Arkuden, the Tosen said, acted as if he alone had the right to determine the destiny of Yala-tene. Her later disillusionment with Tiphan had not altered her feelings against Amero for blocking the Tosen's wonderful dreams for a better world.

Brother of Karada or not, the Arkuden was no friend. If not for him, Tiphan would never have left Yala-tene, her fellow Sensarku Penzar wouldn't have been swallowed by the spirit stones on the plain, Elu the centaur wouldn't have been murdered by elves, and she would never have been captured.

Mara's green eyes widened as the terrible truth crystallized in her mind: The Arkuden was to blame. He was to blame for all of it.

A muffled voice came to her from the tent. Mara stretched out flat on the ground and put her ear to the hide wall.

As usual, the Arkuden was doing the talking.

* * * * *

"I know this is hard, but we must face it. We can't ignore it any longer."

"It's not hard," Karada said sharply. "Ask him what he wants."

Zannian tilted his head toward his sister. "I want to see Nacris."

"No. She's fated to die, so consider her dead and go on."

The former raider chief brought his hands to his head and pushed the bandages back until his face was fully exposed. A single horizontal slash crossed both eyes and the bridge of his nose. The skin around the wound was swollen and mottled by red and purple bruises. He turned his head this way and that, obviously trying to see something, anything, and obviously failing.

He snapped, "If you really wanted her dead, you would've slain her the day she was captured."

Karada found a gourd bottle and pulled the wooden plug out with her teeth. The spicy aroma of cider wafted through the tent.

"She made a good hostage," the nomad chieftain said, and took a long drink.

"And now? How many days has it been since the battle ended?"

"Eight," said Amero.

"So many? It's hard to tell when you see neither sun nor stars." Zannian sniffed the air and held out his hand. "Give me some cider."

She gave him the gourd. He drank deeply from it.

"Let's not talk about Nacris," Amero said. "She is doomed. But you may yet be saved."

Zannian wiped his lips with the back of his hand. "I tried to destroy you. Why would you want to save me?"

Astonished, Amero said, "Because you're my brother!"

"The only brothers I knew are burning now on that pyre."

Karada made a disgusted noise. "This is useless. Are you sure you want to let this yevi-child live?" she asked Amero.

"Yes."

"Kill me and be done with it," Zannian said bitterly. "All the promises made to me turned out to be lies—the Master's, that woman's—" He couldn't call Nacris "mother" any more.

Amero insisted, "You're young. Can you see no other way to live?"

"Think you'll make a villager out of me? I'll fall on a knife first!"

Amero crossed behind Zannian and plucked the cider gourd from his hand. He knelt on one knee beside him.

"A good healer might have been able to save your eyes," he said. "But our best healer's dead. We sent him to talk terms with you, and you cut off his head. Does that mean anything to you, Menni?"

"My name is Zannian!"

Looking up at Karada, Amero said, "Our sister is Nianki. Do you remember that name at all?"

Zannian was breathing hard, clearly distressed, but his voice was loud as he denied it. "I don't remember either one of you! You're nothing to me!"

"You remember 'The Endless Plain.' "

"It's just a song."

"A song our mother sang to us!" Amero put a hand on Zannian's shoulder, his face pale and strained. "If you don't remember, it's my fault. You were just a baby, Menni, two summers old. I put you in a tree to keep you safe from the yevi, but that wasn't enough. I should've kept you with me. I should've found a place for us both—"

"Then you would've fallen into Sthenn's hands or been killed," Karada said bluntly.

Amero sat back, cradling his head in his hands. "I can't help the past, but I can give you a future." Eyes flashing, he raised his head and added, "You were taken in arms. Your life belongs to the one who defeated you, Lord Balif. He's given you to me. I say you shall remain in the Valley of the Falls for the rest of your life. Blind or sighted, you'll learn how to live as a peaceful man of our village, and if you cause trouble—any trouble at all—I'll give you back to Balif!"

Karada stifled a grim smile at what she knew to be an empty threat. Zannian said nothing, so she punched him on the shoulder.

"Say something, boy," said Karada. "What it'll be? If you want, I'll lend you a knife to fall on right now."

Zannian's expression changed from defiant to sly. He licked his parched lips, then said, "What happened to the black-haired girl, Beramun?"

"She's in camp," Karada said.

"Could I speak to her?"

Amero shook his head hard, but his sister answered, "That's up to her."

"I want to speak to Beramun and Nacris."

His siblings argued, but in the end, it was agreed: Zannian would be taken to Nacris. Karada would be present, and when she ordered the meeting at an end, Zannian would go without complaint. Later, Amero would ask Beramun if she cared to visit Zannian. It was entirely up to her whether she did.

Amero touched his younger brother's arm. "Don't take me for a fool," the Arkuden said. "I stood up to you in battle, and I won. If you make trouble or try to escape, I'll deal with you. Brother or not, Yala-tene comes first."

Amero stood. "Let's go back to the village."

"Leave him here," Karada said. "He's a wanderer, he's better off in a tent than a stone hut."

Zannian shrugged. "All places look alike to me," he said without humor.

* * * * *

The Arkuden left. Mara clung to the warm ground, bathed in angry sweat. Her thoughts were confused, muddled, but one phrase echoed in her head—*I'll give you back to Balif!* How could he betray his brother, a fellow human, to the Silvanesti? Didn't he know how they treated their captives? What kind of tyrant had the Arkuden become?

Karada must be made to understand the enormity of the Arkuden's words. Karada trusted her brother too much—and loved him unnaturally, Mara knew. That unnatural love, which blinded her to his true nature, was also the fault of the elves. Her Tosen had told her so.

Chapter 17

The great pyre burned itself out around dawn. The mound of ash and embers slowly lost its dull red aura, but the pall of smoke hovered over the valley like a noxious mushroom, held in by the Ember Wind raging above it. When the funeral fire finally winked out, the last one to leave the scene was Duranix, who had watched over the pyre to the last. He flew back to his cave.

Amero wanted to talk to him, but his hoist had been destroyed during the raider attack. Silent calls for the dragon's aid were ignored, so the only way for Amero to get inside was by the vent holes cut through the roof of the cave. He gathered vine rope from all over Yala-tene. He needed a great deal of it to descend to the cave floor from the high ceiling.

Conditions were improving in the valley. Hunting parties returned with the last of the village's missing children. Every one had been found. Not a single child was lost, because the older children took care of the little ones, hiding out in the foothills exactly as their parents had told them. Likewise, the children and old folks of Karada's band returned, not only hale and whole but staggering under the weight of fresh game and foraged food.

Karada embraced her old friend Targun. "Well done, old man!" she said. "Any problems to report?"

"None, chief," he replied. "The country seems abandoned. All the time we were out there, we saw no one—not a human, not a centaur, not an elf. Just lots and lots of elk!"

"Sounds good. I wish I'd been there."

The grizzled old plainsman regarded his chief curiously. "Was the fight not a good one?"

"Ugly," was all she would say about it.

"When do we return to the plain?"

Karada had been pondering this question herself. She'd imagined her band would fight, defeat the raiders, and depart immediately when they were done. Last time she was in Yala-tene, it was such a strain to be around Amero that she'd left as speedily as possible.

Oddly, she did not feel that way now. The curse was still there, without doubt. She felt it skulking within her, like a hunger pang no meal could cure. But things were different now; the situation was more complicated. Amero had a woman of his own, a woman with whom he shared a history that didn't include herself. There was Beramun, who had become like the daughter she'd never had. Balif too was a considerable distraction. These people filled her days and blunted the ache she felt from her compelled love for Amero.

Lastly, there were Zannian and Nacris. Karada found it hard to care much about the fallen raider chief. She hardly knew him, and what she did know, she didn't like. Still, he was her flesh and blood, and how he lived his life mattered, if only because Amero felt so strongly about him.

Nacris was another matter entirely. She deserved death—even Amero agreed—but it was harder than Karada thought to condemn her. If they had met on the battlefield, sword to sword, Karada could have slain her joyfully. In her present state, crippled and deluded, there would be little honor in taking her life.

Targun was still talking.

"Eh? Forgive me, old man. I was elsewhere," she told him.

"I was asking: How long will we stay here?"

She looked at the sky, still capped by the oppressive

Ember Wind. According to reports from her scouts, the eastern passes and foothills were free of the life-draining wind, so the nomads could return to their beloved range any time they wished.

"Three days," she said impulsively. "We'll leave in three days."

Targun looked disappointed. "So soon? I was hoping to feast the people of Yala-tene before we departed."

"So feast them. You have my good wishes."

Word was spread. In two days, a great feast would be held to celebrate the liberation of Yala-tene and the defeat of Sthenn and the raiders. The morning after the feast, Karada's band would ride out.

* * * * *

Accompanied by Pakito, Karada entered the tent where Nacris was being held. A young nomad woman followed, bearing a steaming basin of water.

Nacris was dirty from her confinement, and her hair was a mass of gray snarls. "Is it my day to die?" she said with strange glee, eyeing her visitors.

"Not yet," Karada retorted. "You're to have a visitor. I thought you might want to clean up before he gets here."

"Who is it? Hoten? Tell him to go away."

"Hoten is dead."

"Then I certainly don't want to see him!" Nacris suppressed a giggle.

Karada sighed and turned to her towering comrade. "You see what she's come to? Crazy as a sun-addled viper."

Pakito looked on sadly and said nothing. Many years ago he'd had a longing for Nacris. She'd been a spirited woman in those days, a doughty fighter and a magnificent rider, better on a horse than even Karada. Nacris had preferred Sessan. Pakito got over his infatuation and took Samtu as his mate (though everyone else knew it was Samtu who'd done the taking). The twisted, wretched creature before him was far from the impressive woman of his youth.

Karada had the water bearer put the bowl in front of Nacris, then the girl gave her a small nub of pumice for scrubbing.

Nacris sat up, her chains clinking. She dipped both hands in and carried warm water to her grimy face.

"So," she said, rubbing loose droplets from her eyes. "Who wants to see me, if not Hoten?"

"Zannian."

Nacris's hands froze, pressed against her cheeks. "Don't lie, Karada!" she said angrily. "If Hoten's dead, how can Zannian still live?"

"He does, and he's asked to see you. I told him he could, so long as I remain in the tent."

Nacris resumed washing, though her hands shook visibly. "It can't be," she muttered. "It can't be. My boy would not live with defeat and disgrace—"

"He's not your boy!" Karada shouted so loudly that Pakito, Nacris, and the water girl all jumped. Her next words seemed filled as much with disgust as with anger. "His name is Menni, and he's the son of Oto and Kinar, as am I!"

Nacris's thin lips drew back in a wide smile. "So you know? I pieced the tale together a long time ago, I did. How does it feel, Karada, to know one of your brothers killed the other—killed the one you love?"

The nomad chief stepped forward, fists clenched. Pakito put a broad arm before her to halt her advance.

With a visible effort, Karada mastered her anger and said a few words in Pakito's ear. His heavy eyebrows climbed his high forehead, but when his chieftain frowned emphatically, he nodded and went out.

Karada dismissed the water girl, then called, "Send the raider in!"

Two armed nomads guided Zannian into the tent. At the sight of him, Nacris gasped.

"What have you done to him?" she said hoarsely.

In answer, Zannian pulled the bandages from his head. His awful wounds spoke louder than any words. The puffiness around his ruined eyes had subsided somewhat, but the bruises were still dark and the red line of the sword cut was crusted and scabbed.

"Poor boy, poor boy," crooned Nacris. "Karada did this to you?"

"No," he said. "The elf lord, Balif, did it in a fair duel."

"Poor boy . . . come closer."

Karada ordered, "Stand where you are."

Zannian advanced no farther but, groping about, sat down cross-legged, facing the sound of Nacris's voice. Nacris regarded his awkward movements with obvious dismay.

"Why did you pretend to be my mother?" he asked quietly.

"It was Sthenn's wish. I could not refuse. Later . . . I did it because I wanted to. You were a bright boy, Zanni, a great warrior. I was proud to be your mother."

"Not a great enough warrior," he said. Tilting his head toward the nomad chief, he added, "Karada says you must die. I wonder why she hasn't killed you yet?"

Nacris snorted. "She can't kill me! Sthenn foresaw my fate. Neither water, nor fire, nor stone shall kill me, and no man living shall strike me down."

Zannian laughed, but the pain of his wounds cut his black mirth short. "All your stratagems were for nothing!" he hissed. "Now you are the prisoner of your mortal enemy! You're just a crazy, hateful old woman. Better you had drowned years ago when the bronze dragon threw you in the lake!"

"A touching reunion," Karada murmured, lip curling in disgust.

"You're hardly any better," Zannian sneered. "I know why you let Nacris live: The hate you share for each other is so strong, so much a part of your spirits that neither of you can bear to live without it!"

"I'm destined to kill Karada!" Nacris declared, trying to rise. Her missing leg and the heavy bronze chain brought her up short, and she subsided.

"You're destined to feed worms," the nomad chief shot back.

Just then, a muffled voice came from outside the tent. Karada peeked through the flaps.

"Ah! Good. Another visitor for the hag."

Pakito had returned with Amero, who ducked inside and stood beside Karada. Brother and sister stared down at Nacris without speaking.

Nacris blinked rapidly. Her jaw worked, but no words came. Making strangled hissing sounds, she struggled again to stand.

"Yes, he's alive," Karada said, pleased by the effect of her surprise. "Your green assassins failed. They killed the wrong man!"

With a shriek, Nacris picked up the water basin and smashed it on the ground. She thrust a jagged shard at Amero. Though he was well beyond Nacris's reach, Karada stepped between them, sword bared.

Losing her balance, Nacris fell over Zannian, knocking him onto his back. The clay shard cut his cheek. He wrenched the fragment from her hand, and they rolled over several times, winding the chain around them both. Nacris seemed oblivious, howling her hatred for Amero and Karada all the while.

"Pakito, separate them," Karada said, appalled.

"Stay back!" Zannian shouted, gritting his teeth as he fought to pin the raging woman beneath him. To

Nacris he said, "Be still, mother, and I'll put you out of your misery!"

"No!" shouted Karada and Amero in unison. Both moved toward Zannian.

But before they could reach them Nacris had worked loose the stake holding her chains to the ground. With a shrill cry, she whipped the heavy wooden peg into her free hand and smashed Zannian in the head. His body went slack. Nacris heaved herself to one knee, facing Karada and Amero in triumph.

Pakito had his stone mace in his hand, but Karada ordered him back.

"Give me a true weapon," Nacris demanded, panting. "Let me die like a warrior!"

Karada's features twisted. "You're not a warrior," she said coldly. "You're the mother of three dozen and one snakes!"

The bronze blade went up. Nacris had her fetters clutched to her chest, protecting her. Karada turned her blade and brought it down with all the rage and pain of her lifetime. When it ceased its shining arc, Nacris's head fell from her shoulders.

Nomads summoned by the shouting burst into the tent. They saw their chief, the Arkuden, and Pakito standing over the erstwhile leader of the raiders. The headless body of the prisoner Nacris lolled at their feet.

Amero knelt by Zannian and reported he still lived.

Pakito said, "Take him to Karada's tent. Bind him, but not too harshly." Two men took Zannian by the hands and feet and carried him out. Pakito went with them.

Alone with his sister, Amero stared at the dead woman, shattered by what he'd heard and seen.

Tearing his gaze away—and forcing himself not to look on Nacris's severed head—he whispered to his sister, "Are you all right?"

"Of course I am." Karada bent and cleaned her bloody blade on a fold of Nacris's shift. "There's one problem solved."

Amero was shaking. "How can you be so hard? Does life mean nothing to you?"

Karada slammed the sword back into its scabbard. "Pity can get you killed," she told her brother. "I have none for her, and neither should you. How many times will you let a mad dog bite before you strike it down?"

He couldn't answer. He could only regard her in silence with wide, shocked eyes.

Her voice softened. "She mentioned a prophecy, an augury made by the green dragon. He told her neither water, nor fire, nor stone would kill her, and no man living would strike her down."

Amero looked down at his feet, his buckskins splashed with blood. "How did he know?" he asked. "How did Sthenn know Nacris would die at the hands of a woman with a bronze sword?"

"He was a dragon," Karada replied, shrugging. "Dragons know too much."

* * * * *

Late in the night, a log raft pushed out from shore. Two people stood on it. The taller one gripped a long pole, with which he propelled the raft out into the lake. His companion stood on the other side. Between them lay a long, hide-draped bundle.

No stars could be seen through the rushing clouds, but the last flickers of the Ember Wind provided a pulsating light to guide them away from shore. When the raft neared the center of the Lake of the Falls, the man stopped poling. The raft drifted slowly under the momentum of his last push.

"This is good," said Karada.

"How deep is the lake here?" asked Harak.

"Deep enough."

He hadn't asked a single question, not even when Karada, cloaked and hooded, had arrived at the prisoners' pen and bade him come with her. A simple job, she'd said. A special task she didn't want her band to know about.

She threw back the hide cover. Underneath lay Nacris, gray hair combed and face washed, wrapped up tight in a fine white doeskin. Only the pale oval of her face showed.

Harak gave a surprised exclamation. He knew he'd helped load a body on the raft, but he didn't know whose.

"Shut up."

Karada moved the body to the edge of the raft. Leaning on his pole, Harak heard the clink of metal. It was then he saw the heavy bronze chain wrapped around Nacris's waist.

"That's a lot of bronze to throw away," he remarked.

"Shut up."

Harak sighed.

Karada eased the body into the water, and it sank without a sound. Immediately, she ordered Harak to take them back to shore.

Nothing else was said until the raft bumped into the pebbled shallows. Stepping off, Karada reminded Harak of his oath to say nothing of what they'd just done, and without a backward glance, she walked quickly up the stony hillside. She disappeared in the deep shadows of the cliffs.

Harak jumped down into the water and dragged the log raft higher onto the beach. It was very late, and everyone in the valley seemed to be asleep. He wondered where the villagers stowed their stock of wine.

Wandering up the hill toward the village, he heard a faint clang of metal and stone. Off to his right, outside the village wall, Harak saw a bright orange light flaring at the base of the cliff. Muffled voices accompanied the sounds of work. He ambled that way. It seemed more interesting than returning to the prisoners' pen.

The light turned out to be a fire, burning inside a broken-down structure built hard against the base of the mountain. Four or five figures were silhouetted against the glare. Unlike an ordinary fire, this one didn't waver or flicker; it burned steadily. Harak made out a new sound he couldn't place: a regular, deep panting, like a bull ox gasping for air after a long run.

Closer to, he spotted the Arkuden in the group. The rest were Silvanesti, including the elf lord Balif. What were they up to? Was this some arcane elven ritual to call up spirit power at the Arkuden's request?

"See that?" one of the elves said, pointing into the fire. "That's the red stage. Now it's ready to pour!"

"Stand back!" said another, but the Arkuden shook his head.

"Let me do it," he insisted. He and an elf inserted forked wooden poles into holes in the sides of a heavy clay pot. They hoisted the pot out of the fire, sidled sideways, and poured the contents into an unseen container. Lapping over the rim of the pot was a brilliant orange-red fluid. Harak's eyes watered just looking at it. The fiery liquid hit its destination, and a loud hissing resulted. Steam filled the air.

Balif glanced away and saw Harak highlighted by the glow of the burning liquid. "Who's there?" he said sharply.

Caught, Harak stepped up boldly and announced himself. Balif drew his sword, though he kept the point down.

"Do prisoners have the run of the valley now?" asked the elf lord.

"Your presence here seems to say so," Harak replied genially.

Amero and the other elf put the hot pot back on the fire. "Never mind!" said the Arkuden, his voice full of excitement. "Come here, you. See what we've done!"

Harak had no idea what to expect. Upon reaching the scene of the strange ritual, he saw they'd poured the brilliantly hot liquid into a rectangular box on the ground. The box was made of wet clay, bolstered by a few wooden planks. A hole in the top, about the size of Harak's thumb, plainly showed where the fiery substance had been delivered.

"I've just cast my first bronze!" Amero exclaimed. "Farolenu showed me how. The secret is forcing air into the fire to melt the copper and tin together—but not too much air."

"You made bronze?" Harak was interested. Here was a task much more rewarding than summoning spirits.

Amero nodded vigorously. "We melted down some scrap and poured it in that mold. When it cools, it will be a sword."

Harak regarded the unlikely looking wooden box with great respect. Like many plainsmen, he had handled bronze, but he had no idea how it was made. Some mysterious process of the Silvanesti, it was said. Now he was seeing it for himself.

He turned to Balif. "Why are you showing a human how to do this? Aren't you afraid we'll make weapons to fight you?"

Amero suddenly looked distressed. It was plain he hadn't thought of that.

"Bronze is a secret humans are destined to learn sooner or later," Balif said, "and though I am loyal to the Speaker of the Stars, I have my own views on the policies of my nation. There are those in Silvanost who want to spread our hegemony from the southern sea to the capes of the north, westward to the Edge of the World and east to the ocean of the rising sun. I do not agree. I believe the true realm of the Silvanesti is what we have now, the forest sacred to us, and continued aggression outside our natural homeland will only result in needless bloodshed."

Balif gave a small, tight smile, adding, "Endless conquest is like burning down a forest to stay warm; it works for a little while but is short-sighted. So no, I'm not worried about giving away the secret of bronze. If the war-minded lords in Silvanost see a bronze-equipped army of plainsmen opposing them, they may recognize at last the wisdom of peaceful neighboring."

The appreciative silence that greeted his thoughtful words was disrupted by Harak. "Faw, they call *me* a talker!" the ex-raider said. "I'm as tight-lipped as an oyster compared to you!"

The mold had cooled enough to be opened. Amero fidgeted about, nervous as a newly mated man. Farolenu and his helpers slipped hardwood wedges into the seam and, in unison, tapped them with mallets. With a slight hiss, the mold split apart lengthwise, falling into two halves. The crudely formed sword, still glowing faintly with heat, lay in the right half of the mold.

"Let it cool thoroughly," Farolenu said. "When cold enough to handle, free it from the mold. Then you can begin filing it to shape and giving it a sharp edge."

"Can you use water to speed the cooling?" asked Amero.

"For short, thick blades, yes. For swords, no. Quenching will make the sword brittle. At the first stroke, it may snap off at the hilt."

The elves and the Arkuden plunged into a deep discussion of metal-working, leaving Balif and Harak far behind. The elf lord yawned and excused himself. Harak took the opportunity to depart, too.

As they walked across the slate-strewn ledge toward Yala-tene, Harak said, "I hear Karada intends to leave in three days' time." Balif nodded, and the ex-raider asked, "What will your people back home make of all this?"

The elf lord's face was unreadable. "Some will hail me for escaping the clutches of barbarians. Others will condemn me for aiding enemies of the Speaker."

He turned away to enter Yala-tene through the south baffle. Harak watched him go, wondering what the Silvanesti was really thinking. Would a noble elf warrior really give away the secret of bronze for such high-sounding, unselfish reasons?

A wide yawn interrupted Harak's cogitations. The doings of chiefs and lords was beyond him, he decided, shaking his head. He went back to his pen to sleep.

Chapter 18

The Ember Wind increased in fury in the days that followed. Vast clouds of dirt were scoured off the windward side of the mountains, darkening the sky and drifting into the valley. Landslides shook the upper passes as the hard-driven dust loosened boulders. To many, it seemed the mountains themselves would tumble down and fly into the air. Amero consulted Duranix, who circled the valley at great height, above the Ember Wind. The dragon reported the brown river of air stretched away far to the north, but it did not extend more than a few leagues east or west of the valley. The Ember Wind would blow itself out, Duranix reassured Amero, though it always worsened before ending. The stronger the wind blew, the sooner it would end.

Beramun found herself helping a band of village women bathe the children. Long lines of yelping youngsters wound down to the lake, where each child was scrubbed head to toe by mothers, aunts, and older sisters. Pumice removed dirt and sometimes a little skin, too.

Talked into the duty by Lyopi, Beramun discovered she enjoyed it. Her hands grew raw from washing, and she stayed wet all morning from wrestling with balky and rambunctious children. After so much fighting and cruelty, it was good to exhaust herself in such an ordinary, useful job.

When the last child was scrubbed clean, the tired women trudged ashore. Hulami the vintner sent skins of wine retaken from the raiders, and never was the drink better appreciated. Loud laughter echoed against the walls of Yala-tene, bringing curious villagers to the parapet to see the cause of so much merriment.

"There's a happy sound," said Jenla, watching from the wall.

"Happy but dangerous," opined Tepa. He looked ten years younger since Jenla had returned alive.

"Dangerous? How?"

"There's a hundred women down there, all made merry by Hulami's good wine. I would sooner cavort with centaurs than try to cross that crowd!"

Jenla laughed. "You've learned a few things in your long life, haven't you?" She left her old friend on the village wall and went down to join the women by the lake.

Preparations for the coming feast were well underway in the nomad camp. Three firepits were dug, and more wood was gathered for the bonfires. The raider prisoners who remained were set to digging the holes and gathering wood. They gave the nomads little trouble. The worst of Zannian's horde were either dead or had escaped with Muwa. Karada, having no desire to shepherd a bunch of prisoners around the plains, wouldn't let Bahco track them down. The sooner the ex-raiders were gone, she said, the better.

The fifty-odd men who remained in the captives' pen chose Harak as their spokesman, as he seemed to have access to Karada and the Arkuden. They wanted their fate settled. Their pen was rife with rumors that they'd be put to the sword before the nomads left the valley. Harak couldn't believe it himself, but he didn't object when his fellow prisoners demanded he seek out Karada and speak to her about their plight. It was a good excuse for him to slip away from the feast preparations, too. No one challenged him. People had become accustomed to seeing him roaming the camp.

Laughter and singing drew Harak to the lake. The impromptu party was breaking up, and women streamed up the hill to village or camp, some weaving a bit as they went. Harak passed unchallenged through the flow of cheerful, red-faced women. He saw many he knew—Samtu, Lyopi, vintner Hulami, and the tough old woman called Jenla, whom Zannian had captured early in the battle. Karada was nowhere to be seen.

He was about give up his search and look instead for a place to stay out of sight until the toil at the firepits was done when a face caught his eye.

It was Beramun, walking slowly up the lakeshore, carrying a baby on her hip. She looked so content and easy with the child that a stranger might have thought it hers. Harak fell into step beside her.

"I'm looking for Karada. Have you seen her?"

Beramun shook her head.

"Whose baby?"

She hefted the year-old boy leaning his head on her shoulder and he gave her a sleepy smile. "This is Kimru, son of Udi and Tana." The names plainly meant nothing to Harak, so she added in a quiet voice, "Udi and Tana are dead. Kimru is an orphan."

"I'm sorry," Harak found himself saying, for reasons he didn't understand. He hadn't killed anyone named Udi or Tana—at least, not that he knew.

"Udi's father, Tepa the beekeeper, has him now. He's an old man, though, and I fear the child will lose him before he becomes his own man."

By the north baffle Beramun handed young Kimru to a village woman. She gave the boy's downy head a final caress and watched until he and the woman disappeared behind the wall.

Sighing, she said, "I will miss him."

Harak trailed after her. "You act as though you aren't going to see him again."

"I'm not."

"Karada's not leaving for another two days."

"I'm leaving tomorrow," Beramun said flatly.

He caught her hand, stopping her. "But why? You have Karada's favor. If you remain with her band, you could be chief some day."

Anguish bloomed in her dark eyes, but she shouted, "I don't want to be chief of anything!"

People nearby glanced their way. Beramun pulled away and started walking faster.

Tall Harak, with his long, lean legs, easily caught up with her. "Where will you go? What will you do?" he asked.

"I'll wander. It's the life I was meant for."

"What about a mate and children? You seem to like children—"

She whirled to face him. "Will you leave me be? I don't want to answer your questions! I'm in this place because men like you murdered my entire family!" She tore at the neck of her doeskin shirt, exposing the green triangle high on her chest. *"This* is why I must go! The green dragon gave me this mark. It binds me to him!"

Harak frowned. "Sthenn's dead. What hold could he possibly have over you now?"

"Just because a viper dies doesn't mean its venom becomes water. Duranix says I'm tainted forever by Sthenn's mark," she said and backed away from him, retying the lacings of her shirt tight at her neck. "What did the green dragon intend for me? Will I end up like Nacris, crazed, eaten up with hate? How can I live among good people knowing I may grow evil in time?" With a violent shake of her head, she added, "No! Better to be a wanderer for the rest of my life. *Alone!"*

She ran. A bit stunned, Harak did not react for a moment. Then his thoughts sharpened, and his choice became clear. He ran after her.

Zigzagging through the rows of tents, Beramun ended up at Karada's. She ducked inside, thinking he wouldn't dare follow.

Mara was there, kneeling by the entry flaps, a whetstone in front of her. She was sharpening the bronze dagger she always kept in her shirt. When she spied Beramun, she recoiled like a guilty thief.

"Where's Karada?" asked Beramun, breathing hard.

"Not here," Mara replied. "What—?"

Harak barreled into the tent, nearly knocking Beramun off her feet.

For a man—a raider!—to enter Karada's tent in such a way was unforgivable. Mara leaped to her feet, presenting the dagger point-first to the intruder. The newly sharpened tip gleamed like gold.

"Who do you think you are?" Mara shouted. "Get out! This is Karada's tent!"

"Shut up, girl!" Harak snapped. Mara jabbed at him, but he stepped nimbly back, unharmed.

"Put that down! I'm not here to cause harm. I need to talk to Beramun."

"Get out!" Mara repeated shrilly. "Karada will hear of this intrusion!"

Harak lashed out with his foot, kicking the weapon from her hand. The blade spun through the air, and he caught it neatly. Mara let out a short, horrified cry and ducked behind Beramun, then continued her furious denunciations.

"Leave," Beramun said, interrupting Mara's tirade. Arms crossed over her chest, Beramun glared at Harak.

He flipped the dagger, catching it carefully by the blade. He presented the pommel to Beramun.

"Hear me out and then I'll go."

Beramun took the dagger. Mara promptly tried to snatch it back, but Beramun thrust her aside. The girl tripped over a pile of furs and fell backward to the floor.

"Don't listen to him!" Mara urged. When Beramun paid her no heed, Mara crawled away. She circled wide of Harak and, near the entry flaps, rose to her feet and dashed outside.

Harak said, "We don't have much time before she brings Karada. Listen to me, Beramun. You don't have to go away alone. I'll go with you!"

The young woman was not impressed. "I know your kind," she said bitterly. "I know what you want. You're no different than Zannian!"

"I don't blame you for saying so, but I'm not like him at all."

She made a dismissive gesture and started to turn away.

"Be my mate, Beramun, and we'll wander the world together!"

The words obviously startled him as much as they did her, but Harak smiled broadly and repeated them. "Be my mate, Beramun. I know you've been asked before, but I'm not a fool like Zannian nor a dreamer like the Arkuden. I've had women before, but I've never asked one to be my mate. Say no and I'll not bother you again, but you must know my offer is honest."

Beramun still held Mara's dagger. Her other hand went to her chest. She said, "What about Sthenn's mark? Don't you fear it? How do you know I won't cut your throat some night while you sleep?"

She didn't say no! Harak thought jubilantly. He stepped toward her. Putting an arm around her waist, he slowly pulled her closer still.

"It would be just like the old lizard to plant an evil seed in a brave, good woman like you. But he's dead, and I don't fear his poison. All his other acts have failed, and he's failed with you, too."

She would not look at him. She whispered, "I won't be the cause of your death."

He took hold of her wrist and brought the dagger up. "Then I'll undo his work."

Her dark eyes lifted, the question in them plain.

"I'll remove the mark," Harak explained.

"No more tricks, Harak, please."

He plucked the bronze dagger from her fingers. "No trick. No lies. Whether you take me as your mate or no, let me remove Sthenn's mark. Once you're free of it, you can decide what you want to do."

A small fire crackled on the hearth. Harak bade Beramun sit by the circle of stones. He knelt beside her and put the blade of Mara's dagger in the flames.

Her eyes widened.

"I saw an old man do this once. His horse had a growth on its withers, and he fixed it this way." Squeezing her hand, he said, "I know you're brave enough to do this."

Wordlessly, she loosened the lacings on the front of her shirt and slipped her left arm out of the sleeve. By firelight, the green triangle looked black and shiny against her tanned skin.

Harak picked up the dagger gingerly. The leather-wrapped handle was hot, but not too hot to hold. The tip of the span-long blade glowed dull orange. "Take a deep breath, and don't be too proud to scream."

Swallowing hard, he pressed the flat of the hot blade against the jade-colored triangle. Beramun twisted her face away and groaned. Her entire body trembled. A sizzling sound filled the tent, but the dragon's mark did not smell like normal flesh burning. Instead, a fetid whiff of Almurk filled their nostrils.

Harak yanked the blade away. Beramun sagged in a faint, so he held her up. It was just as well. Having seared the green dragon's mark, he now needed to excise it forever. He worked quickly, using the knife's sharp tip to cut beneath the foreign color embedded in Beramun's skin. Because he'd cauterized it first, little blood flowed.

At last the evil sign was out. Harak threw it on the fire. He shuddered when the yellow flames changed to vivid green as the last remnant of the green dragon was consumed. A choking stench rose but quickly dispersed.

Beramun's eyes opened part way, and she let her head loll on Harak's shoulder. With great care he lowered her to the furs heaped beside the hearth. He found his hands were shaking.

"Well done."

Startled, Harak turned. Karada stood in the entrance to her tent, arms folded, watching. Behind her were arrayed Pakito and Bahco. Mara's pale face peered between the men.

Harak passed a hand over his sweating brow and sat down by Beramun. "She was afraid the green dragon would compel her to do evil," he said. "I did what I could to help her."

Karada nodded. "She is worth the scar you've given her. But are you worthy of Beramun?"

Harak understood her question. Beramun had no parents, no living kin. Karada was taking on their role, demanding he prove himself to her for Beramun's sake. He returned the dagger to the fire.

Harak hated pain. He'd always thought Zannian and the other raiders who gloried in their resistance to it were stupid brutes. A wise man—a clever man, at least—avoided pain. That's why it existed, so you would know the things that caused it were to be avoided.

When the knife was glowing again, he opened the collar of his worn tunic. Looking straight at Karada, he pressed the hot bronze to his chest, just above his heart—the same place Beramun had borne the mark of Sthenn. He clenched his teeth so hard he was sure they'd crack, and tears filled his eyes. The smell of his own burning skin made him want to wretch, but as he had mastered the noxious ogre drink *tsoong,* so he mastered his sickness.

He threw the burning blade aside. Karada's face swam before him. The tent seemed to waver around him. He fell.

Strong arms hoisted him to his feet.

"Take him out, Bahco," Karada was saying. "Beramun will stay here until she's better."

"Let me stay with her," Harak protested feebly.

Karada clapped a hand to his shoulder. The comradely gesture rocked him like the kick of a horse.

"You won't lose her," she said vehemently. "Not now. That was the strongest mating ceremony I've ever seen. You two are bound for life." She glanced at Beramun, still unconscious on the fur rug. "I knew it would take a lot to win her, but I couldn't have guessed how much."

Bahco draped Harak's arm over his shoulder and bore the ex-raider away. Karada picked up the dagger, still faintly warm.

"Mara," she said. "Come here."

The girl tried to flee but ran into a wall of muscle and buckskin as Pakito barred the way out. Though he looked distinctly unhappy doing so, he held the far smaller Mara fast with one huge hand.

Karada approached, tapping the handle of the dagger into her palm. "One of the worst crimes is when a man forces himself on a woman," she said in a low voice. "I know of what I speak. There've been men who tried to take me. Every one died by my hand."

She stopped at arm's length from the cringing girl. "You come running to me, screaming that this raider is forcing himself on Beramun. I return and find him saving her spirit, if not her life. Perhaps you were sincerely mistaken. I doubt it. The only crime worse than a man forcing a woman, Mara, is a woman lying about it. When you do that, you make us all out to be liars."

Karada put the tip of the dagger under Mara's chin. "If you were one of my band, I'd have you beaten for this."

Mara squeezed her eyes shut. Tears rolled down her cheeks. Karada removed the dagger abruptly. "But you're not one of my band, and you never will be. You came from Yala-tene, and here you will stay. Go, and never le me see you again."

She dropped the dagger. Pakito released Mara. Nearl convulsing with grief, the girl collapsed at their feet.

"Don't send me away," she sobbed, clutching Karada' legs. The nomad chief stepped out of reach. Mara's sob gained volume. "Please! Oh, please! I'll serve you eve better than before! I'll do anything you say, Karada! Any thing at all!"

"Get out!" Karada's voice rose to be heard above th girl's cries. "If I see you again, I'll gut you like a fish! She turned her back.

Large of frame and equally large of heart, Pakito fel sorry for the misguided girl. "Go," he urged gently. H held open the tent flap.

Hiccuping, Mara brushed her tears away. She snatche up the dagger and for a moment stared hard at Karada' exposed back. Pakito would have swatted her like a fly if she' moved toward his chief, but it didn't come to that. Mar slipped the dagger in her robe and darted out of the tent.

"By all my ancestors!" Pakito exclaimed. "I though she was going to go for you!"

Karada shrugged. "I gave her the chance, but the gi has no nerve. I thought she might recover her pride livin with me, the Silvanesti broke her too well. She's just rabbit. A silly, frightened rabbit."

"Poor girl. Will she harm herself, do you think?"

"I don't know and I don't care. She's Amero's prob lem now."

Pakito left. Karada sat by the fire and waited for Bera mun to wake.

* * * * *

Amero kicked loops of braided vine through the hol in the cave roof. As it spilled down, he finished tying o the other end to a cedar tree. A long time ago, rebels from Karada's band had used these holes to enter the cave and attack him. Now they were his means to see his melancholy friend.

He lowered himself through the hole and started down. It was hard work for a man his age, but the privations of the recent war had hardened him, and he reached the cave floor without mishap.

The cave's interior was dark and chilly. Cold blue light filtered through the waterfall, and slender beams of daylight slanted in through the roof holes. The cave smelled strongly of reptile and old smoke. It had been many days since Amero had last been here, but the drinking pool and hearth pit were just as they had been when he used to live here every day with Duranix.

The dragon lay in the back of the cave on his sleeping ledge, a vast mound of coiled bronze muscles. Where once Duranix had had room to spare on the ledge, now his tail hung over the edge, and the arch of his back almost scraped the sloping wall above him.

"I know you're there," Duranix said with a deep sigh, neither rising nor turning to face Amero.

"Is it all right? Or should I go?"

"How would you leave? Are you fit enough to climb that cobweb you came in on?"

The bronze dragon uncoiled, limbs and body seeming to move in different directions at the same time. Amero backed away, giving ground to the massive creature.

"Yes, the cave *is* getting to be too small," said Duranix, answering Amero's thought as he stepped down from the ledge. "How are you?"

Amero sat on the cold hearthstones. "Surprisingly well. I've learned the secret of making bronze, did you hear? Balif's smith, Farolenu, showed me how it's done."

Duranix blinked, huge eyelids clashing together. "My condolences."

Amero's confusion was plain on his face and in his thoughts, so Duranix said, "You've spent a long part of your short life trying to discover how to make bronze. Now you've done it. It's finished. So, what will you try next? Iron?"

"What's iron?"

"Never mind. I've just been having a difficult time imagining the future."

Amero poked the ashes of the long-dead fire with a stick. "There are plenty of problems left to overcome," he said. "The village needs to be rebuilt. We must decide what to do with the prisoners. Hekani has an idea for improving the baffles—he wants to attach permanent ramps to the walls, wooden ramps that can be raised or lowered from within—"

A single claw waved dismissively. "These are your problems, not mine." The dragon sighed, blowing loose ash and dust around. "So much has happened here. It's not the valley I came to a century ago. I thought this was my place. Now I doubt it. There's a wide world beyond this valley. . . ."

Amero quickly changed the subject, announcing that he and Lyopi were to be mated at last.

"Who knows?" he said, grinning. "I might become a father in my old age!"

"It's wise you chose the sturdy female over the black-haired one. That girl is tainted."

Amero wasn't sure about any taint Beramun might have, but he was certain Lyopi would resent being called "sturdy." He asked, "Why so restless? What did you see on your journey?"

Instantly, Amero's mind filled with a crowd of rapidly changing images. He saw flying dragons, dragons on mountaintops and in caves, nesting dragons—in many sizes, shapes, and colors. Like listening to numerous voices all talking at once, he couldn't sort the onslaught of images into any sensible order. Gradually, the cacophony subsided, leaving a single, crystal-clear vision—a slender bronze dragon perched gracefully on a bluestone mountaintop.

"Who is that?" Amero murmured, dazzled by the rush of visions.

As soon as he spoke, the image vanished. Duranix was at the mouth of the cave, his head thrust through the pouring falls. Amero came up behind his left side and tapped on his foreleg.

Duranix withdrew his head from the water and turned to look at his friend.

"Are there truly as many dragons as that in the world?" asked Amero.

"That many and more."

"Who is the small bronze one?"

"No one important." He cocked his mighty head, water dripping from his barbels. "They're looking for you in the village. I hear them calling."

Amero's shoulders sagged. "What can they want now? I told them I'd be gone until morning."

"Your people need you. It's a good thing to be needed."

Grinning, Amero clapped his hand to his friend's massive scaled flank. "Rejoice, then! All of Yala-tene needs you, Duranix."

"You did well enough against the raiders. Perhaps you don't need me as much as you think."

Amero was about to protest when the dragon lifted him gently in one foreclaw. "I'll return you to the village," Duranix said. "What kind of friend would I be if I made you climb that long rope out of here?"

It was like the old days when Duranix plunged through the thundering falls with Amero held close to his chest. He didn't make straight for the ground but remained aloft for a time, circling the lake. Amero grinned as the wind tore at his short hair. From this vantage, he saw blue sky to the north, signaling an end to the Ember Wind. Rather than looking down on Yala-tene below him, Amero kept his eyes lifted, taking in the vistas spread out around him. It had been too long since his last flight with Duranix. Much too long.

At last Duranix landed atop the stump of the onetime Offertory. During the siege, the villagers had torn apart the stone platform, seeking material for missiles or to shore up their weakening defenses. The dressed stone blocks had all been stripped away, leaving only the original cairn of round lake stones.

The dragon closed his wings and set Amero on the ground on his feet. The walled enclosure had a desolate air. Where once devoted acolytes washed the walls and swept the sand around the Offertory to make it pleasing to the dragon (who in truth cared little for what the Sensarku did), now the area was a repository for timbers, stone, and other supplies used in the rebuilding of Yala-tene.

"The nomads are giving a feast tomorrow night," said Amero. "Will you come? Nianki's leaving the next day."

"Human festivities are always amusing. Perhaps I will come."

"Good! See you then!" Amero said, and wended his way to the exit amid piles of logs and baskets of mud for brickmaking.

Duranix lingered atop the cairn, watching until his human friend disappeared from sight. The stone cairn, erected a long time ago when he was notably smaller, began to buckle under his great weight. Like a past that could not return, his perch had to be abandoned. Duranix launched himself skyward, returning to his dark retreat behind the falls.

Chapter 19

The day of the feast dawned fair and bright. During the night the Ember Wind dissipated, and the heavy, muggy air in the valley lifted. Karada immediately sent out hunting parties to bring back any fresh game they might find.

Samtu and a band of six rode up Cedarsplit Gap and returned shortly, bringing bad news. Days of wind-driven dust had carved away the soft limestone in the cliffs and sent waves of broken rock crashing into the pass. According to Samtu, the slide was largely made up of small, loose stones—especially treacherous to cross as they were easily disturbed by feet and hooves.

Hoping the other scouts would bring better news, Karada returned to her tent to check on Beramun.

Beramun had spent a restless night. Even after downing the sleeping draught Karada had sent for, she twitched and moaned in her sleep. At one point Karada touched the girl's forehead and found it blazing hot. Since her wound wasn't visibly festering, the cause of the fever wasn't clear. Now she was asleep. Soon enough, Harak appeared and asked to see Beramun.

The nomad chief was struck by the change wrought in the former raider. From a smooth, arrogant, rather lazy wanderer Harak had become almost likable. Maybe his love for Beramun had transformed him—or maybe, Karada reflected, he recognized that Beramun deserved an honorable mate.

They talked in hushed tones about the girl's condition.

"It's strange," Karada murmured. "Her wound is painful, I'm sure, but it shouldn't cause such distress."

"It was Sthenn's mark," Harak said grimly. "Cutting it out may have done more harm than we know. It's my fault."

"Be strong. I think it was the saving of her." Karada offered to share her meager meal of nuts and fruit with him. He took a handful of nuts and sat beside Beramun's pallet, watching her brow furrow and the sweat bead on her lip.

After a moment, he said, "I have a boon to ask of you, Karada."

She stopped eating to listen. In the same low tone, he added, "The rest of the men from Zannian's band chose me to speak for them."

"Go on."

"It is said you're leaving soon. The men and I want to go with you."

She'd been half-expecting this. "I'll not have raiders and killers in my band."

"Wait, great chief. We're all plainsfolk, aren't we? I doubt anyone in our little pen has killed more men than you or the great Pakito."

"I've never killed an innocent."

His old, cunning look returned. "Never?"

"You won't get far with me, questioning my word!"

Beramun sighed, shifting slightly on her pallet. Karada gestured at Harak. He put aside his uneaten breakfast, and they moved away from the sleeping girl to the entrance of the tent.

Changing his tone, Harak said, "Chief, any men you don't take will fall back into stealing and raiding. I know them. They are not bad, not really. Some are lazy or coarse, but the worst from Zannian's band are already dead or escaped. Those left need a strong leader to turn them around, someone we can follow. You can be that leader, Karada."

Shorn of Harak's flattery, his point about the captives going back to raiding if left on their own was undeniable.

Fifty men could cause a lot of trouble for small family bands wandering the plains. They could make life difficult for Amero's villagers, too.

"Very well," she said. "I will take them, and if they cause any trouble I will deal with them."

It took Harak a moment to digest her blunt statement, then he exclaimed, "Thank you, Karada! You are the noblest chief of all!"

She held up her hand to stanch the flow of flattery. "Harak, I won't be oiled like an old pouch. I will meet with each former raider. They will be inspected by the warriors of my band and by the people of Yala-tene. Any recognized as murderers, plunderers, and other yevi-spawn will meet a swift fate. Those who pass muster can come with us."

"Certainly, Karada, certainly!" Harak said. "I'm sure the men will agree to your conditions. You're even more wise than all the tales proclaim."

"Shut up," she said, but without rancor. Grinning, Harak did.

Hearing them, Beramun turned over and groaned. Her feet kicked at the fur covering her legs. Concerned, Harak went to her and took her hand. Her fingers closed around his with startling force.

He could see her eyes moving rapidly beneath her closed lids. "What is she seeing?" he wondered aloud. "What powerful dreams hold her in such sway?"

* * * * *

The tunnel was endless. Toadstools sprouted in the cracks between the stones of the floor, their yellow gills emitting a weird, cool light. The walls and ceiling were black soil, crumbling and rotten.

Beramun was icy cold. Barefoot, wearing only a tattered doeskin shift, she felt as though she'd been wandering in this bleak place forever. The air was clammy and smelled like moldering bones. She shivered, holding the neck of her shift together to keep out a little of the chill.

She heard footsteps behind her. Though they sounded only when she moved, she knew it wasn't an echo.

All at once she whirled about. For the briefest instant she spotted the outline of *something* in the darkness. The shape melted into the shadows under her probing gaze, but it had been there.

Heart hammering, Beramun turned and ran. Her stride stretched out to bizarre lengths, covering many paces with every strike of her heel. The broad reach of her legs didn't seem to get her anywhere, though. The dimly illuminated tunnel appeared to be endless and straight as a spearshaft.

The footfalls behind were louder than before. Closer.

Suddenly, a hole yawned in the floor ahead. Beramun tried to stop, but her momentum was too great, and she fell into the opening, feet kicking frantically. She flung out her hands and miraculously caught the far side of the hole. Her relief changed immediately to horror. The walls were so soft her feet could find no purchase but instead gouged deep holes in the soft black dirt. The dirt fell away.

Exhausted, she hung there, panting, above what she knew was a bottomless chasm. Footsteps approached, but these came not from behind her but from in front, on the other side of the hole. A face appeared above her.

It was Harak.

"Help me!" she gasped. "I can't hold on much longer!"

"Of course you can't," he said, not moving to aid her. His smile revealed too many wolfish teeth. "Do you know where you are?"

"What? No, I . . . please, Harak!" The fingers of her left hand began to slide off the rim of the hole.

"This is the lair of the green dragon."

A tremor of horror vibrated through her straining limbs. "It can't be! I was in Yala-tene—and Sthenn's dead!"

"Did you see him die?"

"No, but Duranix said—"

Harak threw back his head and laughed. "Little Duranix? You believe one dragon's word about another? How sweet!"

He was neither acting nor speaking like the Harak she knew. As her grip continued to slip, Beramun felt a burning pain on her chest. She looked down and saw blood flowing freely from a deep wound where Sthenn's green mark had been.

When she looked up again, Harak had leaned down, and their noses almost touched. His eyes gleamed oddly. They weren't the dark brown she knew but had a greenish cast. The pupils were vertical, like a cat's—or a dragon's.

Terror rose in her throat like nausea to choke her. "You're not Harak!"

In the blink of an eye, he metamorphosed into the grotesquely tall, misshapen body she knew was his Greengall form.

"Hee hee hee," Greengall giggled, looking down at her and hugging himself with long, thin arms. "You can't be rid of me so easily! Did I live a thousand years to have my neck wrung by that rodent-lover Duranix? I should say not! True, I am much changed, but the genius of Sthenn remains, and I will live again in *your* slender shell of flesh. What an honor for a mere rodent!"

Beramun could hardly breathe. Her fear was so great it made her dizzy. "No!" she said faintly.

"Keep saying that," Greengall-Sthenn said in his ugly singsong voice. "Maybe it will come true! Let go, rodent. Give up. Let go and fall!"

He kept up this refrain, his words twisting through her skull like a snake. She dug her fingers into the lip of the hole, raised her right leg, and gripped the spongy soil with her toes. The earth crumbled, but she worked her toes into the black filth, deeper and deeper until she had enough support to raise her left foot. She began to work it into the dirt, too.

Greengall's face twitched. "Stubborn little female," he said, annoyed. "Still, if you weren't so strong, your body wouldn't be of much use to me."

"You can't . . . have me," she said through gritted teeth. She heaved her right foot out of the hole she'd made. Black beetles, maggots, and blood-colored worms sluiced from the opening in the pit wall. Beramun ignored them and burrowed higher, rising half her own height out of the hole.

Greengall stopped urging her to let go and swiftly backed away, as though he was afraid. Not only did his action gave her confidence to struggle on, it sparked a revelation. He couldn't possess her by force, or else he would simply reach down and capture her.

Only if she gave in would Sthenn control her!

"I know you now," she said, rolling forward, out of the hole. Her breath came in ragged gasps, but her heart beat strongly and evenly again. "The mark you put on me meant *nothing.* It's only purpose was to frighten and dishearten me! It even fooled Duranix. But you have no power over me, except through fear. That's what it was always about, wasn't it? You drink in fear like raiders swill stolen wine!"

Greengall's form altered and shrank into Harak again. "Don't be cruel, brave Beramun!" the false Harak said. "Do you know what it's like to feel your body perish, your powers flicker out like a falling star? This is my last vestige of life! Don't cast me into the darkness, please, sweet, kindly Beramun!"

Beramun rose to her feet. She lifted her hands to brush the dirt from them and realized one now held a bronze dagger. The weapon looked familiar. She closed her fingers around the handle and raised the blade high to strike.

The false Harak's form shifted rapidly as he became first Greengall again, then Zannian, Karada, Nacris, and finally Amero. She hesitated upon seeing this last, but Greengall's telltale eyes remained, framed in the borrowed sincerity of the Arkuden's bearded face.

Beramun struck, burying the dagger up to the hilt in Sthenn's chest. Her target was a spot on his left breast, just above his heart. A stabbing pain lanced through her own chest—

With a cry of pain, Beramun awoke, bolting upright. She was firmly held by strong hands.

"Let me go!" she cried, struggling wildly.

"Beramun, it's Harak! Wake up!" he said, shaking her, then held her at arm's length so she could see his face.

Beramun froze in place, staring at him. His deep brown eyes, flecked with amber, had round pupils, not vertical. His usual smirk was gone, replaced by a look of concern. Behind him stood Karada, her tanned brow likewise furrowed with worry.

"It is you!" Beramun said joyously. "The beast is gone!"

She threw her arms around Harak's neck, and they kissed for the first time.

* * * * *

Riders returned from Northwind Pass and Bearclaw Gap. The narrow northern pass was filled waist-deep with drifted dirt, practically impassable. Forested Bearclaw was still open, thanks to the sturdy trees lining the gorge. The nomad band would have to stretch thin to traverse the winding, wooded pass, but there was no other choice. Karada let it be known the band would depart the next morning through Bearclaw Gap.

The western pass, being much wider and guarded on either side by vertical cliffs, was as clear as always, and Karada's hunters returned through it with elk and deer to augment the feast.

As the sun dropped low over the cliffs to the west, torchbearers ran from pit to pit, igniting tall conical heaps of logs and kindling. Villagers pounded pine stakes in the ground in circles, then wove strips of birch bark between them, making great bowls two paces wide. Into some of these bowls fresh water was poured. Stones, heated in the bonfires, were dropped in the water until it boiled. Herbs and roots gleaned from the high, neighboring valleys would be simmered in this until ready to eat. The nomads had never seen this cooking method before, and they watched, curious and uncertain, as the villagers made their preparations.

The only real shortage in the valley was wine. The raiders had guzzled and spilled huge quantities, and despoiled the orchards until there was precious little fruit to harvest. Tepa tried to remedy this by providing honey from his hives to make mead, but mead was notoriously slow to ferment. In the end, Hulami and Pakito mixed the available wine with crushed berries and water to make a mild punch. Karada and Amero were designated to taste the first cups.

"I've changed my mind," Karada said, making a face. "Hunt down the raiders who escaped. Their crime grows greater and greater."

Amero tasted his and shrugged. "It's not a fine vintage, but it answers thirst." He handed the cup to Lyopi and dipped himself another from the birchbark vat. "Like the walls of Yala-tene, the vineyards need repair, but one day we'll have walls and wine again."

With that cheering thought the feast began. The sky darkened to purple, and the blazing logs sagged into their pits, sending showers of sparks skyward. Whole oxen and elk, which had been brought out on a cross-thatch of tree limbs and set up to roast, filled the air with the aroma of cooked meat. The smell drew Duranix, who flew over the feast site. His belly glowed golden in the light of the setting sun. The villagers raised a cheer for the dragon, which was echoed by Karada's nomads. Duranix landed upwind of the firepits.

Karada hailed him, saying, "The first ox off the fire is yours!"

"Only the first? I thought this was a feast."

There was general laughter, and she said, "The first four, then."

Ox hides were spread on the ground, and groups of villagers and nomads took their ease as the food simmered and sizzled. Children dodged among the adults, chasing fireflies. Someone called for a tune. Six muscular nomads produced reed flutes and began to play a gentle walking song.

Reclining against Lyopi, Amero felt more at peace than he had in many, many days. The expanse of the valley spread out before him, dotted with nomad tents. Above, Lutar emerged from the veil of daylight. It was waning, and its normal red hue was a mild rose by twilight. Just the color, Amero thought, of a ripening apple.

"Something wrong?" asked Lyopi.

"What? No."

"You sighed."

"I was thinking of something Duranix said, about needing challenges to make life worth living. I've made bronze at last, a goal I've chased a long time, but I'm not disappointed I've done it. There are a lot more things to be done in Yala-tene."

"Always more things," Lyopi agreed.

He tilted his head back until he was seeing her face upside down. "Shall we declare ourselves mates tonight?"

Nonplussed, she said, "There's no hurry. Whenever suits you—"

"What better time than this?" he said earnestly, sitting up. "Could you ask for a grander mate-day feast, or finer guests?"

Quietly Lyopi said, "Think of your sister."

It hadn't occurred to him that Nianki might not like to see him mated. Feeling bold (and a little stubborn now that he'd made up his mind), he called to her, sitting a few steps away between Pakito and Samtu.

"Nianki! Will you stand by me tonight and see me mated to Lyopi?"

Pakito looked stricken by Amero's words, and Samtu rolled her eyes, but Karada merely bowed her head slightly and said, "I will."

There was little set ceremony to mating. The man and woman simply stood before their friends and kinsmen and announced their union. Fired with enthusiasm, Amero jumped up, eager to get the attention of every soul in the valley for his declaration.

"Wait here," he said, giving Lyopi's hand a squeeze. "I'd like Balif and Farolenu to be here for this. I'll find them!"

He dashed off, darting between singing and drinking revelers like a child after a firefly. Lyopi shook her head and smiled ruefully.

"Thirty-nine years old and still a boy," she said, speaking chiefly to Karada and Samtu.

"Aren't they all?" Samtu replied.

"No. Truly, he is. Amero's always bringing home the oddest things. He collects sacks of rocks from all over the valley and sits by the fire cracking them open to see what's inside. Sometimes he brings home animals, too."

"He still hunts?" asked Karada.

"No. He brings them home alive! One autumn he brought back an enormous bullfrog from the fens on the west side of the lake. Big as a chicken it was."

"Why?" Samtu asked. "Does he like to eat frogs?"

"No! He wanted to measure how far it could jump!"

The women burst out laughing. After a moment's pause, Karada asked, "How far *could* it jump?"

Lyopi raised her hands and dropped them again in an exasperated gesture. "We never found out. It wouldn't budge, even when Amero prodded it with a stick!"

"Must've been a male frog," said Karada. That set them off again.

Pakito studiously stayed out of the conversation, until their laughter subsided. Then he asked, "Where are the Silvanesti? I haven't seen them all day."

"They've taken to lingering by Amero's old foundry," said Duranix. He'd sated his hunger and moved a bit closer to the fire. By its light, his massive bronze head seemed to float in the air all by itself, his body masked by the deepening shadows. "They were there when I left the cave at sundown."

"Wonder what they're up to?" said Pakito.

"Be calm," Karada said. "They won't cause any trouble. I have Balif's word." She drained the weak wine mixture from her cup. "You know elves. They're up there gabbing at each other, using more words than any decent human would."

"Any decent human but Amero," Lyopi observed dryly. The laughter started anew.

* * * * *

Amero found the Silvanesti, as Duranix had told the others, at the old foundry. When he arrived, still brimming with enthusiasm for his mating day, the elves were busily cleaning and packing their gear.

Balif returned Amero's greeting but declined his invitation to join the feast. The elf lord knew there were still many in Karada's band unwilling to share a cup with a

Silvanesti. As he pointed out, the converse was also true. Few were the elves in Silvanost who would willingly dine with a human. In any event, he and his soldiers were busy preparing for the next day's departure.

The Silvanesti were certainly diligent and organized. Four elves were doing nothing but polishing bronze—sword blades, knives, buckles, gorgets. Others were down by the lake, washing mantles and leggings, while another half-dozen carefully packed their loose gear in bundles.

"Would you and Farolenu come just for a short time, to see me mated?" asked Amero. "It would be a great honor to me." He explained their custom.

"I would be happy to attend," Balif said, bowing. Farolenu likewise accepted.

Amero was ready to lead them back right then, but the elf lord begged for time to change into clean attire. It was agreed to delay the mating declaration until Soli appeared in the southwest. That would give Balif and his bronzesmith time to prepare themselves.

When the Arkuden had hurried away, Balif turned to his nearest elves. "Did you get them?" he asked, keeping his voice low, even though he was speaking in his own tongue now.

"Yes, my lord," said an elf, on his knees packing.

"Show me."

Making sure no humans were in sight, the fellow unrolled the bundle he'd been working on. In it were four bowstaves, bowstrings, and ten arrows.

"How did you acquire them?"

"As you suggested, my lord. We traded bronze and gold to some nomads for them. We have seven complete weapons and twenty missiles."

Farolenu, already pulling on his best tunic and mantle, asked, "My lord, do you think what we're doing is honorable? Aren't we betraying the humans' trust?"

"We are," was Balif's candid reply. "But we have given the Arkuden the secret of bronze. It seems only fair we take something in trade—something in addition to our lives, I mean."

Every elf knew what was at stake. The nomads' bows and arrows could devastate any Silvanesti army in their path. To avoid this disaster, the elves had to learn to use the new weapons themselves. Balif had agonized over his subterfuge, but he felt he had no choice.

"By maintaining a balance, we shall endeavor to keep the peace," Balif promised. "Come, Farolenu, we have been honored with an invitation. Let's do our duty by the Arkuden."

Suitably attired, the two elves departed for the humans' feast. The rest of the Silvanesti worked to complete preparations for their journey home.

* * * * *

A lone figure lifted its head from the soot-blackened ruins of the foundry. Driven out by Karada, fearful of the Arkuden and his supporters, Mara had tucked herself away in a forgotten corner of the foundry. She'd watched Amero converse with Balif but was too far away to register their words. When the Arkuden left, she crawled forward to overhear the elf lord speak to his followers.

Her time as a Silvanesti slave had given Mara only a rudimentary comprehension of the Elvish language, but she understood bits and pieces of what Balif said, and she had glimpsed the cache of nomad weapons. The words whirled confusingly through her head like a dust storm on the plains, coalescing with what she had seen, forming a realization dark and terrifying: The Arkuden must be in league with the elves. He had traded the secret of making bronze for the nomads' bows and arrows. He was a traitor, not only to the human cause, but to his own sister.

Karada must be told. The knowledge would cause her pain, but ultimately she would be grateful to know the truth. Mara would be forgiven and restored to her rightful place at Karada's feet, a beloved daughter of the great nomad chief, and together they would drive the rapacious Silvanesti from the plains forever.

In the midst of this satisfying vision, Mara frowned. The Arkuden had seemed in a great hurry just now. He was obviously bent on some urgent scheme. Silvanesti treachery knew no bounds. They could be planning anything with the Arkuden. Anything at all. Quick action was needed.

Her heart pounded. Resolution flowed through her limbs.

She would do it. She would spare every human on the plain from enduring what she had suffered at the hands of the elves. Most of all, she would save her beloved Karada.

Chapter 20

Plainsmen say Soli, the white moon, is a messenger of change. It hugs the horizon when it first appears and rises into the open sky reluctantly. In spring and autumn it ascends modestly and in winter hardly appears at all above the mountains rimming the Valley of the Falls. Because of its habits, the plainsmen say Soli brings rain in the spring by climbing higher in the sky to pour water on the thirsty soil below, and it carries the green leaves away in the fall (sinking to the its low, winter-time position). Only in summer did Soli linger near the zenith of heaven, keeping temperatures high. It never made sense to Amero that a cool moon rather than the hot sun should be blamed for summer's heat, but that was the lore he'd learned from his mother, a long time ago.

Now, standing with Lyopi between two bonfires, surrounded by the whole of Yala-tene, the nomad band, former raiders, a highborn elf, and Duranix, Amero found himself sweating. It was the fires, he told himself, or maybe all the wine he'd drunk—

Be honest, Duranix's silent voice said inside his head. *You're nervous!*

I guess I am, Amero replied.

The nomad pipers finished their tune, and silence fell over the assembly. No one seemed quite sure what to do next, so Balif, playing the ignorant foreigner, asked, "What happens now?"

"We declare ourselves mates before the oldest person present," said Lyopi. "That would be Jenla."

The gardener, leaning on Tepa's arm, said mischievously, "I'm not the oldest one here." She stared pointedly at Balif.

"But I'm not a human," Balif objected. "Besides, Farolenu is older than I—by two and a half decades."

Amero cleared his throat. "If we're going to be truthful, there's one here older even than the elves." He looked up at the dragon, smiling. "You're past two hundred, aren't you?"

"Well past," agreed Duranix.

"Will you hear our declaration?"

The bronze dragon nodded, a habit he'd acquired since knowing Amero. His scales rang with the gesture.

"Come forward and face us," Amero said.

Duranix clomped toward them, scattering villagers in his way. Framed by the twin bonfires, his metallic scales took on the color of fire itself. He opened his wings to their fullest extent, some forty paces from tip to tip and inflated his broad chest with air.

Amero winked at Lyopi. His old friend was showing off.

"I am Amero, son of Oto and Kinar," the Arkuden shouted, "brother of Nianki and Menni, called the Dragon's Son!"

There was some muttering at the mention of Menni, but the declaration went on.

Lyopi, her chestnut hair free of its usual braid and falling in shining waves to her waist, spoke. "I am Lyopi, daughter of Bydas and Ensamen, sister of Unar."

Her voice broke on the name of her murdered brother, and Amero took her hand, squeezing it gently.

In unison they said, "Know all that we are mated, that all we have belongs to both of us!"

They bowed together to Duranix. "Such a lot of trouble just to breed," he said in his booming voice. Some of the nomads laughed.

"You should say, 'I know you, Amero and Lyopi,' " Amero prompted.

"I know you, Amero and Lyopi," the dragon repeated

dutifully. "Stubborn, curious, passionate, and loyal are you both. Salute!"

He threw back his head and let his jaws gape. Blue-white lightning erupted from his mouth, crackling straight up into the starry sky. The crowd shifted and exclaimed at the display of power.

Amero's own awed expression, as he stared up at the bolt lancing into the stars, dissolved into a frown of characteristic curiosity. Where did it go? he wondered. Did the bolt travel forever until it struck something, or did it fade out in time, like a spark carried aloft from a campfire?

Lyopi tugged at his arm and whispered, "Remember me? I'm your mate."

They embraced and kissed to the cheers of the crowd. The flute players found some drummers among the villagers, and they struck up a fast melody. Round dances sprang up in the crowd as well-wishers flowed past Amero and Lyopi.

Balif was one of the first. "Good fortune to you," the elf said sincerely. "It's been quite an experience for me, coming here. Remind me to thank Karada for capturing us!"

"Peace to you, Lord Balif," said Amero. "Peace in the truest sense. I hope the war between you and my sister is over for good."

"We shall see. Farewell to you both."

Farolenu clasped hands with Amero and presented Lyopi with a small golden charm on a length of woven grass twine. It glittered in the firelight. Amero tied it around Lyopi's neck as she examined it.

"It's pretty," she said, pleased. "A beetle?"

"A spider," said Farolenu. "The symbol of my smithing guild."

He and Balif were soon swallowed in the crowd. Old friends streamed past, wishing the newly mated couple well—Adjat the potter, Montu the cooper, Hulami, Targun,

Pakito, and Samtu. The amiable giant all but wrung Amero's hand off, he was so enthusiastic.

"Being mated is the best thing in the world!" he enthused. "Better than a fine horse or a straight spear!"

"Good to know you rate so highly," Lyopi said to Samtu.

The stout nomad woman eyed her towering mate. "He didn't say it was better than elk steak. That's what he loves most, you know."

"Now, Sammi—" Pakito began. Laughing, she pulled him away so others could approach.

Beramun emerged from the press with Harak. Her left arm was in a sling, and she looked wan. Amero had heard about developments between them from Karada, but this was the first time he'd seen them together.

"Thank you for everything," Amero said to Beramun. "None of this would be happening if it weren't for you."

"I only did what others tried to do. Fate and the Great Spirits let me find Karada."

"I didn't mean that, though you were wonderful on your mission, too. I meant you refused me, and for that I'm grateful."

"As am I," said Harak with a grin.

"Will you be joining Karada's band?" Lyopi asked.

"I go where Beramun goes," he said simply. "I don't much care where that is."

Beramun said, "I don't know what we'll end up doing, but we are leaving with Karada tomorrow."

She and Lyopi kissed each other's cheek, then she did the same to Amero.

They exchanged words with Bahco, Hekani, and almost the entire crowd present. The only conspicuous absence was Karada. To Amero's query, Bahco said he hadn't seen his chief since before moonrise.

Amero realized it was hard for his sister to see him mated and happy. She herself would likely never know a moment such as this.

"I must find Nianki," he said in Lyopi's ear. "I need to see her."

She understood. "Try dark and quiet places. If I were Karada, that's where I'd be right now."

He promised to return to Lyopi's house—their house—before too late. Giving his hand a squeeze, she let him go. Amero slipped into the happy throng and worked his way away from the noise and fire.

He called silently to Duranix, *Have you seen Karada?*

Not lately, but she's near. I can sense her presence.

Amero stopped in his tracks. *You can?*

My senses have grown sharper with the years. Nowadays, her thoughts seem as loud as yours were when we first met.

Dust swirled over the festive mob. Amero looked up and saw Duranix had taken wing.

Going home? he asked the dragon.

Hunting. The trifles you served at your feast only teased my appetite. There's a great herd of elk a few leagues from here. I'm off to roast a few. . . .

Good luck, thought Amero. *Let's talk tomorrow. I have new ideas for Yala-tene I need your help to accomplish.*

Of course you do. Till then.

"Until then," Amero murmured aloud.

The vast bulk of the dragon blotted out the stars as he winged away to the southwest. Amero felt great gladness as he watched the departure. Duranix's responses were more like his old self. Once he became involved in daily life in the village again, the wanderlust of recent days was sure to leave him.

Since Bahco said he hadn't seen Karada in their camp, Amero started his search with the lakeshore from the west baffle back to the old foundry. He saw the Silvanesti sleeping on their bedrolls outside the broken foundry walls, but he found no sign of his sister. Doubling back, he went as far as the old raider camp and the stone towers of the fallen bridge. His feet crunched over the dross of battle—broken spears and throwing sticks, scraps of leather armor. Compared to the life and noise of the feast, the site of Zannian's camp was like a graveyard. Nianki wasn't there, so he quickly left.

The only remaining possibility was the nomad camp. Perhaps she had returned there after Bahco left for the mating ceremony. Amero skirted the fringes of the celebration, as he didn't want to be delayed by well-meaning greetings.

The camp itself was calm. A few dogs tied in front of their masters' tents barked at him as he passed. At one spot he saw something he hadn't seen before—a willow rack laden with cured yevi hides. The yevi pack that had accompanied the raiders to the valley had been devastated during the siege, and before Karada's arrival most had been killed or run off. Nomad hunters searched the neighboring valleys after the final battle, killing every yevi they found. Their gray, shaggy skins were too coarse to wear, but Amero knew why Karada's people saved the hides. Posted in the high passes, yevi pelts served as a potent warning to other would-be marauders.

Amero walked through the camp. Arriving at last at her tent, he found Karada. She was seated by the fire and draped in her white wolf's robe. Their blind brother sat a few steps away, a trencher of meat before him. Amero smiled. Karada must have brought him the food.

"Nianki," he said. She didn't look up, but Zannian tilted his head and turned sightless eyes toward his elder brother.

"Is it done?" she asked, poking the low flames with a stick.

"It is. I am mated at last."

"Good for you," said Zannian. "Is Beramun with you? I heard she agreed to see me."

"I'm alone."

Amero crossed the large tent and sat down at the hearth across from his sister. She dropped her stick into the flames.

"I wish you'd been there," he said. "The whole valley turned out to see us. As the oldest creature in the valley, Duranix played the elder's part."

"We'll be gone by midday tomorrow," Karada said abruptly. "I wanted to be out before then, but Bearclaw Gap is too narrow to allow the band to ride out more than two abreast."

"There's no hurry, you know. Stay longer if you want."

"No, it's time to go. I've stayed long enough, and I can't bear to see you—" She cut herself off, jaw muscles jumping as she clenched her teeth.

"You both sound strange," Zannian said, yawning. "What's wrong? You're talking like a jilted lover, Karada."

"Shut up," she told him.

"Hmph," Zannian said, yawned widely, and pushed his trencher aside. He curled up on a bearskin with his back to them and soon was snoring.

"I thought he'd never sleep," she grumbled. "I put herbs in his wine—the same ones I used to soothe Beramun."

"Don't worry about him. I'll make a gardener of him yet."

She looked him in the face for the first time. "Don't be a complete fool, will you, Amero? Brother or not, he's a savage, bloody killer and will be again if he gets the chance."

"People change."

"No, they don't. Have you forgotten so soon what he tried to do to your village?"

Now it was Amero's turn to look away. "I'll be careful," he promised. "Besides, Lyopi won't let me do anything stupid."

Mentioning his new mate was a mistake. Nianki brought her fist down on a hearthstone, splitting her knuckles. Amero rose, expressing concern.

"Stop!" she said, holding up her bleeding hand. "Pain helps sometimes. I found that out long ago. Don't try to comfort me."

Amero sat down with a thump. Her calm, flat statement—*pain helps sometimes*—sent a chill down his back.

"I only want to be a good brother," he said at last.

"You are good. Most brothers wouldn't have anything to do with a tormented, unnatural sister like me. But you're always kind." She covered her eyes with her hands. "Sometimes that just makes it harder. Your kindness can be as bitter as Zannian's hatred."

The tent was quiet, save for the crack and pop of the fire. Into the awkward silence, Amero said, "What if I asked Balif for help? An elf used spirit power to inflict this curse on you. Perhaps another elf can cure you. I know he'll help if he can. He and I have become friends."

Nianki lowered her hands and gazed wonderingly at Amero. She laughed, a short, harsh bark of sound.

"Merciful spirits! He's not your friend! He's an honorable enemy, no more. Besides, I don't want all of Silvanost to know my problems."

"They may already. Vedvedsica's in disgrace, Balif says. His past doings are a public scandal. If there's a chance Balif could help—"

"Enough! I don't want to talk about it any more! I will be fine." With effort she added in a calmer tone, "Go home, Amero. I'm sure your new mate wonders where you are."

He circled the hearth, bent down, and took her under the arms, dragging her to her feet. Nianki pulled out of his grip easily, though she looked a bit flushed.

"Farewell, sister. I suppose I won't see you tomorrow."

"No. I'll send Zannian to you."

"I'll take care of him."

She nodded. He clenched his empty hands into fists, resisting the urge to embrace her.

"Peace to you, Nianki, for all your life," he said and left the tent. He didn't hear her murmured response.

"Peace to you, Arkuden. Peace forever."

* * * * *

The feast had broken up by the time Amero left his sister. Small bands of nomads and villagers carried on earnestly, but the majority had gone to bed. The great bonfires were heaps of ashes now, with a few bright embers winking through. Heat shimmered above the firepits, blurring the cold stars. Soli was high, gathering in the offering of heat, saving it for the next sweltering summer day.

Amero walked faster. He felt very guilty for having left Lyopi so long, on this night of all nights. Oh, well, he could spend the next decade or two making it up to her. The thought made him grin as he climbed the mound of rubble outside the north baffle.

Compared to the open valley, the streets of Yala-tene were dim and close. By day the stone houses soaked up heat from the sun and remained warm all night. In the winter this was a blessing, but in summer it was close to intolerable. Many villagers abandoned their houses in the warmest weather and slept outside. Some, like Hekani, preferred to camp outside the walls most nights, so long as no rain was falling.

The route Amero followed back to his and Lyopi's house was deserted. He saw no one on the way, met no families sleeping on the cooler dirt path. By Soli's light he could see the crossing paths ahead. To the right was the lane leading home. Sweating from the sultry night and his brisk pace, Amero decided to detour long enough to get a dipper of cool water from the cistern at the Offertory.

As he crossed the lane, he heard the soft scrape of leather on stone. He glanced around and saw nothing. The shadows were too deep.

No need to be so jumpy, he chided himself. There were no Jade Men left, seeking his blood.

The outer walls of the Offertory shone in the moonlight. Lutar was long set, so the pure white light of Soli was bright on the white stones. The upper courses of the wall had been mined away during the siege, but enough was left to shine like a beacon in the night. Amero went inside to the cistern. The Sensarku's drinking gourd was still hanging on its peg. He stirred the water, then filled the dipper.

Clink. Metal on stone.

"Hello?" he called. "Is someone there?"

No answer. He drank the water and returned the gourd to its place.

"Can't sleep?" he said, conversing with his unseen guest. "I can't blame you. It's too hot in the village. Water's good, though. Help yourself."

He turned to go. As he passed through the gap in the Offertory walls, he heard the rapid patter of feet coming at him. Puzzled, he faced the oncoming sound.

Out of the darkness hurtled a slender figure, wrapped in a black ox hide cape. He got a fleeting impression of a pale face wreathed in curly auburn hair. The next thing Amero knew, a span of sharp bronze penetrated his buckskin shirt, then the flesh below his left ribs.

Astonished, he grasped the two hands holding the dagger's handle and forced them back. The blade twisted as it was pulled out. Blood sluiced from the wound, pouring down his leg and over his feet.

"Die, traitor!" said a high, quavering voice.

* * * * *

Duranix devoured six full-grown elk before midnight and then settled down to sleep off his prodigious meal. His heavy, dreamless rest ended suddenly when he felt a sharp pain in his lower left side. The sensation was so strong and so real that he felt along his scaly flank, expecting to find a fresh wound. There was none.

His long neck snapped around, and he stared at the intervening mountains. Something was wrong—deadly wrong.

"Amero," he said, and launched himself skyward.

* * * * *

Karada took her hand out of the fire. Since Amero's departure, she'd been testing herself, seeing how long she could bear a flame against the palm of her hand. Zannian continued to snore behind her.

She counted the thud of her heartbeat silently. One, two, three, four . . . the skin on her palm began to blister. Suddenly, an even stronger pain lanced into her side. Karada gasped and slumped away from the hearth. Under the wolfskin robe the flesh on her left side, between her ribs and hip bone, was unbroken, but it felt for all the world as though she'd been stabbed.

Zannian snorted and stirred. He pushed himself up on one hand, muttering obscenities. "Who did that?" he growled, obviously thinking himself still in command of his raiders. "Which one of you scum poked me with your dagger?"

Karada tied a beaded belt tightly around her waist and grabbed her sword belt. If she and Zannian both felt the stabbing pain in the same spot at the same time, Amero must have felt it, too. Something about that thought filled her with dread. A sense of urgency sent her running from the tent.

She had to find him. She had to find Amero *now.*

* * * * *

Lyopi sat up a long time, waiting for her man to come home. She knew his meeting with Karada would be difficult, but she didn't begrudge him the time it would take to say good-bye to his powerful, troubled sister. Midnight came and went, and still Amero did not return. Patience gave way to annoyance. Certainly, this wasn't the first night they'd spent together, but it was supposed to be an important one. Where was that inconsiderate, overgrown boy?

A sound at the door flap sent her striding to the opening. She drew back the flap, and a bloody spectre barred her way. Lyopi was not easily frightened, but this unexpected apparition brought a cry of surprise to her lips.

The gory vision raised its head, and Lyopi felt her stomach clench in horror.

"Amero!"

He fell into her arms. She backed inside, half-dragging her blood-soaked mate with her. After lowering him to the floor, she felt at his neck for a pulse. It was there, weak and rapid, but he'd lost—by the ancestors!—he'd lost so much blood!

There was a deep wound in his left side, obviously made by a metal blade. No flint knife could make so thin and clean a cut, though it appeared the knife had been twisted in the wound.

All this she took in even as she was frantically wadding a piece of doeskin and pressing it to the bleeding wound. Amero stirred, trying to escape the pain her pressure created.

"Be still!" she snapped, fear coursing through her. "You're bleeding to death!"

He coughed feebly, his body spasming. He said something, but the words bubbled so horribly in his throat she couldn't make them out.

"What?" She pressed hard on the makeshift bandage with her strong hands. "Who did this to you, Amero?"

"Sensarku girl."

He must be delirious. All the Sensarku had died on he western plain with their leader, Tiphan. There were one left, in Yala-tene or anywhere else.

Amero trembled violently. His teeth chattered. Lyopi ulled a fleecy hide over him and cradled his head in her ap. Looking toward the doorway, she shouted for help.

"Lyopi," he whispered.

"Shh, don't talk." She shouted again for help.

"Don't be angry," he said weakly.

"I'm not angry, Amero, but I'll never forgive you if ou die!"

"Duranix . . ."

Tears of terror and frustration were coursing down er cheeks. "I don't know where he is!"

"So many things to know . . . so many."

He exhaled a long, slow breath. It was his last.

* * * * *

Duranix had never flown so fast, not even while chasng Sthenn around the world. He couldn't seem to find ny greater speed, no matter how he canted his wings or notted his tremendous muscles. He would be too late. Ie knew it.

Amero spoke his name, and he demanded, *Why didn't ou wait? I was coming!*

Like a fading echo, he heard: *So many things to know . . so many.* That was all. Though Duranix called and alled, he heard nothing more.

His wings slowed. The throbbing strain in his flying nuscles eased, but a more pervasive and subtle pain held)uranix in an unbreakable grip. He roared at the empty ky. His bellow solved nothing. The pain remained. He lew on.

* * * * *

Karada ran a hundred steps before she staggered to a stop, falling against a tent pitched by the path. Down she slid to her knees, feeling as though she were plunging into an icy river. Vicious cold climbed to her neck then her eyes. When it reached the top of her head, it slowly left her.

Someone was calling her name. "Karada! Karada!"

Her vision cleared. Mara was kneeling in front of her shaking her by the shoulders.

"What? What?"

"Karada, we're safe now!" Mara said, green eyes ablaze "I saved us! I saved us all!"

"What are you talking about?"

"I stopped the Arkuden!"

Cold fury as hard and sharp as flint put strength back into the nomad chief. She seized Mara by the hair and hauled her upright.

"What have you done?" she snarled, shaking the girl so hard her neck bones creaked.

Mara's hands clutched futilely at the strong fingers entwined in her hair, her words punctuated by yelps of pain. "I struck him down, Karada! For all of us! For you! He was your brother, but he was a *traitor!* He gave us over to the Silvanesti—"

Karada uttered a scream of pure anguish, punctuated by Mara's whimpering, and drew her sword.

The tumult awakened the nomads, and they spilled out of their tents. They saw their chief, tears streaming down her face, holding the girl Mara by the hair Karada's sword was bared.

"I'll kill you!" Karada rasped.

"Karada, please, listen! I did it for you! Your fight to drive the elves off our ancestral lands was doomed! The Arkuden betrayed you—"

Up went the gleaming sword. Mara stopped clutching at her hair and threw up her hands as though to ward

:f the blow. It never fell. Karada's sword hand was held armless in Pakito's mighty grip.

"Let me go, Pakito!"

"No, chief. I don't know what's happened here, but ɔu can't kill this helpless girl." He yanked the sword om her hand. Turning, he gave it to Samtu, who stood ehind him, her own weapon at the ready.

"Let her go, Karada," Samtu said. "We won't let her et away."

The nomad chief opened her hand, releasing her hold n Mara's tangled hair. The girl dropped heavily at her feet, 'eeping. When she tried to wrap her arms around the ief's ankles, Karada kicked her until she shrank away. Iara groveled, not even protesting the blows she'd taken.

"What's she done?" Samtu asked, grimacing at the dis-isteful display.

"I think . . . she's killed Amero."

The assembled nomads exclaimed and swore in mazement.

"When did this happen?" demanded Bahco, clutching panther-skin wrap around his waist.

"Just now," whispered Karada.

The nomads looked around, as though expecting to ee Amero's body lying at their feet. "Where? Where he?"

Karada repeated the question to Mara. When the wail-ıg girl did not answer, Karada kicked her hard. Pakito romptly lifted his leader off her feet and set her down ut of reach of the girl. Samtu took hold of Mara's collar nd pulled her to her feet.

"The Arkuden betrayed us!" Mara sobbed. "He traded ur bows and arrows to the elves in exchange for the ecret of making bronze!"

The assembled nomads muttered loudly at that. Pakito ellowed for silence.

"This girl is addled!" he said angrily. "You can't go by

what she says. The Arkuden is a wise and honorable man
He wouldn't betray us to the Silvanesti!"

"There's one way to find out," said Bahco. He dresse
quickly and gathered a few men. They headed to the vil
lage foundry.

Samtu laid a gentle hand on Karada's arm. "Let's fin
the Arkuden," she said. "Maybe this is nothing mor
than a bad dream the girl had."

"My brother is dead," was the flat response. "Sh
killed him."

Pushed along by Samtu, Karada went with Pakito an
two dozen nomads to the village. They found the street
filled with torch-bearing villagers. All of Yala-tene seeme
to be awake.

Karada led them unerringly through the crowd, directl
to Lyopi's house. By the hearth, covered with an elk hide
lay Amero. Lyopi sat by his head, hands clasped to he
lips. She looked up when Karada entered.

"Sensarku girl," Lyopi said weakly. "When I aske
who stabbed him, that's what he said."

Karada nodded. "It was the girl Mara. We have her."

Lyopi turned away, looking back at her dead mate
Karada whirled and walked outside, unable to bear the sigh
of her brother's still, slack face—the face that in life ha
always been so animated, so full of curiosity and vitality.

Spying the trail of blood outside the door, Karada fol
lowed it back to the Offertory. There was more bloo
there, and something else—a bronze dagger. She picke
it up, hands shaking. She recognized the weapon; she'
taken it from Balif the night of his capture. It was th
same one she'd let Mara keep after expelling her for he
false accusation of Harak.

She ran back to Lyopi's house through lanes fille
with stunned, silent villagers. Outside the house, Mar
was slumped on the ground between two angry-lookin
nomads. Karada stalked over. She lifted Mara by th

'ont of her doeskin tunic until the girl's toes barely ›uched the ground.

"No matter what happens, no matter what anyone .se says or does, I'm going to kill you," Karada said. All ›lor drained from Mara's face, leaving her freckles :anding out starkly. She was speechless with terror.

Pakito came out of the house, and Karada thrust the loody dagger at him. "Take this," she commanded. Keep it safe. It's what she killed him with." Pakito care- ılly put the weapon in his belt, then watched his chief 'arily, prepared to intervene should she try to harm Iara.

Karada noticed his scrutiny. Disgusted, she threw Iara at his feet. "Put her in Nacris's old tent. Chain her › she can't run away!"

Pakito gestured, and two nomads spirited Mara away.

Lyopi emerged, supported on Samtu's arm. Tears ran own her cheeks. The breast of her tunic was soaked 'ith them, but her grief was silent. She took Karada's ands in hers.

"The dragon must be told," she said, her voice harsh nd low with anguish. "Who will tell him? Who will tell ›uranix Amero is dead?"

Karada lifted eyes to the night sky, an unnatural chill aising gooseflesh on her arms. "Duranix already nows," she replied.

Chapter 21

Bahco led half a hundred nomads to the elves' camp By torchlight, the men ran among the sleeping Silvanest kicking them awake, then holding them at sword poin A few elves fought back, and a real battle might hav broken out had not Balif intervened. His considerabl presence managed to calm not only his own soldiers bu Bahco's angry men as well.

"What's this about?" the elf lord demanded once som order had been restored.

"The Arkuden has been killed!" Bahco snapped, hi sword still in his hand.

Balif's eyes flickered with surprise and concern. "Hov did it happen?"

After giving Balif the few details he knew, Bahc ordered his men to search the Silvanesti baggage. Balif' protests were overridden as the dark-skinned noma asked, "Is it true? Did the Arkuden trade bows an arrows for the secret to making bronze?"

"I had no dealings of that kind with the Arkuden."

At that moment, the searchers found the hidden bows

"No dealings?" Bahco raged, shaking a bowstave unde the elf lord's nose. "Then what are these—tent stakes?"

Balif drew his robe and his dignity close around himsel "Take me to Karada. I will explain everything to her."

The nomads mouthed ugly threats as Balif walke out with Bahco. The elf lord wanted reassurances the wouldn't harm his elves. Though Bahco refused t make such a promise, he raised his voice for all to hea and said, "If your people behave, my men will no harm them."

Balif surveyed his small, outnumbered troop. "Sit down," he said severely. "Do nothing and say nothing until I return." When they hesitated, he commanded, "Do as I say!"

One by one, the elves complied, sitting down on their bedrolls and closing their mouths into thin, stubborn lines.

Bahco, Balif, and the newly discovered bows went back to Yala-tene. Amid the weeping, wailing crowd outside Lyopi's house, Bahco found his chief. She seemed unnaturally composed. Her icy demeanor alarmed Bahco.

"Mind what you say and do, elf," he muttered. "She's very angry!"

Balif stepped out in front of Bahco and bowed to Lyopi. "Lady," he said solemnly, "my deepest condolences. The Arkuden was a great and wise man. What aid may I give you in this dire time?"

She looked up at him, tears standing in her shadowed eyes. "Amero was sick of war. Please, whatever the cause, do not fight here." Lyopi said this as much for Karada's benefit as Balif's.

Wordlessly, Bahco handed Karada the bows taken from the elves.

She looked at them and her strangely calm face seemed to grow even more still. "So, it's true," she said.

"No, it is not," Balif insisted.

She struck him across the face with a bowstave. The tough fruitwood cracked loudly, and Balif was knocked to the ground. People in the sobbing crowd exclaimed, reminding Karada of Lyopi's stricture against violence.

Balif stayed where he was. Ears ringing from the impact, he put a hand gingerly to his face. The skin wasn't broken, but he would have a tremendous bruise there—if he lived so long.

"Is this how you repay my trust?" Karada shouted at him. "Stealing our weapons? Your treachery has cost my brother his life!" Her face had gone ashen by torchlight, the scars on her throat standing out lividly.

"I did not steal the bows," Balif said clearly from his position on the ground. "Nor did I exchange bronze-making information for them with the Arkuden or anyone else. My soldiers *bought* the weapons from members of your band, Karada. They traded gold and bronze for them. Shall I name the nomads who bartered with us? Better yet, to satisfy yourself of the truth of what I say, examine your warriors. Ask the ones carrying gold and no bows if they have adequate answers for why their weapons are missing."

Karada regarded him wordlessly for the space of three heartbeats, then she exploded into action. She drew her sword and whirled in a circle, howling and slashing at the air. Villagers scattered, and even her own people backed quickly out of reach. Balif was happy he was still on the ground.

"Is there no honor left in Karada's band?" she cried when her frenzy abated.

Silence greeted her question, then Balif announced, "I'm going to stand." He waited for her reaction, but she simply stood there shaking with rage and grief.

He got to his feet slowly. "I did betray your trust, Karada," he said, "but I had reasons for doing so. My people also had misgivings about my sharing the secret of bronze-making. They wondered if I was betraying my sovereign and my race, but there was no betrayal. Beneath the giving of metal and the taking of bows is a more important principle: peace. I did it for peace."

Exclamations of disbelief greeted this. Ignoring the throbbing pain in his head, Balif raised his voice and continued. "By giving you knowledge of bronze, I know I'm equipping you to be even more dangerous. That's part of my goal. By making you more powerful, I hope to dissuade my lord Silvanos and his counselors from warring on you. If we both have bronze armor and blades, the cost of battle will be too high. I sought to bring home examples of your new throwing weapon for the same purpose. If we are equal in strength, no sane mind should crave war."

Lyopi spoke up before anyone else could do so. "I believe you, Lord Balif. I think Amero would have approved of your actions, if he had known. Peace is what he wanted more than anything else—even more," she added, choking back tears, "than he wanted the secret of bronze."

Everyone looked to Karada, waiting for her response. It was a long time coming, but finally the sword fell from her hand. It rang loudly when it struck the ground.

"I'm taking back all the bows," she said, almost inaudibly. "I'll find who traded them to you and deal with them later. Go back to your camp, Balif. Stay there until we leave. I don't want to see you or hear of you until then."

Balif bowed curtly to her, then to Lyopi with more feeling. He vanished into the crowd. People gave way to him slowly, but no one raised a hand against him.

The crowd seemed reluctant to leave. Lyopi begged them to go home, though, and they slowly dispersed. Samtu took Lyopi, who was swaying on her feet, inside the house, and Pakito sent Bahco to post guards around the elves, to keep things calm. Finally, only the giant and his chieftain remained.

Karada picked up a torch left behind by a villager and trudged away, not toward the north baffle and her own camp, but west. Pakito would've followed, but she put a stop to that.

"Go back to Samtu, Pakito. Help her comfort Lyopi. I'm going to wait for Duranix."

* * * * *

Dawn was not far off when Duranix crossed the last line of mountains before the Valley of the Falls. It was the still time, when most animals were asleep. Even so, the valley felt charged as he flew into it, replete with powerful emotions.

He crossed the dull silver triangle of the lake, heading for the village. Before the walls gained distinction from the dark cliffs behind them, Duranix saw a pinpoint of light on the stony beach between the town wall and his cave. Lowering a wing, he descended toward the light, which quickly resolved itself into a burning torch.

He landed. A solitary figure stirred beside the torch.

"Karada," he said, keeping his great voice low.

"Dragon," she greeted him. "He's dead."

"I know." He asked how it happened. Karada explained about Mara. By the time she finished the story of bronze and bows, Duranix was practically speechless with astonishment.

Finding his tongue at last, he exclaimed, "After all we've faced—yevi, raiders, green-painted assassins, wild humans, elves, *Sthenn!*—Amero is murdered by a crazy child with a bronze dagger? Over some bits of metal and bent wood sticks?" He raised one hind claw and drove it down again. The resulting blow rang through the valley. "Where is the justice in that?" he demanded.

"There is none. Good-bye, dragon."

She turned away. There was a strange note of finality in her voice that penetrated the dragon's preoccupation.

"You aren't leading your band out now, in the middle of the night, are you?" he asked.

"I'm not leading them anywhere."

Without warning, Duranix promptly shrank to human form and size, becoming a muscular man with golden yellow hair, clad in a deerskin kilt. He hadn't assumed human guise in a long time, but it seemed appropriate just now.

Long ago, during her first visit to Yala-tene, Karada had seen Duranix both take on human shape and revert to dragon form. It was a remarkable thing to witness the enormous bronze beast compress himself into a human body, no matter how unusually tall and sturdy it was.

Taking her by the shoulders, Duranix gave her a shake. "What do you mean?" he asked. Then, his golden eyes widening, he added, "You are thinking of ending your life, aren't you? You mustn't do that!"

She pulled away from his hands. "You don't understand. I'm already dead. My life was tied to Amero's by more than bonds of kinship. Do you know I felt his death wound?" She put a hand to her side. "It was here, as if I'd taken the dagger thrust myself. I felt his death like an icy wave of water closing over my head. That's how close Amero and I were!"

"Foolish woman! I felt it too! It woke me from a deep sleep. We who loved Amero were linked to him in spirit, not by mere bonds of friendship, blood, or desire. Just because you despair doesn't mean your life is over or that it isn't valued by others."

"I can't live, knowing he's gone," she declared helplessly.

"And if you kill yourself, what will that accomplish? Your spirit will still not be at rest. More importantly, what will become of your people? Who will lead them?"

"Pakito . . . Samtu . . . Bahco . . ."

"Will they be able to stand up to the Silvanesti? Can any of them hold your band together in the face of privation and defeat, as you have?" When she didn't answer, Duranix glared at her, eyes flashing. "So you're not content to take your own life, you're willing to condemn your followers to defeat and slavery, too. What a selfish end! Is that how the Scarred One will be remembered—too weak to survive one blow, one death?"

His words kindled a spark in her at last. She took a step toward him. Duranix returned her angry gaze.

"I am not weak," she said, memories of all she had survived—the deaths of her parents, capture by Silvanesti soldiers, deprivation, loneliness—flashing through her mind.

"Prove it then. Survive. Live as long and as well as you can! You honor your people and Amero's memory by doing so."

Karada closed her eyes tightly, swaying a little. When she opened them again she said, "What about you, dragon? What will you do?"

He looked at the walls of Yala-tene. "I don't know. I'm sick of this place, sick of all the violent, smelly humans who infest my peaceful valley. For Amero's sake, I can't knock the village down and chase everyone away, so perhaps I'll leave." A memory of another place came to his mind. "Yes, I'll go somewhere far away."

She rubbed a hand over her red-rimmed eyes. "My band was leaving tomorrow. I'll have to put off our departure until we've settled some things—the elves, the girl Mara."

"Cut her throat and be done with it."

"It isn't that simple. There's likely to be sympathy for her, once the story of the hidden bows gets around." She inhaled deeply. "And there's Zannian."

"What has he to do with anything?"

"He lives because Amero wanted him to live. Amero believed he could teach our brother to be a peaceful man. I never shared his confidence in Zannian's ability to change, and I'm not so forgiving of the raiders' crimes." She frowned. "But he is my brother, too. And now, my responsibility."

Still in human form, Duranix went with her to Lyopi's house and there viewed Amero's body. With his gray-flecked beard, the man he'd become hardly resembled the inquisitive youth Duranix had plucked from a tree and saved from the yevi all those years ago.

What an evanescent thing is human life, the dragon thought. Was it the brevity of their existence that made them feel so vulnerable, fearful, and violent?

It was a question Amero would have enjoyed discussing with Duranix. No one present could do it justice, so the dragon kept his thought to himself.

* * * * *

Karada called a great council of her band and the people of Yala-tene. The resulting crowd was so large they had to assemble on open ground west of the wall, near the hill where Amero's friend and foundry master, Huru, had fought the raiders and died defending his village.

With everyone present except the Silvanesti and those nomads appointed to guard them, over sixteen hundred people were gathered to hear Karada, Lyopi, and the elders speak. The first matter addressed was how to honor Amero. The village elders suggested an elaborate funeral pyre, either on the valley floor or, as Jenla suggested, on the old Offertory in the village. Jenla's idea was on the verge of being approved when Duranix arrived, still in his fair-haired human shape. He was taller than anyone present, topping even Pakito by a handspan, and caused a stir when he appeared.

After obtaining Lyopi's permission to join the discussion, the dragon-man spoke against the use of the old Offertory. With its reminders of the Sensarku's strange antics, he said this would not be a location that would please Amero.

Lyopi asked what he would suggest.

"Before the cave-in of the storage tunnels many years ago, you humans usually buried your dead," Duranix replied. "I think Amero should be put in a special place in the mountains, sealed forever inside. Then there will always be a place you can come and be near him."

Karada asked if he had a place in mind.

"My cave."

This took the humans aback. Tepa spoke for all when he asked, "If the Arkuden is sealed in your cave, where will you be?"

"Far away," said the dragon. "Once Amero is put to rest, I am leaving the Valley of the Falls forever."

Consternation erupted. Villagers rose to their feet and cried out against this idea. Who would protect them if both Amero and the dragon were gone? Duranix listened implacably, unmoved by their fears.

Karada called roughly for silence. The anxious villagers gradually settled down.

Duranix said, not unkindly, "My friendship was with Amero. Though I think well of some of you, I've realized I can't stay here any longer, minding your small affairs and defending you from your own vicious brethren. I've been too much with humanity these past thirty years. It's time for me to go, to find and coexist with those of my own kind."

They continued to plead with him, wondering plaintively how they would survive without their protector.

"How did you survive before you came here?" he asked vexedly.

"We wandered," Jenla said. "But we can't go back to those ways. Some of us are too old, and the younger ones know no other life than this."

"Then we'll stay here," Tepa said stoutly, grasping her hand. "The soil is fertile, the hunting is good, and the Arkuden's wall is high." He looked to Karada. "And we have friends, if we need them, yes?"

The nomad chieftain nodded curtly, and the villagers' anxiety was slowly replaced by hope.

It was agreed Amero would be placed in the great cave behind the waterfall. Duranix would seal all the entrances. The burial would take place before sundown that very day.

Some of the crowd had begun to move away, but Karada's loud voice halted them, reminding them there were other matters to settle.

"First, the murderer of Amero must be punished," she announced.

Adjat the potter, a distant kinsman to Mara, rose. "The girl has lost her wits," he said bluntly. "She's mad with fear and hatred of the Silvanesti."

"So? Are we just to forget what she has done?"

Intimidated, Adjat replied, "Of course not. It just seems . . . wrong to condemn the feeble-minded."

"Seems perfectly right to me," Karada said. "Murder should be repaid with death. That is the way of the plains."

"This is not the plains, great chief," Hulami the wine-maker said.

They argued fruitlessly a while, until Karada at last turned to Lyopi.

"You were his woman," said Amero's sister. "What do you say?"

"I'd gladly wring her neck," Lyopi said, her voice tired but strong. Though Karada nodded sagely, the village elders looked appalled. Lyopi went on. "But I can't. The wretched girl has known nothing but torment and fear since she left Yala-tene with Tiphan last winter. Maybe he's the true author of this deed—abetted by Silvanesti taskmasters and her oppressive devotion to Karada."

It was obvious Karada wanted to speak, but having asked Lyopi her opinion, the nomad chieftain kept silent.

Lyopi said, "I say exile her. Turn her loose on the open plain and let the spirits of the land and air decide her fate. That's what our ancestors would have done."

This verdict won instant favor from the villagers in the crowd, who were sick of bloodshed. The elders quickly approved exile for Mara.

Karada turned to Duranix in disgust. "Crazed as she is, she won't last five days. Hunger, thirst, savage beasts . . . hers will be a slow, agonizing death," she said. "Their 'mercy' is more cruel than my punishment!"

"Not killing her outright salves their conscience," Duranix said darkly. "That's what matters most to them."

One last important decision remained.

"The man called Zannian, as everyone now knows, is my youngest brother, Menni," Karada told the crowd. "Blinded in battle, he will likely never recover his sight.

It was Amero's wish that Zannian remain in Yala-tene and be treated as his brother, not a defeated enemy. I don't share this view. Zannian is a dangerous man, with no more honor in him than a hungry viper. Now that my brother is dead, Zannian should be dealt with like the snake he is."

Beramun, listening quietly beside Harak until now, stood up. Lyopi nodded for her to speak.

"I suffered as much as anyone at Zannian's hands. His men slew my family and enslaved me. He tried to take me by force, but I escaped. It sounds vain to say so, but I think he came to Yala-tene as much to recapture me as to conquer your village."

Beramun glanced at Harak, who smiled and gave her an encouraging nod.

"I would gladly see him dead," she continued, "but I think the only one who can rightly pass judgment on him is Karada. He's her kin. Let her do with him what she thinks best." Beramun sat down.

Karada looked enormously pleased.

Factions aligned themselves in completely different ways from when they'd debated Mara's fate. The younger people of Yala-tene favored sparing Zannian, while the elders wanted him put to death. Hulami suggested exile for Zannian as well, but in his sightless state, nobody felt comfortable with that idea.

Lyopi stood up to speak. The crowd slowly quieted to hear her words.

"Much as I respect Karada and Beramun, I have to disagree with them," she said. "Zannian should remain in Yala-tene."

Karada opened her mouth to object, but the stalwart Lyopi pressed on.

"I don't believe, as Amero did, that Zannian can be changed. As a vine is trained to a wall, so does it grow, and this raider chief was trained by a hate-filled woman nd a black-hearted dragon. He'll never be as kind as his rother or as noble as his sister.

"So let Zannian stay here," she declared. "Let him ive out his life as a prisoner of the people he sought to nslave. Let him live on our charity! Our pity will be a nore bitter punishment than swift death would be."

Her words, forcefully delivered, carried the day. As he conclave broke up, Karada sought out Beramun and mbraced her.

"You are the daughter I need," said the nomad chief. 'Will you have me as your mother?"

Beramun blushed. "I'm gaining a mate and a mother n backward order! What do you say, Harak?"

Scratching his chin, he said. "If Karada can live with ne, I can live with Karada."

"You're too clever, Wanderer," Karada told him. "But f my daughter loves you, you have my tolerance."

"And your trust?"

"That you must earn."

* * * * *

Wrists tied behind her, Mara was blindfolded and hrown over a horse. Six nomads and four villagers scorted her. They rode west out of Yala-tene at sun-lown. Samtu and Hekani led the group upriver, then nto the open plain. Night was well underway when hey stopped.

Samtu dismounted, pulling Mara off the horse. She ut the girl's bonds and removed her doeskin blindfold. Trembling, Mara fell at Samtu's feet.

"Don't kill me!" she begged. "I did it to save us all rom the Silvanesti!" She looked around at the other iders, eyes roving desperately in search of a sympathetic ace. She found none. "Where is Karada? Let me speak o her. If she hears me, she'll understand!"

Samtu was disgusted. According to Pakito, Karada's last words to the girl had been a vow to kill her.

"The day you see Karada again will be the day you die," she said. She gave the girl a single goatskin bag of water, a flint knife, and a pouch of dried fruit and elk jerky.

"Here's food and water for four days," Samtu continued. "You are exiled, Mara, daughter of Seteth and Evanna. If you ever return to Arku-peli or Karada's band, you'll be killed on sight. Now go!"

Peering fearfully over her shoulder, the girl moved away. At first she walked slowly, then picked up speed, and finally broke into a run. The last they saw of Mara, she was racing through the widely spaced pines, the fading twilight making her appear ghostlike and insubstantial. She was heading for the great savanna.

Hekani turned his horse around. "How long will she last?" he wondered.

"No way to tell," said Samtu. "If she's resourceful—and lucky—she might live a long time."

"Do you believe that?"

The stout nomad woman thumped her heels against her horse's ribs, starting the animal for home. "It no longer matters," she said bluntly.

* * * * *

On the cliffs overlooking the village, Karada stood with Duranix, now restored to dragon form.

"Can you find her?" Karada asked him, her eyes sweeping the dark, distant countryside.

"Yes. Are you at peace with your decision?"

She gave a harsh bark of laughter. "Peace? I've never known it and never will."

Duranix thought this the truest thing she'd ever said. He'd never known a thinking creature less suited to tranquillity.

Rather than leaping into the air, Duranix fell forward off the cliff edge. Spreading his wings, he flew off to complete his final pact with the sister of his first and only human friend.

* * * * *

Zannian entered Yala-tene with a rope around his neck. This was as much to guide him as it was to restrain him. Bahco was leading him from horseback. The nomad was met by Lyopi and Beramun, and he handed the halter to Lyopi. Bidding the women good-bye, Bahco galloped away.

"So I'm in Arku-peli at last," Zannian said. "I wish I could see it."

Lyopi tugged on the braided rawhide rope to get his attention. "I'm Lyopi," she said, "mate of Amero, your brother, once headman of the village."

"Ah, yes. Mated for a day, weren't you? Or was it less?"

Lyopi made a fist, but she only said, "Beramun is here, too."

The name drove the smirk from Zannian's face. He put out a hand. Beramun stepped aside to avoid it.

"I was hoping you would come," he said, turning his head toward the crunch of her footstep.

"I leave with Karada tomorrow. Say what you want, then I'll be going."

"Out here? In broad daylight?"

"It's night, and no one's about," Lyopi answered.

"Strange. When I heard Beramun's voice, I thought it was a bright and sunny day."

Lyopi gave the younger woman a sympathetic, inquiring look. Beramun shook her head, indicating his words held no pain for her. She held out a hand for the rope. Lyopi handed it to her, moved off a few paces, and sat down at the foot of one of the ramps leading up the inside of the wall.

"Lyopi is gone," Beramun said. "Talk."

"My guards tell me you've taken a mate, but they wouldn't say who he was," Zannian replied.

"Strange to say, he was one of your men. Harak."

If she'd slapped him, she couldn't have shaken the ex-raider chief more. His tanned face paled below the bandages around his eyes. His throat worked, but no sound came out. Finally, he forced a smile and said, "I can understand why he wants you, but how did he convince you to accept him? Did he use an amulet, as the nomad tried on Karada?"

She said nothing, refusing to be baited. Zannian took a step closer to her voice. She backed away, and he smiled unpleasantly.

"He's known many women, you know. Cut quite a swath through the captives we took to Almurk. Had a taste for red hair, as I recall, so he's changed just for you—"

She struck him open-handed across the jaw. No dainty girl, she rocked Zannian back on his heels. He laughed triumphantly.

"You must care if you hit me!"

Beramun backed away again, working to regain her composure. "Has anyone explained what's to become of you?" she asked finally.

The odd lilt in her voice gave him pause, but he said jauntily, "With the Arkuden dead, I guess Karada will have my head on stick."

"No."

"What then?"

"You're to live in Yala-tene, forever. The villagers will feed you and take care of you like a child. They'll lead you where you need to go and keep you clean, but you'll never be allowed outside the walls of the town." Her voice dropped to a whisper. "That's what the rest of your life will be like, great raider chief. Every day will be just the same, and you shall live and die in darkness."

Zannian was shaken by the time she finished. He let out a howl, then lunged at her. Lyopi stood to come to her aid, but Beramun waved the other woman off as she easily evaded him.

"I'll escape!" he declared, head whipping left and right. "My eyes will heal, and I'll escape!"

"Your sight will never return. You'll dwell in this village until you're old and feeble as well as blind. And since you've told us there is no more Menni, now there will also be no more Zannian. You're to have a new name, one befitting your new life—Horiden, 'the Sightless One.' "

"Amero wouldn't let you do this!" he said, voice rising high.

"Amero is dead, and this is not my doing. I would gladly grant your wish and take the head from your shoulders, but it wasn't my decision to make."

She expected him to rage or even plead for a warrior's death, but he did neither. He mastered himself, then smiled broadly. That smile unnerved Beramun more than naked rage.

"If you want me dead, then I'm happy," he declared. "And make no mistake—I will see again, and I will escape this blighted valley. I shall forge an even greater band of raiders next time. You'll see! My mistake was getting involved with Nacris and the green dragon. They were twisted by ancient hatreds. I'll create a new brotherhood of true warriors, greater than Karada's band, and sweep all before me. . . ."

So consumed was he by his grand dream that he didn't notice Beramun had left him. Lyopi came and took the rope from her. The women embraced.

"Farewell and be well," Beramun whispered.

"Peace to you, and all your kin," Lyopi murmured back. Behind them, Zannian ranted on. Lyopi squeezed Beramun's arms and asked, "Do me one favor, will you?"

"What's that?"

"Name your first son Amero, will you? He'd like that."

Beramun felt tears start. She kept them in check and smiled.

"I will."

She left the village by the west baffle and returned on foot to the nomad's camp. She never set foot in Yalatene again, nor met anyone who lived there for the rest of her long, long life.

* * * * *

Dawn was near, and still Karada kept her place atop the cliff. She did not sleep, for she did not want to dream. When she heard the rush of wings, she looked up and saw Duranix descending through the broken clouds.

He landed nearby. She saw he had something clutched in one foreclaw. When the dragon opened his talons, Mara's limp form rolled out on the ground.

"I was beginning to think you'd lit out for good," Karada said good-humoredly. She checked the girl. Mara had swooned from fear and the rush of traveling so high in the air, but she was very much alive. Karada quickly gagged her and tied her hands and feet.

Earlier, Duranix had carried Amero's body to the cave they'd once shared. He swept aside the ashes from the old hearth and laid his friend there, piling loose stones over him. Then, with claws and fire, he sealed the outer openings—first the largest one behind the waterfall, then Amero's smaller, personal entrance, where his hoist used to be. Lastly, the dragon closed the unfinished third entrance Amero had meant for Duranix to use when in human form. The cave was now secure, save for the vent holes. Duranix clung to the rocky ceiling with his claws and butted his horned head against the vents, breaking them open into a single hole large enough for him to crawl through.

Now, having returned with Mara, he and Karada would conduct their private justice.

With Karada in one foreclaw and the unconscious Mara in the other, Duranix stepped into the open hole and dropped back into the black cave. The fall into total darkness tested even Karada's nerves. She gripped Duranix's hard-scaled claw until she felt the rush of wind past her ears ease, signaling he'd opened his broad wings and was slowing their descent.

The dragon landed heavily. His massive hind legs took up the shock and spared his passengers. Setting Karada down, Duranix exhaled a small bolt of lightning into a pile of charred wood he'd scraped up earlier from around the cave. A smoky red fire flared.

Clomping across the rough stone floor, Duranix laid the unconscious Mara across the heap of stones that was Amero's grave. Turning his huge, reptilian head suddenly, he said to Karada, "She'll die slowly in here, of starvation."

"Only if she chooses to."

Karada went to the pile of stones. From her belt she drew a short bronze dagger—the same one Mara had used to kill Amero. She put the dagger in Mara's slack hand.

The fire was already dwindling. Duranix picked Karada up in a hind claw and launched himself at the roof. When he reached the opening, he had to close his wings and grip the edge of the hole with his foreclaws. He worked himself through.

Putting the woman down, Duranix covered the opening with great slabs of gray slate and yellow sandstone. He was satisfied, but his companion wasn't, not yet. Karada found a large stone and fitted it onto the pile, closing the last small gap.

They walked to the edge of the cliff. Below them the waterfall foamed and thundered.

"Where will you go?" she shouted over the water's roar.

"I have a place in mind. A long way away, but the company promises to be congenial."

"Human?"

His barbels twitched. "I said congenial. A dragon, if you must know, of my bronze race."

"Female?" she asked. He nodded his horned head, human-fashion.

"I'm tired of humans," Duranix replied. "Maybe in a hundred years or so I'll be able to stand them again."

She looked up at him. "Some of us won't be around in a hundred years."

He brought his huge face close, eyelids clashing like swords. "You'll live longer than I," he told her. "When my bones are dust and my scales gone to verdigris, plainsmen will sing of Karada, the Scarred One, the greatest hunter and warrior of them all. They already make up songs about you."

"I don't listen to such nonsense."

"Sometimes there's truth in nonsense." He lifted his head and spread his wings.

"You're leaving now?" she said. "The folk in Yala-tene will miss saying farewell."

"It's better I go now. Less trouble. Less fuss. Good-bye, Karada."

She put out her hand, touching his massive flank. "Nianki."

Duranix balanced on his rear claws, poised for flight. "Farewell then, Nianki. Be worthy of your honor in all things."

He leaped from the precipice, flying through the cloud of mist perpetually suspended over the falls. For a while his bronze skin glistened in the first, faint light of dawn, then he was so far away all she could see of him was a black silhouette against the indigo sky.

Chapter 22

Nomads breaking camp was always a noisy affair. Amid much shouting and grunting, the rings of tents came down, each hide hut sending up a cloud of dust when it collapsed. As was traditional, the older children struck the tents, under the supervision of the elders. While this was going on, warrior-age nomads saw to their horses and movable gear.

In the center of this maelstrom, Karada sat on her horse, strangely quiescent. She watched the dusty, churning proceedings with a detachment she did not ordinarily feel. Those close to her attributed her reflective mood to Amero's death, and they were right.

Beramun approached on foot, black hair coated with yellow dust. She hailed her chief and adopted mother. Karada smiled down at her and held out a leather-wrapped gourd of cool water.

Beramun rinsed her parched mouth and spat out the resulting mud. "I bring word from Harak and the former raiders," she said. "They want to know where in the column they should travel."

"At the rear," Karada said, taking back the gourd. "We've no horses to spare for them, so they'll walk at the rear, with the travois."

"Harak too?"

Karada sipped cool lake water. She'd grown to like its mineral bite again. "Harak too. I can't favor him over the others, Beramun. They'd hate him for it. If the raiders prove themselves worthy, we'll find mounts for them later on. And no, he can't ride double with you. It's too hard on the horse." Seeing Beramun's disappointment, she added, not unkindly, "Harak will not object, and his good behavior will make him all the more pleasing to his men."

Beramun smiled. The excitement of leaving the Valley of the Falls more than compensated for a temporary separation from her mate.

Looking past Karada at the village, Beramun saw dust rising from the vicinity of the north baffle.

"Someone's coming from Yala-tene," she said.

Karada sighed. "More elders to talk us to death. I've never known folk who talk so much. Wasn't 'good-bye' yesterday enough?"

Beramun frowned, shading her eyes. "There's a lot of them—not just a party of elders."

Karada turned her wheat-colored horse around to see for herself. Sure enough, a sizable troop of people was coming toward them from the village.

"Find Pakito," she said tersely. "Send him to me. If you see Bahco first, send him too."

"Why?"

"Probably nothing. Go on, do as I say."

Beramun sprinted into the chaotic scene, darting to and fro around horses and collapsing tents. By the time Pakito and Bahco returned, the people from Yala-tene were clearly visible. There must have been two hundred of them, all heavily laden with bundles and packs.

Leading the marching villagers was the young hunter Hekani. When he reached the nomad chief, he signaled those behind him to stop. The burdened villagers gratefully set down their bags and rested in the morning heat.

"Greetings, great chief!" Hekani said. "We've come to join you."

"What?" Bahco and Pakito exclaimed simultaneously.

"We want to join your band," Hekani said, sweeping his arm back to encompass all the people behind him.

"What are you talking about?" said Karada. "You're not nomads!"

"We shall be, if you'll have us. Since the Arkuden's death and the dragon's departure, a lot of us felt it wasn't worth going on here. Everyone you see this morning has chosen to leave Yala-tene and join with you."

Karada looked pained, and Bahco said, "Not one in ten of you has a horse! And none of you is accustomed to walking long distances. How will you keep up with us?"

"There must be more horses on the plains," Hekani replied.

"But you're all just a bunch of mud-toes!" Pakito blurted, then looked sheepish. "What I mean is, life on the plain is hard, not at all like living in comfortable stone piles."

"We're not all so long off the plains that we've forgotten what it's like," retorted an older woman behind Hekani. "And life hasn't been that easy in Yala-tene lately."

"We fought Zannian longer than you did," Hekani said proudly. "I'm a hunter myself. As for riding—well, we can learn, can't we? You won't have to take care of us. We have a lot of skills among us—flint knapping, metal-working, tanning, pot-making, gardening. We'll make our own way, and share our skills with your people."

Karada was shaking her head. "You'd slow the band too much." She looked over the composition of the crowd and added, "Besides, if so many young folk leave, what will become of those who stay behind?"

From the crowd at Hekani's back stepped Jenla, the planter. "I came with Hekani to answer that question, Karada."

The nomad chieftain nodded at the formidable old woman, and Jenla said, "As near as I can tell, I've seen fifty-six summers. I know I wouldn't have lived so long, had it not been for the Arkuden and his village. Now

I'm too old to wander, and Yala-tene will be my home until I die.

"Many old people in the village feel as I do. We'll stay in the valley, dragon or no dragon, Arkuden or no Arkuden. We have our gardens, our orchard, and our thick stone walls."

Hekani spoke again. "For us"—he gestured to the crowd behind him—"that's not enough. We want a leader of power and spirit. The Arkuden was strong in wisdom and kindness, but we've learned the hard way that's not enough. Even having a dragon as our protector didn't prevent the raiders from attacking us. The way to be free is to be strong. We want to follow you, Karada."

She took a long time before replying, her eyes sweeping over them. Finally she spoke loud enough for all to hear, "If you think life will be better with me on the plain, you're fools. Stay here. Grow your gardens and live inside your stone walls. That's the best choice for you."

Amid mutters from the crowd, she called to Pakito and Bahco, and the three of them rode off. A short distance away, they stopped and looked back. "They're not leaving," Bahco reported.

The villagers milled about where Karada had left them, watching them from a small hill west of the nomads' camp.

Karada didn't turn around, but said, "Let's see what they're made of. If they can keep up with us, I'll take them in."

"They're not nomads," Bahco objected.

"Neither were you when we met. You crossed the sea in a basket of logs, seeking a new land. Was I wrong to take you in when you asked to join Karada's band?"

He grinned. "No. And we call those baskets of logs 'ships,' chief."

She waved a hand, dismissing Bahco's ships, then twisted right and left on her horse, saying, "Anyone seen our highborn hostage this morning?"

"Balif and his soldiers were waiting for us at sunrise," Pakito said. "I told them to march with the raider-men. Might as well keep all our troubles in one pouch, eh?"

Karada sighed. "As if those were our only troubles! Very well, Pakito, lead the band into Bearclaw Gap. Bahco, hold back a hundred riders, and let the raiders and elves enter the pass ahead of you. You follow them through till we reach open ground again." The two men nodded, and she sent for Targun.

The old nomad rode up to Karada on his dappled mare, the same horse he'd ridden out of the Valley of the Falls thirteen years earlier. Karada gave him charge of the travois and those folk on foot. He asked about the young people from Yala-tene still milling about on the hill.

"Ignore them," she said. "If they can keep up with us, we might take them in."

She gave more orders, and the nomad band sorted itself accordingly. Pakito led the foremost riders into Bearclaw Gap. As they rode away, Beramun, mounted now, cantered up to her informally adopted mother and was told to stay close to "learn how to lead a band."

Beramun put her horse alongside Karada's. Pakito's nomads rode past, waving and calling their chief's name. She did not return their salutes but watched impassively as they passed.

"Don't you answer their hails?" Beramun asked in a low voice.

"Only in battle. All other times I assume a lofty air. It gives them confidence." At Beramun's confused expression, Karada smiled ever so faintly. "A stern face helps them believe I'm thinking deep, wise thoughts on their behalf."

Beramun had a lot yet to learn about being chief. She laughed long and loud at Karada's admission, and all the riders passing gawked at her in surprise.

* * * * *

The elves shouldered their packs and marched out. At their head, Balif set the pace.

"I'm glad to see the end of this valley," Farolenu said, walking at his lord's side. "Too much suffering and sorrow happened here."

Balif made no comment, and they trudged in silence a while. Then the elf lord said, "What will you do first when we get home, Faro?"

"Bathe," said the bronzesmith. "In heated water. And love my wife."

"In that order?"

"Arikina, my wife, will insist on that order. What will you do, my lord?"

"I shall dine on nothing but fruit for thirty days—washed down with the rarest nectar in Silvanost. The coarse food these humans eat has aged me a century."

Farolenu looked forward and back at the lines of humans on foot and horseback. "So many of them," he remarked. "For short-lived creatures, they breed quickly!"

"Too quickly. Our sovereign and his counselors must understand that." Balif spotted the mounted figures of Karada and the black-haired girl she'd taken as her daughter. "Many things need to be explained to the Speaker. Many things . . ."

The elves tramped by the nomad chief. At Balif's command, they fell into matched step, arms and feet swinging in unison.

"Face the honor!" Balif cried. All the elves' heads turned toward Karada, rendering her a salute usually reserved for the highest Silvanesti. If the nomad chief was surprised, she didn't show it, staring ahead impassively with a lofty air.

* * * * *

At the tail of the long column, winding its way across the valley floor to Bearclaw Gap, Targun waited with the unmounted nomads. Most of them were children who rode the travois with the baggage. As he wiled away the time until it came his moment to move, Targun glanced at the crowd of villagers still clustered and waiting on the hill a hundred paces away.

Targun was reminded of how he and his mate had come to Karada's band after the death of their adult son. They'd been as forlorn and anxious as those villagers. His mate was now long dead, but Targun felt moved to do something he rarely did—act without Karada's approval. He picked a boy from the idle nomad children and sent him to the leader of the villagers with a message: *Karada says if you keep pace with us, you're in.*

He could tell when the message was delivered. A few villagers jumped to their feet. The motion spread throughout the crowd until everyone was standing. A cheer went up. Targun pulled the brim of his woven straw hat down and hid a satisfied smile in his gray beard.

Thus did Karada's band depart the Valley of the Falls. Once out of the mountains, she kept her word and released Balif. The elf lord gave her back the bronze sword she'd returned to him before the battle with the ogres and raiders. It was the same weapon he'd used against Zannian. Farolenu had restored the battered blade to shining perfection. Karada accepted the sword without emotion.

"Farewell," Balif said. "Until we meet again, peace to you, as your people say."

"What makes you think we'll meet again?" she asked.

"Our lives are entwined. Haven't you noticed?"

Karada colored, her tan face growing pink

"So we will meet in battle?" she asked with affected brusqueness.

"I hope not. I'd hate to cross swords with a comrade."

He did not salute, but waved breezily as he led his small band away. Karada was silent until Beramun teased, "You've made a friend, it seems."

"He's not a friend," Karada replied stiffly. "Just a very good enemy."

* * * * *

Not long after Balif and the elves departed, Karada relented and let the two hundred men, women, and children from Yala-tene join her band. As Hekani said, the villagers brought with them much learning and many new skills. In one generation, bronze became common, not only for blades and arrowheads but even for homely tools and personal decoration. Raising crops in temporary gardens brought more food to the nomads, and their numbers waxed larger.

In time the nomad band became so large it could scarcely move or feed itself. Small groups split off from the main body to start their own bands in other regions. The descendants of Pakito and Samtu rode far west, beyond the once forbidding Edge of the World, and populated the lands of the sunset. Another group, led by Bahco and his children, returned to the northern seashore. When Bahco died, full of years and rich in descendants, his body was borne back across the waves to his birthplace, the seafaring lands.

Of the fifty men who had been raiders, half became full-fledged members of Karada's band. The others drifted away, becoming lone wanderers or falling back on thievery. Karada gave the task of suppressing the backsliding iders to Harak. It was her way of testing him, and Bera-un's mate did not fail. Every last outlaw was captured killed, four by Harak alone.

The former raider stayed with Beramun always, and gether they had six children. Their firstborn son was amed Amero, and he grew to be a warrior as wise as he as fierce. He was a great favorite of his grandmother arada, and the only one allowed to call her Nianki.

Karada lived to great age, surviving her last brother more than two decades. In later years she left com-and of the band to Beramun and spent her days hunt-g and riding, often alone on the savanna for many ys. Her feats and adventures became entwined with gend. By the time her hair was white, she took a grand-ild with her on these journeys—either young Amero her granddaughter Kinarmun—and from her they arned the ancient secrets and skills.

She ranged far and wide, and many nomads thought ey saw her, silhouetted against the sunset or in a bright reath of stars. The wanderers learned to wave respect-lly to any lone figure they encountered on the plain, nce any solitary rider could be Karada, watching over l the children of the plains.

* * * * *

Far away in time and place, the dull red orb of the sun nk toward the sea. From his perch atop the cliffs, uranix surveyed his circular island home. In the years nce leaving the Valley of the Falls, he'd grown to nmense size, due in part to the spirit power infused into m long ago, but also from the diet of whale and kraken e enjoyed in the waters surrounding the island.

Aloft, Blusidar circled, leading their two offspring in eir first flying lesson. She was a much better flyer an her older, heavier mate, though not as patient with her hatchlings' mistakes. The young dragons' stubb wings fanned hard, trying to keep up with their mother swift progress.

A peculiar sensation filled Duranix's chest. It bega as a small cold spot, deep within the massive layers flying muscle. The feeling spread outward, a creepin numbness more puzzling than alarming. When it reache the tips of his claws and the crown of his horned hea it vanished as swiftly as it had come. He could remembe feeling this way only one other time, and the meaning the sensation was instantly clear.

Blusidar alighted on a ledge above him. She called roug encouragement to the dragonlets still struggling throug the air, then turned with concern to her mate.

"What troubles you?" she asked.

"I fear a friend is gone," he said quietly, meeting he wide golden eyes. "An old friend."

"One of your humans," said Blusidar with a sniff.

"No. Karada was no one's human but her own. Th was her curse and her strength."

Their male hatchling, Seridanax, fluttered by, screech ing for help. Though Blusidar did not approve, Durani caught his small son in his great claws and soothed hin saying, "Don't be afraid, little one. I will protect you."

The Summer of Chaos is over, but the trouble is just beginning.

This is where the new era of DRAGONLANCE® began, heralding a new age and new heroes—The Dragons of a New Age trilogy, by Jean Rabe. These all-new editions of this pivotal trilogy feature handsome new cover art by award-winning artist Matt Stawicki.

The Dawning of a New Age

Volume One

Magic has vanished. Evil dragons conquer the land. Despair threatens to overwhelm Ansalon. Now is the time for heroes.

June 2002

The Day of the Tempest

Volume Two

As the dragon overlords bicker among themselves, a band of heroes stumble upon a new form of magic: the power of the heart.

August 2002

The Eve of the Maelstrom

Volume Three

The most powerful of the dragon overlords is determined to ascend to godhood, and a single band of heroes must find a way to stop her.

November 2002

Dig deep into the War of Souls

Can't get enough of the newest DRAGONLANCE® epic, the War of Souls? Delve into the details of the characters, events, and consequences of this sweeping battle.

The Lioness

The Age of Mortals • *Nancy Varian Berberick*

Learn the legend of the Lioness....

The Lioness is on a clandestine mission from the king of the Qualinesti elves. She must turn outlaw and knit a rebellion from disparate forest factions, aimed at keeping the occupying dark knights off their guard. But another mission arises for the mythical outlaw: she must defeat a mysterious knight-executioner whose sole job is terror.

August 2002

Bertrem's Guide to the War of Souls, Volume II

Sequel to Bertrem's Guide to the War of Souls, Volume I

How far does the War of Souls reach? This collection of correspondence, reports, and essays, compiled by Bertrem the Ascetic, vividly reveals the impact of the War of Souls on everyday occurrences across the land of Ansalon.

November 2002

The Dhamon Saga

Jean Rabe

The sensational conclusion to the trilogy!

Redemption

Volume Three

Dhamon's dragon-scale curse forces him deep into evil territory, where he must follow the orders of an unknown entity. Time is running out for him and his motley companions—a mad Solamnic Knight, a wingless draconian, and a treacherous ogre mage. Is it too late for Dhamon to redeem his nefarious past?

July 2002

Now available in paperback

Betrayal

Volume Two

Haunted by the past, Dhamon Grimwulf suffers daily torture from the dragon scale attached to his leg. As he searches for a cure, he must venture into a treacherous black dragon's swamp. The swamp is filled with terrors bent on destroying him, but the true danger to Dhamon is much closer than he thinks.

April 2002